DARKNESS BEYOND

DARKNESS BEYOND

Marjorie Eccles

SEVERN
HOUSE

First world edition published in Great Britain and the USA in 2021
by Severn House, an imprint of Canongate Books Ltd,
14 High Street, Edinburgh EH1 1TE.

Trade paperback edition first published in Great Britain and the USA in 2022
by Severn House, an imprint of Canongate Books Ltd.

severnhouse.com

British Library Cataloguing-in-Publication Data
A CIP catalogue record for this title is available from the British Library.

ISBN-13: 978-0-7278-5060-7 (cased)
ISBN-13: 978-1-78029-787-3 (trade paper)
ISBN-13: 978-1-4483-0526-1 (e-book)

This is a work of fiction. Names, characters, places and incidents
are either the product of the author's imagination or are used fictitiously.
Except where actual historical events and characters are being described
for the storyline of this novel, all situations in this publication are
fictitious and any resemblance to actual persons, living or dead,
business establishments, events or locales is purely coincidental.

All Severn House titles are printed on acid-free paper.

MIX
Paper from
responsible sources
FSC® C013056

Typeset by Palimpsest Book Production Ltd.,
Falkirk, Stirlingshire, Scotland.
Printed and bound in Great Britain by
TJ Books, Padstow, Cornwall.

Rather more than kin, and less than kind

Hamlet

PART ONE

PROLOGUE

February, 1933

I t was already dark as he headed through the town towards the other side of the river, to what now felt like hostile territory. Coat collar turned up against the rain, shoulders hunched, he moved fast under the pools of gaslight, past the darkened library, closed shops, the public baths, the fire station – familiar old landmarks, most of them, though some were new to him. It still wanted half an hour to opening time for the pubs, and the streets were all but deserted, except for one or two early customers drawn by the smell of the chip shop just beginning its evening frying.

He hadn't expected nostalgia, still less sentiment, and impatience with himself for feeling either made him move even faster, each step taking him further into the dark that was yet to come. It scarcely mattered that it was on the edge of danger, what he was doing, where he was going. Damned if he did what he'd come back here to do, damned even more if he didn't.

He crossed to the far side of the river bridge, sensing rather than hearing the pattering of the rain on the water below. Water under the bridge in more senses than one. Memories unravelling as the current bore with it recollections that were now only echoes, along with resentments that were not forgotten. He'd lived with both for too long to give up now, long before the Armistice fourteen years ago, which had brought peace for some, though not for him.

Since then – since 1918, and once the country's lapsed building trade had received a restart kick – Ladyford Lane, where he now found himself, had become a prime location for the development of several large, expensive houses in extensive grounds. Folbury was a coming area now, conveniently not too far from the Black Country industrial hub, but still on the edge of real, open countryside, and a good proportion of these new homes had been purpose-built for Midland manufacturers, those with aspirations and money to spare: the war and its endless greed for munitions and everything else heavy industry could supply hadn't been bad for everyone. And on the premise that if you'd paid that much for anything, it had to look as though you had, none of the new owners of these properties had lost the opportunity of showing off what they could afford. Mock Tudor facades everywhere, sweeping gravel drives, big landscaped gardens.

The one he sought had an unconventional white wall surrounding the property, an intimation of the surprise standing a hundred yards beyond the open black iron gates, at the end of a straight gravel drive. More of a shock than a surprise it must have been to the neighbouring property owners, landing there like some sort of alien space machine. His lips twisted at the name, Casa Nova, on the gatepost. Quasi-Bauhaus Modernist, an arrangement of cubes with some rounded corners, in dazzling white stucco with a shallow, startlingly blue-tiled roof. Astonishing to say the least in the British climate and unlikely in the extreme for Folbury. Still more so for at least one of its owners.

They were at home, or someone was. Light spilled from the windows as he crunched up the drive, ducked from the rain into the tiled porch and stood for a moment before raising his hand to the blue door. He didn't bother with the bell. Trying the knob and finding it turned, he pushed the door open and walked straight into a spacious hallway lit by a skylight over the stairs, white-painted and furnished only with a sofa covered in zebra-skin, standing on a circular rug and flanked by two long wall-mirrors, bordered in peach and black glass. Screwed to the wall in the elbow of the broad flight of stairs sweeping up to an open landing either side, as if in a Hollywood musical, was the heavy old mahogany hood clock with its hanging weights, a deliberate, ironic fashion anachronism. And to the left, just three feet away, he was looking straight at the oil painting which had once graced Ernest Millar's office, now prominently displayed here. No chance of anyone missing it when they entered the house. He was still staring at the face of his father, inimical as ever, when a door opened and into the hall walked his sister.

'Thea.'

She stood rooted to the spot. One ghost on the wall and another standing in front of her. For several thumping heart-beats, Thea Millar thought she might be going to join them. All feeling left her. The shock of it froze her speech. Then, in a painful rush, one word came out. 'Paul.'

ONE

It's a relief to know that I am not, after all, about to die of shock after what I was faced with when he stepped into the hall – my brother, Paul, who has been dead for over fourteen years. I force myself to take a step towards him – and find I can go no further. We never were a family for embracing, no matter what, and now – especially now – to do so feels unnatural, impossible in fact, even in these circumstances. For where is the joy I should be feeling at seeing him, impossibly alive, here in the flesh? The charged, absurd hiatus goes on, in which anything I can think of saying seems so banal it might almost be laughable, in other circumstances: *'You're not dead, after all . . . Where have you been? . . . Why have you never written and let us know you were alive? . . . What happened to you, for heaven's sake?'*

And even more: *'What in the name of God has made you come back now?'*

It feels hard to breathe, let alone speak. Me, Thea Millar, too outspoken for my own good, and I'm tongue-tied. But Paul is not helping me and in the end I do find it possible to say something. 'Your coat's wet,' is the most I can muster though, holding out my hand for it.

He shrugs the coat off and hands it over, and at last he says, 'I'm sorry, I've given you a shock.' As if that could describe the earthquake which has just rocked me to my foundations. I hang the wet coat up and move stiffly back into the sitting room I've just left, leaving him to follow, walking behind me with that very slight drag of his leg, almost imperceptible to anyone who didn't know him. Waving him to a chair, I at last manage a further few words, as politely spoken as if to a visitor rather than my own brother, this ghost who has no business being here. 'Won't you sit down?'

He sits. 'Teddy not at home?' he asks after a moment or two.

'He's getting ready to go out to a dinner. A Rotary do.' I grasp the excuse and half-rise from my chair. 'I'll get him.'

'Don't disturb him. I can wait.' Another silence. 'You haven't changed much, Thea,' he says at last.

That's an exaggeration, although my mirror tells me every morning that I don't look my age. If there's any truth in it, it certainly isn't down to luck. My once waist-length hair is fair enough to have so far helped to camouflage signs of grey – but I've also gone along with the current fashion and had it bobbed, and I make sure my hairdresser keeps it nicely trimmed. I've always had a good skin and now I've learnt how to use a little discreet make-up, and though I'm by no means as slim as I'd like to be, I don't over-eat and I suppose my figure's still passable. He can't know how many times I look in the mirror and there . . . Thea is not.

In her place there's a woman I don't recognize (and not only because I've had my hair cut), a woman whom most people would say has made an amazing success of her life, even to saving the family fortunes. Spinster of this parish, like so many other women of my generation, on the shelf, a leftover from the war. But settled, at ease with herself. How little they know!

'You've worn well,' he repeats, this time with the glimmer of a smile. I can't say the same of him. Two years younger than I am, he looks not at all well, in the sense of what life has done to him. Seedy is the word that springs to mind. A cheap blue suit, his dark hair lank and a trifle too long. The pallor that was always natural to him now has a sallow tinge. He is still thin, dark and intense, with those high cheekbones and brooding eyes – a combination which always did give him that romantic, starving-poet image, while nothing could be further from the truth – the giveaway being the wry, slightly mocking twist to the mouth. All in all though, there's still that dangerous-to-know suggestion which seems to be so attractive to some women. Less so than it used to be, though, I think, with something new about him I can't yet put a name to.

Under the surface the questions I can't ask – daren't – are seething. I'm afraid of the answers, but I feel a sudden fierce rush of something like the protective love I used to have for him. Almost as much as I had for Teddy.

While I struggle with my feelings, the rain rattles on the windows, the gas fire hisses. He has given up attempts to start a conversation and sits back, taking in the room with fairly obvious incredulity, as well he might. He and I were always so close, close enough for me to predict what he was thinking, but it needs no special connection this time to read his reaction to what he's seeing. It's pretty much the same as everyone else's. The room is thirty feet long, stretching almost the width of the house, light, airy and modern, panelled in maple wood. His quizzical glance takes in the dark, old-fashioned furniture salvaged from the old home, huge pieces at war with the rest of the up-to-date décor, in positions where Teddy would have placed blond wood, glass or chrome. His eyes fall to the faded Turkish rug that used to be in the old hall, the one he used to land on with a running jump from the stairs when he was a boy, so that it took him skidding along the length of the cold marble tiles; then his gaze travels to Mother's rocking chair, still upholstered in its now balding green plush, and finally comes to rest on the massive old mahogany sideboard with its prim doyleys for ornaments, where its raft of photographs used to stand. Absurdity upon absurdity, in this up-to-the-minute, labour-saving, machine-for-living house that Teddy has designed – which to me is a nothing of a house, no more than a set of child's building blocks put together, and just as uninteresting. Keeping the old family stuff was the only reason I agreed to live here at all, which was disagreeable of me, I suppose, since I was well aware of Teddy's plans – he had expected to have furnished the house with things made yesterday. I am not in love, however, with modern furniture, or architecture either. When I think of the old house . . . but then, I hated that, too, didn't I? Yet for reasons other than its ugliness: its cold, high rooms, the kitchen from another age, the echoing bathroom with its massive bathtub encased in mahogany, the blue and white flowered lavatory.

On the whole, perhaps it doesn't matter: the design of the house itself makes what Teddy calls a statement, which is what he intended – it stands as its own advertisement for what he and Millar Homes can offer, and already certain people, those able to afford such, have shown interest in having it replicated for themselves. It serves its purpose for the two of us to live in.

Grandfather's clock in the hall strikes the half-hour, echoed by the soft Westminster chime of his old glass-domed one that rests uneasily on the modern tiles of the fireplace mantelshelf. Six thirty. Have we really only been sitting here for less than five minutes? It seems like half an hour. But a situation that's beginning to feel ever more desperate is saved when the door opens to admit Teddy, ready to go out for the evening in dinner jacket, dickey bow and a white silk scarf draped around his neck.

Paul jumps up immediately, both hands extended, while Teddy's reaction mirrors my own. The colour blanches from his face and he stands stock still. They stare at one another. Paul may think I haven't changed much, but that can't be said of Teddy. Our youngest sibling is now a middle-aged man: affable, easy-going, with a face that is well-disposed to the world in general, a kindly-uncle exterior which, however, gives few clues to what had always promised to be a sharp mind. He has put on weight. He looks prosperous, the successful local businessman he is. The Millar genes have produced a certain family resemblance between me and Teddy which has somehow skipped Paul, but as Father once remarked of him – and in Teddy's hearing, with one of his looks that said everything – 'He's Thea, yes . . . but without her compelling energy, unfortunately.' Maybe remembering that was intentional and is what has spurred Teddy on. Father was adept at being deliberately cruel.

There's no doubt he is just as shocked as I am, but his recovery is better. After the first disbelieving moments, his face breaks into an astonished smile, and he's moving across the room. There is a moment of utter stillness when they meet in the middle. Then a huge, manly, back-slapping bear hug ensues. Unlike my own speechless response, Teddy's now becomes vocal, if somewhat floundering. 'Paul, good God, Paul, it *is* you – or am I dreaming? Tell me I'm not – and what the hell? How many years is it? You've a lot to explain, brother. But first – oh God, yes, you'll have to excuse me, I have to – yes, I must make a telephone call. Thea, get

Paul a drink while I make it. I won't be two ticks, less than that.'

It takes a great deal to make Teddy forsake business commitments, but the Rotary dinner is apparently to be abandoned without a second thought. I make my escape by following him to the door, murmuring something about finding glasses, scotch and soda.

'Cup of tea would be fine, Thea. I don't drink now.'

Outside the door, Teddy's eyes meet mine. Paul, not drinking? He spreads his hands, then crosses the hall and hurries up the stairs, while I go into the shiningly modern kitchen. All fitted cupboards and electrical gadgets, a washing machine and a huge monolith of a refrigerator that hums like an angry hornet all the time. Waiting for the kettle to boil, I remember the half-bottle left over from Ivy Pearson's brandy butter for the Christmas pudding, and reach into a top cupboard for it. I take a large gulp straight from the bottle, probably unwisely, since I'm not used to spirits, but if Paul doesn't need a bit of Dutch courage, I for one have never felt more need of it. It makes me cough, but it brings a sudden rush of warmth, and maybe a promise of easing the knot of pain that's growing above my eyes. Like those other times, I can feel by the crawling on my scalp the beginnings of a storm, a darkness we are all moving towards, that no one can do anything to stop. I take another swig.

Having spun out the tea-making as long as I can, I take the tray back into the sitting room and occupy myself by pouring. I have just handed Paul a cup as Teddy comes back. He has divested himself of his evening clothes and has on a pair of flannel bags and a white cricket shirt under a sleeveless Fair Isle pullover. He looks more like the Teddy of old, the baby of the family, younger than Paul by ten years. He shakes his head at the offer of tea and goes to his pride-and-joy cocktail cabinet. It's of golden maple and has a mirrored interior, pigeon holes and slots for the various implements and ingredients necessary for the serious business of cocktail making. Although he has his back to me I can see his hands are not quite steady as he pours himself a stiff measure. He turns, raising his glass. 'Paul! My God, Paul! We thought you must be dead. Now, come on . . . Where the hell have you been?'

'All in good time,' says our brother.

I remember how he used to take his tea, and I've sugared it before Paul tells me he no longer takes it – he'd got used to doing without in the war and now prefers it that way. He waves a hand at the offer of a fresh cup and drinks the one I've poured anyway.

Teddy is downing his whisky like a seasoned toper and it's making him garrulous. He's babbling, about nothing. He'll be commenting on the weather next. For some reason, he seems now prepared to put off demanding the explanations we are most certainly owed. He takes out his cigarettes and offers them to Paul, who shakes his head. 'No thanks, I don't, any more.'

Not drinking, no sugar in his tea and now not smoking either. I almost expect him to say he's undergone some sort of spiritual and religious conversion and joined the Salvation Army and now devotes his life to good works. Maybe he does.

There suddenly comes a ring of the doorbell. Of all the inopportune moments! I jump up, ready to send the caller away, but Teddy, in the middle of yet another banal utterance, breaks off and beats me to it. He waves me back and goes out with something very like relief.

Voices in the hall. Then a figure fills the space in the doorway. Young, fiercely dark, a bright, brilliant glance from clear grey eyes, a supple, strong body – Matt-like, he hasn't stopped to pick up a coat or an umbrella. Most likely it had never entered his head in the circumstances, and the shoulders of his jacket are dark with rain, his black curls flattened. He should have a towel to dry his hair, he'll catch cold, but I don't imagine the suggestion would be welcome at this moment.

'You called him,' I accuse Teddy. I could shake my dear brother for that, or quite possibly kill him.

'Naturally. He had to know.'

But not yet, for heaven's sake! Not until we know more. Not until my poor boy could have been better prepared than by a bombshell delivered over the telephone.

Paul is already standing up. 'Matthaeus!'

Father and son face each other, the space between them fills with silence until Paul makes a move forward. But Matt gives him a level glance and a cool nod and then turns away and crosses the room, half-sits on the arm of the white leather chair next to me, after kissing me on the cheek. 'Aunt Thea,' he murmurs. It's his normal greeting, but it cruelly, if unintentionally, underlines the rejection. Oh, Matt! He ignores my warning squeeze on his arm, and pats his pockets with paint-stained fingers for cigarettes and matches, decides against it and folds his arms across his chest. I can feel the tension radiating from him, a palpable presence. I wonder just what Teddy has told him.

Matt was eight years old when his father enlisted and has only seen him since on the very few times at the beginning of the war when he came home on short leaves. Eight years old, and he had only just lost his mother. When Paul volunteered to fight it must have seemed to the child as though he was being abandoned by his father, too. Four years he waited for him to return. The end of the war came at last and after that . . . more interminable waiting. No word, nothing. Until now. Matt's attitude is understandable, but I have to wonder if Paul realizes this. Does he even begin to comprehend what the child went through, or what the return of this stranger must be doing to him now?

TWO

Folbury stretched out for roughly three or four miles along the Fol valley. From its busy market town centre, Emscott Hill rose steeply on one side of the river to the Beacon, the town's famous landmark. On the opposite side and rising more gently was Castle Hill, so called on account of the scattered ruins of a medieval castle standing towards the foot. All that was left of the castle now was the stump of a tower and a few crumbling walls on a mound, surrounded by a ditch that still flooded occasionally. But it looked romantic. Primroses carpeted the mound in spring.

Halfway up the hill, a short residential road simply called The Avenue branched off – another post-war development. This time six pairs of modest red-brick semis facing each other, squared off at the end by a much older house, once a lodge to the now non-existent mansion it had served: Fox Close, part of Folbury's history for centuries and on whose land the new homes had been erected.

This old lodge had been unoccupied for years, possibly since before the mansion's last demolished remains were carted away, and in the opinion of some living in The Avenue, it should have been knocked down, too. But the new owners of Number Nine were more than happy with it.

Like everyone else who had any sense, they were at home on this miserable February evening: Detective Inspector Herbert (Bert to his wife and friends) Reardon and his wife Ellen, chairs drawn up to a roaring fire. She was attempting to sketch plans for the garden at the rear, as yet still in its tentative stage, while Tolly, their Jack Russell terrier, occupied his usual position, heavy against her feet.

Boswell's journey into Scotland with Samuel Johnson had failed to hold Reardon; the book precariously balanced on his stomach, his long legs stretched out to the fire, he was asleep. Ellen looked up from her drawing and let herself watch him for a while. In sleep, his eyes closed, he looked vulnerable, as people do, and the war-wound that puckered one side of his face looked more noticeable than it ever did when he was awake. As she watched, he stirred and his hand reached up to touch it, a subconscious gesture, particularly when something he was working on was bothering him. Whatever that might be he was keeping it to himself, though normally he saw no reason not to discuss his work with her (unless it was confidential or particularly upsetting) because he could trust her to be discreet and because she took a lively and intelligent interest in what he did. So much so that she sometimes declared she'd a notion to give up teaching and join the police force herself. She was talking tongue in cheek. Women police? Although Reardon (unlike ninety-five per cent of the Police Force) declared himself for it on principle, she suspected he didn't prolong the discussions because he thought she might just possibly be serious. She'd already shown herself willing to involve herself in previous investigations, but he thought she was better sticking to the job she really loved, teaching French.

As if divining in his sleep what she was thinking, he stirred in his chair. Tonight, he'd looked whacked when he came home at the end of what had evidently been a hard day. The last months had been demanding, moving here from smoky old Dudley, with new jobs for both of them. Ellen now taught French three days a week at Maxstead Court, a girls' boarding school some miles away, while Reardon himself was still busy organizing and getting the new innovative Folbury detective section on to its feet, the sort of task he normally took in his stride. But after a scotch and water, and a meal she'd done her best with, he was out for the count within minutes of lowering himself into his armchair. She let him sleep. He'd been generous with praise for her attempts at a meat pie, after all.

Going back to her sketch, she looked at it doubtfully. Her drawing skills, never up to much anyway if she was honest, hadn't noticeably improved since she'd joined the night school art class. Not that it mattered in this instance – this sketch was only to get some idea of what the old, neglected garden here might become. Brainwaves about what to do with it were in short supply. She didn't seem to be able to summon up much enthusiasm, which was odd, considering she'd always wanted a garden of her own, like the one where she'd helped her father as a child, a small, lush garden enclosed by warm brick walls against which apricots and a medlar grew. This one couldn't be more different. From one side of the house rose the gentle slope of what had once been the drive to Fox Close, but the wind swept across it and it was bare of nearly anything else except an old apple tree. Its scrubby length stretched uninspiringly down towards an old, fallen-down wall at the end. Once there, however, it redeemed itself by giving way to a view she thought no one could ever tire of: during the day, the castle remains and the vista of the old town beneath the Beacon, at night the smoky-red Black Country sky and magic necklaces of lights all the way to Birmingham, disguising the sprawl of its dirt and ugliness.

The garden offered possibilities, but so far, making the inside of the house liveable, at the same time as getting to grips with both their new jobs had been more important. At the front of the house, the two-foot-wide strip under the window was easily managed by planting a few geraniums, and the house's exterior having been smartened up by a lick of paint had gone some way to mollifying its detractors.

The brash young property agent who'd shown them around the house had called it a *cottage orné*, which it wasn't, though it was quirky enough to have fancy chimney stacks and no door at the front, only windows, the main entrance being through a pedimented porch round the side, where once the lodge-keeper had emerged to open the gates for horse-drawn coaches bringing visitors to the mansion. Eager to sell the house, the agent had glossed over what he thought they saw as its deficiencies. True, he conceded, a few modernizations might be needed to make the place over, but the old-fashioned Victorian-panelled doors could easily be 'flushed' at small cost; a modern tiled fireplace-surround substituted for that huge, fuel-demanding grate; the leaded panes in the windows could be replaced with ones that let in more light.

It was Ellen herself, in the grip of immediate love with a house that had looked half-dead when they'd first viewed it, as if waiting to be kissed into life, who'd shown unexpected acuity. She'd agreed with all of these 'defects' and pointed out more, all of which would need money spending on them, wouldn't they? A bathroom to begin with, and a replacement for that awful stone kitchen sink. Reardon, amused, had left her to it and as a result they'd eventually acquired the house at a price they could afford. It fitted them like a pair of comfortable old slippers. And now, the room was warmed by a huge fire burning in the despised fireplace, behind the drawn curtains the rain hissed on to the old lattice windowpanes, and the handsome panelled doors and deep skirtings gleamed with new paint. There was a round oak table, a pair of large wing chairs in which Ellen was lost when she curled up, a comfortable old basket chair and a Knole sofa which cushioned the draughts they hadn't quite got rid of yet. The shine on the wide waxed floorboards was worth (in retrospect) the temporary tennis elbow it had cost her. Lamplight glowed attractively on them, and on the spines of all the books in the now almost completed sets of bookshelves.

They'd bickered amicably about how to arrange all their books – alphabetically by author, subject, or more or less at random, as Ellen wished. 'How do you expect to find a book when you want it, then?' Reardon objected. Order was second nature to him, and he was, after all, the keenest reader of the two.

'Oh, I shall remember where they all are.' Unjustified optimism as it turned out, and she might have to concede defeat, though she still preferred it the way it was, and the delight of unexpectedly coming across a forgotten old favourite.

A lump of coal fell in the fire. Tolly opened one eye and Reardon woke up, blinked and stretched, offered to make a cup of tea. 'Carry on with what you're doing,' he said. 'I'll make it.'

But Ellen had already stood up, shifting an affronted Tolly as she did so. 'No, I will, I'm not getting far with this, anyway.' She had tossed her sketchpad into the chair and before she'd finished speaking, made her way to the door. Except that she had turned the wrong way and walked almost slap-bang into the blank wall opposite.

'What the—?' Reardon, Tolly with him, was across the room in three strides, steadying her with a hand on each arm. 'What happened?'

Ellen rubbed her shoulder. 'I-I don't know. Turned too quickly, I suppose, and lost my sense of direction. I didn't know where I was for a moment.'

'More likely the damned dog sent your foot to sleep and made you stumble.' He threw a look of exasperated affection at the damned dog, who was dancing around, getting under the feet and making a lot of noise in sympathy. 'Shut up, Tolly.'

'If anything was asleep it was my brain, not my foot. I just turned the wrong way. Sit down while I make the tea. I'm still all in one piece.'

He ignored this, steered her back to her chair, sat her down firmly and went into the kitchen. She actually did feel quite shaken, though only because she was bemused. She hadn't crashed into the wall very hard. It didn't take Reardon long to make the tea and as she took her cup from him she asked, 'How could I have been so stupid? I could have sworn there was a door there.'

He looked at the blank wall where more bookshelves were due to be placed, once he'd found time to finish making them. 'I suppose it's a logical place for a door when you think about it. Into the glory hole.'

'Maybe.' She recalled having fleetingly had that same thought herself, though maybe not so fleeting that it hadn't been lurking in her subconscious ever since.

But where would a door lead? To nowhere except into the very small room which Reardon called the glory hole. Not yet touched as far as renovations went, mainly because it seemed like nothing more than an afterthought tacked on to the rear of the house and only able to be accessed, oddly, through an outside back door. At present it was nothing more than the repository for the sort of stuff that accumulates in a removal and hasn't yet found a home.

He was still looking at her with concern. 'Really, I'm all right,' she insisted, which was true. Disconcerted, though. A logical place for a door, yes – why should anyone have to go outside and through another door to get to the room on the other side of the wall? Unless it had simply been added as a lean-to, she'd have put money on the existence of a door there at one time.

So why did the thought make her hair stand on end, as though a goose had walked over her grave?

After what had seemed like weeks of leaden skies and never-ending, tedious rain, the next morning felt miraculous: hard, bright and clear, the sort of weather that made you feel you must get out and breathe it in, just as a thank you. The bedroom windows, however, had been feathered with frost flowers when they woke, and when Reardon had gone outside to fetch coal in, he reported a wind cold enough to take your face off. But he'd had the downstairs fire going for an hour now, the stove had warmed the kitchen and they were breakfasting in its cosy glow.

Today was one of Ellen's teaching days, but her first class wasn't until ten thirty, so there was more than ample time for Tolly's run before she left. She was lucky she could leave him with their neighbour, Horace Levett, who kept an eye on him when she was working, with no worries about being beholden because it was a mutual admiration society there – Horace loved having the dog for company, spoilt him, let him take advantage. All the same, he was seventy-six and she knew he appreciated the fact of an energetic Jack Russell having already worked off some of his superfluous bounce before he arrived. And perhaps, she thought in guilty parenthesis, she could combine the run with that pesky art class assignment that was hanging over her.

'I thought I'd take Tolly up the hill and see what there is to sketch up there at the same time,' she remarked, seeing a way to combine both.

'A bit nippy for drawing, this morning, isn't it?' Reardon said, squinting from behind his newspaper. 'You'll get frostbite in your fingers. You must be keen.'

'Not really, just guilty about not doing my homework. The teacher's expecting us all to have finished the assignment by now and so far only two have submitted anything, poor man.'

'Misplaced sympathy. Watch out it doesn't cause you to freeze to death.'

'Oh, come on, it's just the day for a nice brisk walk up the hill.'

'Rather you than me.'

But he'd read the subtext. Joining the art class had seemed like a good idea at the time, but they both knew Ellen was now only keeping on with it because if more of the initially well-intentioned students lost their enthusiasm and dropped out it would be cancelled. She had once taught WEA classes herself (it was how she and Reardon, her pupil, making up for gaps in his sketchy schooling, had met) and no one was more aware than she of how demoralizing a falling off in numbers could be – to the remainder of the class, as well as their teacher. And she had to admit, it wouldn't take much, if she allowed it, for her to be one of the drop-outs. But reminding herself that the teacher was a struggling young artist and was probably dependant on the extra money the night classes brought in stiffened her decision to make a better try. 'I'm not sure frostbite would make much difference anyway,' she admitted gloomily as she began to clear the plates. 'Whatever made me think I could ever learn to draw or paint?'

'You'd never know if you hadn't tried,' he pointed out, though he didn't seem to think it mattered one way or another that she might not turn out to be the next Leonardo. And even if he was thinking it, he forbore to say that a cookery course might have been a better answer if she was feeling she had energy to spare.

A glance at his wristwatch reminded him he ought to get a move on. Folding the paper, he pushed his chair back. 'Wrap up well, then,' he said, sounding like somebody's nanny, 'it's brass monkeys out there.' He shrugged on his coat, gave her a quick kiss. At the door, he paused for a moment, then turned back and hugged her, hard, and his fingers gently brushed her cheek 'Take care, love.' *And don't go walking into any more walls*, his eyes said, as if remembering last night.

Or maybe that's just me, being sensitive, Ellen told herself. That preoccupied look he'd had for days was back, meaning his mind was quite likely on something else entirely, something

quite unconnected with her. No use asking him what. 'You
take care yourself,' she said instead.

Maybe she ought to have heeded him, she was thinking as she
climbed the hill, the icy wind on her face. She had definitely
picked the wrong morning for sketching, although she was
heavily muffled up in a thick scarf, woolly gloves and the
distinctly unglamorous sheepskin boots which had been
consigned to the back of the wardrobe since she'd stopped
riding pillion on Reardon's now little used motorbike. They
were still useful for this arctic weather.

This was the sort of bracing walk she usually enjoyed, but
struggling against the biting wind, and the thought of sitting
down with a pencil when she reached the top of the hill where
the old house used to stand was becoming decidedly less
appealing than it had in the warm kitchen. The walking was
easy enough. Grass had taken over what must once have been
the drive up to the old mansion; the extra firmness underfoot
being the only indication that it had ever been there at all. But
it felt quite likely she'd be minus her nose and ears by the
time she reached the top. It was so cold she was surprised
even the birds hadn't fallen silent. But after toiling up to the
halfway point turning back wasn't an option.

Fox Close had been an old, old house, its whole estate
surrounded centuries ago by a wall which had now largely
disappeared, its demolished stones carted away, either legally
or purloined for other purposes. There had been gates, too,
but they had been removed when The Avenue was built. One
of the houses actually stood solidly over the place where they
had been, next door to Number Nine, the Reardon residence.
Ellen had no idea whether she was trespassing or not, but
since there was now nothing left to disturb in the mansion's
erstwhile estate, she didn't think a hop over what remained
of the wall mattered.

The grounds could never have been extensive in scope, nor
very ornamental, come to that, but there were mature trees
nearer the house: oaks, some beech and a large stand of tall,
gloomy elms, leafless branches etched against the sky – bare,
ruined choirs where late the sweet birds sang, in the words of

the bard. Today the ruined choirs provided a resting place for dozens of untidy, twiggy nests, and the sweet birds were rooks, restless and noisy, wheeling and flapping their wings around them. Their squawks increased and they rose to the sky in affront when Tolly barked under their chosen trees, his rear-end in the air and front paws furiously digging for what turned out to be nothing more than a piece of rotted, fallen branch. Dropping it in disgust, he trotted off in search of something more interesting, a rabbit to chase if he was in luck. The birds subsided and Ellen turned her back against the wind and scouted around for a place where she could perch and balance her sketch pad on her knees.

It was years since the house had been demolished almost down to its foundations and beneath the stiffly frozen grass and weeds, which now covered most of it, could only be seen the outlines of what must once have been a large residence, its frontage overlooking Folbury in the valley below. Finally she found a sheltered spot, where it seemed there had once been a terraced garden. It offered a view which gave a whole new meaning to Folbury's town centre down below; even the medieval hugger-mugger streets in the old part where she still sometimes lost her bearings made sense at this distance. You could see Town Hall Square and the Market Street Police Station, where Reardon even now was no doubt enjoying a hot cup of tea. She set to work, but ten minutes after rubbing some life into her fingers, she'd succeeded in making only a botched attempt at the streets radiating from the river.

The Fol looked like a flat silver ribbon from here, though with all the recent rain, it must be running higher than usual. Pretty along its banks at various points, edged with willows and balsam, only navigable above the town, which was why the canal, the Folbury Cut, had been built, to run through the Arms Green industrial area and the town before joining the river further down.

Because of the rocks, it was not a river you'd choose to swim in either. And yet, someone *was* swimming there. Really? No, it could be nothing more than a piece of floating rubbish, or a dog possibly, paddling upstream. What looked like a sleek head bobbed up. Not a dog. An otter? Not likely around here.

An arm appeared above the water, then another. It actually was a swimmer, a human swimmer, doing a fast, expert crawl and making short work of the distance to the bank. On a perishing cold winter morning! In the Fol! Ellen couldn't believe that anyone would be stupid enough. Maybe it really was a piece of rubbish being tumbled over that she'd seen. Except that rubbish wouldn't draw itself out of the water and towel itself off. Some people, she thought, sympathetic goose-bumps rising on her arms and an icy trickle running down her spine.

'Well,' said a voice behind her, 'if someone is intent on ending it all, what better way?'

She jumped nearly out of her skin. A tall man, dark, with a sallow skin and a thin face, was standing on the rising ground just behind her and had evidently been viewing the same phenomenon. He didn't look as though he bothered to smile very much, but he sounded pleasant enough. 'Though people do, I suppose. Swim in the sea at Brighton on New Year's Day, I've heard tell . . . but the Fol, in February?'

He spoke as if Folbury rivalled the Frozen North, which it might well do today. Ellen laughed, regaining her equilibrium.

She was very conscious he was making no attempt to avoid looking at the pitiful offering on her sketch pad, and had a silly impulse to cover it up with her arm, as the children did in school.

He must have sensed her discomfiture. 'You haven't got the perspective quite right,' he said. 'Do you mind?' He held a hand out for her pencil and she found herself meekly handing it over. Plus her eraser.

He leant over and with a few rapid strokes the converging lines, which had been confusing her and which she hadn't got anywhere near right, were corrected. Immediately it looked better. A work of art it was not, but it might not turn out to be too totally hopeless to hand in, after all. 'Thank you,' she said, taking the pencil back. 'I'm afraid it was pretty terrible.'

'Not really. I imagine you only need practice.'

Disregarding this obviously polite lie, she asked, 'Are you an artist?'

'Lord, no. I used to draw a bit when I was younger, but I never entirely got the hang of it either.'

'Well, thank you for the help.'

'My pleasure.' He raised his hat and walked away, pausing to pat Tolly, who had rushed up to investigate. It was time she went home, too, now that she had some work on her pad, thanks to the kindness of a stranger. She packed up and walked more quickly down the hill than she had walked up, towards Horace's house where she would leave Tolly, and have the hot drink she knew he'd have waiting for her.

'Another one pushed through the door last night,' Joe Gilmour, Reardon's copper-haired sergeant greeted him as he entered the temporary offices which had been created by the relocation and shuffling around of other offices for what was the still innovative detective section. It was small by any standards, and Reardon's own office was even smaller, consisting of a glassed-in cubicle in the corner.

The police station had actually been designed as part of the town hall, the Victorian edifice which also housed the public library on its other side. The whole, once impressive building was now hopelessly old-fashioned, definitely not up to today's needs, but it was wishful thinking to expect splendid new offices would magically materialize. The force's top brass, with an eye on funds, weren't pushing for it.

'No stamp, pushed through the letter box again,' Gilmour was saying, following Reardon into his office and shunting an envelope across the desk before turning to collect the two mugs of tea DC Pickersgill had just brought to the door. 'Thanks, Dave.'

Reardon shed his outdoor coat and picked up the now familiar missive, his name written in clumsy, pencilled characters: 'INSPECTER REEDEN'. He had no need to open it to know what was inside, but he did. And of course it was along the same lines as the others: 'Ill get you for this Reeden. In a way you wont like'.

He tossed it on to the desk. 'No imagination, our Sonny.' Sonny Murfitt, small-time crook, housebreaker, who else?

'Could be him, I suppose, he's out again,' Gilmour allowed.

He didn't sound too convinced. 'Sonny, writing letters? Hardly his style, is it? And he's not exactly the only one ever to make threats.'

'The only one to make threats so close to home.'

'What does that mean?'

Reardon hadn't felt it worth mentioning, that first threat, made as Murfitt was leaving court after being sent down for six months for breaking and entering. He'd muffed the job as usual and had been nailed red-handed. Protesting his innocence, naturally. Reardon belatedly felt he owed his sergeant an explanation. They were friends after all, as well as colleagues, usually pretty much on the same wavelength, despite their different approaches to most situations. 'His wife died just before he went down, Joe, remember? Cancer. He believes the worry about him caused it.'

'Jeannie? Worrying about him being banged up again?' Gilmour laughed. She'd been a braw Scottish woman, twice the size of Sonny, who'd thought nothing of knocking him about a bit. Heaven alone knew what had brought her to Folbury and Sonny's loving arms. But she hadn't deserved to die as she had and Gilmour sobered. 'Anyway, can worry cause cancer?'

'I don't know. They say it can trigger all sorts. The point is, Sonny believes it did.'

'How do you know that?'

Reardon shrugged. 'He shot his mouth about it enough while he was in Winson Green.'

He had made it his business to enquire at the prison and hadn't been surprised when one of the warders had told him about the grievance Sonny constantly aired. And the threats to Reardon's own wife that he'd made. No one, Reardon included, had taken him too seriously. Such empty menaces were par for the course, a way of venting pent-up frustrations. Anyway, Sonny was a weedy little pip-squeak, and his criminal inclinations were misguided and ineffectual, rather than violent or vicious.

'Hold on a minute . . . you mean – Ellen?' Gilmour said, and instantly became more focused. His little daughter's godmother stood very high in his affections. His own dearly loved wife notwithstanding, if he'd been a knight in the joust, he'd have sported Ellen's favour on his lance. 'Well, it probably means nothing,' he tried, not entirely convincingly. 'You know our Sonny. He's all shout. If it is him sending the letters – if – he's probably hoping to put the wind up you, that's all.'

'Right, so forget it.' Reardon tossed the letter into the wastebasket and picked up the desk sergeant's report of last night's activities.

But when you've just lost your wife to cancer things must take on a different aspect, even to someone like Sonny Murfitt.

Gilmour retrieved the letter from the basket and put it aside. 'Not going to be much help, mind. Even Sonny must be savvy enough to know that fingerprints can be lifted from a letter or an envelope.'

'Want to bet?' But there was no denying Sonny irritated the hell out of him, the way he always said his name wrong – Reeden, not Reardon. The name on the messages themselves had also been ill-spelt in the same way – though a lurking suspicion made him wonder if that wasn't deliberate, if the bad spelling wasn't all too much, which would immediately eliminate Sonny, who wouldn't have known the difference anyway.

'And most of his associates, too,' Gilmour said when he voiced this.

But . . . one of his so-called mates maybe, with a grievance against him? One who knew the trouble he had with Reardon's name and wanted to stir up mischief? Maybe – always supposing that anyone Sonny associated with had more than three-figure IQ between them to figure that out.

'You haven't mentioned anything about this to Maisie, have you, Joe?' he asked. Because if he had, she would have told Ellen, and that might account for the speculative looks she'd been giving him lately, as if she knew there was something he hadn't been telling her.

Gilmour looked hurt. 'No. You asked me not to. But . . . shouldn't you warn Ellen?'

'I already have. In a way. She's wondering why I'm such an old woman all of a sudden, telling her to be careful every time she goes out. But I can't say without going into details and I don't want to frighten her.'

The idea of Ellen being afraid of anything brought a wry exchange of smiles. They both knew she would be more likely to arm herself with a sand-filled sock to carry around, just in case.

Gilmour went out and Reardon turned his attention to what was waiting for him on his desk.

Until recently there had been little large-scale crime in the small market town, but his remit now extended beyond the confines of Folbury itself, to include several communities beyond, into the villages and hamlets of the smiling countryside which could, as one greater than he had once opined, hold more sin than the lowest and vilest alleys of London. Crime in general was on the up and up, here like everywhere else in a country still reeling from the economic effects of a war which had caused a worldwide depression. Men with no work and no prospects, and with families to feed, were prepared to break the law and take the sort of risks they wouldn't otherwise have contemplated – and the ways in which they did it grew ever more imaginative and inventive. Nor was all of it down to the local residents of Folbury, by any means. Not when the use of motor power could get criminals away easily. Increasingly, they were coming in from outside, from the big cities, Birmingham, Manchester, and even London.

'My, it's parky out there this morning,' Ellen said, gratefully sipping the hot cocoa. 'You won't believe this, Horace, but I've just seen someone swimming in the river.'

'Go on!' He moved aside the clock he was currently repairing to make room for his own mug on the table. 'Are you sure?' he asked, shaking his head at such folly.

'Yes, I didn't imagine it.' The stranger who had helped her with her homework had seen the swimmer, too. 'You've a good view from up there, from Fox Close.' She watched Horace spooning more sugar into his cocoa. 'What do you know about it, Horace . . . the house I mean?' she asked.

Horace looked at her over his spectacles. He was a retired jeweller with a sideline in clock repairing, which he had kept up as a pastime after selling his business, something to help fill the days he had found so empty since his wife died. He had lived in Folbury most of his life and was a prime source of information on most aspects of it and its past, and more than anything else, he loved to talk about it.

'You must remember the house. What was it like?'

'Miserable old place,' he answered. 'No loss to anybody when they had it pulled down. For building development, so they said. Although so far they've only built these houses.' By that he meant the semis in The Avenue, one of which he occupied.

'That's the Millars, the building firm? The people who owned Fox Close?'

'That's right. And it's still their land, of course. I've been expecting them to start more building up there any day . . . I hear tell they've finished all the big houses on Ladyford Lane, so they'll be wanting to start somewhere else.'

'It must have been a grand old place, Fox Close.'

Horace laughed. 'Grand? Well, the old chap, old Müller, thought so, I reckon, but nobody else did. When he bought it, off the de Veres that had lived there since Adam was a lad, it had been let go to rack and ruin. He did a lot of building work on it, towers and belfries and fancy brickwork and that. Tell the truth, he didn't improve things to my way of thinking. He'd have done better to leave it and get on with indoors. A mausoleum inside it was, and in the end he died before he ever got round to that. But we all have our blind spots, don't we?' He smiled reminiscently. 'I think he was a bit potty in a way, especially when it came to his clocks, but he was a nice old boy for all that.'

'You knew him well, then?'

'So-so. He loved his clocks, see, old Manfred. That's what he was called. Manfred Müller, started out as a jobbing builder in his young days. Big fella he was. Could lift two loads of bricks without breaking sweat, they said. Hands like shovels, fingers like sausages.'

'That must have been a handicap, tinkering with clocks.'

Horace chuckled. 'He loved 'em like babies, was fascinated by how they worked, but he hadn't got the touch. Course, that's why he had me to attend to them. Dozens he had, and big old things they were, most of them. German, as you'd expect.'

'Not English, then, the family?'

'Not until the son – Ernst I think he was to begin with – changed his name to Ernest Millar. Changed everything else come to that, when his father died, sudden, and left everything to him. I still used to go to the house and service the clocks for him like I used to for his father, but it wasn't the same. Old Manfred always had time for a bit of a chinwag when it came to clocks. He knew a lot about 'em but he was always eager to learn more. We'd talk for hours, and we got to be friendly-like. But the son – different kettle of fish altogether. He'd pay me and thank me for my time, polite enough, but he left me in no doubt I was nothing more than a paid workman. Which I suppose I was, just somebody to maintain the clocks. Well, it's all according.' He bent over to give Tolly's head a scratch and palm him a bit of forbidden biscuit. Ellen pretended not to notice.

'Do go on. I'm interested.'

'Nothing much more to tell.' Horace shrugged, but he had obviously been hurt that his expertise had been undervalued and the temptation to talk about the past, when life had held a bit more colour to it, was too great, and after a minute he went on. 'He was a bible-fearing man, you know, the son, Ernest Millar – up to the neck in all that religious stuff . . . in the wrong kind of way to my mind. Pentecostal, Jehovah's Witnesses, or some such thing. I reckon they had a rough time of it, his wife and family, though she died early. To be honest, he wasn't what you'd call a nice man and it wasn't a cheerful home. I don't think his children were happy at all.' He paused. 'Ah well, it's all a long time ago, best forgotten. More cocoa?'

'No thanks. That was lovely, but I must go.' Ellen stood up. She'd run out of time, and in any case, although Horace was a mine of information about Folbury, he'd only go so far. Gossip was another thing.

THREE

D usk had fallen over the semi-abandoned industrial estate in Arms Green known as Hadley Piece as Wesley Pugh got there, but that wasn't doing much to hide its crumbling dereliction. The whole place fanned his irritation, as it usually did. Apart from the deserted lock-keeper's house by the canal, the odd, still functioning warehouse and the one-storey building where Matt Millar lived and had his studio, little of what he remembered as a once thriving and busy hub of industry remained intact. The fire which had destroyed the ancient corn mill adjacent to the site, a working proposition for hundreds of years, had spread fast to engulf most of the properties around. The mill itself had been gutted, so far devastated that it hadn't been worth saving, and had never worked again, closing several chapters of honourable family history and contributing to the decline and virtual abandonment of the rest of the site. The other businesses had for the most part been light engineering: the small brass foundry owned and run by the owners of the site, the Rees-Talbots; a factory where bicycle frames were made; traditional nail-makers; paint manufacturers; plus several warehouses, only one or two of which were still in more or less casual use.

Years after the fire, the site remained a white elephant. No one had stepped forward with funds to bring it to life again until the whole parcel of land had finally been donated by the owners, the surviving members of the Rees-Talbot family, to Folbury council for the building of municipal housing, afford-able houses for rent. It hadn't happened yet. Money couldn't be found for the purpose, but people like Wesley Pugh, in his capacity as a town councillor and Miss Rees-Talbot herself, who had in fact urged her family to make the gift, had no intentions of allowing the subject to lapse. Wesley wasn't holding his breath about the outcome, but he went on making himself unpopular by harassing the rest of the council and

anyone else who could be of use. Just now he was intent on
a campaign to step up the pressure, but the housing committee
were dragging their feet, to put the best construction on it.

The shed-like structure on the canal bank which Matt Millar
now occupied was one of those which had escaped the fire.
It had originally been taken by Ernest Millar as extra storage
facilities when he was thinking of extending his business.
Nothing had ever come of his intentions however and it had
remained empty until Matt had set up his workplace there.
Ernest had been a cautious, tight-fisted old devil, and it was
more than likely he'd felt he'd been too hasty and had bitten
off more than he could chew in view of the money he'd have
had to lay out in expanding his activities. At any rate,
the builder's yard and offices were still to this day run from
where his father, Manfred, had begun the business, at Inkerman
Terrace, further down the canal.

In the shadowy light the gaunt remains of the corn mill
were stark against the sky at the far end. Empty shells of
blackened warehouses and their landing stages loomed alongside the canal; at the far end the canal basin and the gasholder
beyond could be glimpsed through the span of the narrow
arched bridge. It was a desolate spot even in daylight, and in
Wesley's opinion, the time was long overdue for the whole
lot, including what Matt liked to call his studio, to come down,
regardless of whether the council houses were ever built. He
wondered how the lad could stick it, living and working here.
It gave Wesley the creeps, but it didn't bother Matt, which
was the point, after all.

His light was on, Wesley saw as he picked his way across
the uneven ground, and then noticed with some surprise that
he wasn't Matt's only visitor that night. Someone was just
leaving as Wesley drew nearer. Thinking for a moment he'd
been mistaken, and it was Matt, he hurried to catch him, until
he saw there was no mistaking the way this man moved – in
a middle-aged way, like Wesley himself – quite unlike Matt's
loping stride. Then the man reached the corner of the building
and what light there was threw his face into relief.

Recognition – or what for a moment or two he had imagined
was recognition – ran through Wesley like an electric shock.

Christ! If he had believed in ghosts – which in Wesley's book was akin to believing in witches, fairies and Santa Claus – he might have thought he'd actually seen Paul Millar, long thought to lie among the nameless dead in Flanders fields. He hadn't had any time for the man, for reasons that were buried deep as the bastard's bones, and a stab of the old, boiling hatred rose like bile. The man disappeared around the corner, and he told himself not to be so bloody daft and walked on to the studio.

Ted Millar, having no children of his own, had been bitterly disappointed when Matt had made evident his non-interest in the family firm. He'd always hoped the boy would use his good brain and choose a respectable career, hopefully as heir-apparent to Millar Homes, one day.

'And art isn't respectable?' Matt had grinned and cocked an eyebrow and Ted had lifted his hands in apology. But he hadn't been able to resist reminding his nephew, stating the obvious, that painting pictures (especially the kind Matt painted, the implications there, if unvoiced) was unlikely to earn him a living, especially in the present climate.

'I'm sorry, Uncle Ted. I know how much Millars means to you, but . . . all right, ask me again in ten years and I might have to say different, but just now . . . I have to have a go, don't you see?'

What Ted did see was that this wasn't the plea it seemed to be, it was a statement of intent. It was the only sign of what might be seen as ruthlessness he'd ever noticed in Matt. Well, that was a trait that ran through the family, wasn't it? And Thea at least supported the lad. 'Let him make his own mistakes,' she counselled. Ted sighed and gave in to the pressures on both sides and even dipped a hand into his pocket with offers of monetary assistance through what he saw were obviously going to be the lean years as an aspiring artist. That had been another mistake, but at least Matt had allowed Ted to grant him the use of the old Hadley Piece premises as his studio and the place where he stubbornly chose to live, leading as reasonably orderly a life as being an artist allowed him to do.

Not quite on the latch, the outside door of the studio gave

as Wesley pushed on it. He crossed the empty ground floor to the foot of the steps. 'Matt?' he called.

There was no answer, so he climbed to the top. Matt was standing with his back to the open door, and obviously hadn't heard Wesley. He swung round, his face dark, then saw who it was. 'Oh. Wesley. Come in.'

Wesley was already in and had seen what looked like a letter spread out on the table in front of Matt. Without apparent haste, Matt thrust it back into its envelope and shoved it into a drawer. Not before Wesley had seen what it was; he'd written enough of them himself to know it was a field letter from the Western Front, in an honour envelope, so called because it would not then be read and censored by anyone the sender was likely to know in the regiment before being despatched across the Channel.

'Hang on and I'll get the posters, Wes. I have them ready.'

Posters, illustrations for any firm who needed them for advertising, greetings cards, teaching at night school classes, it was a precarious way of earning a living. But Matt seemed to be doing all right on it – or as all right as he seemed to think necessary for the time being. It was supporting him, if only just, while he built up a reputation for what he considered his real work. Which was likely to be a long, slow job, Wesley thought grimly, though it was no deterrent to Matt's ambition. It meant hard work and not least, a modicum of luck – in the first place, at any rate. A year ago, through one of the teachers at his London art school who'd had a lot of faith in him, Matt had achieved a showing at a fairly well-known art gallery in the West End, and had even sold a couple of his paintings there, but after that more commissions were slow to come in. The trouble was, Wesley knew, his work was too specialized to be universally popular. Wesley himself liked it, went some way to loving it in fact, but the stark, unlovely Black Country factories, canals, smoke stacks, views like those through his window and just outside his door, which were the backbone of Matt's output, were not to everyone's taste or understanding. He admired Matt for his dedication, tenacity, and his sense of always being in charge of himself, but all the same, for a young chap like him, it was no sort of life to be leading, in

Wesley's book. However, since it was what Matt, whom he loved like a son, had chosen, he kept his own counsel. It was what drove him, just as Wesley's own interests outside work drove him. Passions, maybe, in both cases, rather than interests, he was willing to concede, different as they were.

Wesley's Welsh antecedents were long in the past, but they had bequeathed him a fighting spirit and political leanings far to the left. He had read Karl Marx, he took the *Daily Herald*, supported trade union militancy, socialism and rights for the people in any form. The war, for all its traumas, had gone a long way towards sweeping away social divisions but not far enough for Wesley. He had returned from the front with a Military Medal, and as a town councillor was always pressing for action on some cause or other.

'Coming to the meeting tonight, Matt?'

Miss Deborah Rees-Talbot, a slightly eccentric but public-spirited maiden lady with whom Wesley felt some slight if unjustified connection, by reason of their distant and separate Welsh ancestries, had joined forces with Wesley to arrange a protest meeting against the delay in starting the house building. It was to be held in the Holy Trinity parish hall that night and promised to be a lively affair.

'No,' Matt said shortly. 'Sorry, I can't.'

The tone surprised Wesley, though the refusal didn't. He nourished the hope that Matt would one day join him in his campaigns. They could do with some new blood, chaps like him – young and idealistic. Wesley had imagined Matt would be worried that his studio would have to go if the development went ahead. But he'd been wrong. 'I'll find somewhere else,' he'd said with a shrug, and had been quite happy to do the posters advertising this meeting, and several more for next week, as long as he didn't have to involve himself more.

While he went to find a cardboard tube, Wesley leaned against the table and looked round the cheerless room, meta-phorically shaking his head. It was a lonely existence for a young chap. The thought of the man he'd seen leaving the building came into his mind. He suddenly didn't like the idea of Matt living here alone, though Matt, fit and hard-muscled under his shirt, was certainly quite capable of taking care of

himself. But there was something about him tonight which
disturbed Wesley. He was tensed up, as though he had something on his mind.

'Thought you'd have packed it in for the day,' he said,
looking at the posters Matt spread out on the table for his
inspection.

'Just about to.'

The posters were headed HOMES FOR HEROES, a phrase
Wesley and Miss Rees-Talbot had borrowed from Lloyd
George, who, when he was prime minister, had made glorious
promises of social housing, homes fit for those men returned
from the fighting. The posters were bold and eye-catching,
well executed. It would have been surprising if they hadn't
been, and Wesley nodded his appreciation.

'Hope the meeting goes well, Wes. I hear there's a lot of
support, so it should do.'

'Your Uncle Ted won't like it if there's no go-ahead.'

Matt raised an eyebrow and grinned. 'Don't tell me he's
hoping to get the contract? For council houses? Uncle Ted?'

'Why not?' Matt could laugh, but it wasn't as implausible
as it sounded, as Wesley was well aware, working as he did
in his undefined capacity of site foreman/project manager,
Ted's right-hand man at Millar Homes, as Ted was fond of
saying. It wasn't exactly a position with prospects, but Wesley
had never looked for that. What the job did was give him time
and energy for his political activities, and for the other, more
important things which kept him here in Folbury.

Knowing the business inside out as he did, he knew that
now the last house on Ladyford Lane was not far off being
completed, Ted was looking round for other work, and although
as Matt had rightly implied, building council houses wasn't
really his line – still less did they tie in with his ambitions
– such a contract would fill in the gaps until he could get
started on other more lucrative projects. Money was as
tight for Ted as everyone else at the moment, and he'd spent
a lot on that house of his own. Another site of more modest
houses off Emscott Hill was in progress, but worryingly they
were not selling well. 'He's hoping to get the contract, although
he knows it's unlikely. Hurst and Sons are bidding as well.

They're more used to building that type of housing . . . and more anxious than us for the work, so they're bound to undercut. Any road, it won't be disastrous if we don't get it. Ted's had it in mind to start on more houses at Fox Close, at last, so I reckon that's where he'll go next if he doesn't get the contract.'

'I know, he told me, but that was last week. I wouldn't bank on it,' Matt said abruptly. 'He's got more on his mind now.' He turned away and began rolling up the posters and slotting them into the tube.

Wesley waited for an explanation, but it didn't come. 'Sure you won't come to the meeting, Matt?' he asked again.

'I told you, I can't. I'm meeting Imogen.'

'Put her off, she won't mind, not for this.'

'I know she wouldn't, but the answer's still no, Wes.'

Wesley knew when to desist. Matt in stubborn mood was as likely to put off his meeting with Imogen as to abandon his work, and he sighed, though he was glad she was Matt's excuse. He himself had a very soft spot indeed for Imogen Randall.

He turned to go but Matt, for a moment, had seemed on the verge of saying something else, so he waited. 'What's up?'

'No. Don't ask. It's nothing.'

If anyone knew when to shut up, it was Wesley Pugh. But above anything else, that was the last thing he felt he ought to do on this occasion. He braced himself and asked, 'Who was that I saw just leaving here?'

Independence was inbuilt in Matt by now. It went way back, even to when, bursting with pride for his father and his uncle, he had stood at the roadside with the other boys and the women, cheering as their brave fathers, husbands, brothers and uncles had marched off, whistling patriotic songs, to trounce the bloody Huns. His dad wasn't among them, but little Matt was prouder than any of them. Paul had already volunteered, weeks since, and gone away to be an airman, to fly aeroplanes and bomb the bloody Germans. 'I'll write to you, son,' he'd promised, holding him tight. 'Be a good lad. Your Auntie Thea will take good care of you until I come back.' And Matt knew his dad would come home, keep his

promise. It would be like before, when he'd gone away after
. . . after . . .

And he'd come home again that time, hadn't he? Although
too soon after he had, the war had happened, and he was off
again to give the bloody Germans what for.

Matt did his best to hide the fact that his real name was
Matthaeus, and especially that his family had once been
German, before his grandpa changed their name. But he knew
in his heart, with absolute certainty, that not all Germans were
bad. How could they be? One at least had not been – the one
who had been the core of his existence, his mother, Liesl. But
he tried not to think of her, or the way she would make him
laugh with funny stories, the way she smelled so nice when
she hugged him or tucked him up in bed at night. '*Gott segne
dich, mein Kleine!*' God bless, my little one. Most of all,
he would not think about her dying, otherwise he might shame
himself and burst into tears and have one of his frightening
dreams.

'I can take care of myself,' he'd boasted to his father, with
all the passion of an eight-year-old, when Paul went off to
fight. His dad had just patted his head and smiled.

He had lived for those promised letters. It turned out, though,
that Paul wasn't much of a correspondent, and a letter from
him was an event, a few lines, sometimes scored through with
a blue pencil by someone called the censor. Matt had kept
them all, read and re-read them. His Auntie Thea explained
how hard it was for the men fighting the war to find time
and opportunity to write letters, so he tried not to mind. It had
been exciting at first to think of his father as one of the heroes,
but after the big battle of the Somme, when all those Folbury
men were killed, some of them fathers of his own pals, he
lived in daily terror of the telegram which would say that Paul,
too, had been killed, his aeroplane exploding in mid-air and
plunging to the earth on fire. Or wounded, even taken prisoner
by the bloody Krauts, like his classmate Wilf's dad. None of
this happened. His dad, and his Uncle Teddy too, went right
through the war, seemingly unharmed. Meanwhile, Matt
grew older, went to the senior school, tried smoking, learnt
more swear words than 'bloody', and came across a teacher,

Miss Tilley, who encouraged his drawing and painting and gave him the pointer towards his future.

And then at last the conflict was over, and the waiting for his father's return began. Waiting that went on and on until hope dwindled and finally vanished. It was impossible, of course, despite an Armistice being declared, as Thea explained to him, to send every soldier home immediately, and Matt understood this, though he didn't see why his Uncle Ted should have been sent home when his father wasn't. The demobilization of hundreds of thousands of troops was a lengthy, complicated and often chaotic business, said Thea, as so much else seemed to be nowadays, even though the war was over. They would have to be patient.

The worst of it was that the letters from Paul, rare though they'd always been, had now stopped altogether, so what had happened? Thea said that the War Office would have written to them if he had been wounded, killed or taken prisoner. She had tried to seek out and talk to men who had been with him, but nothing came of it. In the end she told him gently that they must try to accept that his father had been another heroic tragedy, one of those thousands of unknown soldiers, sailors and airmen, lost without trace. Killed perhaps in the last days of the war. Matt still had nightmares of him being burned to death in his aeroplane, even his identity tag gone. He didn't care at all by then that this might have made him a hero, he only wanted him home. But he knew in his heart he must certainly be dead.

And then, there he was. Resurrected like Lazarus from the grave. Sitting there, in that uncoordinated muddle of a sitting room that Matt's aunt and uncle had created between them in the house on Ladyford Lane. Looking as if he had every right to be there. And saying nothing whatever about why he hadn't even let them know whether he was alive or dead.

PART TWO

FOUR

A grey dawn is breaking, but the mist hanging over the river is beginning to lift as the kingfisher, a flash of bright blue and orange, emerges from his nest-burrow in the bank and skims low across the water. Momentarily, he hovers over the mass which has just risen to the surface, but it proves to be of no interest to him; under the thick layer of waterweed it's nothing more than a human body. His darting flight to the opposite bank offers a low, bare branch to perch on, beady-eyed and watchful for better prey, while the body, buoyant now with gas, begins to drift gently away.

Passing Cooper's Lock, which is where the Folbury Cut begins – at the point where the river begins to tumble through steep banks, where its shallowness over the rocky bed makes river traffic no longer viable – the body is propelled downriver, occasionally buffeted to one side, sometimes to the other. At one point during the day it nudges the pathless, steep and thickly overgrown bank, and seems as though it might come to rest there, become captured by the overhanging branches of willow and alder. But not for long. It is very soon caught by the flow again and carried mid-stream towards the town, until presently it reaches the weir, slides over and into the choppy waters beneath. For a while it tumbles like washing in a copper before being propelled under Castle Bridge in the town centre. By now, darkness has fallen and no one notices the bundle of old rubbish bobbing about on the water, and as night falls, its journey ends, wedged into a dangerously undercut spot in the narrow path beside the allotments.

'There's no chance we know who he is yet?'

Reardon turned up his coat collar against the wind that was riffling the surface of the water and shivering the dead nettles, old brambles and docks on the earth-trodden path. Here and

there an unlikely promise of early spring gleamed gold
between them, where a few celandines thrust out hopeful heads.
On the path itself, lying there after it had been lifted from the
mud and filth in which it had lodged, was the sodden mass
the police doctor was attempting to examine.

Algae had formed a green scum over the little inlet of water
formed by the deeply undercut bank, though it hadn't entirely
covered the usual river debris which had collected there, along
with what the holders of the allotments lying behind the path
tended to tip into the water, not all of it organic garden waste.
The body had been spotted there less than an hour ago, at about
seven on that miserable morning, doubtless another human
being for whom life had proved too much. Another like that
young woman, pregnant and unwed, who had ended up here
at this very same spot just before Christmas, though neither
would have known or cared about the insalubriousness of their
last resting place.

Reardon's question had been rhetorical. Waterlogged and
bloated as the body was, he wasn't expecting an answer from
his sergeant, nor hopeful of getting one, and he raised a scep-
tical eyebrow when Gilmour answered that yes, the chap who
had found him knew him.

'Knew him? How?' Daubed with mud and slimy trails of
waterweed, the saturated heap was swollen and distorted after
its immersion to the extent that facial recognition was surely
impossible. He was fully clothed, but his pockets hadn't yet
been gone through for indications of anything that would have
revealed his identity.

Gilmour shrugged. 'Search me. But he swears he does.
He says it's a man by the name of Millar, Millar with an
"a".' He paused. 'As in Millar Homes.'

'Not Ted Millar?' Ted Millar was a big name in Folbury.
Reardon knew the man only slightly, having met him no more
than briefly once or twice, and couldn't with any certainty
recall what he looked like, but then, a drowned body didn't
tend to look much like anyone. This one didn't, for sure,
though it was too soon after breakfast to have taken more than
a necessary, cursory look.

'No, it's not Ted. He says it's his brother, Paul.'

'There's a brother?' Something odd in Gilmour's voice caused Reardon to throw him a sharp glance. 'What's up?'

'Nothing – except that Paul Millar's been dead for donkey's years.'

Clearly not, if that's who this was.

'But the man who found him still thinks it's him? And who might he be?'

'Wesley Pugh. Lives round here, in Colley Street, works for Millars as general manager or something like that. Councillor Pugh.'

'Councillor Pugh? Yes, I know who he is.'

'He and Paul Millar used to be mates, years ago, and he swears blind this is him, though he was supposed to have bought it during the war. If Pugh's right, he must've been alive and well all this time, if you can believe that.'

Reardon could, at a stretch. Stranger things had happened. From time to time, men were still reappearing, long after the fighting had ended, after being thought dead for years, missing believed killed – their absences accounted for in different and sometimes bizarre ways. Shell-shocked men, who had somehow disappeared from the battlefield and later surfaced with no memory of who they were, or of anything which had happened to them in their previous incarnations, eventually finding themselves some sort of new life, maybe across the Channel. Men who had seen and experienced more than any human being should – things so bad they had subconsciously shut off their past altogether, until something had triggered their memory responses. As an ex-soldier himself, Reardon knew only too well the horrors that contributed to these lost states of mind. He also knew, as a policeman, that there were those who had deliberately chosen, for reasons of their own, to slip the net, make themselves scarce and not return to their old civilian life after the hostilities ceased.

'I don't recall any stir about it – no mention of him returning, I mean,' he remarked with a frown.

In fact, nothing at all had come to his ears, and apparently not to Gilmour's or anyone else's that he knew of, either, he said, which was surprising, if not actually inconceivable. Because surely the story of a wartime hero returned from the dead would have run like wildfire through Folbury, been on everyone's lips, a sensation greedily fallen on by the local press. And what was even odder: 'He comes back here – after what as much as fourteen or fifteen years, maybe – just to take his own life?'

The police doctor, Kay Dysart, crouching by the body, glanced up quickly, then went back to her business. It was still not yet fully light, and the morning was overcast, piercingly cold and with a hint of more rain on the wind. With a heavy leather coat obscuring her small form, a woolly beret pulled close and with her white surgical gloves making Minnie Mouse hands at the ends of her sleeves, she looked like some sort of strange, burrowing cartoon animal. Being a police doctor, with all the grisly duties that might entail, was still an unusual and unlooked-for job for a woman, but then, Kay Dysart wasn't your usual woman.

'It's a wonder the news hadn't got around yet – about him not being dead after all,' Gilmour said. 'I mean, it wasn't yesterday when he arrived back here, couldn't have been.'

Time must have elapsed between the man entering the water and being found here. A drowned body would sink to the bottom, until putrefying gasses propelled it upwards sometime later. From then on it would float or be borne along by the current until it was either seen and fished out, or as in this instance, caught and wedged into some obstruction to its progress.

'You'd have thought somebody would have wondered where he'd got to again, after coming back like that, wouldn't you . . . his family for a start?' Gilmour said.

'Maybe he died before he made himself known to them.' Reardon wasn't sure he could really believe that.

Nor Gilmour, it seemed. 'Pugh could have been wrong, of course,' he said doubtfully. 'It might be some other poor sod, not Paul Millar.'

'What was the councillor doing along here at seven o'clock in the morning, anyway? Does he have one of these allotments?'

'No. But he walks round this way every morning to collect his paper from the newsagent.'

'When he lives in Colley Street? And the newsagent's on the corner?'

'Sort of constitutional, I suppose. Habit. He knows most of the allotment holders and stops for a chat if there's anyone around. Very well-liked, Councillor Pugh, on account of all he does for the town . . . shouldn't wonder if he doesn't get given any surplus they want to get rid of, a tomato or two, a few beans . . . whatever's in season. There's always more than what's needed, you know how it is.'

Reardon grunted. That was one of the many reasons he'd never taken to gardening. He'd never been able to see the point in sweating over a fork and spade for the sake of producing more food than you could possibly eat.

'He's in one of the huts now, someone took him in for a cup of tea. Hope they've put plenty sugar in, he must have had a hell of a shock, coming across him like that.'

'We'll have a word, as soon as Dr Dysart's finished, and we've seen him taken away.'

'I've finished now.' Kay Dysart stood up, peeling off the rubber gloves, rubbing her cold fingers. She was a small and energetic woman, quickly spoken, inclined to be impatient, and now she said abruptly, 'I hardly suppose you need me to tell you he's been dead for some time . . . hard to say just how long, with the water as cold as it is. Inhibits the bacterial action and stops the gases that bring it to the surface from forming.' The jargon was what was expected of her. 'But I wouldn't bank on the idea that he'd decided to do away with himself, if I were you.'

Reardon gave her a quick glance, then accepted the implied rebuke. He didn't normally jump to conclusions so hastily, but he saw it was true, his first impressions at the scene had been coloured by recollections of that other suicide found in the same place, the young woman who had taken her own life just weeks ago. In this case, however, it need not have been suicide. The poor chap could, after all, have simply slipped and fallen into the water. The path here was dangerously narrow where the river had undercut it, occasionally causing part of the bank to fall in, obscuring it by a green scum of waterweed. Anyone in the habit of using the path must be aware of all that and know to take due care. Paul Millar, assuming that was who the dead man was, presumably wouldn't have known about the present danger, even if he'd been familiar with the path years ago – though why should he have been? And what was he doing here at all? The path led only to the allotments, and further along to the Anchor Lock, the last lock on the cut, where it joined the river. A stronger possibility must be that he had fallen in elsewhere, further back along the Fol and been carried down to here.

'Not suicide then, you think, Dr Dysart?'

'No.' She gave him a level glance. 'Not after I turned him over and saw the wound on the back of his skull.'

'Wound? Accidentally caused, when he fell, you mean?' Or jumped, Reardon's mind was saying, despite what he'd just heard. He wasn't yet quite ready to give up on the idea of suicide. He thought of Castle Bridge, which he crossed twice a day on his way to and from work, and just above it the rocky stretch below the weir. If you jumped from there you wouldn't land on those rocks, some of which jutted above the surface, without some nasty injuries.

'Or a punch-up?' Gilmour said. 'He could easily have fallen in, in a fight, and bashed his head.'

A ruckus here on the riverbank, maybe right here where he was found – where someone had left him to lie submerged in the water until he'd risen to the surface? Given the frequency of brawls and skirmishes on a Friday night, after pay day and a booze-up, that couldn't be dismissed. Tempers flaring, inflamed by drink, somebody going too far.

But Dysart shook her head. 'Look at his clothes.'

Reardon saw what she meant. There was a great tear in a trouser leg and more on his jacket. One sleeve had been almost torn off. All of it consistent with what might happen to a body which had been tossed about among the big rocks which were a feature of the Fol beneath Cooper's Lock. 'Besides which' – she paused – 'he was dead when he went in, I'd say. He's a mess, but I reckon I can still recognize a gunshot wound when I see one.'

For a moment, no one spoke. 'In the back of his head,' she added.

'Then he couldn't have done it himself?'

'He *could*, just possibly, Sergeant. If he'd been something of a contortionist.' She looked from one to the other and then at her watch. 'Sorry, that's a nasty one to leave with you, but I'm only here to certify he's officially dead. And that's as far as I can go, I'm afraid. You'll have to wait for the path report from Dr Rossiter for more details. He won't need reminding to give it priority,' she added. The pathologist, Donald Rossiter, was her husband, though she kept to her maiden name professionally.

Reardon respected Kay Dysart's opinions, which were not lightly given, and he didn't feel a post-mortem would tell him her assumptions were incorrect. She was a good, competent doctor and wouldn't have gone as far as she had if she hadn't been pretty sure. They wouldn't need to wait for official confirmation that what they were now looking at was a murder investigation. For a moment longer, she stood looking down at the body. When she raised her eyes their glances met. 'You were saying he's one of the Millars?'

'We don't know for sure yet, it's only a possibility. If it is, he's been thought dead since the war.'

'Then I feel sorry for his family,' she said abruptly, in the sharp clipped tone that was habitual, which he suspected served to cloak her true feelings about the sorrowful, sordid or sad cases she so often encountered. One of the reasons why Reardon liked Kay Dysart was the empathy she obviously felt but rarely showed. And this was one of those fleeting moments, at the beginning of such an investigation, when he too would find himself contemplating the futility and senselessness of one human being taking another's life. In this case, perhaps even more so. Sadness, that a brave man had faced death in the shape of one enemy, gone through God knows what afterwards and had come home to his family and loved ones, only to meet death at the hands of a different adversary.

He watched the doctor's slim figure walk quickly away towards the street beyond the allotments where her car was parked, while he decided what was to be done. First thing, they'd need to talk to Councillor Pugh, and also have the immediate area searched minutely, though he wasn't hopeful

about that. It had been a wet February, with only the occasional
bright day. Two weeks of rainy weather on a muddy riverbank,
plus the trampling over it of all those who used it as a shortcut
to the allotments, didn't allow much hope of finding anything
useful, even a gun – if this was the unlikely spot where the
crime had been committed.

'Doesn't mean it happened here, does it?' Gilmour said,
reading his thoughts. 'Only that he ended up here.'

It was true, he could have been killed anywhere before being
thrown into the river. That possibility, and the long stretches
of the Fol riverbank where the man might have met his death,
presented more difficulties than Reardon wanted to contem-
plate at this juncture.

It was immediately clear they wouldn't need to spend long
with Wesley Pugh, the man unfortunate enough to have found
the body of his former friend. He had little to tell them, except
to confirm that he had been watching his step as he took his
usual route along the riverbank, mindful of the undercut, and
had noticed as he was skirting it something suspicious in the
water which hadn't been there the previous day. And that he'd
stayed to see it fished out and recognized the body as that
of Paul Millar straight away.

He was sitting hunched on a stool, nursing a pint mug of
tea given to him by the owner of the hut. Inside it was cold,
but at least it was out of the wind and drier than in the
penetrating, clinging damp of the day outside. A lingering
smell of paraffin from the stove mixed with the earthy odour
of the seed potatoes waiting in a box on the bench against
which Reardon leant in the absence of any other seating.
Gilmour had propped himself against a shelf.

If Pugh had indeed known the dead man well, his death
didn't seem to be upsetting him overmuch. Reardon didn't
have him down as a man accustomed to showing his feelings,
however. He was stockily built and muscular, a Celtic ancestry
suggested by the deep-set dark eyes and heavy eyebrows,
prominent nose and thick iron-grey hair worn swept back; a
slightly dour man of few words, except when he was roused
to oratory on behalf of one of the causes he regularly espoused.

A familiar and respected figure in Folbury, often featuring in the local press, he might well have been made mayor, it was rumoured, if his politics had been less left wing. If his hostilities hadn't been so obviously directed towards the self-interest of certain other members of the council. If he wasn't always stirring up something unpleasant for someone.

'How can you be so certain that's who it was?'

'I've known Paul Millar all my life . . . and he was wearing his RFC tie.'

For a full half-minute Reardon gazed at him. '*His tie?*'

The dead man had been fully clothed, but his clothes were sodden, dark and filthy with muck from the river, thick with mud. The less said about his mutilated features the better. And Pugh had been able to recognize a regimental tie?

'Royal Flying Corps. You could buy your lot's tie after the war. I never bothered, myself. I'm not surprised he did though, knowing what he felt about being in the RFC.'

Reardon decided to give him the benefit of the doubt for the moment. Regimental ties were usually of silk, woven in wide diagonal stripes, and perhaps, even in its soaked state, there was a chance that the gleam of silk stripes had been discernible, if not the actual colour. But what kind of person wore a regimental tie as a regular thing, and so many years after the war? Those who liked to think of themselves as one of the elite, perhaps, to show they'd once been a flying ace with the newest, most glamorous of the armed forces, which flew reconnaissance planes and got into dangerous dog-fights with enemy fighters. Originally the Royal Flying Corps attached to the army, it was now renamed the Royal Air Force. Reardon couldn't recall the colours of the tie, but Pugh had recognized them. Or was that the only reason why the name of a man dead for years had sprung to his mind?

Reardon went for a more obvious explanation. 'You knew who he was, so I presume you had met him and spoken to him since he came back to Folbury?'

'No,' said Pugh. After a slight pause, he admitted, 'Though I did have a fancy that I'd seen him. In the distance, that is.'

'Still, it must have given you a shock.'

Pugh's look implied that didn't need saying. 'At first. But

I soon put it down to a trick of the light,' he finally said after a long pause for thought.

This man was going to be a hard nut to crack, certainly not the easiest of witnesses. Not that Reardon thought he was lying, or had any reason to do so, but clearly he wasn't prepared to be forthcoming. He'd answer the questions put to him and nothing more, the sort of witness who had the most patient of policemen growing hot under the collar.

'Where?' asked Gilmour, who was not one of the patient ones. 'Where did you see him?'

'Where?' For a moment, Pugh looked, not so much disconcerted as annoyed with himself for having admitted anything at all. 'I forget exactly where,' he said shortly. 'Somewhere in the town. And I only thought I saw him.'

'And when was that?' Reardon asked.

'A couple of weeks ago, I suppose, give or take a day.'

Which could mean, if Pugh was to be believed, and given what Dysart had said about the time it could have taken for his body to rise to the surface, close to the time he must have died. A fortnight since he was last seen, yet no one had apparently thought to report him missing, after what must have seemed like a miraculous return to life? Was that because he hadn't made himself known, for some reason as yet obscure, either to his family or anyone else, and that no one had been aware that he had returned to Folbury?

'He was thought to have died in the war, wasn't he, Mr Pugh? What was his story?'

Pugh shook his head. 'You'll have to ask Ted about that – and Thea . . . the Millars, his brother and sister. It's not my place to say, even if I knew the details, which I don't.' He contemplated the dregs of his tea, having said his piece.

Reardon was in no doubt that there was more the man might have told them if he'd been so inclined. It would be a challenge, if nothing else, to get out of him anything he didn't want to reveal. But that would take time and no reminders from Pugh were needed as to which direction they should now be heading, pronto. The family of the dead man had to be told before the news reached them by some other means, if it hadn't already.

'You won't find them at home,' Pugh roused himself to warn them. 'They'll both be at work by now. Which is where I should be an' all,' he added, standing up and looking pointedly at his watch. 'It's a good stretch.'

'I'm sorry we've had to detain you, but thanks for your time, Mr Pugh. That's it for now, although we shall need to see you again. We'll be in touch when we do.'

He gave a grunt of acknowledgement and left.

Wesley Pugh was known to be a man of strong passions. Had coming across the dead man really been by chance? In such close proximity to Pugh's own home? If so, why report it at all? Well, he wouldn't be the first person to find a body in a seemingly innocent manner, a double bluff designed to throw the police off the scent and present themselves as an unlikely suspect, but surely only if he knew he was likely to be a suspect in the first place.

Unaware of the stir around the grisly discovery on the other side of town that was to concern Matt so profoundly, Imogen Randall pushed open the door of his studio in Hadley Piece, went in and ran up the stairs.

'Matt! You haven't been swimming again?' she demanded immediately she saw him. 'In this weather?' Closing the door behind her, she looked disbelievingly at him, a basket covered with a white cloth over her arm.

'It's as good a way to start the morning as any. Wakes you up,' Matt replied, coming forward and giving her a kiss. 'You should try it.'

'Well, if ever I was fool enough, I hope I'd at least have the sense to dry my hair properly. Especially on a day like this. What on earth are you thinking of?'

He ran a hand though his thick black hair, seemingly surprised to find it still damp. 'Yes, OK, but you know me. I've swum there every day of my adult life – more or less. Why should I stop now?'

There was a truculence in his manner unusual for Matt, the way he stressed the word 'now'. Because of suddenly finding that he had a father, alive after all, she thought he might have added, but he didn't. Setting the basket carefully on his worktable, she walked across the room to the makeshift kitchen-cum-washroom in the corner, found a towel and went back to him. She watched while he rubbed his hair perfunctorily and threw the towel down. She put her arms around him and laid her head on his shoulder, then reached up and placed both hands either side of his face. 'Matt.'

He looked down into her concerned eyes, wide, brown, fringed with thick lashes and tilted in a heart-shaped face, then very gently touched her hair. It was glossy, toffee brown with gold gleams in it and she wore it bobbed, with a fashionable 'dip' to one side, caught back with a silver and tortoiseshell hairslide. She had the shy, vulnerable look of a young deer, but anyone who thought this reflected her real nature would be seriously underestimating Imogen.

'It's all right,' he said. 'He's gone now. He isn't going to come back.'

'Gone?'

He shrugged, but his eyes had darkened, from brilliant, light-filled grey to dark slate. There was a pinched look to his face and it was pale under the tousled hair, in a way that cut her to the heart. She hadn't met the mysteriously returned Paul Millar, and from the little Matt had told her, was glad she hadn't. She wished fervently that Matt hadn't seen him, either. It had been fearfully sad for him when he was a little boy to have lost his father, but he'd managed to get over it, as all those others who'd lost someone in the war had had to do, and then, to have him return as if nothing had happened – as he apparently had, expecting everyone to welcome him with open arms, even though he hadn't been prepared to explain why he had stayed away so long – was asking too much of anyone, even someone as strong and able to cope as Matt.

He kissed her again, put her gently from him and turned towards the table where he'd been working on some illustrations for a children's story book that he hoped would bring in new commissions. She knew that look: he quite obviously didn't want to talk about his father. 'What's in the basket, Little Red Riding Hood?' he asked, picking it up.

'Mum's sent you some more honey. And some hot-pot, it only needs reheating.'

'I'll warm it up for my dinner. Tell her she's a brick.' Matt had learnt not to turn his nose up at such life-giving offers. Especially Connie Randall's hot pot, plus a jar of honey from her own bees. She was the district nurse and believed in feeding people up and though not entirely approving of her daughter's friendship with him – for reasons Matt very much feared to go into – couldn't bear to see him starving in a garret, as she evidently thought he was. Her hesitation about their mutual attachment wasn't just that she saw him as a struggling, penniless artist, he was sure; mercenary wasn't a word that applied to Connie. Nor did she disapprove of his way of life. She of all people wasn't censorious in any way, and more than that, she was one of those who really believed he'd succeed one day. Down to earth and sensible as always, she didn't see why the commercial side of his work, the way he took on anything that would pay, should be thought of as 'prostituting his art', she told him with a laugh, and he knew she meant it; she understood that taking on such work was simply a way of keeping the wolf from the door until the time arrived when his real work would gain recognition. And if that never happened, so what? He could always get by as he was doing now, couldn't he? Or do as his Uncle Ted wanted, and join the family firm, she'd ventured to suggest. But this was the parting of the ways, as far as Matt's thinking went. Much as his uncle wanted it, and appreciative as Matt was of the affection which had prompted it, his mind stayed firmly negative on that point.

'Matt?' Imogen waved a hand across his eyes. 'Come back. You were miles away.'

'Sorry.' He shook himself, almost literally. 'What were you saying?'

She'd been looking around critically. To her eyes the studio was bordering on . . . well, not quite squalor, but . . . She decided she mustn't make rude remarks about it.

Working in the local hospital as a trainee nurse for the last year, she herself had become forced to work to system and order, and found that it actually did make life so much easier if everything wasn't in a mess and you were able to put your hands on things when you needed them. She liked helping to

care for the patients, but most of the work she did on the wards
at the moment was menial, often disgusting and sometimes
quite boring and she was by no means as sure as she had been
that she wanted to follow her mother into nursing as a career.
She had thought she was, but that was before things had become
serious with Matt, and since she couldn't think of anything
else she wanted to do, it suited her for the moment. She turned
away again and began gathering together the used tea mugs
scattered around, intending to wash them.

'Leave it, Imo,' Matt said, unusually sharp. 'Don't try and
tidy me out of existence.'

'It's chaos,' she said, despite her earlier resolution.

'Ordered chaos.'

She rolled her eyes. But she supposed it wasn't so far from
the truth; she'd been exaggerating, as usual. His working tools,
his brushes, palette knives, pencils, paint rags and everything
else he needed were all arranged so that he could put his hands
on them almost without looking. The rest of the room was
pretty cluttered, it was true, but it had never been a purposely
designed studio, just this big, bare room, once used for storage.
She wished he'd move out, all the same. Hadley Piece and his
isolation there made her jittery, and this place had an insubstantial, temporary feel to it, which was understandable, since
Matt had only ever intended it to serve until he moved on.
Moved on and then . . . well, what about her, then? Would he
ask her to move on with him? Would he at last agree to their
getting married?

He loved her dearly, she had no doubts about that, so why
couldn't they marry now? But Matt wouldn't hear of it. He
had this outdated idea of being able to keep her in the style
to which she should be accustomed, he joked – as if being
brought up by Mum in their little house with no money to
spare had led her to expect the life of a lady and a house full
of servants! When in actual fact she would have been prepared
to marry Matt tomorrow – or even to move in with him without
the benefit of clergy, as they said, if that was what he wanted.
Except that he didn't. Matt was so old-fashioned in some ways,
and he'd been shocked when she'd suggested it and refused
to discuss it further.

He had a way of putting up a barrier when there was some-thing he didn't want to talk about, as he had just now when he'd mentioned his father. Imogen privately thought she was entitled to know more about what had happened after Paul Millar's reappearance that night, and especially about why he'd decided to go away again, but the shutters were up. Matt had chosen to say nothing, and she knew she'd be wasting her time trying to make him say more.

Much as she loved him, she had to admit he could be infuriating at times. Doing unexpected – and sometimes stupid – things. Like swimming in the Fol on a freezing morning in February, for heaven's sake.

FIVE

'They're reckoned to be the biggest builders in Folbury then, Millar Homes?'

Gilmour was too preoccupied to do more than nod as he negotiated his way along the main road through the town, congested as it always was in the general disruption engendered by Folbury's weekly market, with the stalls lining either side of the road, narrowing it to one-way traffic.

After a few minutes of edging the motor along, he was forced to bring it to a halt. There was no getting past the farm cart drawn immovably across the road in defiance of anyone else's right of way – or of Gilmour's muttering impatience for that matter. 'About time they found somewhere else for the market,' he grumbled, tooting the horn and getting nothing but a vulgar response from the carter. But Folbury had held a charter for its ancient market in that place for four centuries, and was proud of it, so it wasn't something likely to happen in a hurry.

He wound down the window while they waited, letting in the noise of the busiest and most enjoyable day of the week: stallholders shouting their wares, exchanging banter with women determined not to be palmed off with shoddy goods, while over and above all came sounds approximating *The Blue Danube*, repetitiously ground out from a hurdy-gurdy on a cart, its handle turned by a one-legged veteran. The noise from it was excruciating, but few who passed could resist throwing a copper into the cap on the ground. The old soldier was doing well today, poor devil.

Reardon fished in his pocket. All he came up with was silver. All the same, he wound down his window and threw it towards the cap. His aim wasn't good; it fell short, but the old soldier was nimble enough to grab it before it rolled away.

Gilmour, who had folded his arms and resigned himself to sitting there until the end of time, almost choked. 'That was a two-bob piece!'

'Was it? Well, I'm not about to ask for change.' It was over the top, but he didn't begrudge it. Anyone whose sacrifices to his country meant playing a hurdy-gurdy all day deserved at least that. 'Go on with what you were saying. Millar Homes . . .'

He wanted to hear as much about the dead man's family as Gilmour could tell him before confronting his brother and sister with the news of his death, and he hoped they might get there before it reached them in other ways. If the taciturn Wesley Pugh had already arrived at Millars, as seemed highly probable considering their own rate of progress, Reardon was reasonably hopeful he would have kept his mouth shut, if only for reasons of his own; but he wasn't the only one by now who knew a dead body had been fished from the river. Speculation about it being one of the Millars was too good a titbit to hope would be kept secret for long. One whiff and the rumour would be spreading through Folbury like a measles epidemic. The groups of gossiping women surrounding them could be talking about it now.

'Millars?' Gilmour repeated. 'Oh, right. Well, not all that big in terms of size, I suppose, not by a long chalk. But well thought of . . . Hallelujah!'

The driver was at last making a leisurely business of moving his cart out of the way. A few minutes later Gilmour was finally able to manoeuvre past, into the less busy streets ahead, put his foot down and continue with what he'd been saying.

The name of Edward Millar, otherwise Ted, wasn't unfamiliar to Reardon. Anyone who read the local newspapers was unlikely to miss a name that appeared on its pages with unfailing regularity, sometimes with a grainy photograph. The remembered image was that of a jovial, clubbable man, prominent in the town's social hierarchy, popular for his active support of various charities, noted amongst fellow Rotarians for his business acumen and his ability to drive a hard bargain. Gilmour enlarged as they drove on: he was well known to be a good boss. You were lucky if you got to work at Millars and you could count on having a job for life if you watched your Ps and Qs. He was liked by his employees and known to be easy-going enough, but at the same time, anyone who wasn't prepared to put in a decent day's work got short shrift. Since its founding by their grandfather, Millars had grown over the years, and though it was still small enough for Ted Millar to know the name of everyone employed there, they'd made their pile and the business managed to keep afloat when all around were sinking beneath the waves of all this post-war economic depression.

After that testimonial, the firm's premises in Inkerman Terrace turned out to be nothing to write home about. Little more, in fact, than a medium-sized Victorian house, end of terrace, plus some land to the side, though no doubt ideal as business and family premises for Manfred Müller when he had started the firm. It was also situated only a step away from Arms Green, a place where no one lived who didn't have to, in its turn not much more than a big stride from the straggling outskirts of Birmingham's vast industrial sprawl. All the same, that one step away from the rows of smoke-blackened two-up and two-downs, crammed in beside factories big and small, corner shops and a forbidding elementary school standing in an asphalt yard, was just far enough for Inkerman Terrace to have stayed on the respectable side of the spectrum.

In fact, the houses in the quiet street were sufficiently substantial for most of the hitherto rundown residential properties to have been taken over and smartened up as business premises by professional people. Window boxes and brass plates proliferated: a firm of solicitors; a doctors' partnership; a dentist. They were the only ones who could afford to keep up such places now.

Visible through the high chain-link fence, Millars' yard stretched out sideways and joined Hadley Piece, those few unlovely acres of land awaiting redevelopment by the town council. The derelict sheds and wharves edging the canal gave it an even more desolate air than usual on this grey morning, compared with which Millars' yard itself was a model of tidiness and order. Timber was propped under open-fronted sheds, bricks were stacked under roped tarpaulins, ladders stood waiting. Above the pair of double gates leading to the yard was a sign with the company's name writ large, but they were locked and there was no other obvious entry.

'Front door,' Reardon said, making for it.

The house had at one time been nice enough – still was. Not big, but square and solid, double fronted, mercifully free of too many architectural frills, its decoration limited to nothing much more than some red and blue stained glass at the tops of the wide sash windows and in the fanlight over the door, and the coloured encaustic tiles flooring the porch. All quite acceptable for its time, though its main attraction for Manfred Müller must undoubtedly have been that piece of land to the side, once an extensive garden and now the builders' yard, with the advantage of the canal and its transport conveniences passing at the end.

Not everyone would want to live over the shop, however, and according to Gilmour, at some stage Manfred had moved his family onwards and upwards, and acquired the mansion at Fox Close. Prosperity had not, apparently, brought unalloyed happiness. There'd been a family tragedy somewhere along the line. Gilmour frowned in the attempt to remember. 'I think old Manfred's son was killed in an accident, but I can't recall the details offhand. Before the war, it must have been.'

There was no doorbell on the front door, just a large brass knob in the centre, but it opened to a push. Facing them was a staircase rising at the far end of a central passageway with two doors off, one of which bore a bell and a notice to ring for attention. From behind came the busy office sounds of a clacking typewriter and people talking. There was no immediate response when Gilmour rang the bell, shifting his weight from foot to foot while they waited, like a nervous boxer anticipating a punch.

'You all right with this, Joe?' Reardon had asked him searchingly before they set out, anticipating what they would be facing and what it might mean to his sergeant.

'Course,' Gilmour had stoutly maintained, not knowing whether he would be or not, Reardon suspected. He hadn't pressed him.

He had his hand raised to the bell again when the door was flung open by a small, dark woman who was flushed, frowning and pushing her spectacles impatiently up into her hair.

'Well, they are very busy this morning, but I'll ask if they will see you,' she said sharply after hearing who they were, as if that were an option. She crossed to the opposite door, gave a short tap and went in, closing it behind her. In a few moments she was holding it open again. 'You can have a few minutes.' She stood aside to let them in, still disapproving, saying 'Shall I bring your Ovaltine, Mr Millar?'

Ovaltine? Gilmour rolled his eyes.

'Later, thank you, Mrs Chadwick.' The crossness on her face was replaced by a smile as she left, shutting the door behind her, though not gently. She needed to smile more, Reardon thought, she was very attractive when she did – if your tastes ran to diminutive dragons who pursed their mouths and had sharply suspicious, bright-blue eyes.

The man who'd spoken came forward from behind the enormous partners' desk occupying the centre of the room. 'Ted Millar,' he said, offering a warm but rather soft handshake. 'And my sister, Thea.' He indicated the woman seated at the far side of the desk. Miss Millar acknowledged the introduction with a cool smile but didn't speak. As if feeling some explanation for the Ovaltine was needed, he added, 'I have a stomach ulcer. I worry too much.' He smiled, bland and flushed with health, not looking at all like a man who worried. He was dressed with casual ease: good brown tweed suit; ox-blood brogues worn into comfortable creases; a soft-collared shirt.

Possibly approaching forty, he seemed younger than his sister by perhaps a decade. There was a family resemblance between the two, the thick fair hair – in his case with a curl to it – and a certain cast of features, but there it ended; she was striking, rather than good-looking, with neat, well-defined eyebrows and a firm jawline. Smart and looking calmly efficient, she wore something in dark blue, the sort of plain and simple elegance that Reardon suspected only came at a price. Not a hair out of place, her make-up discreet and immaculate. An up-to-date Bakelite handset telephone stood as a demarcation between Millar's own untidy, paper-strewn space and that of his sister. There was nothing more in front of her than an in-tray, a blotter and an inkstand. She sat very still but watchful, and sending out the unmistakable message that you wouldn't want to cross her.

'And what can we do for you, Inspector?' asked Millar, resuming his seat when Reardon had given their names.

The office, presumably the dual-aspect drawing room before the house had been turned into business premises, was lit by a narrow side window overlooking the yard and a bay window which faced the street, this last dressed for privacy with crisp white net curtains. The bay itself was filled by a hard and uncomfortable horsehair sofa, on which they were invited to sit. Reardon could feel loose prickles of horsehair which had worked out of the cloth through his trousers as he shifted for an easier position and briefly debated with himself why such a sofa should be thought a welcoming seat to offer visitors who might also be clients. It was in line with everything else in the room, which still bore traces of its previous function as a last-century drawing room: gloomy steel engravings of vaguely Germanic appearance depending on cords from the picture rail; a black marble fireplace; old gas-light brackets still on the wall. They sat oddly with the modern green metal filing cabinets and not least with the model of a very state-of-the-art white house sitting incongruously on top of one of them. As the office of a thriving business concern, it didn't impress, but perhaps that was the intention – to give a subliminal message to customers that their money was unlikely to be wasted. It was no worse than many another office. Compared with Reardon's own at Market Street, it was the last word.

Millar was looking expectant. Clearly, word had not yet reached Inkerman Terrace about their brother and Reardon braced himself for what he had to do. Like every other police officer, it was the one thing he hated most about his police work. However, he'd never found the truth, sensitively stated, to be more distressing than skirting round the subject, and as he usually did, he gave it to them straight, though as gently and tactfully as he could. It was his sad duty to tell them that they, the police, had been called in to make enquiries into the death of a man whose body had been found in the river by the Colley Street allotments. He was sorry to have to tell them there was reason to suspect it might be that of their brother.

When he'd finished, a painful silence ensued. The sort that, as policemen, both he and Gilmour were accustomed to after people had been given such news: stunned disbelief mainly, before the terrible reality set in. But this silence was followed neither by the usual tears, hysterics nor protestations that it couldn't be true. Nor even the usual question as to how it could have happened.

Thea Millar continued to sit motionless. You might have thought the words she'd listened to had had no impact. After a moment, her brother stood up and walked to the fireplace, bent to the coal scuttle and picked up the tongs as if to mend the already heaped-up fire, had second thoughts and put them back again before turning to face the room, his hands clasped behind his back.

'Paul?' he said at last, as if the words were forced out of him.

'I'm extremely sorry, but we have reason to believe it might be.' Reardon waited until Gilmour had added the few details that were necessary for them to know, before apologizing for having to question them to help establish the identification without doubt. There was no necessity, for the moment, to tell them their brother had met with a violent death. Until confirmed by the post-mortem, it couldn't be absolutely certain, so it was kinder to let the fact of his death sink in first, which perhaps it hadn't yet.

Neither of the dead man's siblings were giving indications of the disbelief he would have expected, and certainly not astonishment, at what they'd just heard: that the brother they had mourned, and had long been thought to lie dead on the battlefields of France, had only recently met his death, inexplicably drowned – and here in Folbury, what was more. Shock, however, took people in different ways, maybe they were just one of those families who didn't show their feelings easily.

'I realize how painful this is for you, and I'm very sorry. It must be a big shock, coming after seeing him alive and well when you'd believed him killed in the war,' he said. He added abruptly, 'When did he return, exactly?'

The look that passed between them might have meant anything. He recognized it as the sort of shorthand two people use who have known each other intimately for a long time. Brother and sister, they were obviously close; as well as working together, the two of them apparently shared a home. Neither had ever married, as far as he knew. Did he imagine the slight nod she gave, almost as if granting him permission to go ahead and speak?

Millar was a comfortably built chap, not fat but a little overweight, normally flushed with good living, pleasant and affable. Teddy, as his family knew him. Large, cuddly toys did indeed come to mind when you looked at him, though the image might have been more appropriate, had he not at this moment been so grimly grey-faced, worrying his lower lip with his teeth. Not then as unaffected at what he'd heard as it might have seemed. A faint line of sweat had appeared on his forehead – though Gilmour, too, was surreptitiously wiping his pencil-hand on his trousers and shifting uncomfortably on the slippery horsehair. They'd been invited to take their coats off, but it was still too hot in here even for this miserably cold winter's day. The elderly clanking radiator behind the sofa under the bay window didn't appear to be contributing much; it was the blazing open fire that was throwing out all the heat.

Millar had left his position there, coming back to the desk where he slumped into his chair, as if his legs were suddenly unreliable. He wiped a hand across his face, but after a moment, pulled himself together. 'Yes, it was a shock, I can tell you . . .' he admitted. 'He just walked in, you know, out of the blue.'

'When was this?'

'About two weeks ago, the sixteenth in fact. I can be exact because I had a function that night, which I was forced to cancel.'

'He just walked in here then, without any prior notice?'

'No, no, not here. It was in the evening, we were at home.'

'Home' would be the very modern house in Ladyford Lane which had caused so much comment in the local press, most of it, though not all, adverse. The model of which, very likely, was that one over there, sitting on top of the filing cabinets.

'But in fact, we saw him for less than an hour before he left again.'

'Only an hour?'

'Less than that, and it knocked us both for six, I can tell

you! He . . .' For a moment, he couldn't go on and threw a
look of anguish at his sister. 'He wouldn't stay, he left –
and we've never seen him since.'

'Did he give reasons for not staying?'

'That's what's so hurtful. It was . . . as though the world
had stopped, when he walked in, out of the blue. We could
scarcely take it in, either of us. And then to leave, without any
explanation of where he'd been, what had been happening to
him . . . and, now, oh God, now . . .'

Drowning. Accidental death. Suicide. Unspoken, but envisaged, the implications hung in the air. It must indeed have
been a traumatic experience, that visitation from the dead. Or
perhaps they had believed they were being been taken in, in
some way, and been unwilling to admit it was really him. Men
who had been through hell and back could and did change
immeasurably. Was that why they had apparently kept his
reappearance to themselves, and not broadcast the joyful
news of his return?

Millar was suddenly overcome and put his head in his hands.
Thea pushed her chair back and came to stand behind him.
Still not saying anything, she laid a brief hand on his shoulder
– sympathetic, proprietary . . . or admonishing? He turned his
head, their eyes met, and he reached out his own hand, perhaps
for reassurance. Perhaps she had been warning him.

Thea Millar was a tall woman. Reardon also noticed in a
detached sort of way that she had a good figure and nice legs,
but was wearing the lizard skin shoes which were apparently
the latest mad and, to him, repulsive fashion craze. She didn't
return to her seat but instead perched rather elegantly on the
desk, still with a hand on her brother's arm.

'He was much older than me,' Millar eventually managed
to say brokenly, 'ten years. I always looked up to him, you
know, he was my hero. I even quit my studies and joined up
as he did when the war came.' He couldn't go on.

Reardon let a few moments pass before asking, 'When was
the last time you did actually hear from him?'

It was his sister who answered. Reardon realized it was the
first time she'd spoken. A few weeks after the Armistice it
had been, she said, just before he was due to come home

again. Paul had been sent to a transit station pending demobilization, a time which could often stretch into weeks, sometimes even months, as Reardon had no need to remind himself. He hadn't forgotten how agonizing the wait could be. It had sometimes led to what almost amounted to mutiny among men who were aching to get back home to their families, to forget the waking nightmare of the last four years, and who no longer felt themselves under orders to obey petty rules and regulations.

'We waited and waited for him to come home,' Thea went on, 'and in the end, when we'd still heard nothing from him, I contacted the War Office. I didn't get very far at first, I assume they were under pressure from more than me, but eventually they told me he'd received his discharge papers six months earlier, and they had no further authority over him. But it was . . . unsatisfactory. I had the feeling there might have been a big muddle or miscalculation somewhere along the line and that he must have been killed, unaccounted for, like so many more.'

Silence fell after she'd finished, until Millar said bitterly, 'It might have been better if he *had* been – at least we should have known.'

Gilmour's pencil point snapped audibly. He gave what sounded like a muttered imprecation that turned into a cough. His face as red as his hair, perhaps from the fire, he fished another pencil from his pocket.

Millar looked at him with the embarrassment of one having put his foot in it without knowing how or why, while Reardon threw him a quick glance. He was now looking down steadfastly at his notes.

'So between then and two weeks ago, you'd never heard from him again? And when you did see him, he said nothing at all of where he'd been? What he'd been doing, why he'd stayed away?' Reardon addressed them both. Surely, however brief that meeting, they must have gained some idea?

'Look, Inspector,' Millar said at last, 'all that time he'd been living a hundred or so miles from us, and not so much as a postcard to tell us he was even alive.' He was recovering quickly from the initial shock of what they had just been told, and even beginning to sound a little aggrieved. 'Naturally, we wanted to know what had been going on, but all he would say was to give him time, he would tell us in due course.'

No communication between them? Then how had he known to make for their newly occupied, recently built home on Ladyford Lane? An interesting point. But it seemed Paul had at least left them with one fact. 'He'd been living a hundred miles away, you say. Where was that?'

'Oh, somewhere in London. And how he'd been existing is anybody's guess.'

'Maybe he went back to doing the work he did before the war?'

'I think not,' Thea chose to answer, with a cold little smile. 'Father died just before the war broke out, while Teddy was away in London, studying architecture in South Kensington. Paul had been working in the firm but his heart wasn't in it. He was only too eager to join up when the time came.'

'He'd no interest in learning the building business, but anything mechanical, that was different,' Millar added. 'He was only happy under a car bonnet, with grease under his fingernails. Knew everything there was to know about engines, motorcars – and especially aeroplanes . . . why he went into the RFC, of course. Whereas me – in fact,' he added with a wry glance at Thea, 'my sister knows more about those sort of things than I do. One can only assume he would have found some way of earning a living in that direction since.'

'What about family? Was he married?'

'His wife died, just before the war.'

'I see. Well, let's go back to that night he arrived, two weeks ago. What was his state of mind?'

'State of mind?' Millar stared, then gave a short, unamused laugh. 'Well, not precisely cheerful! Celebration was the last thing he wanted. No fuss. Just to get used to being here again. Or that's what he said . . .'

That sounded reasonable, it was what nearly every ex-soldier had wanted, a need to slip back quietly into their old lives. '"Here" being Folbury, at home with you, we can assume?'

'No, not with us.' Thea turned a cool gaze on Reardon. 'Not even for the night. We tried to persuade him, but he'd already taken a room at the Shire.'

Without comment, Gilmour stolidly wrote the name down, tacitly echoing Reardon's unspoken incredulity. *Paul Millar had booked himself a hotel room.* But if anonymity, no fuss, was what he had wanted, staying at the Shire was hardly the place to choose. It was the best of what Folbury had to offer in the way of hotels, and the one frequented by people most likely to have known Paul Millar in his previous incarnation, and to recognize him. Wouldn't it have been better by far to have kept his head down and stayed with his family until he acclimatized himself?

Reardon looked in vain to see if the bitterness he'd detected at Paul's refusal was reflected on Thea's face as she spoke, whether it was hurt she felt, or even anger. Both would be understandable. Paul had, for reasons still obscure, left them to mourn for all those years, to come to terms and accept as best they could that he must have been one of the numberless soldiers unaccounted for in the carnage of war. Without even a letter sent to assure them he was after all safe and well. He could scarcely have expected they would welcome him with open arms and accept without question a refusal to explain his lack of communication. It was probably why he had decided he would be better off staying elsewhere for the time being.

The huge, round clock fixed above the fireplace, the sort more appropriate to railway stations or schoolrooms, clunkily measured the seconds after Thea had spoken. That loud, deliberate ticking away of the time would have had Reardon climbing the walls, but the two of them had probably lived with it so long they never even heard it.

'You fought in the war yourself, I take it, Inspector, as I did?' Millar said unexpectedly.

Reardon nodded acknowledgement. Oblique references to his scarred face had long since ceased to trouble him. He refused to let it hang round his neck like an albatross, or whatever the analogy should be, despite that was what it felt like sometimes. Yet he was only one of the hundreds of thousands who would bear some reminder of that war for the rest of their lives. He'd fared better than a great many of those who had survived some way or other, better certainly than the one-legged hurdy-gurdy player who'd assaulted their ears in the market place.

'Then I don't have to tell you how difficult it was for some of us to return to civilian life,' Millar said. 'For many reasons.'

Although Ted Millar too had fought in the war, Reardon found it hard to envisage the man he was looking at as having any readjustment difficulties. He struck him as a man who would live very much in the present, taking life as it came. Paul, on the other hand, might perhaps have been one of those men – God knew how many – who had voluntarily 'disappeared' themselves after the fighting was over. Individuals with a shady past, or a life that didn't bear thinking about, who had good reason for not returning to their old haunts – returning never, or at least not until they were ready to resurface under some other guise.

Was Millar inferring this might be what had happened to his brother? But Paul had presumably led a settled and secure life here before his war service. In which case, why should he have felt it impossible until now to return to his home and family? Unless he had been psychologically disturbed by his experiences in the trenches, like many others were now recognized to have been. Shell shock, it was now called. Then his absence could have been forgivable. Otherwise, leaving them without knowledge of his ultimate fate had been a shabby way for their brother to go about things.

'Are you saying,' he began carefully, treading on eggs because this was not something to be suggested lightly to relatives, 'that it's possible his mind had been affected?'

It was a loaded question, but neither chose to take offence. Millar let a few moments pass. 'No, I am not. Paul's behaviour must seem odd to you, but you didn't know him,' he said at last. 'Anyway, does all that matter now?'

It mattered. It mattered very much what this man had been like, what there had been in his character and his life, perhaps something he'd done that had caused someone to harbour enough resentment to kill him. Only by building up a picture of Paul Millar, of his last days, possibly those lost years, and the circumstances which had led to his death, by talking to everyone who'd known him, would it be possible to tell. He foresaw a hard time of it for himself and his officers, if the Millars (and he could believe the same might be true of Wesley Pugh) were an indication of what co-operation they might expect.

At that point Thea Millar relinquished her perch on the edge of the desk and went back to her chair. 'If that's all, Inspector . . .'

But Reardon still had questions. 'A few more minutes, if you please.'

Even as he spoke there came sounds of activity from the yard outside, a small, flat-bed truck pulling in, men's voices, causing Millar to glance briefly out of the window, then at the clock. He drew himself up and said stiltedly, belatedly playing the protective male, 'If you've any imagination at all, Inspector, you must realize how upsetting this has been to us. I hardly think it's necessary for my sister to have to go through it all again.'

'It's not our intention to upset anyone, Mr Millar, but I'm sure you'll appreciate that in any unnatural death we need all the information we can get about the events surrounding it. For one thing, as Sergeant Gilmour said, the coroner will need to establish how and why he died.'

'Isn't that self-evident? He drowned, didn't he?'

'He was found in the river,' Reardon said carefully. 'By the allotments, where Mr Pugh saw him.'

'The allotments – you did say the allotments?' Thea put in suddenly, quite sharply, almost as if the fact had previously passed her by. 'What on earth was he doing there?'

'I was hoping you might be able to throw some light on that.'

'By the allotments,' she repeated. 'And he just fell into the river? Is that what you're saying? Are you suggesting he was *drunk*?' Her manner had been cool all along, but now the frost could have nipped his toes off, if it hadn't been for the temperature of the room.

'A drop too much, maybe? It's a possibility we should perhaps consider.' He didn't say how remote the possibility was after what Kay Dysart had reported.

But Millar said shortly, 'You can discount that. He didn't

drink.' Suddenly, what the main purpose of their visit might be seemed to strike him. 'Further identification, you said? Oh my God, you're not going to ask us to *identify* him, are you?' he asked, turning even paler. 'I thought you said Wesley Pugh had already done that.'

'No, no. That won't be necessary.' Reardon wasn't about to go into details of why Pugh's cursory identification of the dead man simply by his tie was hardly admissible evidence, or why the Millars wouldn't need to be troubled. Relatives were not normally asked to undertake that emotionally demanding procedure until after the body had been cleaned up, and then only if facial disfigurement wasn't too horrific. Neither was an option in this case. The possibility of identifying him by any bodily characteristics he'd had, such as a birthmark or something of that sort, had been removed by his immersion in the river, during which time areas of skin and tissue had peeled away, not to mention the ravages made by the attentions of hungry, aquatic creatures. There remained the need, however, to be sure the dead man was who Pugh had been so sure he was, and not some other, unknown man, and in the circumstances that could pose a problem.

At a nod from Reardon, Gilmour explained about the inquest to establish just how he had died. His sergeant didn't usually have to be so prompted, but in this interview he wasn't showing at his most alert.

Millar didn't question any of this; he only looked relieved that he wasn't expected to undertake the grisly duty of viewing his dead brother's body. Thea, however, offered abruptly, 'Paul broke his leg when he was young and afterwards he always walked with a very slight limp, though it never affected his ability to do anything. It certainly didn't stop him being accepted for service in the RFC. I don't know if it would be possible to tell . . .?'

'Oh, I should think so. X-rays and so on.' She was quicker on the uptake than her brother. 'That could be very helpful, Miss Millar.' He stood up. 'That's all we need for now, but we'll be in touch later.' He felt compelled to add, 'It's a difficult time for you, but rest assured, we shall be doing our best to get this cleared as soon as possible.'

'Thank you,' Thea said stiffly. She was the sort of woman, he suspected, who could not accept condolences easily or gracefully, who would suffer any amount of agony, physical or mental, rather than ask for or accept sympathy. And yet, he wondered if he had been wrong in thinking her unfeeling. In her eyes now he read pain, and something else. Which only might have been – because in this woman it would have been strange if it had been true – apprehension.

Down in the yard, the sounds of activity had increased. A dog suddenly began barking, joining in, enjoying the noise. At the sound, Thea stiffened, her hand went to her chest, then she swung round towards the window, hackles raised like a cat facing the enemy. 'What's that animal doing here?' she demanded, no longer cool and contained.

'It's all right, Thea. She belongs to Billy Sturgess,' Millar said placatingly. 'If he leaves her at home since his wife died, she pines. He keeps her with him in his cab.'

'Obviously not this time,' she snapped, breathing hard. 'And if he can't keep it there he'd better stay at home and pine with it. We're running a business here, not a kennels.'

Millar flushed to the roots of his hair, then it receded, leaving him almost as pale as she was. He crossed to the door and held it open for Reardon and Gilmour to leave, summoned an apologetic smile. 'Let us know when you . . . if there's anything more.'

Gilmour pulled jerkily away from the curb as soon as they were seated in the motor and began driving fast, taking a more roundabout but quicker route this time to avoid the market. It was himself he was angry with, Reardon knew. Normally very much on the ball and ready to play his part in any interview, he obviously felt he'd demonstrated himself as capable of none of this in the past half hour. It was why, before they had set out, aware that the coming interview was likely to be difficult for him, Reardon had given him the opportunity to duck out, but as he'd expected, Gilmour hadn't taken it. Reardon's confidence in his own judgement would have been shaken if he had. He knew what had upset him, but said nothing more as they drove on, waiting until his sergeant was ready to speak, his natural good humour restored, which wouldn't be long, if he knew Gilmour. He was rarely at a loss for words and realistic enough not to dwell on what had gone past.

Eventually he slowed down a little. Reardon sighed in relief and took his foot off an imaginary brake as the drive was resumed more circumspectly. After a few minutes, Gilmour said, 'What were they trying to hide? I wouldn't trust either of them.'

'We can't trust anyone at this stage,' Reardon agreed mildly.

It was a sad but undeniable fact that any murder was more likely to be committed by someone known, and often close, to the victim, than by a stranger. More often than you'd think possible, by some family member, but making assumptions about who was responsible was a big mistake. And it was too soon to make those sort of judgements on anyone after the shocking news they'd just imparted.

They drove on in further silence. Eventually Reardon said, 'You did all right, Joe.'

Gilmour grunted. He knew he hadn't managed to hide his thoughts from Reardon, but hoped he hadn't shown them to Millar, who had, after all, not known he was being tactless – though he'd seemed to suspect he had been.

'Right.'

It hadn't felt right, though, Millar almost saying that it would be better if his brother hadn't come back at all. It had been too close to the bone, the old familiar ache shooting through him. He knew he ought to have come to terms with it by now, he was ashamed that he hadn't, but it still hit a nerve sometimes. Like now. How different it would have been, if the impossible thing had happened, if it had been Micky, his own brother, who had miraculously returned home. Instead of pieces of him being left scattered somewhere on Vimy Ridge.

Wesley, of all people!

I thought I had learnt to control my capacity to be shocked, or to feel more pain, until Inspector Reardon told us that Wesley had been the one to find Paul's body, and to recognize him! He was cautious but I knew what he was thinking, or if he didn't think it now, he soon would. The police aren't satisfied with how Paul came to die, I can tell. They will want to know about their previous association, and it will all come out about that famous quarrel.

I have a lot of time for Wesley, and for the police to suspect him of having anything to do with Paul's death must soon become ridiculous, even to them – surely? A man like him, who devotes so much of his life to making things better for others in the community? Yet Wesley is his own worst enemy when it comes to personal relationships. He won't tell them anything he feels they don't need to know, and they'll very soon be suspecting him of having something to do with it, if they don't already. They'll soon realize he's not one to forget resentments or what he sees as injustices and draw their own conclusions. I saw proof of that once, the first time I ever encountered Wesley Pugh, Paul's friend.

It was also the first time – and the last, I believe – that he ever came to Fox Close. And the only time, in the years since, during which I've come to know him, that I've ever seen him lose his temper. He can be angry, but not like that. It was spectacular. The commotion brought me from the house, to see Paul pinned against the old stable doors – not physically, but by the sheer force of the words being hurled at him by the young man I later came to know was Wesley. Accusing him like an avenging angel: '*Contemptible . . . Despicable . . . Shameful.*' I thought at first it must be something to do with that girl, that Connie – but it wasn't. It seemed to concern someone called Philip. Teddy was standing by, no more than eight or nine years old, a terrified child, and it was when I heard his name also that I whisked him away before Father should appear, waving that stick he'd lately been forced to use, though getting out of the way was as much for my own sake as well as Teddy's. The last thing either of us needed was a repetition of what had happened not three weeks earlier, and its consequences. I was still wearing the bandage round my wrist from that encounter. I shall bear the scars for the rest of my life.

Teddy and I left them to it. The next day, Paul was gone, left home. And within weeks, Teddy was gone also, to boarding school at Westingbury, and I was left alone in the cold, dark, echoing rooms and corridors of Fox Close, alone with Father, and my regrets. Regrets about the chance I'd once had to escape, and not taken. I was barely twenty-two, but for me it was already too late. I had already condemned myself to the life of the spinster daughter.

After what seemed the longest time – although it was only two years, which Paul had spent with the cousins in Germany – he came home, complete with wife and son: Liesl, and little Matthaeus. Tiny Liesl, frail and flower-like, with her pretty, fractured accent. Silly, frothy, light-minded, but headstrong, and with no common sense whatever. But everyone liked her, and for the first time since Mother died, the house was again filled with sunshine.

Since Paul's resurrection (which is precisely what that has felt to be since he reappeared two weeks ago) the weight of oppression has been unbearable. The last years of hard-won peace of mind have gone, forever, I suspect. For the first time in years, I dream at night, those dreams I used to have, when I am chased by a mad, barking dog and I'm running away with lead in my shoes, getting nowhere. I wake to a dread that stays with me all day. I know what a heavy heart means now. It's literally true. I feel it, like a weight dragging me down. Outwardly, I know I look the same cool and capable Miss Millar and I go about my daily business as though nothing has happened, as though our long-lost brother had not suddenly reappeared in our lives for a brief moment, and then . . . was gone again. Only Teddy knows something of what I feel, but there's no comfort to be had there. He has his own demons to face.

SIX

Reardon's office exasperated him more each day. Not for reasons of status, or lack of, but because as a working space it was useless. He shifted papers and files from the spare chair to the windowsill, which only exchanged the available seating. He swore under his breath, gathered his notes together and went into the more spacious outer office.

It was just as well. As he hitched himself on the desk where Gilmour was seated and called the two DCs, Gargrave and Pickersgill, from their own desks to join them, two of the uniformed constables Inspector Waterhouse had agreed to lend him for the duration came to the door, expecting to be included and told what their duties would be. The youngest was an eager recruit to Market Street, a gangly youth who looked no more than fourteen called Imison, whose high-buttoned tunic collar seemed too big for his neck, the other was PC Dawson. Reardon liked Dawson, an experienced copper with years of service, and wouldn't have been averse to adding him to his team if and when the opportunity should occur. But Dawson wasn't interested in being a plain-clothes policeman. He'd made it clear where his priorities lay. As a family man, he preferred the more predictable, routine, uniformed side of the job, even if it did mean night shifts.

'You're all more or less up to scratch on what we've found out so far?' he began when everyone had gathered round, now including Sergeant Longton, who'd ambled up to join them. 'Let's go over it then, so we're all on the same page. Questions afterwards. For a start, the body we have appears to be that of Paul Millar, who's been missing and assumed to be dead for fourteen years, but who had recently made a brief return appearance.' He hadn't finished his brief resume of the few facts they'd already been able to establish before a hand went up. There was always one, and it was inevitably Gargrave. 'When I'm done, Gravy.'

Gargrave, who had eventually resigned himself to everyone, even the gaffer, using the nickname which had followed him down the years from his schooldays, assumed a put-upon expression, but he sat back. Reardon continued, 'We don't have much to go on yet. What we do know so far is that Millar appears to have arrived back in Folbury on the sixteenth of last month, is thought to have checked in at the Shire (which we still have to confirm) then made a short – very short – visit to his brother and sister. For reasons not yet apparent, he chose not to stay with them. Nothing more is known of his movements until his body was discovered early this morning by Councillor Pugh, in the river by the Colley Street allotments. Mr Pugh admits, however, that there's a slight possibility he might have spotted him at an earlier date, somewhere in the town. All right, yes . . . I know.' He'd intercepted the dubious looks: they all knew what the words 'might have' usually meant, coming from a reluctant witness or suspect, and he felt no need to pursue it. 'According to Dr Dysart's estimation of how long the body was submerged, it's probable he died on or around the same day he arrived in Folbury. What I can tell you now is that it looks as though we can rule out either accident or suicide. There seems to be evidence that he met his death violently, that a firearm was involved.' It was the first any of them, apart from Gilmour, had been told of a gunshot wound and as he'd expected, it caused a stir. 'But that,' he added warningly, 'is not yet for public consumption. I don't want this to go any further at his point, is that understood?'

He fixed his glance on Gargrave while he received nods of agreement from all around.

'We'll have more details,' he went on, 'when we get the results of the post-mortem, but until then, I'll remind you again to keep it under your hats. Meanwhile, we get on with some doorstepping around Colley Street. Anyone who saw or heard anything out of the way, or suspicious, over the last two weeks, I want to know about. And if you can gather names of anyone who was associated with him in any way before the war. Especially any hints of why he might not have come back until now.'

The collective lack of enthusiasm was discernible. And Reardon knew why. Doorstepping was boring, but they all knew it was essential, since there was little else to work on yet. But more than that, this looked like being an investigation which had all the makings of the worst-case scenario no one ever wanted to be landed with: a two-week old body with the trail gone cold, no apparent crime scene, no weapon. No witnesses. Nothing known of the victim's life during the past couple of decades. Nothing to suggest why he'd never returned home after the war. 'Any questions, comments or bright ideas?'

No one had. Even Gravy seemed to have forgotten he'd had a question.

A hand rose, diffidently. 'Er . . . doesn't it look as though he might have deserted, sir? And didn't come home because he didn't think it safe?'

It was Imison, the new, eager, young constable, blushing, his ears glowing red. He couldn't know that no one else had mentioned this obvious possibility because they hadn't wanted to put it into words. He was too young to know it as they did: a sensitive subject, often too near home and to be approached with caution. People hadn't forgotten what had happened to men who deserted, those who hadn't been able to face the unspeakable horrors of trench warfare – pursued by the Redcaps, hunted down like animals, sometimes for years. Punished as traitors, sometimes even shot. And if they managed to evade capture, ostracized for the cowards they were thought to be. If Paul Millar had deserted, it was easy to see why he'd kept away from where he had been known. The war and its bitter consequences still loomed large, and in the families of those who had fallen, forgiveness was hard to find for those who were regarded as having abandoned their comrades.

'Good point, Jack,' Reardon said, remembering his name in time, causing Imison to blush more, 'but there's nothing yet to indicate that. His sister last heard from him just before the war ended. She made extensive enquiries when they heard nothing more and was eventually told by the War Office that he had been discharged and they no longer had jurisdiction over him. She suspected some sort of confusion had arisen, that he must have been killed, but there was nothing the family could do about that. They had to accept what they'd been told.'

That created more dubious looks. 'She seems to think there

was more to it, some sort of muddle they were reluctant to admit to,' Gilmour said.

'How likely is that?' Gravy murmured.

'Very likely, take it from me.' PC Dawson exchanged a look with Reardon. He was the only one present, a man of around Reardon's own age, old enough, like him, to have been in the thick of it. 'The fighting might have ended but the chaos hadn't. You had to see it to believe it. The cock-ups were unbeliev-able, though getting thousands of men back home was no picnic for the authorities, I'll grant you. I spent three months myself in barracks waiting for my demob papers before I could go home, and some poor devils spent a lot longer. God knows how many people got fed up and decided they'd had enough and risked coming home without waiting to go through the whole rigmarole.'

'You're right, Stan. All the same it would have been a risk for Millar. The MPs would still have had him in their sights – except that his demob papers were kosher, according to the War Office.' Reardon stood up. 'All right, that winds it up for the moment. Sergeant Gilmour will get on with organizing the door-to-door, Colley Street and around. Anything at all seen either way of the sixteenth, I want to know about it. You'll need to see all the allotment holders as well, though there's not a lot of activity there at this time of year.'

'You'd be surprised.' Longton was a keen gardener, who grew prize chrysanthemums and giant onions in his back garden.

'If you say so, George. Meanwhile, I'm on my way to see what the Shire can tell us. You can come with me, Pickersgill. Gravy, you're with Sergeant Gilmour.'

'Sir.' Gargrave's face was wooden.

Gilmour reached for pencil and paper, ready to organize lists for the local enquiries, repetitive and sometimes thankless as the task was, disturbing folks who didn't want to be disturbed, asking questions people thought they'd no business asking. But action of any kind fired Gilmour even if, as was likely to be the case now, nothing productive came of it. 'We want any sightings of the dead man, anything at all you can pick up,' he told them, 'and don't ignore the nosey parkers.' He had no need to add that someone anxious to pass on a bit of tittle-tattle could lead to a whole new approach. 'We might be on a hiding to nothing, it was a dirty night, the sixteenth, not the sort to be out in unless you had to, but if we don't ask, we'll never know.'

He reminded them again that if Wesley Pugh's reluctant admission of seeing Paul Millar somewhere in the town was correct, there was always the possibility he'd been seen by other people, too, though who would have recognized him, or if they thought they had, have believed what they'd seen? Dead men didn't suddenly come to life. He handed out addresses to be ticked off. 'All right with that, Gravy?' he asked.

'Sure, Sarge.'

Gargrave's face was hidden as he reached for his list, but his shoulders were stiff with resentment, and Gilmour knew it was because he thought he should have been the one, not Pickersgill, to accompany the gaffer to the Shire. But as a natural member of the awkward squad, the DC still had enough nous to see that moaning about what he was told to do wouldn't have been the best idea, in view of the promotion he wanted but was unlikely to get here in Folbury, or not unless things changed significantly. He'd moved here from his native Yorkshire to marry a girl who'd since changed her mind, and it was no secret he was on the lookout for somewhere else to move to.

'Don't forget, Dave, we're only here to find out if Paul Millar really did book in, or for some reason only said he had,' Reardon cautioned Pickersgill as they reached the Shire, a venerable old inn which had recently been undergoing much needed refurbishment. 'It's questionable anyway, seeing as he was so against raising a fuss about his return, but we need to make sure. It can't have been for long, in any case.'

That inexplicably brief visit to his family at Casa Nova, after which they had allegedly never seen him again, threw serious doubt on Paul Millar's stay at the Shire being anything but brief, if at all. But nothing could be taken for granted. 'Mum's the word. No point in starting any unnecessary rumours.'

'Understood, sir.'

Reardon nodded. The caution had been automatic, but not actually necessary. Pickersgill knew when to keep his mouth shut. He was shaping up to be an asset. A serious young chap, steady as a rock, unfettered by too much imagination that might lead to fanciful speculations, his uncomplicated direct-ness sailed straight for the obvious conclusion, which was why he sometimes got to the point quicker than the rest. But Reardon would have given the same warning to any of them.

A former coaching inn which for hundreds of years had been content to carry on in the same tradition as it always had, the Shire was now earmarked to go up in the world. Somebody had been found to put money into it. It boasted new management, there was now a function room with a dance floor and a revamped dining room offering a menu to tempt Folbury to ditch the habits of a lifetime and take the occasional meal out. Brochures advertising places of interest within reach – Stratford-upon-Avon, Warwick Castle et al – were fanned out along a modern, streamlined reception desk, a canny move on the part of the management. Folbury had more to offer as a centre from which to explore places other than itself. Its own attractions were limited to what was left of the town's medieval origins, the castle ruins, a Norman church and a number of quaintly timbered old streets.

The new manager went by the name of Earl Watmough, a man with the slightly haggard looks of an ageing matinee idol trying to stave off middle age. The slightly too-tight chalk-stripe suit, brilliantined hair, the Clark Gable moustache, the would-be attractively crooked smile were too obvious by this time in his life, but to give him his due the rather strained, professional charm was ditched when he learnt who they were, and he showed himself willing enough to do what he could to help.

In fact, he was eager to do so. Because yes, of course he remembered the man they were enquiring about. He recalled him booking in, and his disappearance thereafter, which had posed something of a mystery. He'd walked into the Shire on the off-chance, asking if they had a room vacant, which by good luck they had, and had booked for two weeks.

Reardon suspected that luck didn't have a great deal to do with it. Despite its hopefully risen status, the Shire seemed highly unlikely to have had a full complement of guests, espe-cially at this time of year. In fact there had been four other guests that night. Pickersgill noted down the names and addresses: Mr Cyril Horobin, a government inspector from the Department of Works, a regular who had stayed at the Shire on a twice-yearly basis for years. A Mr and Mrs Harold Lightfoot, an elderly couple who'd ordered champagne with their dinner and the hotel's best room because they were celebrating his retirement as area manager for Lipton's Tea in style, and taking a holiday to explore Shakespeare country. There had been only one other guest, a Miss Cordingley, from Wolverhampton.

'Is she a regular as well?'

'She's stayed here a few times recently.' He was able to elaborate. The lady apparently needed to spend odd days with her pregnant sister, who wasn't well, and each time she visited she had stayed overnight at the Shire. Because, she'd told Watmough, there were no beds to spare at the little house out at Darley End where her sister lived. 'Not surprising, seeing there's four little 'uns already,' he added, rolling his eyes as if to say some people never learn.

'Expensive, staying here,' Reardon commented.

'That doesn't seem to bother her. She has breakfast in her room, which is an extra, and not something we offer as a general rule, but I make an exception in her case. She takes a taxi each time, to and from Darley End, and all. I reckon she's very fond of her sister. And she never has visitors,' he added sharply, anticipating the next question, which Reardon had in fact never intended asking. 'We close the doors at ten thirty. She's a nice lady.'

And willing to talk, seemingly. To Watmough, who evidently saw it as part of his duties to chat with his guests.

'Did you say Darley End, sir?' Pickersgill enquired, checking the addresses in his notebook.

'That's where the *sister* lives, Constable. I told you, Miss Cordingley lives in Wolverhampton, Wednesfield, to be precise.'

'You say you didn't see much of the man we're enquiring about, Mr Watmough,' Reardon said, 'But you remember him clearly?'

'Of course. It's my job. I'd have remembered him anyway, he gave his name as a Mr P. Millar – Millar spelt with an "a". I thought at first he hadn't got it right when he signed the register, but you don't spell your own name wrong, do you? He booked in for two weeks' bed and breakfast, but . . . I've been expecting him to turn up any day, at least to claim his luggage, but he hasn't so far.' He looked a question from one to the other, clearly agog to know what all this was about. Getting no response, he went on: 'I showed him to his room myself and asked him if he wanted dinner that night, but he said no, he was going out.'

'What time was that, when he went out?'

'About sixish, I'd say, and he came back some time during the evening, though I'm not sure just when. We had a Rotary dinner in the function room, so I was busy.' The dinner Ted Millar had been forced to miss, no doubt, Reardon thought. 'He took breakfast the next morning. And that's the last we've seen of him.'

'You didn't think to report it?'

'No, why should I? It wasn't as though he'd sloped off without settling his bill . . . he'd paid in advance – and in cash – unusual, but not something I was going to object to! If he'd changed his mind and decided to spend his time elsewhere that was up to him. His suitcase is still in his room.'

'Did he give his address when he booked in?'

'Not a full one. Just London.' Watmough looked from one to the other, finally unable to restrain himself. 'What's he been up to, then? What do you want him for?'

'He won't be coming back, Mr Watmough,' Reardon told him, and briefly explained why.

'Oh.' Varying expressions crossed his face, chief among them an obvious calculation as to whether this would have any repercussions on his establishment. Eventually, he seemed to decide not, or that it might on the other hand excite a macabre interest, and his face cleared. 'Well, I can't say as I'm surprised. Not that he's dead,' he added hastily, 'but you have to think, don't you? I mean, paying for two weeks and then just taking himself off like that. But it never crossed my mind . . .'

'We'd like to see his room, if you please.'

'Of course.'

The stairs had a new, unsympathetic carpet in a jazzy orange pattern, but clearly, the improvements stopped there. Several doors opened off a dark landing, where miserable wallpaper and brown lino showing signs of wear were in evidence. The door the manager unlocked was to a front room overlooking the main street. Sparsely furnished, but clean and adequate, with a double bed covered in a white Welsh quilt, a dressing table, a wardrobe and a straight-backed chair. A Turkey rug beside the bed rested on parquet-pattered lino. It was freezing cold.

'I don't think he'd even unpacked properly.' Watmough pointed to a small suitcase standing under the window and stood back, waiting for them to begin their search.

'Thank you, Mr Watmough, you can leave this with us,' Reardon told him. 'We don't need to take up any more of your time.'

The manager didn't seem to like the idea of leaving them alone but saw he'd no choice and after a moment he nodded and departed.

The bed had been slept in but remade, and under the pillow was a pair of folded, striped flannel pyjamas. A camel dressing gown, worn almost through at the elbows, hung behind the door. Pickersgill opened the wardrobe, which was empty, as Watmough had indicated, as were the three drawers in the dressing table. Reardon lifted the suitcase on to the chair and tried it. It wasn't locked, but there was nothing inside that needed hiding: a sleeved woollen vest and a pair of long pants, a clean shirt, nicely ironed, two handkerchiefs likewise, and a sponge bag containing soap and shaving tackle. Only one change of underclothes.

'Why d'you think he'd pay for two weeks?' he wondered aloud as he snapped the case shut, ready for taking away, though it wasn't going to yield much in the way of evidence.

'I don't suppose he was contemplating being murdered.'

Quips like this from Pickersgill were rare enough to merit a grin. 'I reckon not, Dave. And not everyone changes their undies every day.'

'No, sir.' He seemed about to say more.

'Well? Something else struck you?'

'Er – not about the victim, sir. It's probably nothing but . . .'

'Spit it out.'

'That Miss Cordingley . . .'

'Who? Oh, right, the ministering angel. What about her?'

'Well, the manager says her sister lives at Darley End.'

'Isn't that somewhere out Maxstead way? A little village?'

'It's hardly even that, there's not above a dozen houses there. Most of them used to be tied cottages to Darley Farm. It's where me and my brother were born, we lived there till I was about eight – till the parents could afford something better. It's true what the manager said, you can't swing a cat in them houses. My grandma still lives there and I'm pretty sure I'd have heard her say if there was anybody had moved in with four kids and another on the way.'

'Interesting.'

'I could cycle out to see Grandma tonight, sir. My mum would be pleased if I did. She worries about her living on her own, though I don't think she needs to, she's nicely set up, really cosy, and she has good neighbours. She's a spry old girl, knows everything that's going on and nothing much gets past her.'

Reardon considered. 'Miss Cordingley pulling the wool over Watmough's eyes, is that what you think? You could be right. The usual reason, I suppose. But if she's having an affair and lying to cover it up, it's none of our business.' Pickersgill looked crestfallen. 'But I don't doubt your grandma will be pleased to see you, Dave.'

He had the rare experience of seeing Pickersgill grin.

They stood amongst the unopened crates and odd bits and pieces stacked in what Reardon called the glory hole, Ellen and a jobbing builder, a man of few words and a maddening refusal to be rushed, called Samuel Trust. Trust by name and trust by nature, he'd announced on their first meeting, shortly after they'd moved in. Ellen had found this to be no exaggeration. He pushed his cloth cap back now, scratched his bald pate, regarded the wall and pondered.

'Do you think there ever was a door there?' she prompted at last.

He walked around and knocked knowledgeably on the wall in several places with his knuckles, stood back and thought. After a few minutes he reckoned yes, there had been one, at one time, indicating its position, and Ellen smiled, justified. She hadn't just walked into that wall because she was confused, then, although just why she'd confidently expected a door to be there was unnerving, to say the least. The builder knocked the wall again, near the floor, and the sound this time was less hollow. Because this was on a lower level than the sitting room next door, he informed her. 'On account of the sloping site, see.'

'That's why the doorway was blocked up, then. Because it was a dangerous drop from the other room?'

'Oh, I wouldn't say dangerous. Ten to one there'd have been a step there, any road. Two, maybe.'

'Why would they be taken away?'

'Rotten, most likely.' He stood, feet apart, on a flagstone below where the steps would have been and rocked it. 'Here, I'd say.'

'Well, we can always put them in again, can't we?'

It seemed they could, and that if the door was to be reinstated, a step would certainly be advisable – he'd go so far as to say necessary, in the interests of safety. While Samuel took out a dog-eared notebook and licked his pencil, cast an eye around and totted up costs in his mind, Ellen scanned the room, trying to see it as it might be, cleared of all the junk. Small and square, with a window overlooking what was going to be the garden; a black, cast iron fireplace set diagonally across a corner. Would it be worth the cost? Maybe with the stone-flagged floor polished, and some bright rugs scattered across, a leaping fire in the small fireplace, a couple of armchairs? Though to what purpose? The sitting room provided all of that already.

'Sound enough,' Samuel pronounced at last with a satisfied nod, having knowledgably checked corners and ceilings for cracks and signs of damp, tapped walls for loose plaster and given the window frame a professional once over for signs of dry rot, woodworm or death-watch beetle, and finding none of them. 'And nice in the summer.'

That at least was true. Opening the window had let the light flood in and revealed the extent of the garden, stretching out to the old ruined wall at the bottom, the apple tree in the corner and the slope of Fox Close's old drive to one side. And with a flash of insight so sudden and brief she might have imagined it, the garden layout, hitherto so elusive, began to take shape and meaning – a drift of purple and yellow crocuses under the apple tree, roses in summer, paeonies, phlox, the scent of damp earth and green, growing things, remembered from when she'd loved to help her father in his garden when she was a child.

She needed to go back to her sketchbook again. And this time, she couldn't wait to begin.

Samuel was looking expectant.

'Well,' she said, cautious about committing herself when it was by no means a fait accompli they were going to do anything about the glory hole or not. Reardon had been cautious: maybe it was always good to have somewhere like this where you could store things you might need later. Very true, of course, but Ellen had cleared out too much accumulated junk in the move here to have much enthusiasm for that idea.

'Have to have the chimney swept before we start, if you mean to have a fire,' Samuel was saying, 'sure to need it, but let's have a shufti anyway.' He prodded open the damper in the fireback that closed the chimney off when it was not in use and a choking shower of soot, bits of old bird's nests and old brick dust fell on to the hearth.

The smell was disgusting. Despite this, he'd no compunction in kneeling and thrusting his head further up the chimney. 'Oy-oy, there's a ledge here. And it looks like Father Christmas left you a present.' He reached up with both hands. More soot descended as he brought forth an old, square biscuit tin.

The rust fell off in flakes as he set it on the hearth and rubbed it with his fingers to reveal what was left of the painted lettering on the lid. Memory rushed back as Ellen remembered one just like it from her childhood. Peek Frean, and something or other shortbread, it said. Damp had removed the rest, and most of the sunny child in the picture. The tin itself, however, still looked more or less intact. No fires, maybe, since it had been stashed there – by whom? The previous occupant, or someone further back? Would it be right to open it, Ellen wondered, before trying to find out whoever it might have belonged to? Vague ideas of treasure trove, and an obligation to report such finds to the coroner occurred to her, though not seriously. This cheap tin box was scarcely likely to have been considered a suitable deposit to hide family heirlooms.

'Samuel, who lived here last, do you know?'

He replaced his cap after shaking the rubbish off it, brushed his shoulders free of more and shook his head. 'If I ever knew, which I don't think I did, I misremember now. You should ask Joe Gilmour's wife . . . Maisie Henshall as was. Her Auntie Clarice worked at Fox Close at one time. She'd know.'

Ellen was reminded that Samuel Trust had been recommended in the first place by Maisie. She thought they might in fact be some sort of distant cousins, though she couldn't for the moment work out just what the connection was. The intricate web of Folbury relationships, woven over decades of complicated association and intermarrying, was something it was as well to be aware of . . . you could so easily put your foot in it and unintentionally offend someone by criticizing or getting on the wrong side of someone who turned out to be their nearest and dearest.

Curiosity was bound to overcome any scruples and she didn't object when Samuel suggested he should have a go at opening the tin. After all, whoever had shoved it up the chimney had either forgotten it was there or wasn't in a position now to claim it, surely.

'Right.' He tried to lift the lid, but it wouldn't budge. A few bashes of his meaty fist, however, resulted in the side of the tin buckling and after that it was easily loosened. Ellen still hesitated. 'Go on, open it, it won't bite, Mrs R,' Samuel said.

'I expect it'll be like the *Treasure Island* chest,' she said with a nervous laugh. 'Empty.'

It wasn't, though its contents did look disappointingly ordinary. Nothing more than a dozen or so faded sepia photographs and a notebook bound in red leather. Despite the rust, the damp didn't seem to have penetrated to the inside of the tin, though there was an unpleasantly earthy, musty smell coming from it. The photographs, about a dozen Ellen guessed as she shuffled them, were mainly of three different children, a girl and two boys taken at various ages, but there were also one or two others, including a posed, rather stiff group of what appeared to be an entire household, a prosperous one, if the servants in the background, the maids in frilly white caps and aprons, were anything to go by. The young woman seated centrally on a chair in front of the group wore a choker-necked blouse and an outrageous, outsize hat of the sort fashionable at the turn of the century, decorated with an enormous ribbon bow, plus a rose and curled plumage sacrificed from at least one ostrich. She was small, fragile looking, with a sweet, delicate face. The baby she held, swathed in a long shawl, seemed almost too much of a burden for her to bear. The girl and boy from the other photographs stood at her side. The girl looked about twelve, plain and serious. She was standing very straight, her thick fair hair hanging past her shoulders, one hand protectively on the baby's shawl. While the boy, in a ridiculously unsuitable white sailor outfit with a large round hat on the back of his dark curls, had a cheeky grin and looked ready to run away as soon as he was released.

This must surely be the Millar family, the last owners of Fox Close. The man standing with a proprietary hand on the seated woman's shoulder was presumably the father, tall and slightly portly, stern and unsmiling, with a drooping moustache, aquiline nose and deep-set eyes under bushy eyebrows. She could easily imagine him being the Ernest Millar Horace remembered.

Samuel had lost interest in the find and presently took his leave after scribbling down a figure in his notebook, tearing the page out and handing it over. A figure higher than Ellen had hoped for, but less than she'd expected. 'Reckon I could fit you in for the job, give it a week or two. See what your husband thinks.'

Reardon didn't know about this visit yet, and now, when he was so involved with his current investigation, was not the time to bother him with it. Ellen folded the paper into her pocket, feeling guilty. She'd acted impulsively in asking Samuel Trust for an estimate, telling herself she needed to find out what the job might entail and the price before presenting her husband with figures. The dust of what the other alterations to the house had cost had scarcely settled yet, not to mention what it had done to their bank balance.

Samuel left and she put the rather brittle photographs care-fully back into the tin and nudged it to one side for later exploration. The red notebook was demanding attention, but she stood turning it over and over, still hesitant. It had, after all, been hidden and was therefore presumably private. On the other hand, if she didn't read it, she wouldn't ever be able to return it to whoever had hidden it up the chimney, would she? She took it to the window and perched on the sill.

It was a small book, about four inches by six. The leather covering was still in fair condition, though the binding was loose. On the first page was the date, written in careful copper-plate, the ink faded to a rusty brown. January the first, 1896, followed by the inscription: 'To Nan, from T, with love.'

The first of January, a new year. Evidently, this had been intended as a diary, but the owner didn't seem to have been very diligent about keeping it. It began rightly enough with several closely written pages, but then the entries gradually became more desultory, and eventually petered out, the original intention and enthusiasm having lapsed, as with diary-keepers the world over. And in between the written front pages and the blank ones remaining at the end, the middle chunk had been raggedly torn out, accounting for the loose binding. As she turned back to the beginning, a sheet of paper, folded over and over into a small square, fell out. She picked it up and opened it carefully, feeling how friable it was in her fingers, and how brittle along the creases. Blank on both sides, it had been used merely to enclose what was inside: a small, soft curl of blonde baby hair.

Ellen let the small square stay open on her outstretched palm, transfixed by a familiar frisson of emotion which turned her heart over. Such a sweet, innocent memory to keep – a reminder of those first baby months as the child grew. Or had the baby died, and this was all the memory the mother had? Had this diary belonged to the woman in the photograph, she of the ostrich-plumed hat, the one holding the baby? And did the soft blonde curl belong to the child?

The paper of the diary was virtually undamaged, Ellen found as she turned back to the beginning and began to read. The words were quite legible, but the handwriting didn't look like the hand of a lady such as the one in the photograph. The letters were large and carefully formed, like a child trying to do their 'best' writing. She felt sure that the person who had written it wasn't used to wielding a pen. Despite its laboured look it read easily enough but her teacher's eye spotted misspellings, and punctuation which was not always correct.

No child had written this, however. If that soft curl of hair had not said so, that much became eminently clear as she read on.

> I do not know how to start this or even why I should. I do not have any engagements or events to record but T says that dosent matter. I can always write about what I feel. What I feel now is being back at school again told to write a composition with a sharp pencil and a new notebook but without an idea in my head. We once had to write The Story of a Penny and I could think of nothing exept that it was large and round and made of mettle and it could buy you a quarter of pear drops with change if you were ever lucky enough to be given one. A Saturday hapenny was plenty for us Pa used to say but then he and Ma had seven of us to provide for.
>
> That was how I got the job here because I was the oldest in our family and used to helping Ma with the little ones. I liked babies anyway and he was so sweet and helpless as they are at that age and so soon to be mother-less poor lamb. Even so I dout whether I would have stayed on after the mother died if not for the other two. Older children though they were they couldnt have managed on there own and they got no help from their father.
>
> I may only be the daughter of a blacksmith but I did not like the way their father spoke to me, and still dont. I am only a paid servant however and in any case he speaks to the children in the same way.

After a few moments Ellen closed the book and put it back in the tin. It was a sad note on which to end, but there was no more. Whatever secrets the diary might have revealed in that middle section had been removed, and most likely consigned to oblivion.

SEVEN

Reardon did as he had said he would, and gave Wesley Pugh a chance to clean himself up and have something to eat after work before he and Gilmour caught up with him again. It was early evening when they stood at the door of the red-brick terraced house in Colley Street.

'I've a meeting at seven, but I can spare a bit of time before I leave,' he warned them when he answered their knock, making it clear where his priorities lay. 'You'd better come in.'

They stepped into the living-room-cum-kitchen which opened straight off the street and Pugh waved them to take a seat at the centre table taking up more than its fair share of space in the small room. He'd just made himself a pot of tea and after a moment's debate with himself, he held it up, raising his eyebrows. When the offer was accepted, he fetched two more mugs from the dresser.

Electricity hadn't yet come to Colley Street and the gas mantles hissed and popped occasionally, casting a yellowish light. The chairs on which they sat were uncompromisingly straight, a strong discouragement to linger over your dinner, and Gilmour grimaced as he shifted to get comfortable. All the same, it was a warm, snug little set-up Pugh had here. Whether he had a woman who came in to 'do' for him, or looked after it himself, it was clean and comfortable. A colourful tab rug stretched in front of a tidy fireplace and a spindle-back armchair with a crocheted wool cushion stood by the hearth. A run-of-the-mill working-class home, but what distinguished it from others of its type was the number of books, as many as Reardon himself owned, stacked on shelves reaching to the ceiling in each fireplace alcove.

Pugh swept to one side the files and papers spread out on the dark green chenille tablecloth, making space for the mugs. The milk had turned the tea a dark orange colour,

strong enough to stand a teaspoon in. Reardon sipped
appreciatively.

'What do you want of me? I've told you all I know,' Pugh
said, taking one of the other chairs. People invariably said that
when faced with questions, though it was rarely true, even if
they thought they had.

'You were the last to see the man you believe was Paul
Millar, and since you told us you used to know him well,'
Reardon began, 'it would be helpful to hear anything more
you can tell us about him.'

If the implication that he'd been less co-operative than he
might have been when they'd last spoken to him wasn't lost
on Pugh, he gave no indication. What he'd said about his
previous relationship with Paul Millar, if it had any truth in
it, implied they had once been good friends, but youthful
friendships didn't necessarily stand the test of time. Pugh
might well have had some reason, such as a disagreement
dating from then, to hold a grudge, and have taken the opportunity to get rid of Millar. After all this time? Perhaps, if he
was a man to keep resentments alive – and something about
the dark intensity of the man said he might be, and would be
prepared to do something about it, should the opportunity
arise. It was Pugh who had found the body and reported it.
That double bluff again? But he wouldn't need to bluff unless
there was some reason to believe he might be suspected.

A slight nod from Reardon gave Gilmour the opportunity
to open the questioning, Reardon had an idea he was still
smarting, annoyed – as he saw it – with his own less than
adequate performance at the meeting with the Millars and no
doubt glad of the chance to redeem the situation. Gilmour
kicked himself if he thought he hadn't come up to scratch.

'We've been in touch with the dead man's family, Councillor
Pugh,' he began, 'and it's looking very likely you were right,
that he is Paul Millar, and he wasn't a war casualty after all.'
Pugh threw him a sardonic glance and drank some of his tea,
waiting for him to go on, as if to say that was what he'd said
in the first place, wasn't it? 'But they tell us that he'd never
been in touch with them since the war ended. Don't you find
that odd?'

'No,' Pugh said shortly. 'Not at all, if you'd known Paul.'

This was the second time that remark had been made about the dead man, Reardon noted, the first time by his brother. 'And you did. Knew him well, I expect?'

Pugh said steadily, 'We were pals once, good pals. At least when we were younger.' He reached for the teapot, topped up his mug and added more sugar.

'But you didn't keep it up? What went wrong?'

'You grow up. At least I did, I hope.' He looked up from his stirring and said levelly, 'We just began to see less of each other.'

'Does that mean you had a falling out?'

'We went our different ways,' he replied after a second or two, avoiding the direct answer, though something flickered at the back of his eyes. 'It couldn't have lasted, anyway, we were worlds apart. Unlike me, and some of the others we went around with, who had to find our own feet, he'd money to splash around. Not a lot, but more than we had. I suppose it allowed him to grow wild, go a bit crazy sometimes. He got to enjoy drinking. He liked the girls, and the girls liked him.'

And once started, Pugh lost some of his taciturnity. Perhaps because what he was telling them had been bottled up for years, though almost certainly it was now being carefully edited – Wesley Pugh's version of what he thought they were entitled to know, or what he knew the police would find out anyway. They'd been schoolmates at the King's School, he said, he and Paul. Unlike the younger son, Teddy, Paul hadn't been sent away to school. 'He was a right old tartar, their father, strict as hell, righteous chapel-goer, teetotal, sign the Pledge when you're young and all that rubbish, but he was no fool. He could see what was happening and I reckon he wanted Paul where he could keep an eye on him. He couldn't bear anybody to go against his wishes, Ernest Millar, and that included his family. And for all he pretended to everyone else that he thought the sun shone from his eldest son's backside, he was no fool. Paul had made it pretty plain that he had other ideas than his father's, see . . . which was that Paul should be the dutiful, stay-at-home son, inheriting the business.'

'Paul didn't want that?'

'Not on your life. He worked with his father after he left school, but it was half-hearted. He had a mechanical turn of mind, clever as a monkey with engines, thought of nothing else. He'd crazy ideas about driving racing cars, dreamt about flying aeroplanes, being a pilot . . . you can imagine what his father thought about that! I reckon that's why he joined the RFC later. I told you he was mad.'

'I imagine none of that sat well with his father's ambitions for him?'

'No. But you could understand Ernest, I suppose. He'd taken over the business from his own father and improved it no end. It was the be-all and end-all of his life. And then, he had to go and marry a German.'

'Paul did?' Reardon asked, after sorting that out.

'You know the family was German originally? Well, Paul suddenly took himself off over there to stay with some of his cousins, without a word to anyone—'

'Why?'

'What?'

'Why did he leave so suddenly?'

'Oh, another bust-up, I suppose,' Pugh said after a moment. He shrugged, but his hand was tight on the handle of his mug. 'He met a girl there, married her without telling his father. The fat was in the fire and not half, as you might imagine. For one thing, Ernest had spent half his life trying to make folk forget the family's German origins. But the row blew over. Paul came back home and as a married man with a wife to provide for, see, he'd no option but to come and dance to his father's tune from then on.'

'That all happened before the war?'

'That's right. But you can't have forgotten how much anti-German feeling there was around, even then.'

No. It was nothing new to anyone whose memory reached back as far as that. Fuelled by fear of the war ambitions of Kaiser Wilhelm – the king's own first cousin! – and his increasingly vitriolic invective against the British, unashamedly whipped up by certain sections of the press, some of the gullible public were easily persuaded into believing anything, however ludicrous: that German immigrants took British jobs;

that anyone who had a German name was likely to be a spy; and that it was acceptable to daub anti-German slogans on their doors, throw bricks through their windows and even subject them to physical violence at times. That German Shepherd dogs, for God's sake, should be renamed as Alsatians. Not that it was all merely hysteria on the part of the British public. German spies had certainly been found and arrested, and immediately the war started the Government had issued a restriction act, whereby all foreigners were rounded up and interned as aliens. They were treated fairly, but none of it stopped the resentments and suspicions of anyone who had foreign connections.

Could this have explained Paul Millar's reluctance to return to his home after the war . . . and the distinct uneasiness his siblings had obviously felt when he did? The war was in the past, they had been building their lives without him, but sleeping dogs weren't always allowed to lie. Were they afraid of repercussions? Ernst Müller had cannily changed his name and become naturalized but that hadn't necessarily been a guarantee of protection.

'I sometimes wondered if that was part of why Paul volunteered so quick to fight . . . to show he was as British as anyone else,' Pugh said unexpectedly.

'What happened to his German wife?'

'Liesl? Oh, she died. Before the war.' He drained the last of his tea. 'Tragedy, so young, poor Liesl. But it happens.' Something said his casualness might be hiding his own situation. He lived alone, from choice or because his own wife had died?

'Then he'd nothing to come back to Folbury for? That might have been the reason why he stayed away so long?'

'Maybe. Who knows?' Pugh scraped his chair back and looked pointedly at the clock. He'd given them long enough. Perhaps he wished he hadn't acted so out of character and said more than he'd meant to.

'So why do you think he did choose to come back after all?' Reardon persisted. 'You must have been wondering about that.'

Pugh shrugged, but he appeared to be giving it some thought

and after a moment or two's hesitation, he repeated, 'Why? Well, to see Matt, of course.'

'Matt?'

'His son.'

Reardon and Gilmour exchanged a look. There had been no mention of a son from either of the Millars when they'd spoken to them, but Reardon was more annoyed with himself than with them. It hadn't occurred to him until now that he'd never actually received a direct answer to his question as to whether Paul had a family of his own. It was such a basic fact about their brother that the avoidance of it now seemed deliberate, though he couldn't imagine why it should have been.

Pugh got up and took his pipe, a tobacco pouch and a box of Swan Vestas from the mantelpiece, but he stood gripping the pipe by its stem, making no attempt to fill or light it. At last he said abruptly, as if the pause had enabled him to come to a decision, 'All right, that was where I saw him. Where I saw Paul, that night, or thought I did. Coming out of Matt's workshop.'

'Why didn't you say so in the first place?'

'Couldn't believe it, thought I'd seen a ghost.' He began at last to light his pipe and the pungent smell of strong twist filled the room.

It had never been entirely credible that he should have forgotten just where he'd seen Paul Millar and Reardon wondered what had made him, unapologetic for his now conveniently returned memory, suddenly decide to tell the truth about his sighting of him.

'Matt Millar? The artist?' Gilmour repeated, making the now obvious connection. 'If that's him, he teaches my wife at night school – and Mrs Reardon, too.'

'That's what he has to do to get a living. You don't get rich being an artist,' Pugh answered sardonically.

'Where can we find him?' Reardon asked.

There was no immediate answer, another indication he might be wishing his mention of Matt unsaid. 'Hadley Piece,' he replied after a moment or two. 'He has a workplace there, calls it his studio, lives there as well.'

'Hadley Piece?' Gilmour repeated disbelievingly, while

saying a mental goodbye to an early supper as he saw Reardon already preparing to get to his feet, no doubt anxious to be on his way there. 'I didn't imagine anyone lived there.'

'Not every building there has fallen down yet,' Pugh said. 'Though most of them have, and the rest should have followed. But let me tell you about Matt, before you go barging in there.' Without giving them chance to agree or not, he went on to explain how the young boy had been left to the care of his aunt and uncle while Paul was away fighting, and had remained with them afterwards, when Paul didn't return to claim his son. 'There wasn't anybody else, but in any case, nobody could have done more for him, they thought the world of him, and still do. Thea dotes on him and Ted's always been proud as Punch. If he'd had his way, he'd be grooming the lad now to step into his shoes at Millars sooner or later. Except that's not Matt's idea of his future. He's a fine young man, knows where he wants to go and he's working hard to get there.' He put the pipe back on the mantelpiece, not gently. 'Look here, what's happened to Paul . . . the lad's going to find that hard to take. I should go with you when you see him.'

'Thank you, Mr Pugh, but that won't be necessary. Nobody's going to go barging in, as you put it. In any case, considering what you've just told us about Matt's relationship with his aunt and uncle, I'd be astonished if he doesn't know already.'

After a moment, Pugh conceded the point and lifted his shoulders. 'As you wish.'

Reardon forbore to tell him the choice wasn't his to make. Instead he asked him about the other young people he'd mentioned, those other friends of Paul's before the war. 'A list of their names would be appreciated.'

'If I can remember them all.'

'Oh, I should think you'll be able to do that. You strike me as being a man with a very good memory, Mr Pugh.'

He threw Reardon a sharp look, but then, as he was opening the door for them he said, 'Look here, it must be obvious to you that Paul and I had our differences, I don't deny it, but that was then, we were only lads. I know the way your minds work . . . and I'm damn sure he didn't get into the river by accident – or by his own intent, from what I knew of Paul.

You're thinking somebody killed him, but for the record,' he finished passionately, his eyes burning, Welsh ancestry to the fore, 'it wasn't me.'

Outside, Gilmour asked with resignation, 'Hadley Piece, then?'

To his relief, Reardon shook his head. 'Been a long day and I for one am heading home. Get a move on and you'll be in time to read Ellie a bedtime story.'

Gilmour did get a move on but not fast enough for him to hop on the number 27 bus he'd hoped to catch, the only one that went his way at that time of an evening. He swore under his breath as he saw it disappearing around the corner, pulled his coat collar up against the cold drizzle and began to leg it home, thinking with rare nostalgia of the bicycle he'd had as a uniformed copper.

Reardon's last reminder was still in his mind – 'Don't forget to chase up that list Pugh promised, there may be people on it who have a better recollection than he says he has' – when he reached the back street he invariably used as a shortcut. Iron gates closed off the delivery yard behind the Co-op, where he'd caught a bunch of toerags the night before, a gang of youths who'd been aiming an air rifle at a target chalked on the wall.

He'd shouted to them to come out and waited until they'd scrambled in undignified though by no means chastened haste back over the gates, defiant and swaggering to show they weren't intimidated. Sent them home with a flea in the ear, especially the cheeky young pup – one of the Bagley clan, of course – who'd been giving him some lip. Scared the living daylights out of them with what an innocent-seeming air rifle could do, and what he'd do if he caught them trespassing again. Seen them on their way and gone on home himself.

It had only been a temporary victory, he knew. He hadn't scared them all that much. Young school-leavers with nothing to do at night except look for trouble. Apprentice-aged lads who should have been at night-school, or indoors doing their night-school homework. But how many of them had been able to find apprenticeships, or any kind of job at all for that matter, when they left school? When the dole queues stretched out of the doors of the Labour Exchange into the street?

This time, he stopped and had another look through the iron gate leading into the yard. There had been no moon last night and only one mantle in the gas lamp further along the street with broken glass littering the pavement below. The lamp, for a wonder, had now been repaired and he was better able to discern what was chalked up on the cement-rendered wall that was the back of the store. Last night, he'd only given it a glance, but the thought of it had occurred to him on and off throughout the day and now, as he paid it more attention, he gave a grunt of satisfaction: it had come to him later, the name of one of the youths he hadn't been able to place just at that time, the one who he'd thought was a bit older than the rest, who should have known better. He told himself he might have known. As he looked again at the target on the wall, he wondered what he should do about it.

EIGHT

Pickersgill was late. Normally a stickler for punctuality, he entered the police station breathless and sweaty after making an unscheduled detour to the back entrance to avoid the press presence at the front: i.e. the hopeful cub reporter from the local rag, who seemed to have taken up almost permanent residence in Market Street. Pickersgill had a highly developed preservation response when it came to recognizing and avoiding anyone from the *Folbury Herald* since his unwise involvement a few years back with one of the staff which could have cost him his career. The rumours circulating about the drowned body of a mysterious stranger had come too late for this week's edition of the paper, but if the reporter got wind of any hint that Millar had been murdered, he'd be away with it to sell to one of the national newspapers.

Speculation about the drowned man was already running like an electric storm through the town since it had emerged that he had once been a soldier – and one of the Millars! – long thought to be a dead war hero. The hearts of bereaved mothers, wives and sweethearts were leaping with unrealistic, doomed and cruel hope – that one of their own lost loved ones might even yet return, somehow, against all odds. Having suffered shell shock maybe, like so many of the poor lost souls who had somehow been returned home, who'd either lost their memory and their wits, forgotten their own name, been displaced, come adrift – and not after all been blown into unidentifiable bits. If this one man could return from the dead, so could Tom, or Dick, or Harry – and what was more, they wouldn't then have drowned themselves, would they?

Pickersgill, red-faced and five minutes late, located Reardon and the briefing he was supposed to be attending in the office of Chief Inspector Waterhouse.

'There's a lot we still don't know about Paul Millar, and

not only the last years. We need to concentrate on when he lived here, before the war,' Reardon was saying. He nodded to Pickersgill to take a seat as he entered. There was only one left, on the other side of the room, overcrowded with Waterhouse himself and several more uniforms who'd wandered in to join those already assigned to the enquiry, and since no one was making any obvious move to let him past, Pickersgill crossed his arms and leant back against the wall.

Because Waterhouse had righteously offered his own office – a proper office, an altogether different affair from Reardon's – for the present discussion, he was taking advantage of his entitlement as senior officer at Market Street to sit in with the rest of them. It wasn't something Reardon was altogether happy with: the CI's pedantry and the way he stuck like glue to the rule book drove him mad, but he could hardly refuse. And he had to remember that Waterhouse's agreement to the continued services of those of his men who'd assisted with the canvassing around Colley Street had doubled the strength available.

Nothing had been gained by the doorstep questioning around there, however, which didn't come as any surprise. The corner shops and the newsagent had been closed by six. A better option for the residents than venturing out into a cold, wet, winter's night had been a comfortable chair by a blazing fire with a cup of tea or a glass of beer, the curtains drawn, reading, doing the football pools, knitting or mending, Henry Hall's dance band on the wireless. No one had seen or heard a thing. Whatever had happened to Paul Millar, if it had happened on that Godforsaken stretch of the riverbank by the allotments, not a soul had been aware of it. Or were prepared to admit they had.

'Meaning that it's very likely it didn't happen there anyway,' Waterhouse commented sagely. 'Only that he ended up there.'

Reardon acknowledged the comment as if it were original, though it had been with him like ear music ever since Gilmour had first made it when the body had been found, as had the nagging follow up of where then had he gone into the water? Which would depend on how far the body could have drifted after surfacing, how long it would have taken to get to where it was found. And the places, strictly limited, he fancied, where it might have been thrown in. Even then it didn't mean he'd been killed there. The boot of a car in which a body might have been transported wasn't out of the question.

'However, we do have a bit more to be going on with since interviewing Councillor Pugh for the second time,' he continued, signalling Gilmour to continue.

Gilmour enlarged. 'Not least, Pugh's relationship with Millar. Close friends when they were younger, but they'd parted company. Reading between the lines, that looks like another way of saying they'd had a big falling out. He's now admitted to having seen him alive on the evening of the seventeenth of February – outside the warehouse at Hadley Piece where his son works – Millar's son, that is. Which means that we now have another time frame. He returned to the Shire the night he arrived, so we're now looking at the day after he arrived in Folbury as a probable date for his murder. Pugh's sighting of him is so far the last one we have.'

'I hope you're not suggesting, Sergeant, that Councillor Pugh could have had any involvement in all this!' Waterhouse protested, his moustache bristling. As the senior officer, he inevitably had contact on a regular basis with people on the local council. Interaction and co-operation between the two bodies was something the higher-ups were very keen on. And whatever anyone thought of Pugh, he had a lot of influence, in quarters where it would be of interest to the police to keep him on their side. Waterhouse knew that the balloon would go up at the suggestion of the councillor being involved in anything so sordid as what was almost certainly an unsavoury murder, when that became public knowledge.

'Not at all, sir.' Gilmour's retrieval was quick. 'Just that Councillor Pugh obviously wasn't keen to renew his old friend's acquaintance.'

Waterhouse looked baleful and seemed about to say more.

'Let's not jump the gun,' Reardon intervened, not perhaps the most fortunate phrase in the circumstances. 'We only know that Mr Pugh states he saw Paul Millar coming from his son's studio at Hadley Piece. We haven't yet had the opportunity to interview Matt Millar, but we shall be doing so shortly – later

this morning, as a matter of fact, which should confirm what
Mr Pugh told us. We don't know for certain yet when Paul
Millar arrived in Folbury, only that he booked in at the Shire
on the sixteenth, went out and returned to spend the night
there, went out again after breakfast the following morning
and never returned. As Sergeant Gilmour has told you, it was
that day, the evening of the seventeenth, when Mr Pugh saw
him.'

'Funny he stayed at the Shire and not with his family,' PC
Dawson remarked, pulling a censorious face. A family man
himself, he obviously couldn't imagine a situation arising
where a missing brother, returned from the dead or not, would
not be as welcome as the prodigal son, with rejoicing all round.

'We can't account for that. Maybe he'd some reason to think
he wouldn't be well received there.'

'In that case why did he come back here at all?'

That was still the biggest puzzle.

'For my money,' Gargrave said, 'it must have been er . . .
well, money.' Before anyone could snigger, he added with
dignity, 'To claim his share of what his father left. The Millars
can't be short of a bob or two.'

'Good point, Gravy,' Reardon said, magnanimous in the
knowledge that his own mal mot had gone unnoticed. 'Money's
a big incentive but we may have to discount it in this case.
His father died before the war, so anything due to him he'd
have received then, one would have thought. It might not have
been all that much in any case. Relations between him and
his father were not all they might have been, at least according
to Councillor Pugh.'

'We could be back with the deserter theory, in spite of what
the War Office claimed,' Gilmour said. 'Still running from the
Redcaps . . . or something worse – someone who followed
him and killed him?'

Waterhouse evidently felt it was time he made his presence
felt again. 'What about his stay at the Shire? Was there anyone
else staying there that night? Someone he might have intended
to meet? I'm sure you've checked there, of course,' he added
with a wolfish smile.

'We have,' Reardon said. 'Some guest at the Shire that night might not have been entirely honest about their reasons for being there, however innocent they might have seemed. We have all their statements. Sergeant?'

When Waterhouse saw the thick file Gilmour produced, he stood up hastily, consulting his watch. 'Then I can leave you to get on with it. I have a meeting with the ACC in five minutes and it's likely to take some time. But feel free to stay here for as long as you need,' he told Reardon benevolently, and with an affable smile all round, took his departure.

The whole room relaxed and loosened up as the door closed behind him. Several felt for cigarettes and lit up. Gilmour opened the file.

He had sent Gargrave, who was good at winkling out details when his interest was aroused, to do the checking at the Shire. The DC had gone with alacrity; it was the sort of job he liked, and did well. Better than doorstepping, any day.

The hotel had just finished serving breakfast when he arrived. He'd unfortunately missed Horobin, the Ministry of Works inspector, who wouldn't be back in Folbury, according to Watmough, until his next scheduled visit to the factories in the area, but he looked a safe enough proposition to be discounted for the moment. Gargrave had managed to catch the holidaying couple, the Lightfoots, who were just settling their bill prior to heading back home to Coventry, having returned to spend the last night of their holiday where they'd started, at the Shire. He settled for interviewing them as they sat by their luggage in the little annexe in the foyer, anxious to be on their way, but willing to help.

On the night in question, they told him, they had taken dinner and then, over coffee in the lounge, they had fallen into conversation with that nice Mr Horobin. The two men had soon discovered a mutual interest in photography. Mr Lightfoot had fetched from their room the new Leica which his firm had presented him with on his retirement to show Mr Horobin, and they had spent a very pleasant evening, the men talking cameras and Mrs Lightfoot knitting a matinee jacket for their latest grandchild. No other guest had put in an appearance.

'But he was here for breakfast.' Mrs Lightfoot was determined to be helpful. She was a small, plump lady with a feathering of white curls, bright brown eyes and a sharp tongue. 'The one you say was poor Mr Millar. He ate nothing. Just had a cup of tea, pushed a slice of toast around and then left. It's dreadful that he was found in the river, but I do wonder if he wasn't contemplating . . . I mean, he didn't look well, and if that was what was on his mind . . .'

'Oh, come on, Flo!' Her husband looked embarrassed, and a little shocked. The news of how their fellow guest had been found had awaited them on their return, and suicide was always the word that sprang to mind in such situations, but it was a shaming way to die. 'You can't say that.'

'I have said it. He didn't look well, and I thought at first he must have eaten something at dinner the night before that disagreed with him, though I must say the fish we had was lovely and fresh.'

'He didn't have dinner here,' Gargrave told them.

'Oh, well, it can't have been that then. It probably was as I said. What an awful thing to have happened, after such a lovely holiday . . .'

'Worse for him, Flo,' said Mr Lightfoot, and before she could embarrass him further, stood up, ready to depart.

Gargrave thanked them and let them go.

As for the other guest, Miss Cordingley, as on the other occasions when she'd stayed, she had taken breakfast in her room before the taxi she'd ordered arrived to take her to her sister's at Darley End. When she settled her bill before leaving, she would usually make a further booking for her next intended visit. Only this time, she'd omitted to do so.

'I think DC Pickersgill might have something to say about that,' Reardon said. 'Dave?'

Pickersgill straightened from the wall. 'Yes, I went to see my gran at Darley End, sir. There's no pregnant woman with four children lives there. And nobody's ever heard of a Miss Cordingley. So I . . . er . . . came back into the office afterwards and did some checking on her home address.'

'And?' Gilmour said.

'No Beadle Avenue in Wednesfield, Sarge, nor anywhere else in Wolverhampton for that matter.'

'So you reckon the lady was up to something?'

Pickersgill said, 'Well . . .'

'You did well to check,' Gilmour said. 'She wouldn't have gone into all that about pregnant sisters in Darley End only to leave her real whereabouts easily traceable. I'll stake anyone a pint if I'm wrong, but I'm betting it was a bit of extra-marital with somebody here who wasn't taking any chances on his wife finding out.'

'We just write her off then, Sarge?' Gargrave put in, evidently feeling his thunder was being stolen by his fellow DC.

'Do we ever write anybody off, Gravy?' Reardon picked up the file. 'There's nothing else we need do at this stage, unless she rings the Shire and makes another appointment. Which, if there is a lover boy here, he might not be keen to have her do, especially if he gets wind of the Shire's connection to the murder enquiry. If we need to, we can try tracing her through the taxi firm that picked her up, but let it rest for now.'

Gargrave wasn't willing to give up just yet. 'If you look at the register, you'll see her writing isn't all that clear. Might have been Beagle Avenue, or even Boodle. I could get myself over there and check, wouldn't take long on my motorbike,' he ventured, with a tentative look at Reardon, whereupon the suggestion died before it drew breath.

He was disappointed. It had seemed like a good idea, negotiating himself a trip out to chase her up further, even if it did mean Wolverhampton.

NINE

I t would give anybody the heebie-jeebies, this benighted spot known as Hadley Piece. Enough to spook even Reardon, though if it did, he wasn't letting on. Gilmour couldn't imagine anyone wanting to work, let alone live here, though it was a long time since anyone had, apart from the person they were on their way to see. The once busy, thriving little business location now felt like a ghost town in a Wild West cowboy film, everything closed or falling down, the sole human beings himself and Reardon as they walked down what had once been the central access road. Adding to the desolation, it was another dreary grey morning. A slight fog shrouded the derelict buildings, clung to their clothes and deadened the sound of their footsteps.

He lengthened his own long stride to keep pace with Reardon's, who was wasting no time, focussed on getting to the coming interview with Matt Millar as fast as possible. Although the lad was sure to know by now of his father's reappearance and death, if not through Folbury's bush telegraph, then certainly through his aunt and uncle, supposing he was as close to them as Pugh had said.

Reardon was very quiet this morning, Gilmour thought, although his preoccupation at this stage in an investigation, while they were still harnessing what facts they could to work out which direction it should take, was nothing new. Gilmour usually found such silence frustrating, even though he knew that when the gaffer did make a decision, he moved fast, but he was rather glad of it just now, being a bit preoccupied himself.

He had been first in that morning and had straight away seen the familiar envelope on top of the previous night's reports the desk sergeant had handed to him as he came through the door. Another of the same anonymous rubbish, and he'd been almost tempted to chuck it into the fire that burned in the front

office. Especially in view of what he'd seen in the Co-op yard
the previous night, and what if anything needed to be done
about it. Interfering with the post intended for the gaffer wasn't
the sort of thing detective sergeants did, and with Longton's
beady eyes missing nothing – not to mention having a good
idea what Reardon would say if he ever found out – had been
enough to scupper any temptation he might have had to throw
the letter on the fire, where it belonged. Gilmour would die
on the barricades to defend Reardon if necessary, but not when
he was in official senior officer mode. That didn't happen
often, but you wouldn't want to be there when it did. So he'd
merely slid the envelope underneath the rest in token protest
until he decided what to do.

Matt Millar had obviously been expecting them. Knew who
they were and admitted them straight away by way of the door
into the empty, echoing ground floor of the old warehouse –
empty that was except for a bicycle with mud on its wheels.
There wasn't much space to get past and Gilmour swore as
mud was transferred to his trousers. At the top of the stairs,
a surprisingly big space opened out, clearly serving as a work-
shop-cum-living-and-sleeping area. Gilmour didn't think his
own system could have taken it, breathing in the smell of turps
and linseed oil while you slept. If it had been with you all
day, you probably didn't notice.

Millar led the way past a battered-looking divan bed and
rudimentary kitchen arrangements – sink, double gas ring,
cupboard, all crammed into a corner. An assortment of damp
clothes hung to dry on a string stretched across the corner.
Personal comfort was clearly an inessential condition in Matt
Millar's lifestyle. But the rest of this light, airy space was
workmanlike enough, even if the order of it seemed unfathom-
able to a layman. It was lit by several big windows. A long,
cluttered table stretched down its length and shelves, similarly
stacked, reached to the ceiling on one wall, with blank canvases
propped against the lower ones. Apart from a few rough
sketches, hardly anything of Millar's work was displayed,
unless the range of glossy photographs pinned to the remaining
wall were his as well. All of them depicted scenes from the
Black Country, which surrounded Folbury on three of its sides

– industrial buildings, canals, locks and bridges, with some charcoal sketches of working people at their traditional jobs of nail makers, glassblowers or foundry workers – which Gilmour liked straight away, plus a few less than appealing ones of rundown slum streets and ragged children.

'I suppose it's about my father you've come?' Millar said, once he'd waved them to seats that were unmistakably packing cases underneath the cloths thrown over them. Perching himself on the high stool in front of his easel, he swivelled round to face them, partly obscuring what appeared to be a work in progress, so that only a few heavy black lines could be glimpsed. 'What is it you want to know? You can spare me the details,' he added. 'I'm aware of what's happened to my father.'

'I'm sorry,' Reardon said. 'I'm afraid it's very sad news for you.'

'Thanks, but I shed my tears for him years ago. I can't pretend a sadness I don't feel.'

Whether the indifference was real or not, the young man was tense as a coiled spring, and evidently on edge. He obviously believed what he'd said – or thought he did – but was he quite as callous as he sounded? A young boy who had grown up believing his father to have been a casualty of war, with a picture of him in his mind as one of the thousands of unsung heroes? And then to have news of him – not killed, wounded or shot down in flames over Flanders mud, but to drown years later in the River Fol? Whatever it was, Reardon could recognize an unhappy young man when he saw one.

'In that case, Mr Millar—'

'Matt, if you don't mind.'

From the way Pugh had spoken of him, Reardon had been expecting to meet a boy – that was how Pugh himself had seemed to regard him – but this was a man, a young man, good-looking and well set up, with an assurance that said he was comfortable with himself and with the path on which he'd chosen to set his feet. Dark hair, fiercely dark brows and thickly lashed, intelligent, grey eyes. A face that was trying not to give away anything of what he felt about a father returned from the grave, despite what he was saying, despite the haunted look in those eyes.

'In that case, Matt, we'll just stick to a few questions. You'll understand it's our business to try and find out anything that might have led up to your father's death.'

'Fire away.'

'For a start, we're trying to trace his movements from the time he arrived in Folbury. We know he turned up at the home of your aunt and uncle, and returned to the Shire hotel where he'd booked in, but we don't know yet how he spent the following day, or not until Mr Pugh saw him leaving these premises at about six o'clock. Perhaps he'd spent the day with you?'

'With me? The whole day?' Matt gave a short, hard laugh. 'Let me put you right. We spent a total of perhaps half an hour alone here just before Wesley came in. We didn't have any more to say to one another than we had the previous night. Not when he wasn't prepared to take the trouble to explain himself.' The wry twist of his mouth robbed the words of actual malice, but he wasn't smiling as he added, 'All he would say was that it was a complicated story, and he'd tell me everything in good time, and that was how it was left.'

'Just a minute . . . the previous night? You'd seen your father the previous night?'

'Yes, of course, at Ladyford Lane – at my uncle's house.'

Gilmour looked up from his notes. 'They didn't tell us you were there.'

'Uncle Ted telephoned me when he arrived. Naturally, I went across.'

'Hotfoot, I should think,' Reardon commented, 'not having seen him since you were a lad.'

'On his last leave in 1916, to be precise,' he said without expression. 'I was ten years old.'

All those missing years, during which he had matured into a confident, self-sufficient young man, running his own life in his own way. Would his father's return have meant changes he couldn't stomach? Paul Millar's decidedly odd, even bloody-minded, refusal to say why he had come back which, if it was to be believed – and Reardon saw no reason to question that so far, they were all telling the same story – must have rankled, with all of them.

'Look,' Matt said suddenly, frowning, 'you think I'm unfeeling, unnatural. You think I should have been overjoyed that he'd returned, and devastated that he's dead. Well, I'm glad he wasn't killed in the war, after all, or suffered injury or anything of that sort, but I didn't know him. Not as a father. I can't pretend something I don't feel.' He had something of the same stubbornness he was accusing his father of.

'What I think doesn't enter into it,' Reardon said shortly. 'That's not how we work. So, he left that night, and later, Mr Pugh came in? How much later?'

'Only a minute or two. He came to pick up some work I'd been doing for him and stayed about fifteen or twenty minutes, maybe less.' He stopped, as if something said before had just struck him. 'He told you he'd seen my father, did he?'

'He says he couldn't believe his eyes,' Gilmour said, 'he thought he must have been mistaken, until he found him, yesterday.'

'Oh God, yes, it was poor old Wes found him.' He looked sick at the thought, showing more upset than he had shown about his father. 'You wouldn't wish that on anyone, would you?'

'No.' After a moment, Reardon changed the subject. 'I notice you're a cyclist, Matt. You don't own a motor car?'

'Me?' He laughed shortly. 'The day I can afford a car will be the day I open the champagne! Why?'

'Just interested. How did you spend the rest of the evening, after Mr Pugh left?'

'I went out. To see . . . a friend.'

'Would you give us the name, please?'

He looked at Gilmour, pencil poised over his notebook. 'Why do you want to know that? And what is this, anyway? If you're thinking I should have gone after my father and stopped him from throwing himself into the river, you have another think coming. He may have been a sorry excuse for a father . . .' He stopped and bit his lip, his face suddenly changing, and Reardon saw he was looking over Gilmour's shoulder.

'He came to see me,' said the pretty young woman who had come up the stairs so quietly none of them had been aware of her until she spoke. Reardon wondered how long she'd been standing in the doorway, how much she'd heard. 'Oh, Matt, is it true what they're saying about your father? That he's dead?'

She ran forward and threw herself into the young man's open arms.

'Imogen,' Gilmour said, 'lovely girl, isn't she?' They were walking back towards where they'd parked the car; asking for trouble it would have been, driving it nearer to where they were headed on this so-called road, which had never been made up properly in the first place and since the site's abandonment hadn't grown any more sympathetic to car tyres. 'Imogen Randall and Matt Millar.'

Reardon gripped his arm and steered him to the left. 'I want to have a look at the canal while we're here.' Gilmour opened his mouth to ask why, but Reardon was answering his question and failed to notice. 'Young Imogen, yes, charming, I agree. Courageous, too, if she's prepared to marry that young chap. It'll be a hand to mouth existence.' He'd liked the look of the girl: slender, with shiny hair, a look of neat wholesomeness and steady eyes. 'And sensible, too, I reckon,' he added, recalling the way she'd spoken when she'd told them proudly that she and Matt were going to be married, and that she'd continue her nursing to help out with finances. He recalled also that Matt, although his eyes had said everything when he looked at her, holding her in his arms and kissing her when she ran to him, hadn't joined in.

'No daughter of Connie Randall would be anything but sensible, I guess,' Gilmour said.

'And who's Connie Randall when she's at home?'

'Nurse Randall, district nurse, everybody knows her and likes her. She's brought half of Folbury into the world, including Ellie. She's the best there is.' He kicked a loose stone out of the way.

'And, Joe?' There was something Gilmour wasn't saying.

'Oh, nothing.' He saw Reardon's face. 'Well, all right, I was just thinking. Connections, sort of.'

'Come on!'

'Reputed connections, I should say. It's reckoned Ted Millar might have his feet under the table at the Randall house, if you get my meaning, but . . .'

'But what?'

'Well, she's older than him, for one thing. And the Millars own a lot of domestic property round about where she lives, including hers, so maybe he's doing nothing more than collecting the rent. You know how the rumours get around. She's still a very attractive woman, Connie.'

Reardon didn't doubt it, if the daughter took after her mother. 'And what about Mr Randall? Some jiggery-pokery going on, is that what you're saying? And what if there is?'

Gilmour looked pained. 'There isn't a Mr Randall. It was Dr, anyway. Married her before the war. Then they both went to work in France when it started, but he was killed right at the beginning. Little Imogen was on the way and Connie came home. Became the district nurse here later. Never married again, though they say she was a bit of a lass in her day, so I shouldn't think she'd be short of offers now. You'd know what I mean if you saw her.'

'And Ted Millar's having a fling with her?'

'I don't think he's the marrying sort.'

Reardon raised an eyebrow.

'No, that's not what I'm saying at all. I don't think he's that way inclined. He likes the ladies – Connie wouldn't be the first, by a long chalk. Safety in numbers is more like it. Or maybe he's happier living with his sister.'

'He's a braver man than I am, then.'

'It might be worth talking to her,' Gilmour was saying. 'Connie, I mean. Pugh brought that list of Paul's friends in this morning. I haven't had the chance to look at it properly yet, but I noticed her name was on it. She could be one of those who might remember something Pugh didn't, or something he chose not to tell us.'

'We'll make sure we do see her.'

They'd reached the canal. The towpath was not in good order at this point. It wasn't well looked after, now that the site itself had more or less ceased to function as a working entity, now that motor transport was being increasingly used to convey heavy goods to and from the foundries, glassworks and engineering works in Arms Green. The path was unkempt and muddy, reverting to nature. It was only the slow, heavy feet of patient draught horses pulling the occasional barge towards factories and warehouses half a mile or so ahead that kept the weeds down at all.

A dank chill rose from the canal and Gilmour turned his collar up then stuck his hands in his pockets as Reardon picked up a flat pebble and skimmed it down the length of the sluggish, mouse-brown water. He'd lost the skill he'd had as a lad, it only hit the surface three times before sinking. He picked up another, but stood holding it, his eyes following the line of the cut as it headed from the first of the locks – Cooper's – towards the ruins of the old corn mill, situated near the far end of his sightline and looking rather picturesque from here. Beyond the bridge the silhouette of the town gasholder was also visible, and beyond were tall, gloomy factories either side, making a dark tunnel before the canal curved and disappeared from sight. From thereon, it took its course through the town, through the junction with the Main Line Canal and on towards the last lock, this one known as Anchor Lock, near the spot in the river behind the Colley Street allotments where Wesley Pugh had found Paul Millar's body.

He said abruptly, 'Get me a map, Joe, a sketch or something. Showing the canal and the river.' It was time he made better acquaintance with the topography of Folbury's river and its surroundings. Gilmour was looking doubtful. 'Can't you do that?'

'Yes, sure. But . . . the canal?'

There was no current in the canal to carry a body along and then there were the locks at both ends. Gilmour gave him a doubtful glance, wondering if he should point this out tactfully, when Reardon said, 'No, this wasn't his point of departure. It was just a train of thought . . . this location, Hadley Piece . . . that studio . . . Inkerman Terrace . . . But since he didn't drown anyway . . .' He threw down the pebble he was holding and rubbed his fingers together, sounding oddly indecisive, for Reardon. 'Well, I don't know.' He added abruptly, 'What do you think that swimming costume was doing hanging on young Matt's clothes line?'

'Didn't notice it.' Gilmour had quickly averted a pained glance from the regrettable assortment of towels and under-clothes on the string across the corner.

'It looked very wet from where I sat.'

'The public baths won't be open this time of a morning.'

'So where else has he been swimming?' A stiff breeze whipped along the canal. 'And *why*, for God's sake?'

Ellen had put away her pencils, paint and paper without too much regret when the announcement had been made that her evening art classes had been suspended. No specific reason had been given, but none was needed, after all, when the identity of the drowned man found in the canal had become public knowledge: almost certainly one of the prosperous Millar family and the father of their class teacher. Poor young man. Ellen had liked him and was sorry for his sake; he'd lost his father and also the income from his night-class teaching. At the same time, she couldn't help feeling relieved that she'd been let off the hook, with time left on her hands. Time to deal with the nagging thought that she ought to do something about that diary she had found, those photographs? Which find, when you thought about it, was a bit unnerving in the circumstances. The Millar name did seem to be cropping up with uncanny regularity just now.

She had given herself a mental shake. If you lived in a house that had once belonged to the family, and in a town in which they were so prominent . . . All the same, the hairs on the back of her neck rose as she looked down at the photo-graphs yet again. How cruel life could be, to think of that little boy with the mischievous grin growing up to have an enemy, or even enemies, who hated him enough to actually kill him, as it seemed someone had.

Reardon hadn't commented much on the diary when she'd told him how it had been found in the biscuit tin; he'd been more interested in the photos. She hadn't been able to show them without telling him how they'd been found, but she was relieved that he seemed to have come round to the idea of doing up the glory hole and was satisfied with Samuel Trust's estimate.

'There's not much doubt that's Thea,' he'd said of the oldest child, the serious, pinafored girl with straight hair drawn back under an Alice band, one hand on the baby's shawl, the other clutching the hand of the boy. 'And I suppose the baby would be Ted. Looks as though their father could have been a bit of a tartar,' he'd added, looking at the unsmiling man standing with his hand firmly on his seated wife's shoulder.

'Yes, that pose says everything.' Ownership, she thought. Restriction. Subservience, perhaps. The woman herself looked to be the sort of sweet, biddable woman men like him had once loved to lord it over. Although Ellen sometimes wondered if things had changed so much since then, since the time when she herself had supported the fight for women's rights. Women might have won the vote, at a frightful cost to some, but the world was not yet as open to them as it was to the male sex, not by a very long chalk. 'From what Horace said, Papa Millar must have been a tyrant,' she'd agreed.

This morning, after he'd kissed her and left for work, not able to say when he'd be home, she thought about the photos again. Ever since Samuel Trust had told her that Maisie's aunt had worked at Fox Close, she'd known that she was going to try to find out more about the person who had started to write that diary – and why it had finished on that inconclusive note, with the bulk of the pages torn out. The diary had been written getting on for forty years ago, but she ought to have tried to find out who the rightful owner was and handed it over before now.

Today was free, not one of her teaching days. She was all ready for tomorrow, with her lessons prepared, and a pile of neatly marked French papers stacked in her briefcase. Tolly had been taken for his walk, the house was tidy and there was a stew ready for supper. And she needed no excuse to visit Maisie, Joe Gilmour's wife, and her little goddaughter, Ellie, never mind they had all spent time together a couple of days ago.

Maisie and Ellen had become close friends ever since their meeting on Reardon's move to Folbury from Dudley, but she'd thought it better to keep back the discovery of the biscuit tin from her until Reardon had been told about it, in case for some reason he didn't want it mentioned. But after he'd looked at the photos, he hadn't said anything when she'd shuffled them back into the tin.

The low, miserable fog which had greeted the morning had slowly lifted, though it was still damply cold. With Ellie wrapped up like a little Eskimo, they'd taken her for an excursion to the recreation ground before lunch. Ellen waited until the child had been put down for her afternoon nap, tired out after a session on the swings and the teapot-lid roundabout, before approaching Maisie with the subject uppermost in her mind. Ellie was an enchanting child, if a wee bit spoiled by her doting father, and with all the demanding, relentless energy of a two-year-old. Truth to tell, she had tired the two women more than herself, and they dropped thankfully into armchairs for a cup of tea and a chat while she slept.

Maisie said yes, her Auntie Clarice had worked at Fox Close. 'I'll ask if she remembers who lived in the lodge, but don't hold your breath at getting much out of her. I'll have to find the right time to ask. Since she married Henry Lendrum, she likes to pretend she was never in service, even though it was for the Millars,' said Maisie, who had herself started her working life as a maid-of-all-work, albeit in very different households to that at Fox Close. She had become friends with the daughter of the house where she finally worked, and with her encouragement and her own love of reading, had educated herself far beyond the limits of her elementary school.

It wasn't the first time Ellen had heard of Auntie Clarice, and how much above herself she'd grown. She'd gone up in the world since the Fox Close days after marrying well, and now she and her husband owned a well-run little haberdasher's in the town, prosperous enough to provide them with a live-in servant girl themselves, plus a fortnight in Torquay every year. They were childless.

'I'd be surprised if she's kept in touch with any of the other servants, but she never forgets anyone – or anything, come to that. She still remembers when I broke one of her best china cups when I was six . . . and I'd only been trying to help with the washing up.' Maisie pulled a face. 'I'll take her a Toblerone

when I go . . . it's like cheese to a mouse, her one weakness
– or so she says.' She smiled, sensing Ellen's eagerness to
follow up on the diary. 'Why don't you come with me? We
could go now if you like, or as soon as Ellie wakes up. I can
leave her with my mum for an hour, they'll both be delighted.
I don't think Auntie Clarice would appreciate sticky fingers
all over her possessions.'

After an initial reluctance, Mrs Lendrum consented to tell them
what she could recall about the last people who had lived in the
lodge, even without the persuasion of the two Toblerones they
had bought on the way, though Maisie's sidelong glance at Ellen
said the reason was just as likely to be because Ellen was the
wife of a police inspector, putting her on the list of acceptable
acquaintances. She couldn't give them much time, however, as
she was due to go out. Ellen assured her it wouldn't take long.
    She inspected the navy pilot cloth coat and smart little hat
of her new visitor and evidently approved of what she saw.
'You'd best come in then.'
    It was a rather grudging invitation, but at least they had a
foot over the threshold of the new-built house, several steps
up from the flat over the shop the Lendrums had once occupied, and she relaxed somewhat when they were sitting in
her front room. She didn't offer them tea. It was the girl's
day off and she herself was on her way to the twice-monthly
gathering known as The Pleasant Hour, when the ladies of
Holy Trinity church took tea and biscuits in the parish hall.
    She was a firmly corseted woman, her hair in a rigid marcel
wave. She wore a maroon moiré dress with a lace collar, and
an air of being very well pleased with herself and her surroundings. Her breath smelt of Phul-Nana Cachou sweets. She was
patently agog to hear why Ellen wanted to know about the
old lodge, but when Ellen simply explained that it was now
her home and she would be interested to know its history and
that of Fox Close, who had lived there and so on, her curiosity
seemed satisfied.
    'But really, I don't know anything about its history. I only
know Fox Close was a miserable old place and I wasn't sorry
to leave when I married Henry.'

She spoke his name as though Henry Lendrum, at present out playing golf, was the Pope, looking round the room he'd provided complacently as she did so. Her fingers stroked the fawn plush of the sofa she was sitting on. The chair-backs protecting them were of crocheted lace. The pair of matching cut-glass vases either side of an onyx clock on the fawn tiled fireplace winked back at each other and the china cabinet in one alcove displayed a pretty china dinner and tea service – presumably minus one teacup.

Whatever she'd thought of Fox Close, however, Mrs Lendrum did at least remember those who'd last lived in the lodge: Fred Probert, the head gardener, and the girl he'd married, who had been employed as nursery-maid to look after the young Millars. Amy Lowden as was, from that blacksmith's disgraceful family in Braddon. Her face registered sour disapproval.

'Disgraceful how, Auntie Clarice?' Maisie prompted.

'Well, that family!' She exhaled a flowery breath. 'Trouble, all of them – except for Amy, she was all right, I suppose. Big lumps, like their father, all brawn and no brains, five lads and their Elsie. Their mother couldn't do anything with any of them. Always up to something or other, they were, in some sort of bother.'

But Amy the blacksmith's daughter hadn't done so badly for herself, it seemed. Well enough, in fact, for Mrs Henry Lendrum to allow her to remain on her Christmas card list. She went to find the address.

TEN

Reardon had decided it was time to address the matter of the will Ernest Millar had left. Gargrave's opinion that the murder of his son must be all to do with money wasn't just Gravy being Gravy – he'd rightly latched on to the fact that if anything stronger than sex was a motive for murder, money was. And the Millars had money – family money, handed down. However much the idea of Paul being cold-bloodedly killed by any of his family turned Reardon's stomach, he couldn't allow it to be discounted – if any of them could be considered as suspects, given the lack of evidence or credible motive so far.

The premises of the long-established firm of solicitors, Purbright, Purbright and Brownlow, were so Dickensian they were almost a cliché: Victorian red-brick on the outside, the outer office into which the main entrance led, and where two women worked, was dimmed with the passing of years, the accumulation of dusty law tomes on shelves and the bundles of papers tied with red tape which occupied every surface, including the floor. What furniture Reardon could distinguish was old enough to be antique but lacked any trace of personality. Just old and a bit battle-scarred, making the modern typewriters and the telephone sitting on one of the desks look like brash modern intrusions, as though everyone working there ought still to be writing with quill pens. What had been good enough for the first Purbright was evidently a good enough working environment for his great-grandson.

Reardon happened to know, however, that Charles Purbright himself, whom he had met in court and out of it several times, lived in a newish and expensive riverside house in spacious grounds on the outskirts of the town, no doubt replete with accoutrements that were equally expensive. And like the typewriters, the man himself stood out amongst all the dusty, musty fustiness, wearing bespoke tailoring in charcoal worsted with a barely discernible pinstripe, doing its best to disguise an incipient paunch. He was smiling and bonhomous, smoothly shaven and balding, wearing heavy spectacles with thick lenses. His shirt was Persil white and he wore a discreetly striped tie. He looked as though he'd emerged from the bath not half an hour before.

'Come in, come in, Inspector, good to see you,' he greeted Reardon amiably from the door of his private office. He was ushered in, offered a warm handshake and waved to a chair. He had been expected and by the time he was seated, one of the women from the front office, grey-haired, droopy grey-cardiganed and of indeterminate age, had appeared with coffee things, plus a plate of digestives, all set out on a snowy tray-cloth. 'Thank you, Miss Bancroft, that looks nice. You can leave it, I'll pour,' Purbright said kindly.

Miss Bancroft blushed and backed out self-effacingly to be part of the general frowziness. Reardon, who wasn't a coffee man and would have preferred tea, accepted a cup in the spirit it was offered, but declined anything from the plate of what he privately regarded as artefacts made from stable sweepings.

This inner sanctum, though no more modern than the outer office, had a lighter, less Dickensian air. For one thing, it had a large window with a bowl of hyacinths on the sill, a wifely exhortation, no doubt, to brighten up the office. For another it was extremely orderly, in keeping with Purbright himself. Intercepting Reardon's glance at a slightly less than tidy pile of papers on his desk, he shuffled and squared them, restoring order by placing them neatly between the telephone and his pen tray.

Known to be a busy man who got things done, he didn't waste time in getting Reardon to the point. He went straight into what he knew the police must be here for. 'Upsetting for the Millars . . . not to say more than a bit of a poser for you. Could have knocked me down with a feather, Paul turning up here like that. What can I do for you? I'm happy to help – if I can, that is,' he offered, mildly curious.

'Paul turned up here, at your office?' Reardon took him up quickly, hoping this might be the answer to how Paul had spent at least some of the time before visiting his son at Hadley Piece.

Purbright soon disabused him of that notion. 'Good God, why would you think that? Here in Folbury is what I meant.'

'Well, we haven't yet found out why he did come back, or where he'd been, and certainly not how he'd been earning his living. Unless he was getting an annuity, money in trust or something like that – and had some reason to see you about it?' Purbright adjusted his spectacles and threw him a very sharp look. 'I understand your firm's acted for the Millars for a long time.'

'Since old Manfred Müller came to us in my grandfather's time, yes.'

'But you've had nothing to do with Paul since he left Folbury? In a professional sense, I mean?'

'There was no reason we should.'

'No monies to administer?'

From a man who was not normally lost for words, the response was slow. The solicitor's heavy spectacles made his expression hard to read. At last he said, 'I presume you don't know about the old man's will?' Reardon murmured something non-committal. 'You're thinking Paul might have gone through what his father left him, then come home like the prodigal son, hoping to scrounge more? Well, let me scotch that first to begin with. His father didn't leave him anything.'

'Nothing?'

'Not a penny.' He let that sink in while he picked up another digestive biscuit and munched it with evident relish, lowered the level of coffee in his cup and leaned forward to top it up. It wasn't bad, as far as coffee went, Reardon had to admit, but he declined a refill.

'You don't look amazed, Inspector.'

'I'm not – not really.' He realized he wasn't surprised at all, after what they'd already been hearing about father and son. 'Still . . . I know the two of them had a stormy relationship, but wasn't that a bit harsh?'

'You'd have to have known Ernest Millar not to think that. Which you didn't, of course. To be truthful, he was . . . let's say he wasn't a man you could like, not by any stretch, but there were faults on both sides, as there always are. Paul didn't go out of his way to be accommodating.'

'Refusing to go into the business, for instance?'

He didn't seem surprised Reardon should know. 'That . . . and other things. But it wasn't until he upped and left that Ernest changed his will in a rage and cut him out completely. Finally had enough.'

'But he was forgiven when he came back? After a couple of years or so, I understand? Complete with wife and child.'

Purbright leant back in his ample chair, steepling his hands together in a lawyerly way. 'Frankly, I didn't have much time for Ernest Millar,' he went on after a moment or two. 'He was a miserable old devil at best – he didn't even trust banks, not completely. He could be vindictive, too – a hard man, for all his so-called religious principles. Maybe he blamed himself for how Paul had turned out, too much rope, too much money, who knows? But forgive him? I don't know about that. When he came back Ernest did agree to have him in the firm again, although it was an uneasy compromise. For one thing, he wouldn't give Paul any responsibilities, and who could blame him? Paul didn't show any more enthusiasm for the business than he ever had. And in the end, he backed the right horse, didn't he, old Ernest? Choosing Ted, I mean. Look what he's done for the firm. Not to mention Thea,' he added with a careful look at Reardon. 'The sister, you know. She stepped in and saved the day during the war, when there was no one else. Ernest was dead by then and the two brothers were away fighting. Ran the whole caboodle herself, without ever having so much as set foot in a builder's yard before. Splendid woman. To do that, even after what her father had done . . .'

'Which was?'

'Left her with but thirty per cent of the business in his will, the other seventy to Ted.'

In certain masculine circles, that was only too likely to be considered a perfectly reasonable provision for a daughter, Reardon knew. The sort of thinking which said that Thea was bound to find herself a husband willing to keep her, so what was the point in leaving anything much to her?

Purbright's tone, however, didn't sound as though he went along with that. It confirmed the sneaking suspicion Reardon had always had, that the solicitor, a shrewd and astute lawyer whom he liked and respected, wasn't entirely the establishment figure it suited him to let people think he was. 'Thea never got the credit she deserved. But maybe she's never wanted it. Women don't on the whole, you know. Prefer to play second fiddle. Or run the show from the wings. Manipulation, maybe?'

Reardon conceded that point, as far as Thea was concerned. The impression left with him from their first meeting had been that her part in running the firm was certainly a major one, although it was Ted who was generally thought of as the one who ran the show. Ted, the younger brother, who was now one of the town's hierarchy, on equal footing with people like Purbright and other professionals, the local doctors, dentists, all the well-to-do businessmen. Rotary. Freemasons, no doubt.

'So after the spell in Germany and his coming back,' he said, 'Paul stayed here until the war took him away again, never to return . . . until now? He let his family believe him dead all these years. What do you think brought him back?'

The solicitor considered. 'I became fed up with urging Ernest to revoke that will and rewrite it, to leave Paul something, after he came home. But he was a stubborn old fool and all he would say was we'd better see how Paul shaped up this time around before doing anything drastic. There was a wife and son to think of by then, but he procrastinated over changing that damned will for years and he died before he could do it. People will do that,' he finished, shaking his head. 'No one ever believes they're going to leave it too late to sort their will out.'

Reardon thought of what Purbright had said earlier. 'If Paul was short of money, maybe he came back this time hoping to get something from his brother and sister?'

'My dear chap, you can't seriously believe that?' Purbright's tone indicated the likelihood wasn't worth the time discussing it, which seemed odd, given the trouble and wrangling he must regularly have to deal with over wills and inheritances.

A slightly awkward hiatus fell. Eventually Purbright spoke again. 'In all fairness, one should really try to see it from Paul's side, I suppose. Frightful tragedy it was, unimaginable.' Reardon's eyebrows rose. 'To lose your wife so young, I mean . . . it broke Paul's heart. She had been the reason he came back to work with Ernest, of course . . . he needed to support her and the boy . . . he took it badly when she died and simply did the disappearing trick once more, took himself off, God knows where, leaving the boy in Thea's care.'

'He went away *again*? Making three times in all?'

'Not for long, that time. It was 1914 and it was evident by then to us all there was going to be a war. When it was declared he suddenly reappeared back home . . . but only to announce that he'd enlisted in the Royal Flying Corps. As one might have expected, given his passion.'

Reardon calculated he and Paul had probably been more or less of an age. 'How well did you know him?'

'Oh, not that well. We went to the same school and knocked about together occasionally afterwards, but I wouldn't say I knew him well. He wasn't my type, and we didn't have much in common. He thought of little else but motorcars.'

Reardon said nothing for a moment or two. 'Did you like him?'

Purbright took a moment, then answered steadily, 'No. I didn't. Not really.'

'Any particular reason? Just the incompatibility?'

'It wasn't that.' He pushed a few biscuit crumbs which had landed in his saucer around with his finger, then looked up. The light caught the lenses of his spectacles and made his eyes appear enormous. 'To be truthful, I wasn't too keen on the way he treated some of the girls we knew.'

'Oh? I had the impression he was very popular with women.'

'Well, he was a handsome devil, and you know how it is with women . . .' A rueful smile accompanied the remark. He obviously knew himself to be no oil painting – but still, look at the wife he had ended up with! Reardon had met Diana Purbright once, though their acquaintance hadn't gone beyond the introduction stage. A county type, and any deficiency in the family looks department, she made up for it. Stunning. Tall, blonde, well dressed. Expensive, no doubt. On the other hand, she hadn't done too badly for herself either, married to a successful solicitor. Lawyers never went hungry.

'Are you saying Paul was violent with women?'

'Goodness, no! I wouldn't say that, not at all – not physically. But he left them . . . bruised, if you know what I mean.'

'Left them? So perhaps that was the reason he went to Germany that first time? Not a row with his father?'

'Oh, there was that all right! When he announced he was off, I wouldn't have liked to be there when it happened. But after all, that sort of row had become par for the course and they always blew over, or just went on simmering below the surface. You know how it goes in families. But I don't think that was the reason he took himself off.' He paused and poured more coffee.

'It was over a woman, then?'

'I would say not. But if it was, it couldn't have meant all that much to him, seeing how quickly he married Liesl.'

'On the rebound, perhaps?'

Purbright raised his shoulders and spread his hands, a curiously Gallic gesture, and then said unexpectedly, 'No. It certainly wasn't that. He adored Liesl. It wasn't like the other girls he'd messed around with, it was the real thing. What little I ever saw of her, I could see why he'd been attracted. She was lively, a lot of fun. Not blessed by overmuch intelligence, if we're being truthful, but still I could see she was . . . oh, something special, you know. She must have been, to get him to knuckle down, more or less, and work with his father again for all those years.'

After considering it for a moment, Reardon said, 'Wesley Pugh . . . Councillor Pugh. He was Paul's closest friend at that time, yes?' Purbright nodded but looked wary at the abrupt change of subject. 'There seems to have been a falling out between them around that time.'

'I daresay. Wesley Pugh was no easier then than he is now,' he said dryly.

That wasn't anything Reardon needed to be reminded of, recalling his own sessions with Pugh. It was an observation anyone might have made, knowing the man's reputation. He didn't go out of his way to make himself popular when it came to raising difficult issues over anything he considered amiss, the civic injustices he made war against, and Charles Purbright had no doubt come up against him many times in the course of his work. 'I hope you're not suggesting Paul rushed off to Germany simply because of a disagreement with Pugh?' Purbright laughed, and then shrugged. 'Even if it was, it's all history now, anyway, youthful indiscretions and so on, so why rake it up?'

Because you know as well as I do, Reardon thought, that past events cast their shadows long after the event, and what happened then could be the reason I'm sitting here now asking all these questions. 'It was because of a girl, then?' he persisted.

'No, I am not saying that, because I really don't know. There were rather a lot of girls,' he added, blandly and ambiguously.

It didn't matter that he was lying, or prevaricating if you preferred, Reardon thought as he made his way back to Market Street and a cup of tea to compensate for the coffee he'd drunk. Purbright had become suddenly cagey, and Reardon couldn't help wondering what, apart from his lawyerly caution, could have made him so. Had it been anyone else but Purbright, he would have thought he had personal reasons for being evasive.

You could probably throw a five-mile rope around Folbury town centre and still have a few yards to spare. That didn't include the outskirts of course, which were spreading further and further outwards towards the green countryside. Reardon wasn't sure how he felt about that. He'd liked Folbury the way it was from the moment he'd first seen it. Its layout meant that the town had a plethora of alleys and byways and little hidden courtyards, giving it individuality, and the more familiar he became with everything and everyone on his patch, the more like home it had begun to feel. By now, this side of the town was imprinted like a map in his mind; he needed to familiarize himself just as much with the other side, where the river ran, and he reminded himself to get hold of that map he'd asked Gilmour for.

As he opened the door from Market Street, he saw Longton at the front desk was busy with a customer, the burly sergeant's name for anyone who came voluntarily into the police station. 'Lady to see you, sir,' he broke off to say when he saw Reardon. 'Name of Randall.' Jerking his head towards the door behind him to indicate where she could be found, he turned back to the customer, in this case an irate old gentleman who was complaining about the rubbish overflowing the waste bins in the park.

'Nothing to do with us, I'm afraid, sir. Best advice is to make a complaint to the council.' Longton's big, impassive presence was oddly reassuring to customers as a rule. It wasn't working this time.

'And do you think they'll listen? They don't empty them often enough, that's the problem. Cutting back on expenses, they say! What I say is . . .'

The old man was showing signs of becoming apoplectic. Reardon silently wished him luck with Longton, who could stonewall with the best of them, left his coat and went on his way. The querulous voice followed him as he went to the all-purpose room which served for interviewing 'customers', suspects, witnesses. It was ill-lit by one grimy, high-set window, the walls were painted a sickly, institutional green, it was always cold and smelt of stale smoke, sweat, fear and often worse, and sometimes, Reardon thought, despair. Wrongdoers apprehended and dumped in here against their will brought their own misery with them.

In contrast to this, the young woman in the tweed coat buttoned up to her neck, woolly beret on her head, who was perched on one of the two wooden chairs beside a table scarred with cigarette burns, had brought a breath of the outdoors in with her. The cold air had whipped colour into her cheeks. She looked clean, fresh and glowing with health.

'Miss Randall!' For some reason, Reardon had expected it to be her mother, whom he still had to meet, waiting for him.

'Oh!' she cried, jumping up. 'Inspector Reardon, I'm so glad you're here. They weren't sure how long you'd be.'

'Please sit down, Miss Randall, and tell me what I can do for you. Can I get you a cup of tea?'

'Oh, Imogen, please, and no thank you. I haven't got much time. I'm due at the hospital soon.'

Her coat fell open slightly as she sat down, showing the striped blue-and-white cotton of her probationer-nurse uniform. She was breathing quickly and twisting a pair of fur-cuffed leather gloves in her hand. She didn't seem in a hurry to speak, despite having little time, but he waited, suspecting it was nerves holding her back. At last she said, 'It's about Matt. Matt Millar.'

He had guessed as much.

'I just want to say that I hope you didn't get the wrong impression yesterday. I could see that you and your sergeant both thought he should have been more upset than he seemed to be about his father.'

'I'm sorry you felt that way. We weren't there to judge. We only want to find out the truth.'

'He . . . he didn't mean what he said, you know. About what he feels. Not really . . .'

He said gently, 'It hadn't escaped my notice.'

'Oh.' That seemed to surprise her. 'It's been a terrible shock for him, and with things not going too well just now . . . for us, I mean, Matt and me . . .' She looked unhappy. She blinked and her eyelashes were wet.

'In what way aren't they going well for you?'

'It's nothing, really, I suppose. Oh, well, it's my mother, you see. It's not that she doesn't approve of Matt. She likes him very much, I know, and anyway she's not the sort to go around disapproving of people. It's just that, well, she thinks I'm too young to know my own mind. About us getting married. And Matt . . .' Her voice wobbled. 'Oh, he can be so stubborn, so *stuffy*! I wouldn't mind us being poor. Honestly, I wouldn't. But nobody seems to believe me.'

'If it's not an indelicate question to ask a lady, Miss . . . Imogen – how old are you?'

The blush ran up from her neck. 'I'm seventeen.'

Only just, he suspected. Her mother undoubtedly had a point. And maybe Matt had, too. Barely seventeen was very young to realize what that sort of permanent commitment could mean.

'She thinks I don't know my own mind. And, you know, I sometimes wonder if Matt thinks that, too. But they're wrong, I do know it's right for us. We love each other and I won't ever change my mind about that.' She looked at him with wide, serious eyes. 'I do realize what it will mean, the money and all that, I really do. And anyway, I don't think age comes into it, but if I must wait until everyone thinks I'm old enough, I will.'

He wasn't at all the right person to make judgements on something like this, but as he looked at her and saw the steadiness in those clear brown eyes, a maturity he hadn't expected to find, suddenly he was on her side. Perhaps maturity wasn't always a matter of age, not with people who were wise beyond their years. Which he thought Imogen Randall might well be.

'Well, anyway, that's what I came to say.' She pushed her chair back, ready to leave. 'To tell you that Matt, of all people, couldn't have had anything to do with . . . with what's happened to his father.'

What, other than that young man's rather intemperate words, had made her think he had thought Matt could be guilty? He'd been careful, as you always had to be with witnesses, not to level accusations before there was reason to do so. It must have taken some courage to come here and he wondered why she really had. Behind what she was saying was something very troubled and uneasy.

Halfway to the door she turned and said rather forlornly, 'I know Matt must come round to my way of thinking soon, and my mother really does like him, so I expect she will too, in time.' She sounded as though she was trying to convince herself, but then she added, 'She's very upset for him, about his father, you know, and about Uncle Wes finding him in that horrible way, too. She doesn't show it, but I know she is.'

'Councillor Pugh is your uncle?' There it was again, that intricate web of relationships in this town which constantly knocked him off balance.

Her brown hair swung against her cheek as she shook her head. 'Not my real uncle . . . His wife, Auntie Cora, was Mum's best friend.'

Another surprise. *Was.* Wesley Pugh was not the confirmed bachelor Reardon had taken him for, but a widower.

'She is really upset,' Imogen repeated. 'They've known each other a long time, you know, Uncle Wes, Paul and my mother. In fact, I think they – Paul and my mum, I mean – were sweethearts at one time . . . sort of Romeo and Juliet, you know,' she said, smiling, like any young woman her age, half in love with the romance of the idea. 'Oh, it was years ago, before the war,' she added, as if that sort of thing only happened in the Dark Ages. 'When they all went about together, you know.'

'All? Who are we talking about?' She wouldn't know that Pugh had already told them about that group of friends, of course, and that her mother was on the list.

'Paul, Mother, Uncle Wes, Auntie Cora and a few others. They've all known each other since they were children. Not Mr Millar though – Ted, I mean – he was much younger . . .' She stopped and gave another little laugh. 'Uncle Ted, I suppose I shall have to call him, when Matt and I get married . . .' She bit her lip. She was as stubborn on that point as she'd accused Matt of being, and wasn't about to forget or give in easily. 'He wasn't one of that crowd, but even so, he's always kept in touch with Mum. He's ever so nice, always around, wanting to help – with money, especially, though he should know by now that's not on with someone like my mother.'

'And Miss Millar? She's a good friend, too, I take it?'

'Oh, Thea.' She paused. 'Well, no, not really. We don't have much to do with her at all. Oh goodness, is that the time? I'll have to run, or I'll have Sister after me. Thank you for being so nice, Inspector. And you won't forget what I said about Matt, will you?' she said, her eyes pleading.

The letter – another – was burning a hole in Joe Gilmour's pocket. He'd been first in again that morning and when he saw it, before allowing himself time to dwell on the consequences, he had picked it up and stuffed it inside his pocket. Just what they didn't need right now, another of those pesky missives which had seemed to have stopped, but obviously hadn't. And then he'd made up his mind what to do about it.

He wasn't able to get away before late afternoon and by the time he came to where the Murfitts lived, a row of run-down houses in a scruffy, half forgotten, neglected part of the town, it was almost dark. He could see through the thin curtains that the gas had already been lit.

It was Kenny, the oldest Murfitt boy, who answered the door. A strapping lad, handsome and tall like his mother had been. Seventeen and trying to look older in a sharp, chalk-striped suit and a tie knotted so tight it looked in danger of throttling him, comb tracks visible in his Brylcreemed hair. His dad wasn't in, he said immediately, when he saw who it was at the door, and tried to shut it. Gilmour already had his size eleven in the opening. 'It's not your dad this time. It's you I want to see.'

'Me? I haven't done nothing!' But he was wary.

'Either let me in or you come down to the station. I'm not fussy which.' Gilmour stepped forward and Kenny had no option but to back away. Feigning indifference, he shrugged, turned his back and sauntered away, Gilmour following, into the all-purpose living room where the family Murfitt spent their lives eating, cooking their meals, washing at the corner sink and taking baths in a tin bath in front of the fire on a Friday night (at least when their mother had been alive) and sometimes sleeping. Someone was sleeping there now. A recumbent figure under an outdoor coat lay on the sofa, swore and turned its back when prodded by Kenny.

'Geroff.'

'Shift yourself, Malc. It's the rozzers.'

'Only one,' said Gilmour.

Kenny swiped a pile of comics from a chair to the floor and threw himself down, leaning back with hands shoved in his pockets, legs outstretched while the brother eventually heaved himself up. Rubbing his eyes, he swung his legs out and swore again when his bare foot landed on a greasy ball of chip paper which hadn't reached the fireplace. The fire had gone out anyway, some time since judging by the mountain of cold, unraked ash spilling on to the hearth.

Malcolm, shoeless and wearing only trousers and a once white vest, balanced himself on the edge of the sofa and hitched up his braces. He was another big lad, built like his brother, but pale and pinched-faced like his father, with nothing of Kenny's flashy good looks. He had a vacant stare that made Gilmour wonder if he was all there, or if it was only that he'd just been dragged from his daytime dozing – the way the lad's days usually went, he guessed, doing nothing all day until it was time to go for the fish and chips.

In the course of police work, experience soon taught that sitting down in unlovely surroundings like this wasn't a wise option, even had an invitation been offered. It wasn't, and Gilmour remained standing in the centre of the room. He couldn't help remembering how Jeannie Murfitt had been a formidable housekeeper, making the most of what she had. Able to feed the five thousand on an Oxo cube, as they said here in Folbury. She had kept even this dump clean and shining and she'd have given the pair of them a rare old clatter round the ears if she could have seen it now. There was a more than likely possibility that it hadn't been touched since she died, ten months ago. Dust and grime lay everywhere, there was no room for one more pot in the sink or draining board, so the overspill had been left on the table. A mismatched pair of socks had been pinned to a string stretched across the fireplace to dry. The air was noxious with stale cigarette smoke, the smell from the greasy cooker, a faint trace of gas and Malcom's sweaty feet. Sonny's philosophical shrug at the prospect of his foreseeable future being spent in Winson Green the last time he'd been apprehended needed no more explanation.

Malcom was coming round, still looking bleary-eyed. But Kenny was the one Gilmour wanted, and the one he assumed was the more intelligent, if only marginally, of the two boys – the most sharp-witted, at any rate.

'Where's your dad then, Kenny?' Either keeping out of sight upstairs or had made a quick back door exit, he suspected.

'I dunno. Why should I?'

Why indeed? Sonny's periodic disappearances, whether to serve his sentences or on the kind of illicit business which had led up to them, ever since his sons were born, had been as immutable a feature of their lives as Christmas and the opening fixture of Folbury Wanderers.

'He's gone to fetch his wages, from work,' Malcom offered suddenly.

'Work?'

'Nightwatchman at Pratchett's warehouse. Started last week.'

Gilmour managed – just – not to laugh out loud. 'It restores your faith in human nature,' he said instead, not sure if he meant Sonny's, or the gullible firm who were taking him on.

He knew Pratchett's. They were a holloware firm who'd recently taken the opportunity of acquiring more machinery in a bankruptcy sale and had needed to take on additional warehousing for it, all in the expectation of an uplift in the country's economy and an expansion of their own business – unjustified optimism in both cases. But then, the intelligence of anyone employing anyone with Sonny Murfitt's history as a nightwatchman or anything else had a serious question hanging over it.

'Right, then.' Kenny heaved a sigh. Pushing his chair back he crossed the room to prink at the cheap mirror hanging from a nail near the sink. 'You'll have to excuse me now, Sergeant Gilmour,' he said with exaggerated politeness, 'I have a date.'

He adjusted the folded handkerchief in the top pocket of his double-breasted suit jacket. Where that suit had come from was anybody's guess, given that nobody in this house had had any paid employment for years as far as Gilmour knew, and how Kenny managed to keep up his smart appearance was something else. Maybe he took after his ma, rather than his feckless dad. But whatever it was, Gilmour knew he was wily as a box of monkeys. It wasn't the first time he'd come under the eye of the law.

'She'll wait, Kenny, whoever she is. I've a few questions and I haven't started yet.'

Kenny sighed again and from habit looked at the metal alarm clock on the mantelpiece, which in probable want of a wind-up had long since stopped ticking, before remembering the suspiciously new-looking watch on his wrist. 'Oh God, look at the time. What questions?'

'A good beginning would be where you got that watch.'

'What about it?' He hadn't expected that and couldn't find an answer. Then he looked at it and found inspiration. 'Oh, this! Me Dad bought it with his first week's wages.'

'Generous dad.' That watch was worth twice a nightwatchman's weekly pay packet. Kenny threw himself down on the chair again and Gilmour said suddenly, 'Where do you keep your writing paper, Kenny?'

'Writing paper? What the heck should I want with writing paper?'

'Specially since he can't write,' Malcolm sniggered, showing more signs of life.

'Shut your face, Malc.' But Malcolm's eyes had slid to the battered sideboard. The vacant look had been replaced by another. Shifty, and no more appealing. It was then that Gilmour knew he'd picked the wrong brother.

It was Malcolm who'd been in the Co-op yard. A big lad, enough like his brother to be taken for Kenny in that light. As the gang of young hoodlums had emerged into the dimly lit street, he'd been the one who'd hung back, not one of the ones ready with cheek, a difference which ought to have alerted Gilmour. He turned to face him. 'All right. What about that airgun, then, Malcolm?'

Startled that the attention had been turned on him, Malcolm almost squeaked, 'What airgun? I haven't got no airgun.'

'The one you were using in the Co-op yard.'

He went all colours, then after a long pause he said sulkily, 'It were Dennis Bagley's, not mine.'

That stacked. A Bagley. The young pup who'd cheeked him, youngest member of that extensive clan, none of whom were strangers to Market Street police station.

'And who's the artist, then?' Malcolm looked blank. 'The one who draws bobby's hats.'

By the light of the repaired gas lamp, the second time he'd looked into the Co-op yard, Gilmour had seen quite clearly that the target figure which had been drawn on the wall – a crude outline of a human figure, arms, legs, a circle for the head – had been topped by something clearly meant to be a police helmet.

'That were Dennis an' all,' Malcolm admitted sullenly after a minute, but he was looking worried, and not necessarily because of snitching on his mate. The shifty, sideways look he slid at Gilmour was clearly mystified – he'd let them off lightly the other night, hadn't he? Why was he bringing all that up again? But this wasn't the neighbourhood's Bobby Oliver, used to giving them a clip round the ear and a telling off if he caught them up to something they shouldn't be doing before seeing them on their way. This was a sergeant, a detective what was more – which might be a different matter.

Malcolm began to look hot and bothered. 'It were only a laugh,' he muttered.

'Well, Malcolm, what other laughs have you been up to that you want to tell me about?'

Kenny chose that moment to chip in and defend his little brother. ''ere! You leave him alone. He hasn't done nothing wrong.'

Gilmour ordered him to be quiet and before either boy realized what he was doing, lunged for the sideboard and one of the top drawers which Malcolm's glance had given away, and where he guessed what he wanted would be, along with the tide of life's detritus, the unwanted, broken and useless bits and bobs people keep, just in case. He yanked it open and lo! There it was, the same cheap, lined writing paper that was very familiar.

He held it aloft and felt in his pocket for the letter he'd picked up in the office that morning. 'Did you write this letter, Malcolm, and the others?'

'Me?' Malcolm tried a defiant look at Gilmour, but what he saw there made him give up any pretence and mutter, less certainly, after a struggle with himself, 'No . . . well, what if I did?'

'Threatening letters, Malcolm.'

Kenny jumped up. 'What have you been up to, you daft little—'

'I told you to shut up, Kenny. What were you up to, Malcolm, incriminating your dad, making out they came from him?'

'What?' Patently bewildered, Malcolm was having trouble with that, possibly with the word 'incriminating'. But watching his face turn from uneasy to scared Gilmour knew he'd been right and could make a pretty good guess why. Hurt and angry after the loss of his mother, he'd been listening to Sonny's grievances and had lashed out with those letters, aiming a random dart at the man who'd put his father away while his mother was dying. With no expectation of ever being able to carry out the implied threats and no thought that his actions might have consequences. Not having the nous to see the letters would immediately have been connected to his father, simply because he didn't know Reardon was spelt any other way than it was pronounced by Sonny: Reeden.

And yet . . .

The letters had shown some initiative, at least, and he'd actually summoned up the energy from somewhere to put pen to paper. Malcolm's basic problem was boredom, no job, nothing to do but hang around the house or lounge about on street corners. Despite his aggravation, Gilmour could feel sorry for both these lads, and a lot more like them, the mates they hung around with. They'd never had a chance. And the future wasn't too rosy either.

'What are you going to do to the stupid git then?' Kenny asked truculently, giving his brother a disgusted look, having at last absorbed something of what was happening.

'I don't know,' Gilmour said truthfully. He waved the pad he was still holding. It would prove nothing, anyone could buy one at Woolworth's, but that hadn't dawned on either of them. Malcolm's eyes skittered away as Gilmour stowed it safely inside his jacket as though it was vital evidence.

The whole thing was a pain in the backside, certainly more trouble than it was worth to have the lad hauled up before the magistrate. There would be no more letters, and although Reardon had shrugged them off as nothing to bother about, implying the implied threat to Ellen had been bothering him no more than an annoying fly that refused to be swatted, it gave Gilmour a buzz to know he could tell him it was out of the way now.

Malcom was looking as if he was going to cry.

'If you've any sense at all in that thick head,' Gilmour said before he left, 'unless you want to go the same way as that dad of yours, spending half your life in clink, you'll keep away from that lowlife Bagley lot. They're bad news. And,' he added for good measure, tapping the letter, 'any more of this and you're for the high jump. Got that?'

Making his way back to the station, he bethought himself of Stan Dawson. The constable ran a club for youngsters that kept them off the streets, where they played football and could learn boxing and fitness training. Whether Malcolm could be persuaded to stir his stumps and attend was another matter, but it might be worth a try.

ELEVEN

The most appealing part of Folbury – if you discounted its lack of modern amenities – was the maze of small lanes and alleys around the steeply sloping Stonegate. The picturesque scene formed by the quaintly crooked houses and twisting lanes attracted visitors and was mainly why the area had escaped demolition when part of the high street had been pulled down to make way for the new Odeon.

Connie Randall lived in one of the ancient cottages, in a narrow lane which ran off Stonegate at a right angle, paralleling the main road into Birmingham in the valley below, where the adjacent railway lines and the River Fol ran alongside. The houses here were a pretty mixed bag, the earliest ones being timber-framed, centuries-old dwellings with overhanging upper storeys, and the newest a terrace of four small, pretty, Victorian workmen's cottages in red brick, with several decades of styles in between.

A nameplate was screwed to the bulging plaster wall of one of the older black and white houses: *Nurse Randall, District Nurse*, it read, above a bell which callers were instructed to ring. Gilmour did so, hunching his shoulders against the wind whipping nastily around the corner. It was four o'clock on the day following his visit to the Murfitts. The afternoon was drawing in, not quite lighting-up time yet in the streets outside, and the weather showed no signs of any improvement on the previous day, or indeed much of the last weeks.

Light spilled out on to the pavement as the door was answered by Connie Randall herself, a comfortably built woman with a ready smile, looking younger than the age she must be. She was still in her dark blue nurse's uniform dress, but she'd removed her apron, and her outdoor coat, cap and Gladstone bag could be seen tossed on to a chair in the passageway behind her.

She recognized one of her visitors immediately. 'Well, Joe

Gilmour! Sergeant, I should say, I suppose, shouldn't I?
Nothing's wrong with your little girl, I hope?'

'No, no, Ellie's lively as a cricket.'

'Glad to hear that. Keeps you on your toes, I expect, Sergeant?'

'You could say that.' Gilmour's face lit up with the proud,
besotted grin any mention of his daughter brought to his face.
'And Joe will still do nicely, Nurse.' Remembering he was
here in an official capacity he hastily introduced Reardon and
gave the reason for their call.

'Oh. Oh, yes,' she said, her face falling into grave lines.
'Well, don't stand out there in the cold, then. Come away in.'

'Er – you might want to lift your bike inside, Nurse, the
wind's getting up,' Gilmour suggested. He waved towards
the yellow-painted sit-up-and-beg bicycle with a basket
on the front, a familiar sight around Folbury, now propped
up against the outside wall.

'I suppose I'd better, in that case. I left it there because I
may have to go out again any time soon.'

Gilmour lifted the bicycle in and propped it in the place
against the wall she indicated. It didn't leave much room in
the narrow entrance and they had to squeeze by as she led
them into a low-ceilinged back room overlooking a surprisingly long garden. The curtains at this side of the house hadn't
yet been drawn. A bird cage, home to a golden yellow canary,
at present miserably hunched on its perch, was hanging in
front of the wide window, beyond which could just be seen
in the gathering dusk three white beehives at the bottom of
the garden, on the slope to the road and river below.

'I was about to make some tea. You're welcome to join me,'
Mrs Randall said, waving them to sit down. 'Just helped to
deliver twins, so I need it, though it wasn't too bad, considering. Not as if it was her first time. Better than the last,
anyway, a breech delivery with complications, that was.' There
was a twinkle in her eye; she was quite used to strong men
blenching at the mere mention of obstetrical details, which
was perhaps why she was teasing them, while putting off,
perhaps, what she knew was to come. Inviting them to take
their coats off, she went to make the tea when they accepted
the offer.

While she was gone, Reardon took stock of the pleasantly haphazard room, as he always did, for what it would reveal of its owner. It wasn't large, and beams ran across the low ceiling, but the old dark furniture against the cream walls gave it a cosy atmosphere. A couple of lamps glowed in the corners, there were flowers, a small bright fire, a pile of newspapers on a coffee table and shelves set in either fireplace alcove, filled with an assortment of books, ornaments and framed photographs. The sofa had squashy cushions and a gentle sag, but it promised comfort.

Reardon always took notice of the photographs in a room. These were mostly of Imogen at various stages, and a pen and ink drawing of her he guessed might be the work of Matt Millar. Other photographs showed a younger version of Mrs Randall in nursing uniform, wearing the starched and frilled cap of a senior nurse, and a snapshot with her arm around the shoulder of a shorter girl, both of them holding tennis racquets.

'That's my friend Cora and I, when I was slimmer,' she said, coming back with the teapot. She smiled a little sadly and Reardon remembered that Cora was the name Imogen had mentioned, Wesley Pugh's wife. She looked pretty, but not memorable.

'Little Ellie must be – what, two by now, Joe?' she remarked, pouring tea.

'Two and three months,' he beamed.

The question gave him the opportunity to keep up the small talk while the tea was dispensed. Reardon didn't interrupt until he judged it had gone on long enough. When he came back to the purpose of their visit, her face grew sad. 'It's all so incredible – Paul turning up like that after everyone thought he was dead. And then, to think . . . Poor Paul. And how awful for Ted . . . and Thea, of course. I can't begin to understand it.'

'Neither can we, Mrs Randall. But it's an unexplained death, and we need to take a look at anything that might have led up to it, talk to as many people as we can who knew him. I'm sorry about what's happened to him. I know you used to be special friends.'

She gave him a straight look. 'If you know that, you've

been doing your homework, so you must know we were more than friends.'

He hadn't expected such frankness, and she smiled faintly at the expression on his face. 'Don't get me wrong. We were very young, but we didn't act like the young do nowadays, since the war. Free thinking – or enlightened, as they see themselves. It wasn't at all like that with Paul and me – just a boy and girl imagining themselves in love, nothing more.'

Which left a lot open to interpretation, in view of Paul's reputation with girls – if both Wesley Pugh and Charles Purbright were to be believed.

She was watching him and didn't seem to like what she evidently thought was going through his mind. 'Look,' she said, 'there were a few of us used to go around together, as you do at that age, me and a few other girls, with some of the local lads. One or two of the boys from the King's School joined us sometimes, the ones who weren't too snobbish to mix with the hoi-polloi, that is. Some of them kept up after we'd left school – Wesley Pugh and Paul and one or two more. Naturally, we paired off a bit.'

'You didn't get to know Paul through his sister then?'

She pulled a face. 'Thea? Not likely. We weren't posh enough for her ladyship. Not like her brother. He didn't put on airs, even though they lived in a big house and he was at King's, and the fees don't come cheap there. He and I . . . he was different, a bit wild sometimes, scary in a way, I suppose, but it was . . . exciting.' Reardon thought there might be a lot more than just a remembrance of the sweet romance pictured by her daughter Imogen.

'But you fell out, you quarrelled.'

'Quarrelled? I don't know who said that,' she came back quickly. 'It wasn't anything more than what my mother would have called a lovers' tiff.'

'But serious enough for Paul to pack up and leave the town.'

Again the straight look. 'Don't read anything into that. It was just the sort of thing Paul did . . . running away from anything unpleasant.'

Did he detect a trace of bitterness? He couldn't be sure. She began fiddling with a packet of bird seed she'd picked up from a table by the side of the sofa. She glanced at the cage, where the doleful canary, still silent, had hidden its head under its wing. Its silence was oddly disconcerting. Canaries were supposed to sing, weren't they?

He watched as she poured seed into the holder clipped on to the cage. 'Come on, Pippie, buck up.' The bird still didn't move. Then as if in answer, it suddenly began to sound off, shrill and piercing. Could two ounces of fluff and feathers burst your eardrums? She laughed, picked up a velvet square and draped it over the cage. 'Sleep tight, Pippie.' A merciful silence ensued. 'I thought he wasn't well.'

It had been a diversion, intended or not, but it was time to get back on track. 'Can you tell me what it was you and Paul disagreed about?'

'No,' she said decisively, 'I can't. It doesn't matter now, it has nothing to do with what's happened to him, and it didn't matter then, after a while.'

'Was it anything to do with Wesley Pugh?' he persisted.

'Oh. Oh, someone *has* been talking.'

'Mr Pugh himself admitted they'd had a disagreement. He didn't say what it was about.'

'No, he wouldn't, not Wes.'

He waited. She picked the teapot up, poured the last dregs into her cup. It must have been stone-cold, but she drank without apparently noticing. At last she looked up and said tiredly, 'He wouldn't say, because he wasn't the only one involved, you see.' She sighed. 'All right, you're going to find out sooner or later, somebody's going to tell you. It was partly my fault.'

She stopped, then went on hesitantly, 'You have to under-stand . . . Wes, he and I . . . you know, before I met his friend Paul, his best friend until . . . until they went their different ways,' she finished, though Reardon thought she had been going to say something else. 'You'd never have thought they'd be such friends, they were so different, chalk and cheese, but it didn't seem to make any difference.'

'We've seen Mr Pugh's books,' Gilmour said. 'Obviously he's a reader, and he doesn't seem very keen on aeroplanes or automobiles . . . but that's how it works sometimes, doesn't it, opposites?'

She smiled a little. 'You're so right. Paul never so much as picked up a book if he didn't have to, whereas Wes . . . he was the clever one, you know, that's how he won a scholarship to King's. His parents could never have afforded to send him there otherwise. They were farmers out Emscott way, but only tenant farmers. Nothing to leave poor old Wes when they died. Not that it bothered him greatly, with his views.'

'How did the two of them come to fall out?' Reardon asked, guiding her back.

Leaning forward, she picked up the poker and stirred the fire. The flames leapt and threw a softening, rosy glow onto her face. At last she said, 'Wes was such a sweet boy, you know. Full of Marxist ideals, fierce about wanting to put the world to rights, but kind and gentle really. I've known him all my life and . . . well, it had always been sort of him and me, if you see what I mean, until Paul came on the scene, and . . . I suppose it made him jealous.' She bit her lip. 'The thing is, you see – oh, this sounds so bad, but I'd begun to feel Wes was taking it for granted, that we would get married some time – no, fairly soon – and that wasn't what I wanted at all . . . or not just then. I wanted some fun, and to see somewhere other than Folbury. I'd set my sights on training to be a nurse and I was already enrolled.'

A small chirrup came from under the velvet cover on the birdcage. Reardon hoped it wasn't going to deflect her. Another chirrup. Pippie revving up, seemingly not fooled that it was bedtime. But silence prevailed again as Connie continued, 'Wes just couldn't see why that was so important to me, you know, and we began to have arguments. I told him he was wasting his life, when he could have gone to university and made something of himself – his headmaster wanted it – but he said his father needed his help on the farm. Which might have been true, but then his father died and even when he was free, it didn't make any difference. One night we started arguing, one thing led to another, and you know how it happens, you say things you don't mean. He said he'd seen how I looked at Paul and he supposed he wasn't good enough for me now. I told him he didn't own me, and it ended with me walking away. If he'd come after me and apologized it might have been different. But he didn't.' She looked again at the fire, as if seeing the past all over again in its glowing heart, and not particularly liking what she saw. 'To be honest, there may have been a bit of truth in what he'd said, because Paul was . . . well, Paul. You know, he had that, what do you call it – charisma? It was all so intense . . . too much so, though at the time it only seemed to make everything more exciting.'

'So what happened between him and Wesley?'

'Oh, Wes confronted Paul, told him to leave me alone. Paul lost his temper and Wes . . . he has a temper, too, on occasions, though it's usually more of a slow burn. I'm afraid they came to blows, but they managed to stop before they actually killed each other. I was fed up with the pair of them, to be truthful. I told Paul I didn't want to see him again, either. It didn't go down very well.'

'He left everything and went off to Germany? Because of that, and an argument with his best friend?'

She gave him a speculative look. 'Neither helped. But to be honest, I feel sure the fight was triggered by something else. I don't know what had happened between them just about then, but something had . . . they were barely on speaking terms. It was so unlike them, but I daren't ask. And then, because of me, it all blew up. Nobody knew where Paul had gone for ages, until he let them know he was with those cousins in Germany.' She shrugged. 'He stayed and married someone else there and by the time he came home again, I was nursing at the Middlesex in London. I became a ward sister,' she added, so casually he could see she was proud of it – and rightly so, if what he'd heard was true of the Middlesex, the crème de la crème of teaching hospitals. 'I met my husband – he was a junior doctor – and we worked there until the war began, when we both went over to France. And that's all there is to it,' she finished, 'for what it's worth.'

By no means sure about that, Reardon nevertheless thanked her. 'You've been very helpful.'

'Have I?'

'Just one more thing, Mrs Randall.' She'd been open enough, more than he'd expected. But something was out of kilter, he didn't quite know what. For one thing, though she knew Paul had come home and then drowned, a bizarre situation in itself, she hadn't expressed any surprise. He hadn't felt compelled to enlighten her on the true circumstances of his death; they would be made public soon enough. For now, he had one more question. 'When was the last time you actually saw Paul?'

For a moment he thought she was about to be evasive, but she surprised him. They had in fact last met in wartime France. 'And that,' she said, the memory lighting her up, 'was amazing! One of those things that can only happen in a war.'

'When you were nursing there?'

'Yes. My husband had joined the RAMC right at the beginning and I followed him to France as a nursing sister. I was working at the base hospital in Etaples when I heard a rumour that the Pals regiment from Folbury had arrived at the transit camp. Can you imagine? There were people in that regiment I'd grown up with and hadn't seen for years, a boy from next door, even young Teddy! He knew Paul was stationed only a few miles away and he tried to get word to him, hoping we could all meet. Who would have believed such a set of coincidences?'

Reardon had no difficulty in believing it. Stuff like that happened all the time. The randomness of war, the way it not only kept people apart, but threw them together in totally unexpected ways and places. He himself had once come face to face in a noisy canteen in a little French town with a distant cousin he hadn't seen for years; and arriving at the military hospital, after the incident on his motorcycle, he'd encountered his own doctor from home.

'We were a bit crazy that night, we all went out to one of the bistros in the town – me without permission, but I didn't care – and a lot of red wine was drunk. Teddy wasn't used to it – as you might imagine, with his family – and he was barely twenty, after all, poor boy, facing God knows what, and he was well on the way to getting drunk. And then just as we were thinking Paul hadn't got Teddy's message or wasn't able to come, he arrived on a motorcycle he'd borrowed. As usual he was immediately the centre of attention,' she added, her eyes misty again.

'You said Wesley Pugh was there as well?'

'Yes. He was working nearby, too, as a stretcher bearer.'

'It must have been quite a reunion, all friends from the old days. Differences forgotten, I suppose?'

'Between Wesley, and Paul? Well, we were all older and a bit wiser perhaps. It didn't seem to matter any longer. Friendships, especially such old ones, are very precious, aren't they? They certainly were at that time, when none of us knew whether we'd still be alive the next day. As it happens, my own husband died only a few weeks later.'

'I'm sorry. Doctors were sadly no exception.'

'That's true, but he wasn't killed, although he was working at a front-line clearing station. There was a typhoid epidemic – not unknown in the appalling conditions in the trenches – and he was one of the victims.' Momentarily, she looked away, but after a moment, she went on. 'Well, that night. There was no awkwardness between them, you know, between Paul and Wes, I mean. They hadn't seen each other since they had joined up but they were just as they'd always been, years ago – except that Paul was quieter than he used to be. At one point he tried to talk to Teddy, who was a bit maudlin by that time. He took him outside to try and sober him up before he passed out, and they were gone a long time. I don't remember much else that went on. Except for one thing,' she added after a moment. 'It sounds strange now, but I've never forgotten it. At one point, one of those weird silences fell . . . angels passing overhead, isn't that what they say? Just for a flash of time, when every-thing seems to stop, sort of suspended. The whole place went absolutely silent, I suppose it was only for a moment or two, and then we all began talking again, as if it had never happened, but I know I wasn't the only one who had felt it.' She had been speaking quite calmly, but now she faltered. 'We none of us ever saw Paul again after that night.'

Lost in the memory, there were sudden tears in her eyes. Reardon didn't see any point in keeping her talking much longer. The last half hour must have been harrowing for her – and her working day probably hadn't yet finished.

Joe Gilmour I'm all right with, Connie told herself after they had gone, but his boss, the other one with the dark eyes, the searching look, he's different. He understood more than I'd like. I should have kept it to myself, I always have until now, and I don't know what made me come out with something I've kept behind closed doors for half a lifetime.

But now the doors are unlocked anyway, and what has lain behind isn't going to stay there. If I'm being truthful, I'm not sure I want it to any longer. There have been more than enough secrets, for too long.

All the same, what *I* want doesn't matter – it's not up to me.

I ought to get myself something to eat before the telephone rings and I have to go out again. But I feel incapable of moving . . .

I can still see it: that night, the way all eyes turned to Paul as he came in, shouldering his way between the mass of khaki bodies and the crowded tables. My heart went into my mouth. The light of my life once. Why had I ever let him go? Because he wasn't good for me. Brought out the worst. We had been bad news together.

And now, there we all were. Paul, brilliant, charming as always, though the war had already changed him, as it did everyone, sooner or later. That haunted look they all had when they came back from the front line. If they ever did come back. Teddy, young, with eyes over-bright, whom I have come to love, for all his faults. And Wesley. Wes, whose conscience would not let him do work other than as a stretcher-bearer. And me, welcoming a reprieve not only from the unthinkable pain and grief we nurses had to face day by day, but also from the disaster my marriage had become, to a hand-some young doctor who'd walked down the wards as if he owned the place, with that arrogant stride, heels ringing, as if he expected all the nurses to fall down and worship. Which they usually did. Me included. Until I recognized him for the womanizer he was, when it was too late.

There, that night, in France, across the flickering candlelight, among the appalling racket of drunken Tommies singing war songs to an out-of-tune piano, French girls on the make, the exotic smell and flavour of garlic in the food, the air still full of that strange silent moment when the world had stopped, I looked from one to the other and made my decision – this time final, irrevocable, unregretted then, and unregretted ever since. I knew rightness when I met it now, felt it was true, though I knew it was impossible, out of reach, that we were stirring up trouble, even before we walked out into that brilliant, starlit, eerily quiet night.

Later, the guns started their ominous thunder again, and the sky took on a different brilliance. We scarcely noticed, we were blind and deaf to everything but each other, and hearing a different music.

She is my cherished memory of that night, my darling Imogen, our lovely daughter.

'Whatever he's been up to lately, Paul Millar was a bad lad in his youth, wasn't he?' Gilmour sat astride his chair, arms folded across its back, facing Reardon's desk. Like that, his legs seemed to take up less room. 'So what about Pugh – still suspect number one? Would he let something as trivial as a quarrel over a girl rankle for all these years?'

'Not being Pugh, it's hard for me to say. But people do.'

Reardon picked up a large, smooth pebble he used as a paperweight. It had a vein of quartz running through it which gleamed silver when you held it to the light. Ellen had picked it up in the garden and thought it looked lucky. 'Why do you think she's so against her daughter marrying Paul's son?' he asked suddenly.

'Connie?' Gilmour didn't have to think long. 'For one thing, Imogen's barely out of the schoolroom. And he's a struggling artist. Not much of a prospect. Or maybe she thinks marrying into the Millar family isn't the best idea in the world. They don't exactly have such a reliable history, when you think of Paul – or what his father seems to have been. Bad blood?'

'Are you sure that affair with Paul was as pure and innocent as she made out, Joe? If the reason he left Folbury that first time was because he was in it too deep with her?'

Gilmour lowered his chin on to his crossed arms and frowned at the floor. He liked Connie Randall and didn't want to believe what this was leading up to. 'She's a good woman,' he said defensively after a minute.

'I don't doubt it. But she was young once.'

'Thirty years ago – and Imogen's *seventeen*,' he objected.

'Born 1916. And Mrs Randall has just told us she and Paul met again in 1915 when they were stationed in France, only a few miles apart.'

After a second or two, Gilmour took his scowl off the floor. 'Even if it's true, what would killing Paul resolve? It doesn't provide a motive for anyone. Being dead wouldn't alter the fact that they still had the same father. If they had.'

TWELVE

Saturday was a half-day for most of Folbury, when work ceased at midday and the weekend respite began. Reardon managed to catch Thea Millar at the office before she left, when he rang to say he had more information about their brother. They were busy at Inkerman Terrace at the moment, she told him, but the offices would soon be closing and she would be home later. Perhaps he could meet her at Casa Nova this afternoon?

'Mr Millar will be there, too?'

There was a pause. 'Afraid not. My brother's playing golf.'

'It's rather important,' he said, mildly in view of what he was thinking.

'The golf's rather important, too, Inspector. He's playing with a client we're hoping to do business with.'

And that took precedence, of course, Reardon thought sourly. Typical of what he suspected about golfers and their reasons for joining clubs. Thea Millar was taking it for granted that her brother would rather not risk losing business through offending his golf partner than be there to hear what more was to be told about the tragic event which had suddenly erupted into their lives.

'I have some new information for you.'

'Is it about the post-mortem?' she asked after a moment. He said it was. 'Then Teddy doesn't need to be there. It will come better from me, in any case,' she finished decisively.

He debated whether to leave it until he could see them together, but as far as he was concerned, postponing what he had to say was not an option. 'If you say so, Miss Millar.'

So it was later that afternoon when he arrived at Ladyford Lane and Casa Nova, less than a brisk ten-minute walk from Market Street police station in the town centre. At first sight, the brilliantly white house with its blue-tiled roof, futuristic among the surrounding mock-Tudor facades, seemed oddly familiar, until he recalled the model he'd seen standing on the office filing cabinet at Inkerman Terrace. Casa Nova! How tacky, and the house itself about as far a cry from Fox Close where brother and sister had been brought up as you could get.

And yet, as he crunched up a drive running ruler straight through a half-finished garden where paving slabs stood waiting to be laid, it struck him that the house was actually rather appealing. Its asymmetrical assembly of geometric shapes, the windows wrapping around corners, the lack of superfluous ornament was refreshingly different from any other building he knew of in Folbury. That bright white-and-blueness – which admittedly might have been more appropriate to some place baking under a Mediterranean sun – brought a touch of warmth and the exotic to the briskly cold spring day.

In this frame of mind, he was almost expecting the door to be opened by a French maid in a frilly cap and apron, not by this small, thin, elderly woman in a crossover pinafore, wearing a hairnet and old tennis shoes, truculently enquiring about his business in a strong Folbury accent.

'I have an appointment with Miss Millar at three thirty.'

'She'm not here yet.' She stood, arms akimbo, a small Cerberus guarding the entrance, making no move to let him in.

Unless he wanted to wait on the doorstep, he decided he'd better show his police card, though it wasn't really any of her business.

After inspecting it, she nodded, her eyes avid with curiosity, and she sounded just a shade less hostile as she handed it back. 'I reckon you'd best come in then. Don't just stand there. You'll have us all catching noo-moany if you don't shut that door.' She stomped off, her tennis shoes making flapping noises on the floor tiles. Assuming he was meant to follow across the hall, he did so and found himself in a big kitchen, where machinery hummed and something savoury was cooking. A lot of stainless steel and shiny paint, reminiscent of the last time he was in the mortuary.

'Sit you down then. Never late, Thea isn't.' By now it was nearly twenty to four.

Reardon looked around for a chair. Seating seemed as though it might not be regarded as a high priority in this streamlined machine of a kitchen, but he spotted a couple of high stools almost hidden under the window near a little flap table and he hitched himself on to one.

She looked at him, her eyes narrowing. 'You sure her said half past three? It was supposed to be four when you was expected.'

She'd known when he was expected all along. He was pretty sure he hadn't got the time wrong, but he said mildly, 'Maybe I was mistaken.' It scarcely mattered, his time wasn't about to be wasted if, as he suspected, this crotchety old dame wasn't averse to a bit of useful gossip.

'You'm welcome to wait but I've no time to stop, I've to get on with me straightening up afore I go home. Since you're here, I don't suppose you wouldn't say no to a cuppa tea?'

'You're right, thank you, I wouldn't say no, Miss . . .? I didn't catch your name.'

'I didn't give it. It's Ivy Pearson. Mrs.' She switched a chrome electric kettle on and while it boiled, went back to finish the task he seemed to have interrupted, the scrubbing down of a pastry board within an inch of its life.

That accomplished and the tea made, she reached into a cupboard for a mug for herself and a cup and saucer for him, matt white with a solid black triangle for a handle. It was too wide across the top. He began to drink immediately she set it in front of him, before the tea had a chance to grow too cool to enjoy, and discovered the triangular handle was impossible to hold with any comfort.

'Good smell, Mrs Pearson,' he said appreciatively, manoeuvring the cup down carefully on to its saucer. 'Pie?'

'Teddy's partial to a nice steak and kidney.' She sniffed, but looked slightly mollified. Her tidying almost finished, she swept a damp cloth over a tiled work surface as if she were attacking it. Considering the energy she was putting forth, Reardon decided that she was more robust than she looked and probably not as old as he had thought at first sight, either. 'It's for tonight, only to heat up when they'm ready for it. Thea's no hand at cooking.' She sniffed. 'Or it'll keep till

tomorrow, if he don't come home tonight. Which he might
not,' she added cryptically.

He stowed away that little nugget of information for further
use. She'd dried her hands and now leant back against the sink,
arms crossed, which seemed to indicate she'd finished her work
for the moment and also, he hoped, showed a willingness to
talk. Thea and Teddy, she'd called them. He didn't think
the familiar use of Christian names was simply the Jack's-as-
good-as-his-neighbour attitude prevalent since the war had
supposedly put society on a level footing. It was more than
likely she had known them from childhood. 'How long have
you worked here, Mrs Pearson?'

'Here and at Fox Close, nigh on forty year, so help me.'
She picked up her mug and came across to hitch herself agilely
on to the other stool.

'Long time, forty years.'

She shrugged her bony shoulders. 'Jobs ain't that easy to
come by, and when your husband's signing on, it's Hobson's
choice. My Norm used to work for Millars an' all, see, brick-
layer he was. Till he got his back and they said he was taking
too much time off and give him his cards,' she added spitefully.
'I wouldn't work as nobody's skivvy if it wasn't for that.'

He wondered why she'd been kept on, when resentment
and dislike seeped from every pore. He decided she'd enough
nous to keep that from her employers – and she was obviously
a good worker. Guilt also came in all sorts of forms, and
perhaps employing her helped to ease the Millar conscience
at having had to sack Norm.

'I take it you've known the family since they were all
children?'

'That I have. And never thought it'd a come to this.' She
gave him a quick, sideways look and leant across the table.
'It's Paul you're here about, innit? Drownded himself, has he?
Well, you never knew what he'd do, that one. Jumping down
the stairs and sliding on me polished floors, climbing trees till
he fell and broke his leg! A right handful, he were.'

He recalled the photographs Ellen had found in the rusty
tin box. The boy standing next to his father, clutching his
sister's hand, who had grown to be the sort of man who had

been willing to abandon his family, his own son above all, leaving them to grieve for all those lost years. Yet unlike the father, Ernest Millar, with that arrogant look to him, the boy's mischievous grin was the sort to charm birds off trees had he been so inclined. 'A handful, but a bit of a charmer, was he?'

'Sometimes. Not always.' She slid him a sideways look. 'None of them was.'

'More of a rebel?'

She pursed her thin lips, maybe wondering whether she had already said more than she should. He wondered again just how old she really was. Her face was wrinkled and seamed with cracks, like an old plate, but considering the energy she'd been putting out, it was surely deceptive. At last she said, 'If he hadn't married her – that Liesl. I knew as her was trouble soon as I set eyes on her, I did.'

Her face said it all. If Ivy Pearson had her knife into you, you'd better look out, although at a guess she had probably disliked Paul's wife simply because of her nationality and he had no intention of going into all that.

Her glance fell on the clock, no doubt anxious not to over-stay her working hours, and she began to clatter the tea things together.

'What time do you finish, Mrs Pearson?'

'When I'm done. About now, as a rule.'

'You're not here in the evenings, then?'

'No.' She gave a sideways glance, debated, then said, 'Except that once. A week or two back, when I come back for me wages. Like a fool, I'd gone home and left the money on the shelf yonder. Norm gets one on him if he don't have his pint up the Glassmakers of a night . . . and he had a few on the slate already.'

Despite his 'back', being out of work but not needing to give up his drinking because his hard-working wife was doling out money, feckless Norm seemed to have it made.

'They had visitors,' Mrs Pearson went on. 'They was shouting too much to hear me, and I have me key, so I just stepped in and picked up me money and left. I knew Thea would have noticed I'd forgotten it and tucked it under the tea caddy for safety, and she had.'

'What day was this?'

'What day? Heavens, that I couldn't tell you. Half a minute, though, it must've been a Tuesday because that's when my friend Gertie comes round for a bit and I wanted to get back.'

'You didn't by any chance hear what they were arguing about?'

She looked indignant. Of course she hadn't heard. She didn't go listening at keyholes, did she?

But she'd heard enough to think the incident worth reporting.

Maddeningly, at that moment there came the sound he'd been listening for, a car drawing up outside. Mrs Pearson's mouth shut as if a zip had been drawn across it. 'Here's Thea now,' she then said. 'I told you her wouldn't be late.'

The clock on the wall now said five minutes to four. She couldn't get him out of the kitchen fast enough.

Thea came in, holding a pair of driving goggles and unwinding a long scarf from around her head. She was wearing a leather coat – and trousers, a wartime innovation that still raised matronly eyebrows. She was flushed and looked windblown, her hair mussed up, and in Reardon's eyes looked younger and far more attractive than when he'd last seen her. The open-topped car drawn up outside was a red Alvis Tourer that would have turned Gilmour green with envy.

She offered him a seat in the big sitting room before going to tidy herself, hoped he hadn't been waiting long. Was that an apology for being late, or was she accusing him of being too early? He knew he hadn't made a mistake and wondered if she'd made him wait on purpose, just to remind him of his place.

Fighting gravity in a big leather chair too low for comfort, built more for lying back in than sitting upright, feeling it would put him at a distinct disadvantage when it came to what he had to say, he looked around for a higher seat. He didn't find one, apart from, strangely, an ancient rocking chair, which didn't seem a much better bet, for different reasons. As well as being a rocker, it had sagging springs, a decided list to one side and stuffing poking from its rubbed velvet arms. He gave in, stayed where he was and took stock of the long, low room where the big windows curved round the corners at each end and let in the cold winter light.

The décor was a continued expression of the outside – glass and blond wood matching the smooth maple panelling on the walls, pale leather chairs. The only colour came from a large rug at the far end of the room, emerald green patterned with scarlet lightning flashes. But things other than the shabby rocking chair were strangely out of kilter, in the shape of heavy, ornate old stuff from another era, awkwardly placed here and there about the functional room, as if it were in a furniture depository. Perhaps that was why it was here, incongruous amongst all the twentieth-century stuff, just being stored temporarily while someone found somewhere better to put it?

After a few minutes Thea returned, having divested herself of her driving attire. Hair now smoothly brushed, wearing a soft woollen dress, long-sleeved, with a matching velvet collar and cuffs, the colour of olives, that made her eyes look more green than the blue he had thought them. Plain and simple, but again very obviously expensive. No jewellery.

He was glad that she seated herself in the twin of the one he was occupying, bringing them to equal levels. She didn't seem to find it uncomfortable, and certainly looked more at ease than he felt, with her hands folded across her lap. They were strong hands, large but shapely, white and well-kept, with long fingers and pearly nails and he saw he'd been wrong about the absence of jewellery, noticing the ring she wore on her left hand. It was easily missed though, a thin gold band and a very modest twist of three small diamonds, like an engagement ring, but worn on her middle finger.

She waited for him to begin, calmly prepared for anything he had to say, for which he was mildly grateful. If anything could make his grim task somewhat easier, that would. He began to tell her what the post-mortem had revealed.

The pathologist had delivered the results in person, suspecting there would be questions to answer. What it had revealed had confirmed the leg-break which Thea had mentioned, no doubt from the tree-climbing accident Ivy Pearson had just spoken of; there appeared to be little doubt now about the identity of the body. As to the cause of his death . . .

'I'm sorry, but there's no easy way of saying this. Your brother died, I'm afraid, from a gunshot wound.'

It was several seconds before she answered. '*What?* You did say gunshot? He shot himself?' It seemed not so much shock as confusion she showed. 'You mean – it was . . . suicide?'

'No, I'm afraid not.' He continued gently, 'Miss Millar, he was shot in the back of the head.'

She drew in a breath and stared at him for several moments. 'Well, even so, that's not impossible, is it?'

'Not impossible, no, but highly improbable. And he could hardly have thrown himself into the water afterwards.'

'Perhaps he . . . perhaps he toppled in.' She bit her lip at the lameness of that. 'Someone else, is that it? But who could possibly want to do that to him? And what sort of person would have a gun?'

He couldn't answer the first question, but as to the second . . . For a start, practically anyone who'd had access to them in the war, and that meant a lot of people.

'It was a service revolver.' A Webley handgun, issued to officers, airmen and police as being more convenient than a rifle, identified by the bullet which had not exited but had been found lodged in his head, but he didn't tell her that. 'All guns should have been surrendered at the end of hostilities, but not all were, I'm afraid.' Far more than he cared to think about; some kept, however mistakenly, as souvenirs, out of date now and highly dangerous. Others smuggled over for more nefarious purposes.

'Can you think of anyone who might have wished him harm, Miss Millar? Any enemies?'

'Enemies? Paul?' He caught a look, a change in her face, but then it was gone. 'How should I know that? Have you forgotten how long it is since I last saw him?' she reminded him sharply.

The news had shocked her, but not as much as he had expected, and she was fast recovering herself, or at least she wasn't letting any sadness show, any more than she had when they'd first been informed of the discovery of Paul's body. As he watched her, she put up a hand to smooth an imaginary strand of hair back and her sleeve fell away, revealing an ugly, crescent-shaped scar just above her wrist. Pinpoints of light reflected from the tiny diamonds in her ring as she hurriedly pushed the cuff into place. He told himself that after all, she had had time to absorb the initial shock after being told that their brother was dead, well and truly dead this second time; perhaps she regarded the means almost as an irrelevance. The workings of Thea Millar's mind were not easy to read.

However, worse was to come for her. As gently and tactfully as such news could be imparted, he told her what else the post-mortem had revealed.

She heard him out without interruption. By the time he had finished, what little colour was left in her face had drained away, leaving it ashen. The green-blue eyes looked stricken. The silence now was not calculated. She seemed incapable of saying anything.

Why the devil couldn't Ted Millar have abandoned his golf and been with her? Reardon thought angrily, feeling suddenly, uncharacteristically, slightly helpless. He should have brought Gilmour with him; he was better at dealing with women. 'Are you all right, Miss Millar? Would you like Mrs Pearson to bring you a glass of water?'

She answered with a shake of her head and sat up straighter. 'Are you sure?' was all she could say.

'I'm afraid so, yes.'

She gave a slight nod, sitting with hands folded, trying to absorb what she'd just been told, what the post-mortem had revealed, as well as the cause of his death from the gunshot wound. He couldn't help but marvel at her control. He was not disposed to like Miss Thea Millar all that much from what he had seen of her so far, but anyone who could summon such self-control after what she'd just been told deserved respect.

'Your victim didn't drown,' Rossiter had said, confirming Dysart's findings. 'He was dead before he went in. The gunshot did for him.' Then he had added, 'But he was going to die anyway.'

'So are we all, sooner or later.' Gilmour held up a hand immediately regretting the flippancy they all used at times to counteract what didn't bear thinking about, although Rossiter had that effect on most people. A dedicated and serious chap, a dry, sandy-haired Scot without much sense of humour; but it was a serious business, being a pathologist. Unlike his wife, Kay Dysart, he had a measured and considered way of speaking, but he was no slouch as far as his job was concerned and Reardon appreciated that he hadn't wasted time before performing the autopsy, and what was more, getting the results to them as soon as possible.

'In his case, Sergeant, sooner,' Rossiter said severely. 'His lungs were in a sorry state, could have seen him off at any time. His condition wasn't helped by smoking, but I should say it's more than probable he'd also been gassed at some point during the war.'

'He was in the Royal Flying Corps, Doctor,' Reardon told him. He might have faced being shot down from the skies by a German fighter pilot, but he hadn't fought in the trenches and been subject to a gas attack which could have affected him for the rest of his life.

'Hm, well, that's interesting. But if his aeroplane had ever caught fire – which they did, of course, with some regularity, those paper kites – it might amount to the same thing. He could have suffered from smoke inhalation which would have affected his lungs in the same way. The end was nigh anyway for the poor devil, before someone helped him on his way. You'll see the full details on my report.'

'Poor devil,' echoed Reardon. And what an end! 'Would he have known? That he was terminally ill?'

'Maybe not acknowledged – if he was one of those who deny there's anything to worry about until it's too late. But he must have known something was very wrong.'

Could this have been the reason he had returned to Folbury? Intimations of mortality? Even the worst of villains had been known in these circumstances to want to make peace with their maker, guilty at something they wanted to get off their chest. Perhaps Paul Millar had had a need to make amends to his family, to ask their forgiveness for past misdeeds, and to receive their sympathy when they knew he was a dying man? Maybe his home town was the only place he had to go, like a wounded animal returning to its lair to die. Whatever it was, he had made promises to them that some explanation of why he had come home would be forthcoming – and hopefully, some account of what had been happening to him during those missing years. But he'd left it too late. Maybe he'd lost his nerve and hadn't been able to bring himself to tell them of his fatal illness. Reardon hoped he hadn't been expecting to remain here and be nursed by his sister. Thea Millar was not his idea of a latter-day Florence Nightingale.

But whereas the initial news of his death, the manner of his drowning and the circumstances of his being found – even the news that he had been shot – had been received with what he considered an unnatural calmness, he couldn't have any doubts that this last had been a shattering blow. Thea Millar was obviously shocked and maybe suffering.

Then suddenly, with something very like relief, she said, 'Then despite what you say, he *must* have shot himself. He had every reason to, if he was . . . he had every reason. You need look no further for . . . for a murderer.'

He could feel pity for her, clinging on to hope that wasn't there, preferring even suicide to the idea of murder. 'Then you would have to ask, Miss Millar, why did he come home, just to shoot himself?'

Why did he come home? Well, who ever knew why Paul did anything? I might have answered the police inspector. But there are some things you do not say. Cannot.

He left half an hour ago, the policeman. I find myself walking across the room, back and forth, unable to stop and sit down, unable to think. My handbag, where's my handbag? My old crocodile bag that never leaves my side? At last I find it, under one of Teddy's stupid 'functional' chairs which slide back from under you of their own accord when you attempt to stand. The inspector clearly found them as incomprehensible as the rest of the furnishings. And yes, it's time this old stuff from Fox Close went. Insisting on them being kept as a protest against this house of Teddy's (childish and untypical of me in retrospect, I must admit) it has run its course.

It's so habitual to take the photo out that my fingers find it automatically, I don't have to look. It's in the inside pocket of my bag. I feel the shiny surface, the tiny cracks that have developed over the years with too much handling. The image of the little boy he was is faded and spoilt, but it's too familiar for that to make any difference now. The minutes tick by and all I can do is sit there and hold it, swamped by the memory of the lost years: my growing-up years, spent in keeping the balance in that house, ensuring that no one went over the top.

We fled Fox Close like lemmings after the accident, all of us: Paul, myself, Teddy and of course, little Matt, escaped to hide ourselves in the only other place we knew . . . Inkerman Terrace, the family home where the business had begun. It had been enough for our grandparents, Manfred and Clara, and though it felt incredibly small and cramped to us after the many rooms and spaciousness of Fox Close, none of us, least of all me, regretted leaving the gloom and misery that had hung like a pall over the old mansion.

But it wasn't long before Paul took himself off again – to where that time I've never known, a typical Paul reaction to trouble of any kind. He stayed away six weeks, didn't come back again until the war started, when the thunder of guns was beginning across the Channel and the bricks of Fox Close were already crashing down, the demolition crew having moved in to raze it to the ground – by instant mutual consent among the three of us, with Father no longer there to say us nay.

I could not say I was surprised when Paul announced that he was not home for good, that he had volunteered for the RFC. I suspect that for him, the war – which had been confidently predicted to be over in a few months and the Germans put in their place – had actually come as a reprieve, at a disastrous point when life had suddenly erupted into chaos and the world had disintegrated around him. An excuse to escape again, even war seeming less of a catastrophe than the events which had shattered life as he had come to know it. Whatever the motivation, he responded to the call to arms and enlisted in the Royal Flying Corps – of course, what else? – and very shortly was sent off to fight for king and country. Teddy, who was little more than a schoolboy, barely a couple of years or so into his architectural indentures, threw everything up and volunteered also, though it was the army for him. It infuriated me at the time – but who could blame him, after all? Their departure meant leaving me to scrape together the remnants of our former life, of course, but they'd scarcely given that a serious thought, either of them. Thea always coped, didn't she?

I was left to run the business as best I could, without any experience – but I did it. I had promised Mother on her deathbed I would be a good sister to the boys, and I have always tried to do whatever has to be done, whatever it is, no matter what the cost, and this included keeping the business going for them. I often wonder how Father would have reacted to what I was able to do. Apoplexy, probably. Although he knew I had a better brain than either of his two sons, he would no more have thought of putting me in charge of his precious business than a monkey on a stick.

My life at that time was not at its happiest. But I grasped the chance I would never have had otherwise and kept the firm going, learning as I went along from those trusted employees who were still with Millars, because they were too old, or otherwise deemed unfit, to fight. I listened and learnt how to manage the buying of supplies for what little work we had in hand, and how to keep track of the monies owing to us. I organized the firm's day-to-day running more efficiently than it had ever been done before. I made acquaintance with our bank manager, who after some misgivings about my capabilities, turned out to be a great ally and a tower of strength. Above all, I learnt how to bargain like a market trader to secure profitable contracts for the army huts and temporary hospitals which had to be thrown up in a hurry to accommodate the unprecedented, terrible avalanche of broken and wounded men as they were brought back from France. I never turned away any other building work that was going, either. That was mainly how Millars as a firm survived, and there was a thriving business for Teddy to come home to.

That's how it was. I sometimes wonder if the shape of our lives is predestined, its pattern evolving like the web the spider is programmed to spin, but I prefer to believe our destiny is in our own hands. Even before the fighting really and truly began and robbed legions of women of the chances of marriage and motherhood, I was already a confirmed spinster in the eyes of other women. Little did they know. And little did I care whether they did or not. The three tiny diamonds winked on my finger and I knew it was not fate that had decreed my future, but myself. I soon learnt to cope with the regrets I had. Apart from everything else, it had also given me something I would never otherwise have had: the chance to love and take care of Matt as if he were my own son, the child I longed for but would never have. The little boy that he was, the man he has become. So like, and so unlike, his father.

It tears from me, then, a hoarse whisper that scrapes my throat. '*Why did you have to come back and do this to me? To take away my reason for living . . . was that it?*'

I gaze once more at the photograph, for the last time ever. Then I tear it up in silent fury, so fiercely my fingers ache. The pieces scatter on the floor, and I leave them where they lie.

THIRTEEN

'I met him, you know,' Ellen said, looking up from the piece of toast she was buttering. 'At least, I think I might have.'

Sunday morning, and Reardon was taking time to enjoy his favourite breakfast of the week before he left, on this supposed day of rest. The sacrifice of a weekend wasn't calculated to be welcomed by anyone, including Reardon himself, but Ellen knew that he had a meeting with the newly appointed super in Dudley, who'd made it plain that he was giving up his own Sunday morning because he expected cut and dried plans for the way forward in the new case to be presented to him. He was due for a disappointment, Reardon said sourly. Expecting plans at this stage was akin to trying to make an omelette without eggs.

'Met who, Ellen?' he asked absently, applying himself to bacon and fried tomatoes.

'Your man, the poor chap you pulled from the river.'

His fork stayed mid-air. 'You met Paul Millar. My God. How? Where? And how did you know it was him?'

'Well, I didn't know, he didn't introduce himself.' She described her unexpected encounter with the stranger who'd appeared when she'd been sketching up on the hilltop, in the place where once Fox Close had stood.

'Ellen, he could have been anyone,' he said sharply. She had the distinct feeling he'd only just stopped himself from warning her about talking to strange men, as if she were someone careless of her own safety, a child, or a headstrong adolescent, before something like remorse made him apologize. 'Sorry, love, I didn't mean to jump on you. I reckon I've been a bit touchy lately. All sorted now though.' He gave a short laugh. 'Thanks to old Joe.'

Which was no more enlightening after all, since he didn't explain what it was, but she smiled and gave her attention to pouring more tea. Worrying about your husband was all part of being a copper's wife, especially when he was a detective; she'd learnt you had to accept that, for the duration of any serious investigation at any rate, you had to take second place. You were there in the background. Not forgotten or abandoned, by any means, but temporarily put aside – in your own interests as well as those of others.

She was relieved when he merely said again, though not with the same emphasis, 'Ellen, he could have been anyone.'

'Very likely he could, but how many strangers do we get in Folbury, wandering up there in the ruins of Fox Close, the Millars' old home?'

'You never mentioned it.'

She hadn't spoken of the meeting to Horace, either, when she'd related the swimming incident. The encounter with the stranger hadn't felt to be of any consequence, after all. The man hadn't introduced himself to her (and why should he?) before sloping off pretty quickly – and not necessarily because he didn't want his presence advertised. 'It's only just dawned on me that it might have been your man, but I don't think it's so unlikely, from what you've said,' she defended herself, refilling his teacup and pushing it across. She added slowly, 'He was nice, you know, he helped me to make my homework at least passable.'

Well, the homework wouldn't be bothering her any more, but it was sobering to think that the man she had spoken to must have been her art teacher's father, and that he was now horribly dead, the happiness of his sudden homecoming shattered, before there'd been any chance for his family to reunite, or to learn the story of those missing years. The mystery of that lay with the dead man himself.

Thinking of this, something else occurred to her. 'You know, there was something a bit . . . odd about him. Perhaps it was his face . . . it was so . . . well, I can only say, sad. Though maybe that's understandable in the circumstances.'

His plate, with the last of the fried tomatoes uneaten, was pushed away. Too late, she saw that breakfast wasn't the time to be reminded of when he'd last seen the face of the victim and what it must have looked like. It didn't seem to be that, however which had bothered him. 'What do you mean, understandable?'

'I don't know. Making a sort of nostalgic pilgrimage . . . or something, to the old house, and finding nothing left but a few stones? It must have been a bit harrowing.'

'Not if he was the sort of man I've been hearing about. From what I'm gathering, Paul Millar was the last person . . .' He stopped himself. That was the impression he was slowly gaining, but what did he know? He was beginning to think Paul Millar might have been as unknowable a person as the rest of the Millar family. Until he'd spoken with Thea yesterday, they'd seemed to be taking the shattering event which had happened to them as if it were a disturbing inconvenience, a ripple that had momentarily disturbed the tenor of their lives. On the other hand they had, as Matt had put it, shed their tears for him long ago. But heartbreak could happen twice; hearts that had broken could be mended, and re-broken. Clearly, however, the return of the hero hadn't been wholly welcome, for whatever reason.

Ellen picked up his plate, put it down again. Sat down. 'You know, I don't think it's as crazy as you might imagine, what I said. From where I'd set up my easel, you could see someone swimming in the river . . . yes, I know! I know it sounds completely mad, this sort of weather, but they were. He'd seen it, too, and said something about some people having a death wish, but in a funny sort of way. I thought it was a joke, but maybe it wasn't, perhaps going up there was a sort of last goodbye, as if he had . . . well, a premonition or something.' She stared. 'What have I said now?'

A line of damp clothes slung across a sagging string to dry. Underwear, a shirt, a towel . . . a wet swimsuit.

'Whereabouts on the river was this?'

'Directly below Fox Close.'

According to the map Gilmour had now supplied, that would be a spot on the wider, calmer waters upriver from Cooper's Lock, before the sharp bend in the river and the rocky, unnavigable stretch of water began. On the map, it had been marked as a spot often used by swimmers – in better weather than the present, one hoped – just off a scrubby acre or two known locally as The Laverocks. Easy of access, the river widened there into gravelly shallows at its edge. There had been talk of developing the area into a municipal park and recreation ground, another good intention which, like Hadley Piece, had come to nothing in these lean and depressing times.

'What's wrong?'

Easy of access, his mind said again. He put aside the disturbing notion of how easy it would have been to introduce a body there and let the current take it away – and how monstrous the idea was that Matt Millar would have found it possible after that to swim there.

He also remembered that he'd been too preoccupied, since that session with Thea Millar, to have told Ellen what the post-mortem had turned up, as he'd fully meant to do. She would want to know. Fox Close, those who'd once lived there and those who'd lived in this house, had caught her imagination and concern. 'It wasn't a premonition he had, Ellen, it was a certainty. He knew he didn't have very long to live at all.'

'What?'

He repeated what he'd had to tell Thea Millar.

'How terrible,' she said when he'd finished. 'How unfair.' The bitter irony of surviving four years of hell in the war and heaven knows what afterwards, returning home at last and then dying in such a vile way. Her eyes wide, she stared across the table, over the remains of his breakfast. 'And pointless, too. Whoever killed him surely couldn't have known. They'd only have had to wait . . .'

'I know.' Unless it had been imperative he should die quickly, before the reasons for his reappearing became apparent.

She said soberly, 'Let's just hope you get him soon – whoever it is.'

'Hope's not an option.' He pushed his chair back and went for his coat. 'We will,' he said as he kissed her goodbye.

He could have wished he felt as confident as he'd tried to sound.

After he had left, Tolly had had his run and she'd later eaten her solitary sandwich lunch, Sunday stretched out emptily for Ellen. She ought not to put off any longer that visit she should make, but she was in two minds about whether to risk it today, knowing what Sundays meant to some people. Day of rest, church attendance, having company for Sunday tea. But she hadn't much else to do today and the week ahead was full of work commitments. She could, after all, if circumstances warranted it, simply return the biscuit tin, saying where she'd found it, and depart.

The home of Amy Probert, née Lowden, now a widow, proved to be one of the rash of suburban bungalows off the Kidderminster Road, behind the ribbon development stretching insidiously further out of the town. Owning your own house in Northam was what a lot of people aspired to. It was a nice area: ornamental trees had been planted at intervals in the pavements, the bungalows were well built red-brick and the proud owners cared for them well. The handkerchief-sized front gardens, surrounded and separated by low privet hedges, showed evidence of careful tending.

Having driven past the quiet Sunday precincts of Oak Avenue and Sycamore Grove, and finally reaching Chestnut Crescent and a spot where she could park the car, Ellen found number twelve to be no exception to the general rule. The windows shone and the front step had been recently scrubbed, the knocker polished. The woman who answered was equally well scrubbed. Mid-fifties possibly, small and rounded, neatly dressed in a hand-knitted red jumper and a brown tweed skirt that gave her the look of a sharp-eyed little robin. She was clutching an apron she'd just pulled off and a good smell of baking wafted out when the door was opened. Better the day, better the deed? Ellen wasn't sure whether she found that reassuring or intimidating.

She was given a suspicious look when she introduced herself. She had a feeling it might be because the name had rung a bell and Mrs Probert was wondering if her visitor was anything to do with the police, and if so why she was here. It wouldn't have been surprising that she'd registered the name – how many Reardons after all were there in Folbury, where responsible people made it their business to know not only how their rates were spent, but who was in charge of keeping law and order? Ellen's explanation that she had obtained Mrs Probert's address from Mrs Lendrum only gained her another sharp look.

She invited Ellen to step in, however, after a moment or two's hesitation, and showed her into the front room facing the road. Neat and square, cold yet a little stuffy, it was another room used only for high days, holidays, funerals, and entertaining guests at Christmas. Clean, tidy and bland as a furniture shop window. Biscuit-coloured wallpaper and a single, small picture over the fireplace, hung so high you'd have a serious crick in your neck, making the effort to look properly at the Spanish dancer it depicted.

No Lendrum house this, and Mrs Probert was no Mrs Lendrum.

'Oh yes, I remember Clarry Henshall,' she replied in a way that said who wouldn't, 'from when we both worked for the Millars. Done well for herself, hasn't she? Henry Lendrum, eh? It didn't surprise me when I heard. She always thought a lot of herself.' Realizing she was letting her tongue run away with her, she suddenly recollected her manners. 'Well. The kettle's just on the boil. Would you like a cup of tea?'

'Thank you, I would, very much.'

'Sit yourself down then, I won't be a minute.' At the door she hesitated, summing up her visitor before giving a slight nod that apparently indicated satisfaction. 'If you wouldn't mind coming into the back. I've a Madeira cake in the oven, nearly ready.'

The 'back' proved to be a good-sized, homely living-room/kitchen twice the size of the front room, filled with the warm, delicious baking smell. Comfortable old chairs and a sofa, with a big square central table, a modern gas cooker and a sink under the window, it was everything the front room was not. Baking equipment occupied most of the table. A batch of scones just out of the oven was cooling on a wire rack.

Mrs Probert waved Ellen to a seat, cleared a space and busied herself setting out cups and saucers, fetching butter and milk from the pantry. Scones buttered and dispensed, and tea poured, she let herself flop into a chair opposite Ellen. 'You've come at the right time. I'll be glad to take the weight off my feet for a bit,' she admitted.

She was thawing and ready to be friendly now, but obviously bursting with curiosity, calculating what had brought her unexpected visitor here and not able to prevent her eyes straying to the brown paper carrier bag Ellen had brought with her.

'Lovely scones, Mrs Probert. You've a lighter hand than me,' Ellen parried, playing for time. She wasn't now quite so sure about the wisdom of bringing back something that might well have been deliberately left behind in the first place. Belatedly, she saw its return might not be altogether welcome.

At least she had hit the right note by praising the scones. They were mouth-wateringly light and fluffy, and Mrs Probert beamed. 'Practice. Mr Probert used to like one or two with his tea. And when the kids were little I'd be making them every day – biscuits and cakes an' all. Nothing lasted two minutes with them lads around.' She smiled again. 'Kept me busy, and no mistake. But would you believe it, now I've a bit of time to myself – with my hubby gone and the boys all married – I'm still at it I make cakes to sell to anybody who doesn't have the time to bake . . . they're cheaper than shop-bought, so I'm not short of customers.'

'How many boys do you have?' Ellen guessed that now the ice was broken, she would welcome the opportunity to chat.

'Three. My stepsons,' she added quickly, getting embarrassing misconceptions out of the way from the start. 'Mr Probert – Fred – was a widower when I married him, and we weren't fortunate enough to have any of our own, but they were good boys and I loved them like my own, still do – and now their children as well, though they all live away now. I've always liked children.'

The world of sadness lying behind those few last words was all too recognizable. Ellen finished her tea rather quickly, accepted a refill and took another scone to please Mrs Probert. After which, and when the tea things had been removed, she felt the time was right to approach what she'd come for and bent over the carrier bag.

Carefully, she extracted the biscuit tin, holding it in one hand while she spread the carrier protectively on the lino, being careful of any remaining flakes of rust. Mrs Probert gave a small cry and put her hand to her mouth when she saw the tin. 'Where did you get that old thing?'

Ellen explained that she was now living in what had been Fox Close's lodge.

'You live there?' The way she said it started uneasy feelings in Ellen. Remembering that non-existent door, goose pimples rose on her arms. Was there something wrong with the house? She told herself it was only surprise on the part of the other woman, it meant nothing. 'I just wanted to return this, when I heard you'd once looked after the Millar children. Photos you might want to keep.'

Amy Probert bent over the tin and lifted them out with obvious pleasure, fingering them lovingly. 'Yes, I would like to keep these. But I don't want that old book,' she added, seeing what lay beneath. 'How did you find it?'

'We haven't needed the room at the back of the house since we moved in, but we're thinking we might do something with it, and the builder came across the tin.'

She nodded. 'I won't say that house wouldn't be better with a bit more space,' she allowed. 'We couldn't have lived there much longer, not with three growing lads. They had to sleep in that room, even though it was . . . well, it wasn't what you'd call convenient, only having an outside door.'

'There was never a door from inside then?'

'There was once, before we lived there, but it had been bricked up and some dangerous steps taken away. A door would have been useful.' She rubbed at a piece of unbaked scone she'd missed on the tabletop, fetched a cloth to wipe it clean and sat down again. 'It hadn't been lived in for years before us. I'm surprised they didn't knock it down when they demolished the big house. Nasty old place it was.' It wasn't clear whether she meant Fox Close or its lodge, maybe both.

'I believe the original intention might have been to demolish it sooner or later, according to what the house agent said – until we came along and bought it.'

'We didn't stay there long, but Fred missed his garden when we moved. There wasn't much of a one in Onslow Road, and he had to take one of them allotments on Colley Street. Couldn't abide not having fresh veg for the table, Fred couldn't. That's why we bought this bungalow,' she added proudly, 'when the boys had grown up and we'd saved enough to afford it. The garden here's great for that, and lovely in summer.'

'I'm hoping to do something with the lodge garden, too,' Ellen said, not feeling the necessity to add that growing vegetables wouldn't be a priority. Later, perhaps . . .

'He'd have been tickled pink at that.'

Mention of the Colley Street allotments had given Ellen the opening she needed to broach the subject they'd so far been skating around. 'You've heard about Paul – Paul Millar – Mrs Probert?' The other woman nodded, her lips pursed. Ellen said, 'My husband is in the police and he's in charge of the investigation.'

'I wondered if that's why you'd come.'

'No, no, that's not why I'm here!' Ellen hastened to put her right. It was in no way in order for her to question this woman about a major investigation. On the other hand, there was nothing to say she couldn't listen if Mrs Probert wanted to talk – and she obviously wasn't averse to doing that.

'Terrible business,' she was saying. 'You think life can't throw any more at you, and then it does. It beats cockfighting. I mean, Paul . . . believing him killed in the war and then for this to happen! I can't understand it . . . if anybody could look after himself, it was Paul.' Her fingers worried a nub of wool in the weave of her tweed skirt. 'It was a big part of my life, looking after that family.'

She picked up one of the faded photos, showing a little boy in knickerbockers and Eton collar. 'That's him, when he was about six or seven, looking as if butter wouldn't melt, when he was such a little rip! This one's Teddy, same age. Trying to be like his big brother as usual. He thought the sun shone.'

The little boy with the curly fair hair and the cherubic face sat astride the low branch of a tree, although having attained the position, he didn't look too happy about it. He appeared to be clinging on for dear life, one arm still around the trunk, and Ellen could almost see his lower lip trembling.

Mrs Probert was looking at the family photograph, the one which included all the household, letting her finger rest on the image of her younger self when she found it, and for a long time over the baby's mother. 'She was never strong, the mistress, not made for having children, and then . . . well, she never recovered from having Teddy, died before he was three months.' The young Mrs Millar did indeed look a frail, insubstantial creature under the absurdity of that hat. 'It was a sorry situation, but we managed, down to Thea as much as anybody . . . proper little trooper she was, the way she looked out for them boys as they got older. She's the one kept that family together. Their father was no help – too wrapped up in his own concerns.'

'He must have been upset at losing his wife.'

'Not he! Angry, more like – furious she'd left him with three children, one of them a babe in arms, which he'd never so much as look at.' She stopped and bit her lip. 'I shouldn't be talking like this. It's not right to speak ill of the dead, and he was a righteous man – within his own lights, if you get my meaning. Preacher at his chapel and you know what they can be like . . . hellfire and damnation, my Fred used to say. He could frighten the children sometimes, he was the old school – children should be seen and not heard. Real strict, but fathers were in them days, weren't they? Not like now, not even a smacked bottom when they deserve it.'

'You mean he was cruel to them?'

'Oh, no, not physically! But there are other ways,' she said, tightening her lips.

Ellen could think of nothing to say and Mrs Probert, suddenly angry, burst out, 'You think I'm exaggerating? Well, how about this then?'

And out it came, a painful memory she'd perhaps lived with too long. She touched the photographs, fanned out on the table, and went on in a rush. 'It goes back to Teddy's birthday, nine or ten he must've been. He was a happy little soul, you know, no trouble, but I suppose he was lonely sometimes – being so much younger than the other two. Well, he was longing for a kitten or a puppy, but the master, he wouldn't hear of animals in the house. So what does Paul do but get hold of a mongrel bitch, telling Teddy it would be all right as long as he kept it in the lodge. Nobody else but Paul would have dared to do that, but he never thought, Paul didn't. The lodge hadn't been lived in for years and the master never went there, did he? Except he did, that one day, a bit later.'

'What happened?'

'I wasn't there at the time, there was only Teddy and Thea, but I heard all about it after, when they brought her back to the house.'

Her. 'Thea?'

'Yes. Soon as the master saw the dog, he said it would have to go – be put down. Took hold of its lead to take it away himself. But Thea wasn't having that. She went to grab the lead herself, there was a right to-do and well, between them all, that's when it happened. The master had taken to using a stick for his rheumatics and it was knocked away, he fell down that step and in the commotion the dog bit Thea, badly, on her arm. I don't suppose the poor thing knew what was happening, who it was biting, it just went mad in all the excitement. Teddy loved it, but it wasn't a good-tempered dog in the first place. What else could you expect, kept tied up in the lodge, left barking its head off all day? I expect that's how the master got to know of it . . . somebody must've heard it and told him.' She pleated the corner of her apron. 'We had to get the doctor for Thea – and have the dog seen to.'

'It *was* put down then?'

'Had to be, after that, didn't it? But it wasn't right, was it? And Paul should have known that. He wasn't a child.'

She fell quiet after her outburst, her face saying everything: that she'd spoken too openly; that she was glad she had; that Ellen could make what she wanted of what she'd heard. 'Well, it all blew over after a bit. Paul got round his father, like he always did. It doesn't matter now, anyway, best forgotten. I left Fox Close soon after. They wanted me to stay on, I'd become more of a housekeeper and cook than a nanny by then, you know. But everything had changed. Paul took himself off to Germany, Teddy was sent away to school. Besides,' she said, smiling, 'Fred had asked me to marry him.' She looked at the clock and the oven where her cake was nearly ready and Ellen saw it was time to make her departure.

'Thank you for the tea, Mrs Probert.'

'It's you I have to thank for the photos. I'm glad you found them . . . daft place to keep that tin, but Fred didn't like me writing in that diary, thought I was wasting my time, so I used to keep it out of sight, on that ledge up the chimney. It was where they used to hang hams and bacon and that to smoke, before our time, we never lit fires in there. Truth to tell, I forgot I'd left it there when we moved, and I couldn't go back for it. I was sorry about the photos but that old book, it was best left where it was. There's things best not written down for all the world to see. Let the dead rest in peace. Take it, I've got no use for it now. Burn it, I should if I was you.'

She hadn't made any move to touch the tin and looked at it as though it were a box of snakes. To please her, Ellen picked it up and put it back in the carrier bag, leaving the photographs on the table.

'It's been good to talk, Mrs Reardon,' she said as Ellen left. 'There's been too many secrets, for too long.'

FOURTEEN

The beer was as good as it always had been in the Goat and Compass, insalubrious as the pub itself was, an ancient establishment tucked away in a side street in Dudley, surviving only, Reardon suspected, by the excellence of its beer and a particularly potent cider they served. It was dark and cramped and it didn't do to look too closely into the corners – nor at the surly landlord, come to that. Percy Sweet, said the name over the door, so you had to believe it. He was an ex-wrestler, a huge man with a totally bald head except for a fringe of hair at the back, above his neck. If he thought you were looking at him the wrong way, he might refuse to serve you. But the Goat was too near the police station to be frequented by characters who had cause to avoid police company, and for that reason had always been their meeting place of choice when they wanted a quiet talk.

Ex-Detective Superintendent Howard Cherry sat nursing his pint, pork pie consumed – and with such relish Reardon wondered if he was feeding himself as well as he should since his wife had died – looking forward to a good gossip.

He finished his own lunch, an uninspired corned-beef sandwich, then sat back likewise, listening with half an ear while Cherry went on with the burden of what he'd been saying for the last five minutes.

'You should have been sitting there, Bert,' he finished. 'In my chair, I mean.'

It was a subject they'd covered more than once before Cherry's retirement, and one his old boss already knew the answer to. But even now that Cherry had actually left the force and his position had been taken by a young Turk from London, police school trained and patently ambitious to go even further than where he was now, the subject was still on his mind. 'Why have you never gone in for it, promotion?' he went on. 'You'd have been a natural. Better than bloody Knott.'

'Too rich for my blood.'

They both knew that wasn't true, or only partly so; but promotion wasn't what Reardon had joined the force for. To tell the truth, he was never entirely sure why he had; it was just something he'd known he wanted to do and thought he was cut out for, maybe if only to try and bring some sort of order into a disorderly world, and later, when he became a detective, to pit his wits against those who thought themselves wilier than the police. But he knew now he'd gone as far as he wanted to go, while he could still enjoy doing the work he did, where he wasn't entirely desk-bound. At times like the present, when there was a serious enquiry going on, you had to accept that your time wasn't your own, but otherwise the job was more than enough to absorb and satisfy his energies, mental and physical. More than any of that, since meeting and marrying Ellen, Reardon needed no reminder that he had another life outside the police force. He could never have put his marriage at risk as Cherry himself had done by the demands of the job, though Ellen wasn't another Alice Cherry, always complaining about unsocial hours and low pay, when she'd married a policeman, knowing what she was letting herself in for, after all.

Cherry sighed, evidently seeing he wasn't getting anywhere with his arguments. 'Well, anyway, Folbury seems to suit you,' he said unexpectedly, and then changed the subject. 'So what had Wonder Boy to say?' He knew Reardon had just come from a meeting with the man who had taken his place and couldn't wait to hear about it. He had become, as Reardon had always suspected he would, one of those coppers who although retired couldn't yet let go – which was the reason he'd asked his old boss and friend to meet him here. Putting that aside for the moment he let the conversation turn to where Cherry wanted it to go, to Knott, one of the new breed of policemen, well-educated young chaps who could see the way the wind of change was blowing through the police force and creating new opportunities for its personnel. Ambitious and manifestly not destined to stay in the lower orders.

The meeting today had been hurriedly slotted in to brief Knott on Folbury's new investigation. After the pleasantries were over, it hadn't taken Reardon long to see the new super wanted to keep it as low key as possible. He couldn't help wondering how much of this was due to the status of the Millar family in Folbury, and Ted's connection with other worthies there. He wondered if Knott played golf. He would bet he did.

It soon became evident Knott had decided that, given the circumstances, the odds were stacked against them in this new investigation. It could turn out to be that disaster, an unsolved murder, and though he paid sharp attention, he wouldn't be inclined to support fruitless enquiries. 'Intriguing case, and good luck with it, Reardon,' he said when Reardon had finished. 'I know it's in capable hands with you and I trust you'll keep me well informed and not be slow to request assistance if you need it – extra manpower and so on.' This last was a seemingly magnanimous offer, but one to be honoured more in the breach than in the observance, Reardon suspected. And clearly Knott had no intention of interfering personally if he could help it. 'Bit of a mystery, of course, chap turning up like that,' he'd added redundantly. At the same time, a sharp look in his eye warned Reardon to beware. He shouldn't underestimate this man; for one thing, this meeting had probably been engendered as a test of sorts, to see how he, Reardon, was shaping up to his still fairly new responsibilities.

It had lasted another half an hour but hadn't reached better heights than that. Knott stood up when a not-too-surreptitious glance at his watch indicated that the time allocated had expired. He pushed his chair back, stood up and shook hands. 'I know I can rely on you for a good result.' His pleasant tone and his smile didn't hide a warning: if that didn't happen, the future of Folbury's much-debated detective division could well be of less duration than its existence. It had been created, pushed through by Cherry, not without a good deal of opposition from the upper echelons, solely to lift the load from the increasingly overworked Dudley division; Reardon didn't feel it was in his interests to remind Knott of this.

Nor did he think now that Cherry needed to hear a full account of what had gone on at that meeting. His old-fashioned style of policing being poles apart from Knott's, it would only irritate his old boss further, and that wasn't what Reardon was here for. In any case, Cherry's next words confirmed he well knew that in the middle of a murder enquiry, Reardon wasn't likely to have had the spare time to have fixed this meeting for his old chief's benefit.

'All right, what is it you want, Bert?' he asked, filling his pipe, a noxious invasion of human rights in Reardon's opinion, though ultimately it was unlikely to make any difference to the rich mix of smoky, beery, sweaty-humanity fumes that made up The Goat's general ambience. Once lit, Cherry puffed away contentedly, a sign that he was preparing to be co-operative. He'd always been a mine of information about anything to do with the wide-flung area of his remit. Give him a lead or two and he'd recall chapter and verse of nearly every case he'd ever worked on. Like many another copper whose job had been his life, his memory was phenomenal and went back a long way, hopefully as far back as the stint he had spent in Folbury as a young constable.

Disappointingly, however, he didn't at first recall anything of the Millar family. 'I wasn't in Folbury but a few short weeks.' Just a temporary placement it had been, before he'd been drafted elsewhere.

'They weren't called Millar then,' Reardon said. 'It was Müller.'

'Oh, hold on, then. Müller – that's different. I do remember that name, now I come to think. German, wasn't it? One man and a dog outfit?'

'Yes, it was Müller, Manfred Müller, but the son changed his name before the war, to something more acceptable.' Like a lot more, including the royal family, now Windsor rather than Saxe-Coburg-Gotha. 'It's Millar now, Millar with an "a".'

'Wise move.'

'And they've come a long way since then. It's old Müller's grandchildren who run the firm now, and they're in a fair way of business by all accounts.'

'And one of them's been up to summat?'

'One of them's been found murdered.'

'Go on!'

Reardon told him all he could about the case. It didn't take long. There wasn't, after all, much to tell.

Cherry's pipe had grown cold as his thought processes worked. 'It's coming back to me. Didn't I hear the German had bought that old mansion up on the hill . . . what was it called?'

'Fox Close.'

'That's it! Big old place, nearly falling down. Caused a bit of talk, him buying it, if I'm not mistaken. They still live there, do they, these Millars?'

'No. It's been demolished and new houses built on part of the land. You remember, when we moved to Folbury, we thought of buying one, Ellen and me, but the old lodge had been left standing and it was for sale as well. As soon as she saw it, Ellen fell in love with it.' He grinned. 'The new houses didn't get a look in after that, as far as she was concerned.'

'Is that right? Didn't realize that's where you lived.'

You've forgotten, thought Reardon, surprised, we did let you know.

But it was Fox Close Cherry was interested in. 'Knocked down, was it? Well, who wants a white elephant like that? They can't survive nowadays. I suppose the old chap bit off a bit more than he could chew, buying it.'

'That seems to be the general opinion. I believe he did have a lot of work done on it, but he died suddenly before he could finish. Bad heart, I suppose.'

'It wasn't the accident, then?' Cherry stared at his pipe, which had gone out. 'No, course it wasn't . . . I'm a generation out. I reckon it must have been the son that was killed in that accident.'

'Ernest Millar?'

'I think so, if that's his name. It happened after I'd left Folbury. Motor car crash, it was. Nasty. Went out of control and ran away down some hill or other and ended up in the river. I think – no, I'm sure – his wife was killed, too.' Cherry frowned and raised his eyes to the smoke-pickled ceiling, annoyed that the cogs of his memory weren't clicking into action as smoothly as he would have liked.

'Was anyone else involved?'

'Not that I know of, but I told you I'd left the area before it happened. I misremember all the details, if I ever knew them, which I don't think I did, but as I say, it made a bit of a stir all round, that's how I happened to hear of it at all.' He mused. 'But summat's sticking in my mind. It'll come back to me. I'll let you know when it does.'

The detectives' office had a Sunday somnolence hanging over it when Reardon arrived back, an indication this wasn't the sort of investigation demanding frenzied activity before the trail went cold. Only Gilmour was there. Although it was his day off, too, he had come in and was waiting for Reardon, ready to compare notes.

Reardon didn't feel he had much to tell. The outcome of his meeting with the new super had been predictable and he was disappointed that he hadn't obtained more from Cherry. It was only when Reardon came to his mention of the accident in which Ernest Millar had died that Gilmour's interest sharpened.

'I knew there'd been something I should've remembered!' He was frowning. 'But I can't recall the details. It was just before the war, I must have been about fourteen, still at school, and you know what lads are like at that age.'

'Get someone round to the *Herald* and see what they can scout out. A motor accident like that, it would've been big news for them . . . leading family and so on. Must be in their archives.'

'Not that far back, it won't. They had a big fire, before your time, when they still had grotty old premises in Scorby Street. The whole lot went up one night. Spectacular it was. I remember a gang of us lads watching the fire brigade from as near as we were allowed. Lucky it didn't spread. We didn't have the *Herald* for weeks.'

'Somebody there must remember that accident though.'

'Sure. I'll send one of the lads round to ask.' He picked up a sheet of paper from the desk. 'This list Pugh's given us, it's fairly detailed but he can't vouch for what happened to all of them. I got Maisie to have a look at it with me last night, see if she could fill the gaps.'

'Which of course she wasn't able to do.'

Gilmour gave a wry grin. There wasn't much the females

of the Henshall clan didn't know or remember about other local families. What an aunt didn't recall, a grandmother would. A sister might have been to school with that girl who'd grown up to be no better than she should be, a second cousin twice removed who'd emigrated to America was said to be already a millionaire. Between them there wasn't much they didn't know about who lived where, who'd married whom and what they were up to.

Pugh had produced about two dozen names. Boys and girls who'd grown up together, been chums in the golden decade before the world had been turned upside down. 'We're going to have our work cut out,' Reardon remarked.

'It's not as long as it looks. A good few of them aren't going to concern us now.'

It made sad reading. Five of them indisputably dead: killed at Arras; dying of wounds sustained at Ypres, and mentioned in dispatches; missing, believed dead, awarded a posthumous Military Medal; two brothers, killed on the same day in the Somme slaughter.

Others on the list had also died, but from natural causes: a woman who'd succumbed in the Spanish flu epidemic which had swept the country just after the war; and a young man who'd been a consumptive.

Among those who remained were Thomas Turnbull, who now, with his wife, ran a pork butcher's shop, with a nice line in faggots, sausages and pies, and John Merryweather, music-shop owner and organist at the parish church. Most of the rest had moved out of the district or were otherwise lost to the Henshall clan, leaving only a clutch of spinsters who might once have married any one of those lost in the fighting.

'Neither of these two look promising, do they?' Gilmour said. 'Tom Turnbull lost a leg and walks with a crutch, and John Merryweather's blind, poor devil.'

'Not promising as suspects, no . . . and thirty years and more since they were all pals together – but some folk have long memories. We'll have to make do with what we have.' Reardon glanced at the paper again. 'What was it made them all hang out together?'

'Most of them were in a youth group attached to the chapel

– Bethesda, where Ernest Millar was a local preacher. I reckon
the big attraction must have been the table tennis, darts, tea
and buns, stuff like that.'

Reardon put his finger on the last name on the list. 'Who's
this?'

'Mrs Seddon, Dolly Seddon, she used to teach me at one
time . . . leading light in the Gilbert and Sullivan Society.
Maisie dragged me to see *HMS Pinafore* last Christmas, when
she was singing Little Buttercup. Powerful voice she still has,'
Gilmour added with a laugh, 'even though she must be eighty
if she's a day,'

'Eighty? What's she doing on the list then?'

'I added her name myself. She was the one who ran that
youth group. She knew them all and she might tell us something useful. I thought I'd go and see her tomorrow.'

Reardon nodded agreement. And looked at his watch. 'I
reckon Evensong should be ending about now. I'll go and see
if I can catch this Merryweather chap.' Pugh had put an
asterisk beside his name, to indicate he'd been a close friend
of Paul's. 'Holy Trinity's on my way home.'

'It is if you go the long way round.'

'It'll save time in the morning.'

FIFTEEN

He was beginning to feel seriously in need of his supper, and a quiet evening to clear his mind of the events of the day, leaving room for fresh thoughts, and he hoped the music he could hear as he walked up the flagged path between the headstones in the graveyard attached to Holy Trinity was the last hymn.

It was a dark night. There was no moon and the church loomed, a solid blackness in the yew-filled churchyard. Its tall old windows, lit from behind, hung like banners of rich medieval colour above the emerging spears of the thousands of daffodils that would in a few weeks make the churchyard a sight to uplift the spirit after a dreary winter. They were truly magnificent when they were in bloom; even Gravy had grudgingly admitted they were all right. Not as good a show as some he could mention in the Yorkshire Dales, mind, but not bad.

He reached the entrance and slipped inside, grasping the iron ring of the heavy oak door tight while shutting it as quietly as possible on the closing notes of the hymn. It made a slight clanging noise despite his efforts, but the congregation, not large, was now shuffling to sit again, and only one old woman turned her head to give him a cursory glance.

Slipping into a pew at the back, he settled himself on the hard, too narrow seat as best he could while the service reached its close, willing himself to let his mind go blank. He wanted to start afresh on the coming meeting, without the faint, lingering unease about Cherry – the man he'd worked with ever since joining the police, his mentor and later his friend – intruding, as it had seemed insistent on doing ever since they'd spoken. A lapse of memory, he told himself, was something that happened to everyone at times. But Cherry? No, he wasn't allowing himself to go down that road just now.

He leant back, letting the church ambience wash over him, the smell of old stone and dry timber, and possibly a lingering trace of High Church incense: a red sanctuary lamp burned in the chancel, there was lace on the altar. The rector's voice was mellifluous: '. . . as the shades lengthen, the evening comes, the busy world is hushed, the fever of life is over, and our work is done . . .'

How long was it since he had sat, not in this church, but in any church, following the rituals and listening to those lovely, once-familiar words? Not since the most bitter war the world had ever known. Not since he had questioned the existence of any God who could let that happen.

He sat where he was until the congregation had trickled out and then walked down the carpeted central aisle to the front as the last notes of the organ voluntary died away. The organist swung round on his stool as he approached. 'I've been thinking, Rector—' he began.

'I'm sorry, Mr Merryweather, it's not the rector,' Reardon said quickly. 'I'm a police officer, Detective Inspector Reardon. If I might have a word?'

He extended a hand without thinking, then almost drew back when he remembered, but Merryweather had sensed it was there and met it with a firm clasp. He was a big, good-looking man, with a rugby player's physique and a strong, craggy face, with nothing obvious there to indicate that he was blind.

'What can I do for you, Inspector?'

'I'm investigating the death of a man named Paul Millar. I believe you were a friend of his?'

They were directly facing, and it was disconcerting to be reminded that Merryweather wasn't studying his features as Reardon was studying his. He was silent for so long, Reardon wondered if he might not have heard. 'So it's true, then? He was killed?' he asked at last.

'I'm afraid so.' It hadn't taken long for that to become common knowledge once it had been confirmed. He was bracing himself for when the national papers got hold of it.

Silence lay between them until the organist said, 'Anything I can do . . . of course. Though I doubt I can be of much help, it's so long since I saw Paul. The last time was when we shook hands and said goodbye before we both joined up.'

'That's part of the problem we're having, Mr Merryweather. Nobody appears to have seen him since then, apart from the one or two occasions when he came home on leave early in the war. Where he's been since the Armistice is anyone's guess. Hence the focus for us on his life before then – before he left Folbury and joined up, when he was a young man. Anything that might give us a lead on what led up to this. That's where I'm hoping you may be able to assist us.'

He sensed a slight drawing back. 'It's going to be difficult, talking about him and . . . and what's happened to him. I was, after all, his closest friend.'

'I understand.' Reardon reflected that the same claim had been made by Wesley Pugh, albeit in a different light.

'We can talk better if you're sitting down, Inspector,' the organist said suddenly. He pushed his stool back and stood up, overtopping Reardon, himself a six-footer, by a couple of inches. He touched Reardon's arm lightly and unerringly guided him to the front pew where he waved him to sit, taking his own seat a few feet further along, half-turned towards Reardon.

The silence surrounded them as he collected his thoughts, the distinctive, enclosed silence of an empty church, broken only by sounds still coming from the back. There had been no sign of the priest since he'd disappeared into the vestry; that was the verger, gathering hymn and prayer books, turning out lights. The acrid scent of the extinguished altar candles cut through the sweeter one of spring flowers – the shop-bought kind, arranged at the chancel no doubt by the devoted ladies on the flower rota.

Another light went out. He wasn't going to have long before it would be locking-up time. It struck him suddenly that he had perhaps been in too much of a rush to get another visit over and done with, that this wasn't the ideal place for the sort of conversation he wanted to have. Better to have waited, perhaps, until he could have spoken to Merryweather either at home, or in his music shop. If it wasn't a suitable time to talk, he could see him when it was more convenient, he told Merryweather.

'Here and now will do very well. I have a church key, and I live nearby. I'm in no hurry.'

Reardon recalled there had been no mention in the notes he'd read of him being married, and the lack of haste suggested he lived alone and there would be no one expecting him home for supper. He felt slightly sad for the man, though less guilty at detaining him.

The verger called out something from the back and Merryweather answered that he would lock up. Goodnights were said, the verger departed, leaving them alone in the empty church. Reardon retrieved the thread of what Merryweather had been saying about his friendship with Millar. 'Paul seemed to have had a lot of friends,' he remarked. 'No enemies that you knew of?'

'Enemies? Paul? Good Lord, no. He didn't have any enemies. Everyone liked him.'

Reardon let this familiar eulogy pass: the victim who was immediately elevated to sainthood on his demise. Sometimes, it was even true. Merryweather at least seemed as though he genuinely believed it of Paul and wasn't merely spouting a mawkish sentimentality. After he'd spoken, he sat easily in the corner of the pew and stretched one casual arm along its side, revealing his Braille watch, a bulbous contraption with a hinged cover and raised dots that enabled him to read the time. A minute, passed, then he said in a low voice, 'You would imagine, wouldn't you, that after seeing so much carnage, one would become accustomed to violent death, but . . .' He broke off. 'Were you in the last lot, Mr Reardon?'

'Yes, I was.' It was a question that never needed to be asked of Reardon by those who possessed their sight. 'But one never does become accustomed, thank God.'

'Even though you're a policeman?' As soon as it was said, Merryweather followed it with a sober: 'Forgive me. That was crass.' He let a second pass. 'So what is it exactly you want from me? How can I help?'

'Let's start with how long you'd known Paul.'

The slight reserve Reardon had sensed had gone. He was now seemingly more than willing to be co-operative; after thinking it over for a moment or two, he began to talk freely of the time when he and Paul had known each other, how they had met at school and become firm friends, perhaps in more detail than needed. Reardon didn't stop him, he wanted to know what the guarded response meant when Wesley Pugh's name came up. Although they had all been pupils at King's, that highly thought of, prestigious school, Pugh had been there only by virtue of winning a scholarship, according to Connie Randall, whereas Merryweather had probably been one of the fee-paying pupils. His accent was cut-glass; Reardon learnt that his father had been a high-ranking cleric. He'd gone on to Oxford after the King's School to take a music degree and obtained a commission in the Royal Navy when war was declared.

Any or all of this might well have made for unbridgeable differences between himself and a boy like Pugh, but counter to this was Merryweather himself, who was impressing Reardon as a man without that sort of prejudice.

'Mr Merryweather—'

'I'm usually called John,' the organist said with a smile. 'Such a mouthful, Merryweather.'

Reardon didn't much like conducting interviews on such friendly terms, not unless the interviewees were at least a generation younger than himself, but he could hardly say so. 'As you wish,' he said, continuing where he'd left off, with an inward instruction to himself to by-pass the necessity by avoiding either Christian or surname in future. 'As you knew Paul so well, you must have been aware that he and his father were not always on the best of terms.'

'That's an understatement!'

'Mainly because Paul had had other ideas than joining the family firm, I understand.'

'That's right. Cars, aeroplanes were his passion, a phase both of us went through for a while. He dreamt of flying, being a pilot.' His tone became reminiscent, slightly wistful. 'We'd go to car rallies, aerial shows . . . Brooklands, when we could afford it . . . Sometimes, not often, his sister came too. She loved cars too.' He laughed shortly. 'Paul had a mad idea of crossing the Channel for the Monte, the Monte Carlo rally, but that was pie in the sky . . . we never got that far. We were a bit obsessed. Young men. You know how it is.'

Only too well. Reardon's own youth had been coloured by something very similar. Except that he had been driven by the need to earn his living, he hadn't had a father able to fund him, and his ambition had eventually resulted in nothing more exotic than owning a second-hand motorcycle. Still, it had been his, he'd obtained it through his own efforts, and he'd revelled in it. He'd been so motorcycle mad he had in fact done his bit as a despatch rider over there in France during the war years, until the incident which had landed him in hospital for months. And even that hadn't stopped him from buying another, bigger machine as soon as he was discharged from hospital, deemed fit enough to ride again. An inseparable part of his life it had been until recent years, until the purchase of the small car he and Ellen now shared. He hadn't been able to relinquish the bike altogether, and for a moment there, the mention of motorbikes had given him a pang for his lost love, now languishing under covers at the back of his small wooden garage. Bit by bit, he'd reluctantly been forced to the conclusion that his days of careering about the wide-open countryside on two wheels with the wind on his face were behind him, but it didn't stop him having regrets.

'I understand Paul was part of the Bethesda chapel youth group. Were you a member, too?'

Merryweather gave a short laugh. 'My father was rector here at the time, and an honorary canon of Worcester cathedral. He was reasonably tolerant, but he'd have had a fit if I'd even suggested joining the Bible-punchers, as I'm afraid he called them. I wouldn't have joined anyway . . . my music practising didn't allow for it. That mattered far more to me . . . even more than fiddling around with cars. But Paul . . . he was always talking of leaving his father for something in that line, though to be honest, he would have found it difficult not to have cash in his pocket – he didn't work for nothing at Millars, he had a wage like everyone else, and a little car of his own. Of course, he knew that meant strings attached . . .' He hesitated. 'I suppose in the end, everything came to a head, the usual thing, this time with Paul throwing in the towel and heading off to Germany. We lost touch for a while.'

Either Merryweather wasn't going to say anything about Paul's upset with Pugh over Connie Randall, or he hadn't known about it. It was becoming evident that the secretive streak in Paul had made him adept, even then, at keeping the various strands of his life in different compartments.

'But you did meet again?'

'When he came back from Germany – which he did eventually, after he'd married, but we didn't see much of each other. I was up at Oxford and afterwards I was too busy trying to earn my living as a musician to have time – or money – for messing around with machinery. We only met perhaps half a dozen times after that – times when I came home to visit my parents. We'd have a drink together, to catch up, that sort of thing . . . as I said, the last time was just at the beginning of the war. He asked me why I wasn't enlisting in the RFC as he was, and I laughed and said I valued my life too much. Unlike me, he was always a bit reckless, defying authority, as long as . . .' He broke off abruptly. He had said more than he meant to say. As long as he didn't have to face the consequences?

'It was the navy for me . . .' He paused, unconsciously fingering the big watch. 'We'd no idea, had we? Torpedoed by a U-boat on convoy across the North Sea. But I survived.' He shrugged although his voice had dropped an octave and the unseeing eyes stared straight ahead, seeing God knows what.

It hadn't all been trench warfare, thought Reardon. Men dropping from the skies like burning torches. Sinking in the icy North Sea. The darkness that would never lift. Nobody wants to remember the war, but we all do, even those who never, ever speak of it.

'He'd rather shocked me, you know,' Merryweather went on in his normal voice, turning to face Reardon once more, 'by saying, well, he didn't value his own life too much just then, either, though I knew it was because he was still raw after the accident.'

'We're talking about the car crash when his mother and father were killed?'

A moment passed. 'His mother? No, Paul's mother died when he was a child, not long after young Teddy was born.'

'I understood there were two people killed in the crash – Ernest Millar and his wife—'

'Ernest was killed, but it wasn't *his* wife, Paul's mother, who was with him. It was Liesl who died. Paul's wife.'

How easily misconceptions could arise: accepting Cherry's mistake about the generations, with other things going on in his head so he had allowed it to slide past him, forgetting that the Millar children's mother, Ernest's wife, had died when Teddy had still been an infant in arms. He'd been aware that Paul's wife had died young, too, and he blamed himself for not enquiring into what circumstances. She had died just before he went to war. It could provide the strongest reason yet put forward as to why, when the fighting ended, he had not wanted to come back to his old life in Folbury.

He arrived home feeling jaded and his mind full of the meeting he'd just had with Merryweather, but his mood lifted at the good smell of roast pork and the sight of a pie just out of the oven. Thank the Lord for an intelligent wife! Not born with a wooden spoon in her hand and a natural inclination to cook, like Maisie, Gilmour's wife, it hadn't taken Ellen long to work out the best way to a man's heart, etc. She'd applied herself to learning how to cook, with her usual enthusiasm. Sometimes she was successful, and sometimes she even admitted she might be beginning to enjoy it.

He put his arms round her and smelt the sweet, familiar smell of her skin and the lily-of-the-valley scent she used. He didn't tell her that her apron also bore traces of the odour of roast pork and baking apples. What was wrong with the glorious smell of good home cooking?

He suddenly wished it had been possible to say to John Merryweather that he had understood the difficulties of returning to civilian life; that he too had returned home with a scarred face – and a disillusioned mind. But it was better not to. He'd been infinitely more fortunate than Merryweather. He had returned to find a renewed friendship with a woman who had kept faith with him during the war, a friendship which had quickly blossomed into what they had now, something so all-encompassing there just weren't any words for it.

Ellen drew away. 'A scotch before we eat?'

'How do you manage to read my mind every time?'

'Maybe because at this time of day it's always open at the same page.'

'Only if you join me, then.'

Over supper, she asked, 'How's it going?'

'Early days yet, love, but we'll get there,' he answered, again with the downbeat feeling that although it was true, he'd already been saying this too many times just lately, and with just as little conviction. And yet, the conversation with Merryweather had started a new train of thought. Which he didn't want to think about too much before talking it over with Gilmour, in case it lost its initial impetus.

After they'd finished eating, Ellen made herself comfortable with a cushion on the floor by the fire, her back to the sofa. Tolly flopped beside her on the side nearest the fire, away from the draught that came from under the door. 'Self-preservation should be your middle name,' she told him, lifting him firmly to her other side and saying to Reardon, 'I went to see Amy Probert today.'

'Amy Probert?'

'The woman Maisie's Auntie Clarice told me about, the one who used to live here.'

'Ah. The writer of that diary you found up the chimney.'

'Yes, the one who looked after the Millar children when they were small, according to Auntie Clarice. I went to return the diary.'

'And what did she have to say?' He asked because he could see she was dying to tell him, even though he felt that he'd really had enough of the Millars for one day. 'Carry on. I'm all ears.'

She told him what had been said and how Amy had reacted to having the diary returned.

He raised an eyebrow when he saw her frown. 'And . . .?'

Ellen hesitated. 'Paul didn't go away to school, he went to King's, am I right?' He nodded. 'Amy said Teddy was sent away. I wonder why.'

'Maybe their father just thought it offered better schooling than King's – though if he did think that, he was a fool. It's a damn good school, from what I hear.' But Wesley Pugh, he recalled, had said Paul might have been there only so his father could keep an eye on him.

'She said Teddy was *sent* away, not that he went. As if he'd been packed off or something.'

'Sent away, went away . . . just a different way of saying the same thing?'

'Not in the way she said it. Especially since she'd just told me about something rather horrible that had happened.' She hadn't been able to get the story of the dog incident out of her mind. Her hand went out to stroke Tolly behind the ears as she told him what Amy Probert had said.

'Interesting,' Reardon said thoughtfully. 'Thea still has the scar on her arm – and she doesn't like dogs. Scared for ever probably, after what happened.' Little wonder the barking dog in the Inkerman Terrace yard had caused such an unaccountable outburst from her when she'd heard it. 'Not a pretty story, is it?'

'It upset Mrs Probert, just remembering it. I probably ought not to have gone and stirred things up. I only thought she might want the photographs.'

He gave her a thoughtful look. 'Was she pleased to have them?'

'Oh yes, I'm sure she was.'

'There you are then. You did the right thing.'

'I hope so.' She picked up a piece of mending and began stitching the lace on the hem of a slip. Reardon's book stayed open on his lap. Boswell was proving to be harder going than he'd expected. Something was unsettling him. It was a not unfamiliar sensation, a quick stab of excitement that usually meant something had occurred or been said, or done, its significance not understood. He'd learnt better than to drive it away with over-thinking. Try to capture it and it would slide from his grasp like a slippery fish. If it was important enough it would come back to him.

SIXTEEN

Dolly Seddon had long since retired from teaching. She'd been an institution even when Gilmour had been her pupil. One of the more popular teachers, she was generally regarded as a good sort; she sometimes even made jokes. Eccentric in her dress and sometimes in the methods she used to teach, she kept good-humoured order in her classes. On the other hand, she wouldn't stand any nonsense and you were punished if you did wrong, though not with the cane, like old Pa Siggins, the hated headmaster who took Standard Six. She was Dolly to all the pupils, though not to her face.

Gilmour supposed now that Mrs Seddon had been quite unusual in that she was married, unlike the other female teachers on the staff, though it would never have occurred to any of her pupils to think it strange, or indeed to imagine any of the staff might have a life of their own outside the school gates. Teachers were just teachers. Gilmour hadn't known then that she was married to the dentist at the far end of the high street.

The detached villa-type house where Arthur Seddon, now deceased, had lived and had his dental practice was one of the prosperous properties built along the formerly quiet high street which had meandered dozily through Folbury on the way to Birmingham until, as the town grew, shops began to be squeezed in between, wherever there was space or when a house could be demolished. By now, commerce had triumphed, the high street was a hive of activity, there were even up-to-the-minute traffic lights installed at one of the busy junctions and most of the residential properties which remained had been divided for two families, or otherwise designated.

Mrs Seddon's house was situated towards the end of the high street, where the shops began to peter out and it became the Birmingham Road proper. It was still fronted by a yard or two of space fenced by iron railings and occupied by dusty, overgrown laurels.

Surprisingly, there was only one bell, suggesting she was still the sole occupant, and indeed she opened the door herself. It was a handsome door, high and wide, rather like the woman who stood there. A woman nearly as tall as Gilmour himself; still larger than life in every way, she seemed to fill the doorway.

He had telephoned to make the appointment, just saying the police would like to speak to her, not giving his name, but she recognized him at once, though he reckoned it must have been going on for thirty years since she'd last seen him. His ginger hair. It usually was.

Not entirely, it seemed. 'I'd know that cheeky grin anywhere, Joe Gilmour,' she said, welcoming him in with a beaming smile of her own. 'Very good at getting you out of trouble, it was . . . and now you're the one chasing the troublemakers. I hope you're not after me.'

He didn't find her that much changed either. Still the same colourful personality, an impression reinforced by clothes which owed nothing to fashion, past or present. A loose red dress, multiple necklaces, Turkish beaded slippers. Her eyes were still bright and lively. She couldn't have been young when she'd taught him at Wardley Street. She had in fact eventually become headmistress, when the numbers of pupils in each year winning coveted scholarships to the two Folbury grammar schools (boys' and girls') had shot up from practically none to at least a dozen. Gilmour had considered himself lucky enough to have won one of them, even if it was by the skin of his teeth.

The room she showed him into was as warm and colourful as Dolly herself, filled with old furniture, untidy with everyday living – books, newspapers, dozens of photographs, mainly of children – and, he thought, a lingering smell of cigarette smoke. Tea was waiting, keeping hot under a knitted cosy. He guessed it had been brewed some time since, judging from its colour as she poured. Reardon would have approved. Gilmour sipped it bravely, though it felt to be taking the enamel off his teeth. The chocolate biscuits were spot on, though.

'We saw you in *HMS Pinafore* at Christmas, Mrs Seddon, Maisie and me. We really enjoyed your performance.'

'Thank you, that's nice. You won't get another chance. It was my swan song. The old voice isn't what it was.'

'They'll miss you in the G and S.' He was sure this was true. She'd been much in demand for the contralto parts, especially the comic ones, for years.

'What about you, Joe? I must say, I never thought to see you in the police! You married Maisie Henshall, didn't you?'

'And we have a little girl now, she's two,' he said, producing the photo from his wallet where it lived. It was duly admired, and they chatted until they'd drunk their tea and nearly all the chocolate biscuits were gone and he judged it time to tell her he was one of the officers enquiring into the death of Paul Millar.

Like everyone else, she would have heard about the discovery of his body, if nothing further. He didn't suppose Paul had ever been a pupil of hers, though. Prep school and King's School educated, Wardley Street Elementary was a long way from that. Yet she didn't seem surprised the police were enquiring of her.

'I understand he used to go to the youth group you ran at Bethesda?'

'Under pressure from his father at first. But he soon came of his own accord, like the others who weren't regular chapel attenders.'

'It was open to outsiders?'

'It was started by the minister, but chapel membership wasn't compulsory. I was roped in to run the club, but I only did it for a short while. It seemed like a good idea at the time, but it wasn't really my cup of tea. It was a strain and I was glad to leave as soon as they were able to get someone else to run the club.'

'A strain?' Gilmour laughed. 'After teaching at Wardley Street?'

'Oh, it wasn't that I couldn't handle it! Most of the young folk were from families of the congregation anyway, so they'd no option but to behave themselves, but the others . . . it was somewhere to go in the evenings, free lemonade, tea and a bun – and a chance to meet the opposite sex,' she added with a smile. 'But they could get a bit rowdy . . . ones like Paul and Wesley Pugh and their cronies.'

Cronies he noticed, with its derogatory connotations, rather than 'friends' or 'pals'. 'Did you have trouble with them?' he asked, though not able to envisage a situation she wouldn't have been able to deal with.

She sighed again. 'They were only boys, that's what I tell myself. Wesley was all right. Easily influenced, though you might not think it now.' She quickly corrected herself. 'No, that's doing him an injustice. Paul had a way with him, you know. I think it was more that he seemed to Wesley to be everything he himself wasn't, and perhaps wanted to be, and that was why he shut his eyes. Both of them did, he and my Philip.'

He followed her gaze to the cluttered mantelpiece where a silver-framed photograph had a prominent place amongst various knick-knacks, postcards, a pot of pencils, a letter half-tucked behind the clock. The photo showed a boy of about fifteen, thin-faced and pale, looking nothing like his mother. 'Your son?' He had never envisaged her with children of her own.

'Yes. He was at Kings, one of their scholarship boys, the same as Wesley. They were very close. He was clever, exceptional in fact – and I say that as a teacher, not as his mother. He was our son, but I'm not exaggerating. He was a certainty for Oxbridge.' The animation had left her face, leaving her looking her age. Her eyes when she looked at the photograph were moist with unshed tears, and he couldn't help noticing the past tense.

'The war?' he asked gently.

After a while she said, 'He isn't dead, Joe. He's in New Zealand, where he's lived for the last thirty years. I only hear from him on my birthday in July and a card at Christmas.'

He realized now that the unfamiliar stamp on that envelope behind the clock must be a New Zealand one. He could see how painful the subject was for her and he balked at pushing her further; at the same time, he didn't think she would have told him that much if she hadn't wanted him to know the rest. 'What happened, Mrs Seddon?'

'Oh, it was all so stupid! They were only boys,' she repeated. 'Philip hadn't yet left school. But that's no excuse. They were old enough to know better.'

After that she fell silent for so long, looking into the glowing embers as if seeing the past, that he asked the question again. When she answered it was almost to herself. He had to strain his ears to catch. 'He did an unforgivable thing – Paul, I mean – or he would have done, if it hadn't been for Philip. The boy never really knew what he was doing.'

He was losing track. 'The boy? Philip?'

'No, no. Young Teddy. Teddy Millar. His father used to bring him to the junior Bible class he led on Sunday afternoons, before the adult one. Morning Sunday school and evening service as well. Oh, I know, I know!' She'd seen his expression. Sunday school once a week had been more than enough for Gilmour.

'What about Teddy?' he prompted.

'Well, you know, after the junior class was over, the boy was left on his own, to wait in the office for his father to take him home after he'd finished the adult one. It never seemed to bother him, he always had a book with him, or a pencil and paper – he liked to draw. He was never any trouble to anybody . . .' She paused, reluctant to go on. 'It was Mr Millar's – Ernest's – responsibility to look after the chapel finances, and he kept the money, from the collections and so on, locked up in a cupboard in the office, but the keys in a drawer, foolish man. Anyone could have got into it. There was never much there, but all the same it was a temptation. You've heard of the Monte . . . the Monte Carlo rally, I suppose?'

He nodded and she went on: 'Paul was determined to go. How is it boys are so obsessed with cars? Only he'd spent his allowance, you see. It was meant to be a great lark. He had a plan – if you could call such a hare-brained scheme a plan – for the three boys, Paul, Wesley and . . . and Philip, to drive there, and he knew there was cash in the cupboard. If he'd stopped to think, even for a moment, he would have realized a few pounds couldn't possibly be anywhere near enough, for a start . . . well, Teddy was only a child and he would have done anything for Paul . . . and no one would have noticed what he was doing while he was alone in the office, waiting for his father.'

'You're saying Paul got Teddy to steal it for him?'

'"Borrow" was the word that was used. Teddy did as he was told, took the money, put it in his satchel and ran outside to give it to Paul, who was waiting, with Philip.' She sighed. 'But when it actually came to it, Philip was suddenly appalled at what they were doing. He snatched the money and went back inside with it, dragging Teddy along with him. It was too late. The Bible class had finished early and Ernest Millar was already in the office, looking for Teddy. The child was speechless with terror by then and Philip . . . well, he couldn't let him be blamed. Or wouldn't. So he just handed the money back.'

'He took the blame himself?' Gilmour was staggered. He also wondered if Philip could have been as intelligent as his mother thought him, if he'd expected Ernest Millar to swallow that.

'I know what you're thinking, Joe. I don't suppose Ernest Millar believed Philip for one moment. He *must* have known Paul was at the bottom of it, but his pride wouldn't allow him to admit it. And to do Paul justice, he did come forward when he saw how things were going, but his father chose not to believe him – or not in public. All he would allow was that since the money hadn't been lost, he would overlook it . . . as long as Philip didn't associate with Paul again.'

'What about Teddy? And Wesley Pugh? They could have told the truth, surely?'

'Teddy was too terrified to say a word. And I don't know whether Wesley was actually involved, or knew what was going on. I'd like to think he didn't, although I do know his friendship with Paul broke up about then, so perhaps he did. He was a decent boy, just young. Maybe it opened his eyes in time, made him see what a fool he'd been.'

'And . . . Philip?'

'Philip. Well, God knows why he'd ever allowed himself to go in with the scheme in the first place. That wasn't how he'd been brought up. It left him with a load of guilt, bitterly ashamed that he'd been so irresponsible. His father and I knew something was wrong, but we only learnt the truth later, when he told us he wanted to leave England and try his luck in New Zealand, live with his godfather. We were shocked, but he couldn't be convinced that it was all a storm in a teacup, would be forgotten next week. Yes, Joe, I know it was an extreme reaction, but that was Philip, always too thin-skinned, too sensitive. Nothing we could do or say would persuade him otherwise. I hoped he'd be back home when he realized what a fool he'd been, but he found a job over there, trained as a teacher, and he's never returned. I've learnt to live with it, what else is there to do after all? But it broke his father's heart. He wasn't well when it happened and I watched him die, slowly, never forgiving the Millars, Paul in particular, to the day he died.'

Gilmour shook himself free of a brief, mad moment, seeing the letter with the New Zealand stamp tucked behind the clock, one of those twice-a-year letters, birthday and Christmas, and imagining Millar's past catching up with him, even from the other side of the world. Logistics were against it, even if imagination wasn't. It was simply a coincidence too far to imagine Philip Seddon had been conveniently in Folbury when Paul had made his own return to his home town.

Afterwards, retelling the tale to Reardon, he knew that although what he'd learnt had revealed an interesting slant on Paul as a very young man, it hadn't thrown much light on what had led to the present situation and he was still more inclined to focus enquiries on events less remote. 'Wouldn't you think they'd have pressed Paul for more information on where he'd been living – the Millars, I mean?' he said restlessly. 'North London, didn't they say? There must be somewhere there where they build cars, or aeroplanes, somewhere or other where he might have worked? We could've set up some enquiries if they had.'

'Well, they didn't, and we can't,' Reardon said irritably. 'He could have worked anywhere, doing anything, and not necessarily in the place where he lived, what's more. North London covers a lot of ground. We still have options to exhaust here first.'

It was beginning to sound like a mantra, and Gilmour rolled his eyes. 'Getting less by the hour.'

Reardon nodded absently. His mind was still on what Gilmour had just heard from Dolly Seddon. 'I wonder what part Pugh really played in all that?' he said.

He was still wondering that several hours later. He had been staring too long at notes, reports, his own tentative scribblings, and the words were beginning to dance on the page. Somewhere, if he looked long enough, a pattern must begin to emerge. So far it remained obscure. His eyes itched, he rubbed them, and when he took his hands away, he realized the outer office was dark. It was after six, everyone else had cleared off and he was the only one still working. He shuffled his papers into order, stood up and stretched. He was about to reach for his coat when the telephone rang.

'Working late as usual, Bert? I thought I'd catch you,' Cherry said. 'I've remembered a bit more about that accident.'

As he walked home across Castle Bridge, Reardon fancied the weather had taken a turn for the better. In contrast to the previous weeks, the air seemed to have a softer, balmy feeling to it, as if spring really was on the way at last. But it was only the beginning of March and not to be trusted, and a chilly mist hung over the water. The Fol was never a quiet river, or not here at any rate, but tonight it seemed calmer, less restless. It was a dark night and the gas lamps set at intervals along the bridge reflected on the water below. Further along, mirror images of the lighted town were reflected. Tonight he didn't stop to look, still thinking of the last few minutes and what Cherry had told him. He was walking quickly when he heard running foot-steps coming up behind him, overtaking, someone else wanting to get home before it began to rain again, no doubt. Someone who came close – too close. His trained reaction was automatic. He didn't need to think, just grabbed the hand that was seizing his coat, near his pocket. He whirled round as whoever it was tried to pull away, and heard a voice saying, 'No, please!'

It was a girl. She was young, plump and clearly not used to running. She was panting heavily, and her round face was an alarming shade of red. 'Please, I'm so sorry. Please, could I have a word?'

So many pleases, such a look of entreaty mixed with embarrassment. She couldn't meet his eyes.

He removed the hand still clutching his coat. 'What do you want?' he asked, more gently than he might have done had she not said at the same time, their words overlapping, 'It's . . . it's about Paul Millar, Inspector.'

She knew who he was, she knew something about Millar. How come? She looked about eighteen, twenty at most, Imogen Randall's generation. But he could see she was earnest, agitated, and he didn't like the ragged way she still breathed, though she appeared to be calming down. 'I shouldn't have run like that,' she gasped. 'Asthma. But I wanted to catch you. To tell you something.'

She'd have been wiser not to have grabbed him like that, either. His response had been instinctive, police-trained, and he might well have landed her flat on her back.

Castle Bridge on a cold dark night, with people hurrying homewards past them and several throwing curious glances, was no place to talk. He was on the point of telling her she should come into Market Street the following day if she had anything to say, but he had a quick change of mind. However much a waste of time it might turn out to be, he should listen now to what she had to say.

'You look as though you could do with a cup of tea, Miss . . .?'

'Hallam. Jenny Hallam.'

'Let's get inside, under cover.' He jerked his head in the direction of the tin-roofed shack at the far end of the bridge and began to walk towards it.

'All right,' she said, and accompanied him meekly.

The little eating place, Stringers, had looked as though it was falling down for years, but somehow it remained standing, dirty, dishevelled-looking, unappealing. Inside, though, it was spotless. Scrubbed wooden floors, one bare-topped rectangular table, likewise scrubbed, and straight, hard chairs squeezed around it for eight people – the largest number Stringers allowed to be accommodated at one time.

Mrs Stringer, round, unsmiling and uncompromising, served a hot, hearty meal to first-comers every day at midday to a menu of her own choosing. You had to be early to get a seat, willing to share the table and to take what was on offer. She'd previously closed at one thirty but she'd lately taken to re-opening at four for an hour, to serve tea, sandwiches to order, slices of seed cake or slab cake stiff with fruit, but the new venture didn't appear to be as popular yet as the dinner-hour one. Folbury folk were used to having their tea at home.

On this dark, windy evening the place was empty of other customers. Reardon bought two cups of tea and on second thoughts, a slice of slab cake for Miss Hallam. She looked as though she liked cake, plenty of it, he thought uncharitably, thinking of the single malt, his evening meal and Ellen waiting for him at home. Then he thought, too late, as he joined her chubby form at the table that maybe cake hadn't been such a good idea. But he was glad to see her breathing was steadier and her colour more normal. He could see now that she was pretty, with a pale skin and freckles on the bridge of her nose. Her hair was light brown and wavy, just now curling in damp tendrils round her face. Her eyes were large and blue, but very troubled.

She sipped the tea gratefully but only toyed with the cake. Evidently, what she had to say was too much on her mind. He let her take her time and it wasn't long before it all came out in a rush.

'I work at Purbright's,' she began, 'and I saw you when you came in the other day. I have to talk to you, because of Eva – Miss Bancroft. She'd never tell you herself, she's far too shy.'

Bancroft? Oh, yes, the grey-cardiganed lady who had brought in the coffee. He remembered her, and someone else sitting at a desk in the reception area, this girl no doubt. 'I wouldn't otherwise,' she went on, 'not for anything. I wasn't sure whether I should or not – I don't want to lose my job – until I saw you on the bridge and then I knew if I didn't do it now, I might not do it at all. I mean, Mr Charles – he's always called that to avoid mix-ups, because his father's only semi-retired and still comes into the office for an hour or two every day – well, Mr Charles is a good boss, he's very kind and I like working there, but still, it's not right.'

'What isn't right, Miss Hallam?' asked Reardon, his patience tried. It was evident that breathing problems weren't enough to stop her from rattling on, it was late and he wished she'd get to the point. 'Just take it easy, start at the beginning.'

'Oh, Jenny, please.' She blushed, hesitated, popped a piece of slab cake into her mouth and chewed. It seemed to give her courage. 'It's Eva, Miss Bancroft, you see. She's been so nice to me since I started working there. I've been there six months, but I'm afraid I'm still not very good. It's hard to keep a job, you see, when you have bad asthma.' Even mention of it made her wheeze a little. 'I have to go sick a lot and so I never get the chance to learn a job properly, but my dad's on the dole and with the little ones we need the money at home. But it's different at Purbright's. Eva understands, she's so good, she covers up for me when I make mistakes . . . and I *am* getting better,' she finished earnestly.

'You said you had something to tell me about Paul Millar,' he prompted. Her breathing was becoming noisy again and he was beginning to feel sorry for her. She seemed like a nice girl if not, he thought, all that bright.

'Oh. Oh, yes.' Her face flushed and her plump cheeks wobbled. Then suddenly she pushed her plate away and took a deep breath. 'Mr Purbright told you Paul Millar never came to the office, didn't he?'

'How do you know that?'

'He must have done. He tried to pretend to us it wasn't Paul Millar who came in that day, but we knew it was. Eva knew, anyway.'

Reardon felt slightly winded. It took a minute to sort out what she'd said. 'Which day was this?'

'It was the seventeenth, the day we make up the accounts.'

'And what made you think it was him?'

'Well, I didn't know who he was, of course, just the gentleman Mr Charles was expecting, that he'd told us to show straight in, but Eva knew him. She'd known him when they were both young and she recognized him straight away. It gave her the shock of her life to see him, when everyone had thought he was dead, killed in the war. But he just looked straight through her when she spoke to him and said that Mr Purbright was expecting him and then Mr Charles came out of his office, shook hands with him and they went inside and shut the door.'

'Could Miss Bancroft have been mistaken? People change—'

'She swears it was him. Their families went to the same chapel, she and Paul were in Sunday school class together for a while. Well, she went in later to take some letters for Mr Charles, and he could see she was upset and asked her why. She said straight out that the man that she'd seen was Paul Millar. But he told her she must be imagining things, reminded her that he was dead, and he said the man was called Swann and he was there to talk about buying a house.' She ate some more cake. 'But she was right, wasn't she? Everyone's saying the man who was found in the river was Paul Millar. And that he's been . . . murdered,' she whispered, her eyes wide as saucers.

Reardon didn't like what he was hearing very much at all. If this Miss Bancroft wasn't letting her imagination run away with her, or even just airing some sort of office grievance, and was so sure, Purbright had lied blatantly, perhaps never expecting he would be caught out in such a way. That was something Reardon would never have expected of him, a man he'd hitherto liked and respected. But he wished he could recall at what point the lawyer had suddenly become very cagey when he'd been speaking to him.

SEVENTEEN

'Is she sure, this Miss Bancroft?' was Gilmour's first reaction when Reardon told him next morning of the disturbing encounter he'd had on the bridge with the young woman.

'Jenny Hallam thought so. She said they'd known each other since they were children.'

'But why the devil should Purbright have pretended he was someone else? What's he been up to, then? *Purbright?*'

'I don't know.' The picture of Charles Purbright as a pillar of the community, a respected solicitor with a reputation as a keen lawyer, straightforward and renowned for his commitment to his clients didn't precisely square with what Jenny Hallam had told Reardon, the lie she swore he'd told about meeting Paul. Dangerous to run too far ahead with speculation about something that may or may not turn out to be true, but she'd no reason not to tell the truth, and if she was right, Purbright had also lied to Reardon. 'He brushed off the money question when I raised it. Swore there was no inheritance for Paul in Ernest Millar's will.'

But supposing that wasn't so: that the old man *had* in fact at last made provision for Paul, Reardon mused, perhaps leaving a legacy or some trust fund to be paid over to him at some time in the future, when marriage and fatherhood might hopefully have induced more responsibility, what then? It was a possibility, given the complex relations between Ernest Millar and his son.

And what if, before the time it was due to be implemented, Paul Millar had disappeared from the spectrum? Gilmour wanted to know.

Misappropriation of funds was the answer that came very easily to mind, however difficult to believe in view of Purbright's probity. 'He wouldn't be the first dodgy lawyer, nor the last.' Even as he said it, Reardon was reminded of that high-priced home of his, one of those desirable riverside

properties the other side of town – and built, incidentally, by
Millar Homes, if memory served him correctly. Children at
exclusive schools. Not to mention his expensive wife . . .

And if the impossible had happened, and Paul had somehow
found out that something dubious had been going on, and
had confronted Purbright, what would the solicitor have done
about it?

'Do we have another suspect then?' Gilmour's mind was on
the present dearth of them, until he saw an answer to his own
question. 'No, of course not. For one thing, the gun was army
issue and he could never have been in the army, not with those
bottle-bottoms he wears.'

'It's not out of the bounds of possibility that he would know
how to get hold of a gun. Nor do you need twenty-twenty
vision to pull a trigger and fire at close range.'

The possibility was there, but any further speculations on
the solicitor as the killer of Paul Millar were interrupted by
Pickersgill at the door, showing what was for him excitement,
saying there was a woman waiting downstairs who had
something to say about the murder. 'They've put her in the
interview room. She won't give her name.'

They were both on their feet at once. Someone with something they had heard or seen that they'd suddenly remembered
– or decided they'd better tell, after all? Not Jenny Hallam,
obviously. Reardon felt again that swift buzz of excitement,
this time with a dead certain gut feeling. Before even seeing
her, he knew who she would be.

Following Gilmour into what Pickersgill had euphemistically
called the interview room – actually the same claustrophobic
little space where Reardon had talked to Imogen Randall – he
saw the same chair she'd used was now occupied by a middle-
aged woman sitting very upright, her gloved hands clasped
tightly over her handbag, a small holdall at her feet. She was
nothing like he'd expected: no Jean Harlow peroxide blonde
with plucked arched eyebrows and a mouth drawn to a scarlet
cupid's bow. How mistaken could you be? But that was how
it went sometimes; you built up a picture and the reality didn't
match. He gave her good morning and a smile, introduced
himself, drew up the chair on the opposite side of the table,

while Gilmour followed him in, carrying another, borrowed from the front office.

'Thank you for seeing me,' she said, obviously nervous, but as polite as if he was the one doing her the favour. She hesitated, then said abruptly, 'I'm Mrs Millar. Emily Millar.'

After a moment, with things suddenly coming together after a quick reshuffle, Reardon got his breath back. 'Mrs Paul Millar, I take it?'

Not Cordingley, then, as he'd so confidently expected. Not the Shire guest who didn't have a pregnant sister living at Darley End, nor an address in Wolverhampton. He was rather glad he hadn't made a fool of himself by addressing her thus before she'd given her real name.

Her head was bent over her gloved hands and when she raised it to give a brief nod in answer to his question, he saw that she was on the verge of tears. Soft brown eyes with thick dark lashes, a striking feature in an otherwise nice, but unremarkable face that gave away her age in the few wrinkles and a slight sag under her chin. 'I've only just found out,' she said shakily, and then surprised him again by adding quickly, before any sympathy could be expressed, and as if she had to get it over with straight away, 'I was staying at the Shire the night before Paul died.'

After a moment, he hazarded, 'As Miss Rita Cordingley.'

'Yes,' she admitted, startled that he should know. 'My maiden name was Cordingley.'

Emily Millar, as she now was, was middle-aged, on the verge of being plump, her face unpainted and her brown eyes shadowed. She had on a tweed coat that might have been fashionable once but had long since given up any such claims, and her brown felt hat could be said to be serviceable rather than becoming. What hair had been allowed to show under it was brown, too, ordinary mouse brown. She looked decent, but very slightly shabby. The leather of the handbag she clasped so tightly was rubbed and the left forefinger of her fabric glove had a small, neat darn at the tip.

'You stayed at the Shire hotel the same night as Paul Millar . . . your husband?' She nodded, her lips pressed together. 'But you used another name. You didn't acknowledge each other. Why was that, may I ask?'

Her eyes suddenly swam. She groped for the handkerchief tucked up her sleeve. 'I'm sorry . . . it's all so . . . so complicated.' The words were choked. Underneath he detected the flat sort of accent he associated with East Anglia.

He'd spoken more sharply than he'd intended. He pulled himself up short and tried a softer approach. 'Don't distress yourself, Mrs Millar. I'm sorry, too – about your husband. You do understand how he died, and that we're investigating his death as suspicious?'

'Of course,' she whispered.

'If you feel up to it, would you like to tell us more about why you're here?'

'That's what I came for. But do you think I might have some water first, please?'

'Are you sure you wouldn't like a cup of tea, Mrs Millar?' Gilmour asked, jumping up.

'No thanks, water would be fine.'

While he was gone, Reardon asked, 'Do your husband's relatives know you're here? In Folbury, I mean?'

She looked a little scared, slightly bewildered and said rapidly, 'No. I don't know them. I've never met them.'

'I see.' It was no more than he'd suspected.

Gilmour reappeared with the water. He'd brought three custard creams on a plate as well, which seemed a bit odd, but Emily Millar with her big brown eyes and her look of hopelessness was bringing out his chivalrous instincts, never far away. She took a long drink from the tumbler and looked at the biscuits but didn't touch them.

'How long have you been married, Mrs Millar?' Reardon prompted, since she seemed in danger of losing the impetus to speak which had brought her to see them.

At that she roused herself, as if recalling what she was doing here. 'Thirteen, nearly fourteen years.' She mistook his silence for disbelief. 'I do have my marriage lines to prove it.' She twisted open the clasp of her handbag. He waved a negating hand, but she dipped into the bag, nevertheless. 'If you don't believe me, take a look at this. I brought it along because I knew you would doubt me. It belonged to Paul, he gave it to me.'

A ring lay heavily on her palm. 'That's not a woman's ring,' Gilmour said tactlessly.

'I know, but he thought a great deal of it. It's too big for my finger, so he made me wear it on a chain round my neck.' Reardon wasn't sure he liked the sound of that 'made me'. 'But I don't want it, you can keep it. I have other things of his I'd rather keep.'

She passed it over and he had to wonder why she thought they should have it, while understanding why she didn't want it herself. He couldn't see Ellen, for instance, thinking it had much to recommend it. Fashioned from some dark metal that might have been tarnished silver, it was decorated with a kind of starburst made by two double bars crossing to form an X, with what looked like a flat barb or hook at the end of each bar, eight of them in all. It was weighty and as he looked, he began to think he might have seen something like it before, though he couldn't think where. He'd no idea why she'd brought it, what she thought it might prove. The decoration was odd-looking for a ring, not very attractive. Was it supposed to represent something, or maybe it was a good luck charm? It looked unusual rather than expensive. He thought of his neighbour, Horace Levett, who might know, if it should prove necessary to find out.

'I believe you, Mrs Millar,' he said, putting it to one side. 'And thank you for coming in. What is it you have to tell us?'

She didn't seem to know where to start, so he kicked off. 'All right. Before we get on to why you were staying at the Shire that night, maybe we should talk about what your husband has been doing since he was last heard of, since the end of the war. You were married for thirteen years, you say?' he encouraged, since she still didn't seem able to speak.

'Yes,' she said at last. 'We met after the war.'

It had given her a start, though she faltered for a while. Gradually, however, her voice steadied. She gave the facts bare and unvarnished, in a way he guessed hid a pain and sadness she was trying not to show.

She had been a young war widow when they met, she said, one of the countless thousands of young women who had once expected nothing more of life than to be wives and mothers and were unprepared for anything else when their husbands were counted amongst the dead. Her own husband had been killed early in the war, and at a loss what to make of life without him, she had left the town of Downham Market in Norfolk where she'd been born, and gone to work in London at a forces canteen for servicemen on leave, where at least she felt useful, she said.

She paused to take another drink of water, and Gilmour asked, 'Was that where you met Paul?'

For the first time, she smiled, just a little, revealing good, even teeth. 'No, we actually met later. In Green Park.' The fleeting smile vanished. 'It was a bad time for me, and that day was so beautiful, which somehow made me feel worse. You see, I'd stayed on in London after the canteen closed, when it wasn't needed any more. I'd found work in a hotel, but it was just drudgery really and my lodgings were awful. I thought I was going to have to go back to Downham and live with my mother again and listen to her saying I told you so, you should never have gone to London.' She managed another ghost of a smile. 'Well, anyway, I must have been sitting there on that bench for an hour or more. I'd lost track of time, and then suddenly a man sitting at the opposite end of the seat spoke to me. I'd no recollection of him coming to sit there, he could have been there ever since I'd sat down. He said, "Pardon me, but you look as miserable as I feel. Would you like another handkerchief?" I hadn't realized until then how much I'd been crying, and I was so ashamed, I got up to leave but he reached out and touched my arm. "Don't go," he said. "Stay and be miserable with me, if you can't smile."

'Well, I looked at him and somehow I knew that he wasn't just trying to pick me up. I'd grown used to men trying that on, working at the canteen. And he didn't look miserable, he looked . . . lost, and sad. I stayed, he listened to me and told me something of himself . . .' She stopped, unable to go on.

'You became friends and later, you were married.' Reardon helped her out.

'Yes, that's how it was. Just a few weeks later in fact.' She began to move the plate with the untouched custard creams back and forth. 'It sounds so . . . so cheap, put like that, but it wasn't. We'd both been married before, to people we loved very much, so there was nothing terribly romantic about it, we weren't what you'd call "in love", but we did come to love each other, in a different way. He was good to me, you know, made me stop working at that awful hotel, and though we never had much money, we managed on his wages.'

'Where did he work?'

'He'd found a garage that was pleased to have him. He'd always been very good with engines and so on, ever since he was a boy, so he didn't mind – and the money wasn't too bad.' She picked up a biscuit, then put it back on the plate without even looking at it and took another drink of water.

Over her bent head, Gilmour and Reardon exchanged a glance. A garage mechanic. What a different life from that which had once stretched before Paul Millar. What hopes and expectations diminished.

The tumbler was nearly empty, and Gilmour asked if she wanted more water, but she shook her head and went on. 'The only worry we had was Paul's health. It wasn't good, he'd been gassed in the war, you see.'

Gassed? Gassed was what happened to men who had fought in the trenches, not in the air. It was what the pathologist, Rossiter, had originally thought when he'd seen the state of Paul's lungs, although he'd later agreed that flames from a burning aeroplane could have resulted in much the same long-term symptoms. 'Wasn't he in the RFC, Mrs Millar?'

'Oh, yes he was, to begin with, but he got himself transferred to an army unit.'

Neither of the Millars had mentioned this, but it was possible this was how the 'mix-up' that Thea had referred to had happened. 'Wasn't that unusual?'

'I suppose it might have been, but the RFC, which he'd joined, hoping to fly, was still only a branch of the army at that time, before it became the RAF. He knew everything about aeroplanes, and he did fly for a bit, until he had a slight accident, nothing much, but it meant a medical, and some doctor or other decided his eyesight wasn't good enough for flying. He found that quite ridiculous, and I must say I agree. He

never needed glasses, not even for reading, but if that was
what they said, what could he do? He told me he argued, tried
to appeal, but it was no use. They made him a mechanic. It
made him very bitter and angry, although personally I think
he was lucky. Not having to fly, I mean.'

It was an understandable sentiment: the survival of those
who flew what Rossiter, with some justification, had called
paper kites, had been nearly as much a matter of luck as skill.
Engines that were sometimes uncertain, the whole a light
wooden framework with a cellulose-doped cloth covering,
highly flammable, was no protection in single combat against
a German fighter pilot armed with a machine gun. Crashing
into a tall building, if not exploding, bursting into flames
mid-air was by no means unheard of. Nevertheless, that's what
Paul Millar had hoped to do. Delegated to looking after the
machines he'd hoped to fly, servicing them for other daredevil
young men to pilot must have been gall and wormwood to
him.

'Did he ever say why he never came back here to Folbury,
or contacted his family after the war?'

'Not really, but I could see why he didn't. His wife had
died and there was no one . . . that was something I could
well understand. I left Downham Market when Alfred – my
first husband – died and I could never have gone back to where
I'd been so happy.'

Tears threatened again. She groped for the handkerchief
tucked up her sleeve. 'I'm sorry, I don't know why I'm getting
so upset. It's not as though I wasn't prepared. But I would
never have expected him to die the way he has.'

'Did you know he was so ill, then?' Reardon asked carefully, aware that this might prove to be another added pain.

'Yes, I knew,' she said sadly, 'and so did he. He'd been
told he hadn't long to live and I'm sure that's why he came
back here. There were things he had neglected to do, he said.
He had to come back and see them put right.'

'Was it concerned with money?'

'No. At least . . . I'm not sure, but I don't think so.'

'And you . . . you came too?'

After a hesitation, she admitted she had, though alone and

not entirely willingly. 'Paul could be . . . a bit . . .' Searching
for a word, she came out with 'persuasive'. He wondered what
she had been going to say. Intimidating? Manipulative? Or
even frightening? Even Connie Randall had felt that about
Paul, though she'd been very young at the time she'd known
him. Emily was looking highly embarrassed at having said so
much, as if she might be having second thoughts about coming
here at all. It had taken courage, he could see, but he didn't
want to lose her now.

'Persuasive in what way, Mrs Millar?' he asked gently.

She shook her head, not answering, and bent her gaze on
the gloves she'd removed and was twisting into a ball. He let
her take her time and eventually she looked up. Perhaps he'd
underestimated her. A fierce blush had swept her face, but now
her chin was raised and when she spoke her voice had taken
on a new decision.

'You should understand . . . there was something eating
away at him, it was like some sort of sickness. Not his physical
sickness. Hard as it was, I know he'd accepted that he was
going to die, but other things had begun to prey on his mind
– all of it . . . all that had happened here, his wife dying in a
terrible accident, and most of all, I think, why he'd let his
family think him dead.'

'Did he contact them?'

'He couldn't, I think. He used to say he'd made a new start
in London, with me, and it was better that way. I sympathized
with that. You know, the longer one stays away, the harder it
becomes to go back. But then he had a letter from someone
– don't ask me who, or what it was about – and after that he
would sit brooding for hours, he even took to walking the streets
at night. That was when it all started, the plan he made. I refused
to do what he wanted at first, but it upset him so much, in the
end I promised, though it all seemed so . . . so silly and rather
pointless, to tell you the truth. Though I suppose everything
changes, things must look different to you if you're living
under a death sentence.'

She looked infinitely sad and took another sip of water. 'It
seems you know most of it already, all that business about me
staying at the Shire, a different name, having a pregnant sister,

a taxi to pick me up and all that.' She flushed again. And
repeated, 'It was so ridiculous, so unnecessary. I didn't after
all need to excuse my movements to the management, did I?
But he insisted no one must have any inkling as to who I was,
why I was really there, and he made me promise.' She stared
into the distance then added so quietly she was hardly audible,
'I almost convinced myself he'd dwelt so much on whatever
it was that was getting at him that he wasn't quite in his right
mind and didn't properly know what he was doing.'

Maybe that had been true. Maybe. But in Reardon's opinion,
such a demand exacted by a dying man constituted an
emotional blackmail that was very clear-minded indeed. A
short silence fell until Gilmour asked, 'What exactly did he
want you to do here, Mrs Millar?'

'Not much, really, when it came down to it. Just find out
what I could about his family, which was easier than I thought
it would be. I kept my eyes and ears open . . . went to the
local paper and looked up back issues and found his brother
was never out of the news for long. I went to the recreation
ground where the children play . . . it's surprising what you
can pick up talking to the mothers as they watch over their
children on the swings. Of course I never went to that place,
Darley End, but I still had a lot of time to spare so I let the
taxi that came for me take me a little way out of town
and then I caught a bus out to Halesowen.'

'*Halesowen?*' Gilmour repeated, as if it were the ends of
the earth.

'It's where my friend Joan lives. We shared digs when we
were working in the canteen in London. Paul had it all worked
out . . . he knew what good friends we were, that she'd let
me spend as much time as I wanted in her flat during the day
while she was at work. She's not married and lives alone . . .
and she's not one to ask questions.'

It seemed to Reardon that a more sensible course of action
would have been to stay with her friend and go into Folbury
only when she needed to do what her husband had asked of
her, but she shook her head when he suggested that.

'It *would* have been better, of course, if it weren't that . . .
well, Joan calls it her flat but it's really only a small bed sitter,

nowhere for overnight guests.' She gave a long sigh. 'What was it all for? All I found out was that Millars was a good business firm, and that the family home had been demolished and his brother and sister were living in a very modern new house he had built. That was easy enough . . . that house, Casa Nova it's called, isn't it? . . . it's the talk of the town. And that was it, until . . . I'd no idea Paul was going to come here himself, that he'd be there that . . . that last night.'

'The sixteenth?' Gilmour asked, with a look at Reardon. 'Where did you meet?'

'We didn't, not that night. I'd no idea he was there in fact, staying in the same hotel. But the next day, he was waiting as I got out of the taxi, at the place where I'd told him I usually boarded the bus for Halesowen, by the Three Tuns. I had the shock of my life, seeing him there, when I'd thought him still in Stoke Newington. I thought the whole point was that he couldn't be seen in Folbury himself. He saw I was angry, but . . .' Her voice broke. 'I couldn't be, not for long, not when he was so . . . so broken up. Oh, he was! We sat in the bus shelter and he promised he'd explain everything soon. He only had someone to see later that day and then it would all be over.'

'Did he say who that was?'

'Yes,' she said steadily. 'His son, Matthaeus.' And the pain in her eyes told them that had been the first time she had heard that Paul Millar had had a son.

Later, after she'd been persuaded to have a cup of tea and had eaten one of the custard creams, she picked up the holdall at her feet, ready to leave. Reardon had managed to persuade her that a visit to Paul's son, even with the best of intentions, was not a good idea. They could hardly stop her if she was determined on it, but he didn't think Matt Millar was yet ready to receive a hitherto unknown stepmother, even one as well-disposed towards him as Emily insisted she was. He said now, 'We shall need to see you again, Mrs Millar.'

'I was intending to go across to Downham Market, to stay with my mother,' she said, looking at the overnight bag. She hadn't shown much enthusiasm when she'd spoken of her mother previously and didn't now; but staying with her was presumably the only alternative to a sad, empty house back in London.

'We can fix you up with somewhere here to stay,' Gilmour said.

Sergeant Longton was unmarried and lived with his mother, who took in occasional paying guests. She was a warm-hearted woman, easy to get on with, who had obliged them before. She was also an excellent cook, as George's girth testified. Emily Millar would be comfortable there.

She suddenly looked exhausted and no one was surprised when she gave in and agreed.

PART THREE

EIGHTEEN

Gilmour was fully occupied the next morning with preparations for the court appearance he was due to make later in the afternoon. The case involved a break-in at a local off licence, where the thieves had set on the owner and knocked him to the ground before scarpering with the takings and some of the stock while he was still out for the count. The thieves in question were a couple of well-known local villains and the owner was claiming to have recognized them. That the alibis they were producing were derisory, coming as they did from half a dozen of their mates, wasn't going to speed up the proceedings, not with Mrs Agatha Wellborne as presiding magistrate. Tireless in pursuit of the truth, she would leave no stone, however unlikely, unturned.

Gilmour worked in his shirtsleeves, jacket over the back of his chair, his hair on end where he'd run his hands through it, his face as red as his hair.

Reardon, immersed in his own paperwork, left him to it until the clock reached midday. He went to sit on the edge of Gilmour's desk, swinging his leg, making room by shoving aside several of the empty coffee mugs that decorated it. It had been a long time since breakfast. 'Fancy some lunch, Joe?'

'Lead me to it!' Gilmour was immediately rejuvenated, simply by the prospect. He could eat like a horse and still keep trim and fit because he was rarely still and burned off calories like a boiler furnace.

The prim little cafe around the corner was normally quiet at lunchtime. There was no beer, such as that served by Percy Sweet in Dudley, but the tea was hot and strong, and the waitress was nicer. They mainly served light lunches of the poached eggs on toast variety, but also pasties and pork pies, so good they couldn't have come from anywhere else but Turnbull's. Which reminded Reardon to ask if anyone had yet spoken to Tom Turnbull, who had been on that list of Pugh's.

Gilmour made a face. Nothing had come of Pickersgill's visit to the pea-and-pie shop the ex-soldier and his wife ran, other than a parcel of faggots and pigs' trotters handed to him on his way out, which Pickersgill, being a fussy eater, had generously distributed round the office. Turnbull, it seemed, hadn't been one of Millar's special pals, had known him only slightly. 'Like nearly everyone else we've spoken to,' Gilmour said gloomily. The list had in fact grown from the original one given by Pugh, one contact leading to another, and all had been followed up, however unlikely, but the results had hardly been worth the effort. 'Everybody seems to remember the name, but no one seems to know much more about him than that. Too far back.'

Gilmour was hoping that now they had obtained from Emily Millar where Paul had spent his last years, Reardon might be persuaded to tackle the enquiries from that angle. But the gaffer had that something-mulling-over-in-his-mind look. Unlike Gilmour himself, who threw out theories as they came to him, Reardon, once he had an idea going in his head, liked to keep it to himself until he was sure it made sense. He waited until the waitress had departed after serving Welsh rarebit to two elderly ladies at the next table, the only other customers, before pressing his point. 'What Emily told us . . .' he began, through a mouthful of Cornish pasty.

But Reardon pre-empted him. 'Yes, what Emily told us helps to fill in the hours of what had to be her husband's last day.'

Neither needed prompting to recall the details of how those hours had been spent, in so far as they knew them. The first evening Paul had arrived in Folbury, out of all the people who had previously known him, he'd apparently only visited his siblings at Casa Nova. Although the account they'd given of what had gone on there might well be apocryphal, there must still be time unaccounted for. The following morning he had almost certainly been the man making what Ellen had likened to some sort of pilgrimage to Fox Close. It now also turned out that he'd met Emily briefly in the bus shelter that afternoon, and later he had (if Eva Bancroft had been correct in her assertions) called at Purbright's office. Lastly, he had been seen leaving his son's studio by Wesley Pugh. There was nothing so far to suggest he'd made any attempt to contact Pugh himself, or Connie Randall, come to that. On the face of it there was no reason why he should have done so. His close connection with both had been severed years before he'd finally left Folbury, but they had once been important to him and the question nagged. Reardon still felt there had to be a link somewhere.

Not to be put aside either were those raised voices Ivy Pearson had heard the night following his arrival in Folbury. And not least the second visit he had told Emily he must make to his son that day.

Emily's appearance out of the blue, and what she had to say, had initially seemed like the breakthrough they'd been hoping for, but when it came down to it, what she'd told them hadn't taken them much further along. True, her story had indicated some sort of starting point for looking into those last unexplained years of her husband's life, the possibility of finding anyone or anything that might lead to the discovery of his murderer, but when they'd pressed her for details, they'd drawn a blank. Paul had had no enemies to her certain knowledge – nor many friends either if it came down to it, just the people at the small garage where he'd worked until he'd finally quitted a couple of weeks ago on the grounds of his ill-health. Clearing the way, Reardon thought, for his ill-fated return to Folbury. Everything Emily had told them about Paul and his preoccupations during his last weeks pointed to his home town being the place where the circumstances which had led to his murder had originated.

Which brought them back with nice circularity to precisely what it was that had brought him back – that letter Emily said Paul had received. It had evidently been enough to prompt him to find out, via his wife, what the situation was in Folbury before he took what must have felt like the huge step which would at last bring him home. Suggesting he had very good reasons indeed to be wary of what he might have to face. Someone, then, had known enough about him to have his address and write to him.

'Purbright,' Gilmour said. 'Had to be.'

'But he definitely said he'd had nothing to do with Paul since before the war. No need for it, since old Millar hadn't left him a farthing, in trust or otherwise.' Knowing as he said it that in view of what Jenny Hallam had said, Purbright's word was no longer to be trusted without reservations.

He pushed his chair back and stood up. 'I guess it's time for another word with him, see what he has to say for himself. We'll go this afternoon. Or I will,' he corrected, belatedly remembering that Gilmour would be in court.

PC Dawson was talking to Longton at the front desk when, on his way out to see Purbright, Reardon's ear picked up the name. 'Millars?' he queried, halting. 'What's going on?'

'They've had a break-in on site, up where they're building those houses off Emscott Hill. Cement mixer pinched,' Longton informed him.

'Wasn't the site secured?'

'Chain-link fencing – and a lot of difference that would've made! Damn gyppos, brass neck for owt, they have. Drive a lorry straight through it and pick up what they want, halfway to Timbuctoo before you can say Jack Robinson.'

The gypsies always got the blame, and not always without justification. They didn't all live in horse-drawn caravans nowadays, and they'd have found no difficulty in 'acquiring' a clapped-out lorry where a few more bashes from a chain-link fence would make no difference.

'Right, then, Stan,' Longton said to Dawson, 'on your way. Inkerman Terrace first.'

'I'll come with you.' Disregarding the sergeant's raised eyebrows, Reardon followed the constable out to the waiting car. Purbright could wait a bit longer. Each time he'd tried to see Millar since his visit to Casa Nova with his brother's post-mortem details he'd been fobbed off; Millar, it seemed, was a very busy man. Too busy even to cancel a business game of golf in favour of learning how and why his brother had died. This would be an opportunity to find out how he'd taken that news.

When they reached Inkerman Terrace, they were told that everyone was up at the site – or everyone they would need to see, which amounted to Ted Millar himself, and Wesley Pugh, who'd gone up there with him. It was half-past twelve, and Miss Millar was not available, either. She had left to keep a lunchtime hairdressing appointment ten minutes since.

It was the dragon lady they were speaking to, Mrs Chadwick, no less snippy but slightly less formidable than before. The frown was still in evidence, but she wasn't in a hurry to see them off the premises. As they were leaving, she followed Reardon to the front door. Dawson went to the car at the kerbside but as Reardon set his foot on the top step, she put a hand on his arm to stop him. It was very clean, with rosy pink nails, and small and soft, but she had a firm grip. 'We've had things missing from sites before, you know, but we've never had a detective inspector to deal with it,' she said accusingly. 'I was under the impression it was the . . . the murder case you were dealing with. You're not thinking this business has anything to do with that, are you?'

He turned to look at her. 'You never know,' he said mildly. 'Stranger coincidences have occurred.'

'Oh, coincidences!' she exclaimed with a look that suddenly breathed fire and smoke. 'I suppose you'd say it was coincidence that Ted's . . . that Mr Millar's brother happens to have turned up alive when everyone thought him dead.'

'No, I wouldn't, Mrs Chadwick. But I'd say that him turning up here alive could be the reason he's now dead. Why do *you* think he returned?'

She looked taken aback, but not for long. 'How on earth should I know? But if you think he . . . if you think anybody here had anything to do with that, you're barking up the wrong tree. They've done nothing.'

'Then they've nothing to fear, Mrs Chadwick, have they?'

It was an exit line that left a lot to be desired, but she wasn't able to summon up a better reply either.

Dawson was a steady driver. He kept his eyes on the road and his concentration on where they were going while they carried on in silence, but his mind was elsewhere. Eventually he gave a dry cough. 'Er, is it in order for me to say something, sir?'

As far as Reardon was aware, it wasn't a request that anyone at Market Street normally found necessary to ask of him.

'Go ahead. You're not in the army, Stan.'

'It's just that I wouldn't take too much notice of what Maura Corrrigan says, if I were you, sir.'

'Who the devil's Laura Corrigan?'

'Maura, not Laura . . . Sorry, I forgot – Mrs Chadwick, Corrigan as was. I went to school with her.'

The little dragon. 'Did you indeed? Well, she hasn't told me anything to take notice of or not.'

Dawson looked uncomfortable. 'No, but I just felt I ought to say.'

'Say what? Is she not to be trusted?'

'It's not that. Only . . .' He stopped, then burst out suddenly, 'They're all the same, these religious types, aren't they? Divorce is an unforgivable sin but it's all right to commit adultery as long as you confess it to the priest. Then you can go on doing it. What I mean is . . .' He stopped, seeming not to know what he did mean. The stoic, sensible and unflappable Police Constable Stanley Dawson, who'd seen it all during his years of service and never wasted words, always came up with reports that were succinct and to the point – if short on inspiration – was floundering.

'Stop the car, Stan.'

Dawson threw a sideways look but did as he was bid and drew into the kerb.

'What's all this? I hear what you say, but it seems to have damn all to do with anything.'

The constable drew in a deep breath. 'I'm sorry, I don't suppose it has. It wasn't called for, what I said. It's just . . .'

Reardon could take a guess by now at what was coming, but he left it to Dawson to tell him. A staunch family man with strong principles, strait-laced, his main fault was that he was inclined to see everything in black and white, no shades of grey in between.

Presently, he sighed. 'She lives at the other end of Marlin Street from me. Married to this chap Chadwick, Arthur Chadwick. The wife says you can't blame her looking else-where when you see how he treats her. He works the sand and gravel pits just above Cooper's Lock, you know?'

Reardon nodded. 'I know where you mean.'

'She works at Millar's during the day but the old skinflint still has her down there at his office, doing his books and that for him of a night. Right miserable sod, he is – but he's still her husband, isn't he?'

'She's having an affair with Ted Millar, is she?'

Dawson studied the steering wheel. 'I shouldn't have said anything.' His hand went to his pocket but came out empty. He knew the gaffer's views on smoking in the car.

Reardon sighed. 'Wind the window down and have a fag if you need one. But for God's sake come to the point, we haven't got all day.'

Dawson took his time over lighting up. Exasperated, Reardon said, 'What you're saying is, Ted Millar is now a better offer than Mr Chadwick?'

'I reckon so and if, like, she was asked to give him an alibi . . . or anything . . .'

'And why should Ted Millar need an alibi?'

'I don't know,' Dawson said. 'But if he did, she'd give him one.'

'Since we're not even close yet to knowing when or where Paul Millar was killed, isn't the question of alibis academic?'

Decidedly so. Of their chief suspects (the only realistic ones so far, Reardon reminded himself) Pugh had spent the rest of the evening, after leaving Matt, at a public protest meeting, and the Millars had passed it quietly at home, Thea writing letters, Ted catching up with the day's news, as was his wont, in the *Daily Telegraph*. Matt had been with Imogen.

'I suppose so.'

Apart from Dawson needing to let off steam on what was evidently a personal prejudice, this new aspect of Ted Millar's personal life wasn't helping much. It had already become clear that he liked the ladies – particularly those who wouldn't threaten his bachelor existence – including, if Gilmour was right, Connie Randall, and now Maura Chadwick, nee Corrigan, dispenser of Ovaltine.

An attractive woman. He saw the Irish in her now. The blazing blue eyes, the dark hair. That was where Ted Millar had been on Saturday, not playing golf, he'd take a bet on it. If, of course, Millar had actually been told of Reardon's request for that meeting at Casa Nova, if Thea had deliberately kept Millar out of the way. It will come better from me, she'd said.

When they reached the site, at the end of a lane off the main road, it was evident there wasn't much left of whatever security had been there originally. A large section of the fencing lay flattened to the ground near the entrance, tempting enough for anyone except Dawson to drive straight through. He by-passed the chance and drove circumspectly through the gates further down, which had now been opened.

A large sign advertised that Millar Homes were quality-built houses ready for immediate occupation and could be secured with a ten per cent deposit. They were a smaller version of those surrounding Reardon's own house in The Avenue, on what had been Fox Close land. Not such an enviable address, but easier to sell. That didn't appear to be happening just yet, however. The hopefully predicted housing boom wasn't showing signs yet of having reached Folbury and it looked as though the prosperous Millar Homes might be having the same problems as everyone else. Only two of these were finished, as yet unoccupied and presumably unsold, standing like wall-flowers at the edges of a dance floor, waiting to be claimed. Foundations had been laid for the next pair, but it appeared that further work on the site had been suspended.

They stepped out of the car into a low, cold drizzle. Millar and Pugh were the only people about, both muffled up against the weather, as they stood watching the police car approach. Pugh's greatcoat was a well-worn, ex-army British warm. Millar sported a tweed cap and his coat had an astrakhan collar. Both wore gumboots, a protection which the newcomers had failed to appreciate might be necessary, the local soil being red and sandy, quickly absorbing even the biblical amounts of rain they'd been blessed with lately.

In any case, it didn't seem that they would be expected to tramp very far over the site, muddy or otherwise. 'Inspector Reardon. This is a surprise.' Millar extended a hand, ushering them into one of the two finished houses, whose front room was apparently being used as a temporary site office.

The card table they'd set up, and a single chair, left practically no room at all when the four men were inside. The whole place was so small it was actually difficult to envisage furniture for a family fitting in. Well, two hundred and fifty pounds, though more than a year's wages for some, what could you expect?

Dawson chose the windowsill to lean against while taking down details of the missing cement mixer. It was a formality soon done. No one had any expectations of its return. Millar appeared to be taking it philosophically, and Pugh said, 'We shouldn't have left it here anyway. Asking for trouble.' He had been very quiet until then, his default condition, a man who saw no reason to waste words. He was now looking first at his watch, then at Millar. 'If that's all there is, I'd best be off.'

'Of course, Wes, you don't want to miss your bus.'

'I'll be in tomorrow.' He nodded to Reardon and Dawson and presently, having changed his rubber boots for more conventional footwear, could be seen through the window striding off down the lane. Millar's car, in which they must have arrived, was standing outside. Yet he was sending Pugh home by bus?

Perhaps feeling that needed an explanation, Millar said, 'The bus for Lipcott passes here in a few minutes. It's visiting day at Rosmere.'

Rosmere Hall. The erstwhile lunatic asylum, still called that by many, had been where, in years gone by, patients sent for a 'cure' had been known to be kept, sometimes for years, sometimes until they died. But during the war a wing had been taken over for rehabilitating shell-shocked soldiers returning from the trenches and the place had been kept open ever since as a hospital for what was now called the treatment of nervous disorders.

'His wife,' Millar added, looking after the departing figure. 'She's been in there for years, poor woman, with her nerves. And now, on top of everything, she's got terminal cancer. Wes is a brick, visits her twice a week, without fail, always has done. Though not for much longer, I gather.'

Pugh, then, was not yet a widower. The permanent hospitalization of his wife – Connie Randall's friend, Imogen's

Auntie Cora – must be what had kept him in Folbury, and
perhaps went some way to explaining why a man of his intelligence and education had been working for Millars for so
long in a job patently below his capabilities. Perhaps it was
an easier option in the circumstances than holding down a
more demanding position. He seemed to be held in regard at
Millars: whatever had happened between him and Paul clearly
had not extended to the rest of the family.

'Well, Inspector,' Millar said, turning from the window
as the man disappeared down the lane, shoulders hunched
against the rain which was now starting to fall steadily, 'don't
tell me you're here to investigate a missing cement mixer. I
assume you have some news for me?'

Reardon shook his head. 'Afraid not.'

'My God, it's been over a week now, and you're still no
nearer finding out who killed my brother?' It was what grieving
relatives always expected after such tragedy, a quick solution.
As if solving an unexplained murder was no more difficult
than joining the dots in a children's puzzle. But some aware-
ness that he was sounding more aggrieved than grieving must
have struck him. 'We had no idea he was . . .' he said
awkwardly, then stopped abruptly and stared at the window,
where the rain was now rattling against the panes. 'He was
going to die, anyway, wasn't he?'

'According to the doctor, yes, I'm afraid he was.'

'Oh God, if only we'd known!' He turned away, hiding his
emotion.

Ted Millar had aged since they last met. In that forlorn way
fresh-faced, boyish looking men could suddenly look like
elderly children. 'We could have made him stay with us.
Looked after him,' he added wretchedly. Unlike Reardon, the
notion of Thea Millar as a sisterly carer didn't seem out of
the way to him.

'We haven't been idle, Mr Millar. There has been . . . a
development.'

'Development? What?'

'Not at liberty to say more, I'm afraid, at the moment,
but it might have some importance.' The time had not yet
come to surprise any of the Millars with the news of Emily's

appearance. He had little doubt that sort of shock, the advent of a hitherto unknown sister-in-law into the family, would be anything but welcome news to either Ted or his sister, but it was Emily Millar he was thinking of, reluctant to subject her to any more distress.

'You've discovered where he'd been hiding all these last years?' Millar hazarded, seemingly unaware of the implication that his brother had needed to hide.

'No, but what we have found out is that he had . . . let's say a complicated past.'

'That's not something I find surprising.' For a second, asperity threatened to replace the anguish. 'What had he got himself mixed up in?'

'I'm talking about his past here in Folbury, before the war.'

'I wish you luck of it then. I don't suppose anyone remembers him much, it's so long since he left, or has ever seen him since.'

Was he showing a certain amount of relief? He said it as though a lifetime had elapsed, though it was certainly true that nearly everyone they'd seen had tried to make them believe their memories were shrouded in hundred-year-old cobwebs.

'On the contrary, one or two people did see him when he arrived back here.'

'They did?' If he was feigning surprise, or hiding alarm, it was well done. Surely he knew by now that at least Wesley Pugh had caught sight of Paul, even before he found him dead?

'You and Miss Millar apart, of course. You saw him the night he arrived.'

'As we told you.'

'So you did. But Mr Millar, are you sure you didn't see him after that? We have reason to believe he went back to your house again, the next night.'

Millar had begun moving towards the door with Reardon following, until they were standing below the front step, where Dawson was waiting. He stared at Reardon, then pulled the fur collar of his coat up around his ears and shook his head. 'No, Inspector,' he said, sad but sure. 'The last time we saw my brother was that night we've already told you about.' He pulled keys out of his pocket, patiently waiting for them to leave.

Reardon turned to go. 'Is that your motor over there?' he asked. The small, elderly Morris was a popular model, reputedly reliable but in no way the glamorous accessory of a man who had designed and lived in Casa Nova, with its new-fangled furniture and streamlined kitchen.

Ted smiled wryly. 'It serves. The family genes have passed me by when it comes to machinery, as I've told you before. I've no interest in cars, I leave that to my sister.'

He stood watching them as they walked to their own car and drove off down the lane.

Reardon had intended dropping in on Purbright unannounced, but it was getting late by the time he'd been driven back to the station. He left Dawson to park the car and went into the office to telephone, and discovered, as he'd half expected, that the solicitor had already left for home, since he and his wife had a function to attend that evening. He didn't leave a message.

NINETEEN

You had to keep going, no matter what, Connie Randall told herself, no matter how bad you felt, no matter what appalling news had just thudded onto the doormat. Take hold of yourself. Think of other things. Stick to routine and get through by doing what has to be done each morning.

She had already checked that her bag was properly stocked, and now she rescanned her list of calls: old Luther Freeman first, to dress his ulcerated leg and get him comfortable for the day; on to young Joyce who had TB and wasn't long for this world, poor little wench; check on Maggie Price to make sure she wasn't already getting out of bed after that difficult delivery in order to make her idle husband's breakfast, put up his sandwiches and see her brood off to school.

It only remained to make her usual morning visit to the three white beehives at the bottom of the garden to check that all was well. But when she got there she suddenly found herself brought to a standstill, staring at the hives, unseeing, forgetting what she'd come for. It took a while before it came to her and she was able to move. Automatically, she went and gave a tap on each hive, put her ear to the side. A slight hum reassured her all was still well with the colonies, that feeding them sugar to get them through the rest of the winter probably wouldn't be necessary. The bees led structured, ordained and instinctive lives with rules for survival: they would cluster together to keep warm when the temperatures fell; they would abscond from the hive if anything went wrong; they would kill the queen when she had outlived her purpose. They killed the useless drones, too, after they'd done their job of mating.

Suddenly, her tight-held equilibrium threatened to give way altogether. She shivered and forced herself to sit down for a moment on the wooden bench outside the hut, holding on to herself. The sun touched her face. Today, at last, it was beginning to feel warmer, especially here in this sheltered spot. It was mid-March after all. Was she imagining it, or could she smell the earth warming up, see the first faint greening of the trees that led from here down to the river?

The river was where his body had been found. Not in bloodstained Flanders mud but here, in Folbury, in the disgusting gunge by the allotments. Not drowned, but *shot*, they were saying. Her heart gave a dreadful lurch.

It had been a mistake to stop: the images flooded back again unbidden, as strong as they had been doing ever since she'd first heard that Wesley had come across Paul's body. She'd kept them hidden all these years but now, after what she'd just found out his morning, she could hold them back no longer. Through the tears she watched a cloud drift across the sun, felt its shadow as the trees and fields below once again became the dead grey landscape that the flat, low-lying farmland of northern France had so soon become as the fighting progressed. The seasons had made little difference to the general misery, but there had been shafts of hopeful sunlight, and human nature being what it is, brief, precious moments of happiness, even then. It had been this time of year when they had all met in that little *estaminet*, for that last time . . .

The ringing of the doorbell brought her abruptly back to the present. It was faint at this distance, but her ears were attuned to door knockers, bells, the telephone – anything that might be a call to duty. She blew her nose, left the bees to their own meaningful lives and hurried down the path.

It was that detective who stood on the doorstep, Joe Gilmour's boss, the Inspector Reardon who was in charge.

Oh, Lord! she thought. Joe Gilmour I'm all right with, he's predictable, but this one, the dark one with the steady eyes that miss nothing, and that searching look, he's different. He understands more than I'd like, he made me talk too much when they were last here. What does he want now?

Reardon had come wanting nothing more than the retrieval of his fountain pen, which he might possibly have dropped. As good an excuse as any, if one should prove necessary. Not that excuses were actually needed. It was in fact what he and Gilmour had talked about after their previous visit which had made him, on impulse, take this small diversion on his way to work. The conversation had been at the back of his mind ever since. It made no sense to believe that Paul Millar had been murdered because he might have been Imogen's father, but he was anxious to know why her mother was against the match with Paul's son.

There was no immediate answer to the bell, and he thought he was out of luck, that Nurse Randall had already left on her rounds, but as he was about to turn away, she opened the door. She was quick to tell him after his request to speak to her that she was just leaving.

'I won't keep you long, Mrs Randall. I know it's early, but if you can spare a few minutes, just a quick question or two.'

'Again?' She shot him a suspicious look but led him into the sitting room, where Pippie welcomed them with a flash of golden plumage and a shrill greeting.

'I see he's in voice again.'

'Yes, he's perked up.'

She'd been crying. Her eyes were red-rimmed, the tip of her nose was pink. 'Forgive me, Mrs Randall, but is anything wrong?'

'No,' she replied angrily, 'why should there be?'

He thought he could guess why and sensed that the anger was with herself for letting it show. But then she gave a sigh that was almost a sob. 'I'm sorry, that was so rude. You must excuse me, I've just read about . . . about Paul.'

The *Herald* was there, front page uppermost, tossed on to a chair, the news filling the front page.

'They're saying he was . . . that somebody *shot* him. Is that true?'

'I'm afraid it is.'

She gave an odd little shiver and looked away, not wanting him to see her face. He sensed a tenderness and sadness for the dead man that might after all be a great deal more than just a memory of adolescent first love.

'I think you could do with a cup of tea, Mrs Randall.' Nurses reputedly drank copious quantities of tea, didn't they? At the same time, it occurred to him that brandy might have been a better suggestion.

'No, I'm all right, really. It was just a shock. And anyway, I have to go out,' she repeated.

'If it's not urgent, then I think you should take time to sit down for a while,' he said more firmly. 'I won't keep you long.'

She hesitated, closed her eyes for a second, then let herself sink down on to the squashy sofa. He took a seat opposite and she said again, 'I'm all right.'

He saw that she was, or soon would be. She was fast regaining her usual command of herself.

'That's why you're here, of course,' she said after a moment. 'To talk some more about Paul. But I can't tell you more than I've already told you. Have you . . . have you found out who it . . . who killed him?'

The inevitable question again, but he was patient. 'Not yet, but we will.'

She swallowed. 'How is he taking it – Ted, I mean? He must be devastated.'

He nodded. 'Miss Millar – Thea, too.'

'I expect so. Perhaps if I went to see them . . . but no, I can't.' She saw his eyebrows raise. 'She wouldn't thank me. She doesn't like me because I won't stop Imogen from seeing her precious Matt. She thinks she's not good enough for him.'

'She's mistaken, I think.'

A small smile appeared, but it transformed her face. 'I'm glad you think so.'

At that moment, his hand in his pocket met that old, heavy ring Emily Millar had handed to him, absently pushed in amongst his loose change, where it had stayed. He drew it out now and showed it to her. 'Have you by any chance ever seen this before?'

She craned forward to see what it was and gave a choked little gasp. 'Where did you get that? Oh!' She faltered. 'Oh, God, don't tell me – he wasn't . . . wearing it, was he?'

'No. No, he wasn't. But it was Paul's wasn't it?'

'Yes, it was.'

'The decoration's . . . unusual.'

'He told me it was an oriental motif to protect against scorpions, it's used on kilim rugs as well as jewellery and so on.'

'He was superstitious?'

'Not really. But it was his birth sign, Scorpio. and he liked to think of it as a personal crest . . . or insignia, or whatever you like to call it.' She eyed the barbed, double X, stylized symbol on the heavy ring with a sort of fascinated repulsion. 'He gave that to me, with a silver chain so I could wear it round my neck.'

She didn't ask how he'd obtained it, and he didn't think she'd want to hear about the other woman whose neck the ring had also hung from, much less that she had been Paul's wife. Unless this was a replica of the one he'd given Connie.

'He never took it off his finger before he gave it to me. I hated it, but I wore it,' she said with a hint of bravado and a grim little attempt at a smile, 'or at least until I threw it back at him.'

'You *threw* it?'

'When we had that quarrel I told you about before. I had a temper in those days.'

At that inopportune moment, the front door opened. Imogen, hungry and tired no doubt after her night shift. She came into the room on a rush of cold air, cheeks blazing, breathless, snatching off her hat and tossing it onto a chair, rushing immediately to Connie and folding her arms around her.

'Mum,' she said, and only then did he see she had tears in her eyes. 'Oh, Mum, it's Auntie Cora. I've just seen Uncle Wes and Mum . . . it's over.'

Connie stood as if the news had poleaxed her. A tired, barely perceptible little whisper escaped her. 'Oh, Cora, Cora, my dear . . . at last.' And then, more urgently: 'Is he all right . . . your Uncle Wes?'

'Of course he is, Mum. You know him.'

Imogen held her mother, rocking her as if she were the child. Over her shoulder, her glance rested on Reardon. She must have seen him when she came in, but it was as though his presence hadn't registered until then. 'It's my auntie, Uncle Wes's wife,' she told him. 'She died a couple of hours ago.'

The day was already well under way as he walked back up Stonegate, shops opening, wares being set out ready for another busy day. This one had scarcely begun and already it had hit Connie Randall hard: firstly by opening the newspaper and reading that Paul had been shot to death, then hearing that her dearest friend had died. Feeling distinctly de trop, he had made his excuses and left as soon as he could.

He could have wished he hadn't chosen this time to bother her, if it hadn't been that for one thing. After talking to her, he knew now why the ring in his pocket had seemed familiar. And for another . . .

The certainty that had now come to him quickened his steps up Stonegate.

TWENTY

Charles Purbright had believed until now that he had pulled off the previous meeting he'd had with Reardon pretty successfully. The few dealings he'd had with the inspector before then had told him he wasn't easy to fool, though that wasn't what Purbright had intended, or not deliberately, when he'd denied Paul Millar having visited him. Now, with Reardon back in his office, asking more awkward questions, he found himself sweating slightly and hoped to God it didn't show.

There was little point in further denying the meeting now. The inspector knew. Purbright hadn't reckoned on Eva Bancroft recognizing the man she'd known only when he was a boy. He couldn't prove that his visitor had been the man he'd said was called Swann – a name snatched from the air – and anyone talking to Eva would know within minutes that she wasn't lying. She'd worked for Purbright's for over thirty years and was utterly loyal, and he knew she was incapable of dissembling. He was, however, certain the information hadn't been passed on by her, or not directly, and old George Wilkins, his chief clerk, was at present absent with the bronchitis which got to him every winter. Which left only the new girl, Jenny Hallam. And she had been starting to show signs of promise, too, after a beginning which had been anything but great.

He shook hands with Reardon when he came in, offered coffee, which was politely refused. The inspector hadn't booked an appointment, taking Purbright by surprise and leaving him at a disadvantage, a situation he didn't like to find himself in. He always made sure his briefs were thoroughly prepared. However, he could, when the need arose, be as slippery as some of the clients he represented, and for a while he took refuge in being at his most lawyerly: urbane and smooth, and citing client confidentiality when Reardon requested details of the man who had visited him, admitting nothing and skirting further questions with practised skill.

He knew he'd sailed close to the wind. Too close. Charles Purbright, respected lawyer, upright citizen, all round good type. He had acted unethically and he, a solicitor, had lied to the police. He couldn't now for the life of him imagine why he had, except that he'd been taken unawares, then as now. Huffing a little, he repeated his previous assertions, that he had not known Paul Millar was alive . . .

'Until he wrote to you.' Reardon sounded tired.

Purbright stiffened. Dammit! Until now, since that first meeting with Reardon, he'd been confident that he'd been quick enough to shuffle out of the inspector's sight that letter with the damning scorpion motif; Paul, still typically dramatic, hadn't given up the flamboyant habit of drawing it on his correspondence. But it was evident now that Reardon must have seen it. He huffed a little more but finally spread his hands and capitulated, admitting that it was Paul who had first written to him. 'I assure you, there are good reasons why I kept his visit quiet.'

'Tell me.' Reardon eased himself into a more comfortable position and almost wished he'd accepted that offer of coffee as he prepared to listen to what was certain to be a lengthy justification. He'd experienced Purbright in full flight before now, but thankfully, they weren't in court today.

'It's an unnerving experience, I may tell you, receiving a letter from the other world,' the solicitor said. 'Or that's what it seemed to be . . . except that it turned out Paul Millar was very much on this planet, alive and well and living in London. At first I suspected some kind of hoax, especially when he requested me not to mention the letter to anyone. He suggested we meet in London, since he didn't want to take the risk of anyone here seeing and recognizing him. Well! Naturally, I refused to do any such thing. I was not, I wrote back, at the beck and call of someone who might or might not be the late lamented Paul Millar. If it was so important, he should come to see me – though I couldn't imagine what he thought to gain from doing so – meet me on my own terms, here in my own office. He didn't reply.'

'He did come, however?'

'Eventually. He changed his mind and we made an appointment. When he turned up I was frankly shocked. He looked older, naturally, but also shabby and, I thought, not altogether . . . Let's just say there was a wild light in his eyes I didn't like at all. He didn't tell me what he'd been up to for the better part of what . . . fourteen, fifteen years? Nor did I ask.' He steepled his fingers and pressed them against his lips. 'It was very clear, however, that whatever else he'd been doing, he'd been brooding over what had happened in the past. Resentment's not very pretty, Inspector.'

'What did he want?'

'Money, as you rightly thought. I told you his father had failed to change his will before he died. There was nothing Paul could have done about that, and in any case I suppose it was of minor significance then, compared with the tragedy of losing his wife. But a long time had passed since then and he'd now come up with this irrational idea that his brother and sister owed him something. He was after all the eldest son, and he'd convinced himself they should give him a share of the inheritance. He had this idea that I should approach them on the grounds that they had a moral obligation to hand over. If they would not, he was prepared to instruct me to act for him and take them to court. Not a chance! I told him. Nothing would ever come of it. Nor would I help him. Absolutely not. If he chose to go along that road, he must find someone else to act for him. I refused to have anything to do with it.'

'And he was angry?'

'We had words,' he said dryly. Then his face registered almost comic surprise. 'Oh, just a minute! You don't imagine, Inspector, that I . . . took the argument further?'

No, when it came down to it Reardon acknowledged that he'd never really been able to go so far as to believe that of Purbright, but he did wonder why the man had felt it necessary to conceal what he was now telling with no apparent reservations.

'Why did you not tell me this before?'

For a long time, he said nothing. 'I saw no reason for

upsetting the Millars. They are social acquaintances, friends in fact.' And then, with a straight look at Reardon, as if deciding that since he had gone so far he might as well go the whole way, he added, 'Thea, especially.' Another pause. 'We go back a long way, Inspector, she and I, if you understand me. But we were very young, I was struggling, finding my way, not yet qualified, and her family didn't approve. She wouldn't go against her father and I didn't blame her. There's not many who would have dared to! I suppose we could have gone ahead, regardless, but there was the little brother she wouldn't leave either – Teddy. And anyway, one didn't do that sort of thing, not in those days. We didn't, anyway. Later, I married, and I now have a wife and two children I love. But I'm still too fond of Thea to upset the applecart.'

Reardon was astonished how easily the revelation had come. But it didn't say everything. He thought of that modest little ring on Thea's finger. Besides, something else Purbright had just said had made him remember that telephone call from Cherry.

'Tell me about the accident. When their father died.'

The solicitor raised his brows. 'It was a long time ago.'

'But you remember it?'

'Of course I do. It wasn't the sort of tragedy you forget. Both Ernest and his daughter-in-law were killed. She was taking him to a meeting with a client the other side of Birmingham. Ernest didn't drive, never had, and anyway he was crippled with rheumatism by then. It need never have happened if she'd been more experienced. She'd only just learnt how to drive.'

'In that case, how did she come to be acting as his chauffeur?'

'I don't suppose he would have refused, if she'd offered,' he said dryly. 'She could apparently twist all of them – even Ernest – round her little finger. I only met Liesl a few times, but I could see why. Everyone liked her. She was . . . not exactly beautiful, but pretty. Not clever, but certainly not boring. A bit of a good-time girl, actually. Come-hitherish, know what I mean? The sort to turn men's heads. I imagine she set Fox Close alight.'

And what had Thea, the plain, dutiful daughter, made of that, Reardon wondered. How would she have taken such an addition to the family? 'How did the accident happen?'

'If I remember rightly, they'd barely left the house, and for some inexplicable reason Liesl decided to take the short cut down the hill to the main road.'

Reardon tried to visualize the terrain up there on the hill where the old house had stood, where they sometimes took Tolly for his run. 'There's an overgrown lane that runs to the bottom, is that the one you mean?'

'It was overgrown even then.' It had, he explained, been one of the original coach road entrances to Fox Close, not used for maybe a hundred years or more. 'It must always have been a bumpy ride for coaches and certainly never fit for motors. It was madness for her to try and drive down there and it was a mystery why she did, except that it was something Paul used to do sometimes, for devilment, one supposes, or bravado, knowing Paul. His passengers might have found it exciting, if terrifying – like a roller coaster or some such – but I suppose he knew what he was doing, and they had always reached the road safely. Only this time, with his wife driving, something went wrong.'

The rest was soon told. As the car was bumping down the lane, Liesl had lost control of the steering, the motor had gathered speed. Then the long plunge down the lane, across the road at the bottom and into the river running alongside. Liesl and her father-in-law had been killed instantly. But Teddy, he added, had survived.

'Teddy. Yes. What was he doing there?'

'He wouldn't have been there at all if it had happened a day earlier . . . he'd only just come home from his college in London for the summer vacation and according to what I heard, had gone along with them for the ride. He must have a charmed life. The motor was an open tourer and he was thrown out, escaped with nothing more than a broken collarbone and some spectacular bruises, if I'm not mistaken.'

That was what Cherry's telephone call had been about. The fact which had been eluding him had eventually surfaced and he'd remembered that someone in the car had escaped being killed. And that survivor had been Teddy.

'Paul was devastated when it happened.' Purbright finished. 'It was his car Liesl was driving and he blamed himself, not Liesl.'

'For allowing her to drive it?'

'Or for some fault in the engine? The car was a total wreck, just a heap of metal, and they never found out what had caused the crash. Perhaps Liesl lost her nerve, panicked when something went wrong. Perhaps the brakes failed. Who knows?'

'Brake failure on a motor that belonged to Paul, that he maintained? From what I've heard, that doesn't sound very likely.'

'I've heard of more likely scenarios,' Purbright agreed.

Reardon's head was full of the day's events as he left the office for home that night, among them Purbright's astonishing confession of his connection with Thea, which had led him to make that ill-judged lie. The interview had given him another piece which clicked smoothly into place in the puzzle he'd already half completed; not just another piece of sky, but one which fitted so neatly into one of the missing spaces that the picture was now losing its formlessness and beginning to make sense. Tomorrow, he would need to check on the details of the inquest which had been held after that accident.

Things were beginning to fall into place. Means, motive, opportunity, he was beginning to see them all, but the most slippery of these was motive. Slippery and . . . all right, he was convinced by now that he knew *why* it had all happened, but the *how* and *where* were still eluding him, just beyond his grasp. And where any leads as to which direction anything useful was to come from still remained obscure.

When one did come, it was in a form, and still less a source, he would never in a million years have considered.

He'd barely stepped out of the police station door when he sensed someone sidling alongside, and for a flash of a second he felt a sense of déjà vu, living that moment on Castle Bridge over again. Until he caught the whiff and knew this was no

Jenny Hallam. He swung round so quickly the person staggered away.

It was a dark night with no moon but still, he was instantly recognizable. Hair growing low on his forehead, furry eyebrows, squashed up features giving him the look of a ferret. Disreputable ex-army greatcoat, too big, sleeves covering his hands. Voice wheedling, head reaching somewhere in the region of Reardon's shoulder. Outward appearances were said to give no indication of what was going on inside a person, but in Sonny Murfitt's case this was debatable. He looked what he was: furtive, sharp, slippery and with a feral scent you could smell a mile off.

A first glance said there was something different about him today. Less scruffy? Hardly, unless it was the light from the blue lamp above the police station entrance throwing an eerily clean cast on his face. Reardon couldn't put his finger on what it was until he remembered the sky had fallen and Sonny was no longer in the ranks of the unemployed. Whatever it was, something about him inclined Reardon to stop. 'What are you after, Sonny?'

'Summinck to ask you, Mr Reeden. Our Malc. What's going to happen to him? He's upset, and I'm worried sick.'

Reardon knew that Gilmour had left the two Murfitt boys with the impression that Malcolm had been lucky to be let off so lightly. Kenny at least was streetwise enough to realize that the business of hauling his brother in and taking official steps over the letters he'd sent wouldn't be worth police time. Having their ears boxed by the local copper for some misdemeanour or other and warned to behave in future was what they'd grown up with and expected. It was part of what bobbies on the beat were there for, and presumably detective sergeants also. Gilmour reckoned he'd done as good as, and put enough wind up Malcolm to scare him from attempting anything of the sort again. Somehow, Sonny had found out about the business and now seemed to have got it into his head that dire consequences awaited his miserable son.

'He didn't mean nothing, Mr Reeden. And if I was to tell you what I seen t'other night . . .'

Who did he think he was kidding? This wasn't Sonny having

a change of heart regarding his son's welfare. This was Sonny storing up points for himself. Fondly imagining he might be able to call on them next time he was likely to be brought before the Bench. He had a hope.

'What if it has to do with that murderer you're looking for?'

Despite himself, Reardon stopped.

They were still standing a yard or two from the door to the police station here in Market Street, in full view of the public. It wouldn't take him a minute to haul Sonny inside. But that would mean more interest than he wanted to arouse at that moment. Yet . . . even though this was Sonny Murfitt, if there was the remotest possibility of a glimmer of light on the investigation . . .

'OK. Let's talk,' he said after a minute, and headed for Anchor Passage, a few yards away.

He let Sonny shuffle along behind, towards the narrow alley that twisted itself down towards the canal at the bottom, any view of which was blocked by the brick wall at the end, constructed to link the premises either side and prevent access to the rear. The narrow space provided privacy, often for after-dark purposes not akin to the one it was now being used for. A perfect place for being trapped, if Reardon had had any intention of stepping more than one pace inside. 'Come on, Sonny, let's get this over with. It's been a long day and I've had enough, so don't waste my time.'

The number 27 bus trundled across Town Hall Square. Its lights swept the passage and revealed something now blocking the entrance: Kenny, accompanied by a huge, ugly, shaggy creature the size of a donkey, part wolfhound, part lion as far as Reardon could make out in the dim light. He took an involuntary half step back before realizing it was a dog and that Kenny had it on a short lead. It growled menacingly and bared its teeth.

'He don't like you, Inspector,' Kenny said with a smirk.

'I don't much like him, either. Where the devil did you find him? The zoo?'

'I wouldn't go hurting his feelings, Mr Reeden, if I was you,' Murfitt Senior warned. 'He's my mate down at Pratchett's, aren't you, Cuddy? Chained up all the time he is, but he's a big dog and he needs his exercise before eight o'clock, when we're on duty, him and me. Strong as a bull, needs our Kenny here to keep him in order.'

The very idea of Sonny restraining anything larger than a pussycat was laughable. With the dog straining on the lead until it looked to throttle him, Reardon wouldn't even have bet on the chances of someone the size of Kenny, if it came to a real tussle. But suddenly, Cuddy gave up, barked once, a sound like a factory hooter, and then flopped down, put his huge head on front paws like meat plates, and yawned. All bluster, then. Or just biding his time.

'I'll tell you what I saw if—' Sonny tried again.

'If nothing.' But Reardon had a sudden, if belated, moment of clarity. Pratchett's warehouse, where Murfitt was now employed, was one of the few buildings still in use on the Hadley Piece site, like the one where Matt Millar lived and worked. He turned back towards the police station. 'You'd better come inside.'

This wasn't what Sonny had envisaged, and began to turn away, but Reardon had a hand on his arm. 'And no, not you and the dog, Kenny. You take him back where he belongs. Sergeant Longton's of a nervous disposition.'

In view of their own activities, the Murfitts of this world reported nothing unless it might be of some use to them. It was only now, hoping for some sort of payback, that Sonny had at last seen fit to come forward. He was prepared to tell them what he'd seen on the night of the seventeenth, when he had been fulfilling his unlikely duties as nightwatchman at Pratchett's warehouse.

You wouldn't have turned a cat out on a night like that, and it was hard to envisage Sonny braving the elements to scout around outside when he could have been sitting comfortably inside his no doubt snug little cabin, smoking and nursing a mug of tea over his football pools. But that was what had happened.

It was Cuddy who'd alerted him, he said, Cuddy who lived outside on a long chain with a kennel to shelter in if he felt like it. He'd heard a disturbance further along, had run the

length of his chain and begun barking and leaping at the
perimeter fence. In the end the noise had forced Sonny out
into the rain where, above the racket Cuddy was making, he'd
heard a high-pitched sound, a shout maybe, a shriek, a yell.
Hard to tell what it was. It might have been the wind.

'Like the sound of a gun going off, maybe?' Reardon asked.
No, nothing like. But it had made him look harder, and through
the rain, when the wind had parted the clouds, he'd seen people
manoeuvring a body out of what he unflatteringly called
Millars' old shed.

What had made him think it was a body? Well, he hadn't
thought they was shifting carpets that time a' night!

It was only when Kenny had told him what was in the paper
about that murder, and that young chap living there, that he'd
known it must've been what he'd seen – that Millar what was
murdered, he'd said confusedly.

As to what they'd done with the body – chucked it in the
canal, he supposed. He hadn't seen what happened next. There
was no moon and it had been black as the devil's arse out
there. All had gone quiet, except for the wind, and the rain,
still bucketing down. So he'd gone back inside.

Reardon sighed. If you wanted to conceal a body you
wouldn't dump it in the canal, whose sluggish waters would
keep its secret only until the process of decomposition made
the body rise to the surface. After that, the absence of any
current to carry it away would ensure it would soon be noticed.

Sonny was aggrieved that his story hadn't been received
with more enthusiasm. 'Can't I go now? I can't tell you no
more and if I'd known you was going to keep me here that
long . . . they'll sack me if I'm late . . .'

They were all tired. It was hot and airless in the cell-like
room. Both officers were in their shirtsleeves but Sonny had
refused to be parted from his coat, as if fearing he might not
get it back again. Reardon leaned back in his chair, stuck his
long legs out and shoved his hands in his pockets and stared
at the unpromising material sitting on the opposite side of the
table. Gilmour sat as far downwind of Sonny as he could get.

Clearly they weren't going to get anything more out of him.
They let him go, telling him that as long as Malcolm behaved

himself, nothing more would be said on the matter. He wasn't satisfied, but it was all he was going to get.

Gilmour held the door open for him and stayed there, wafting it to and fro to clear the air. 'Phew!' He came to sit down. 'So what do we make of that? A joint effort, Matt and Ted Millar . . . and who else but Pugh?'

'He was at that meeting,' Reardon reminded him, referring to the public meeting which had been called against the long-delayed municipal housing development at Hadley Piece. The meeting, however, had purposely been arranged to start and finish as early as possible because no one would have come otherwise. A whole evening spent sitting on hard chairs in the draughty parish hall wasn't an enticing prospect. Murfitt's shift started at eight o'clock, so it was possible Pugh could have been one of the three he had seen moving the body.

Body? Discounting any embroidery, how much could they really rely on anything said by Murfitt, a natural stranger to the truth? If he'd been telling even some garbled version of what had really happened, it was possibly for the first time in his life. How identifiable at that distance, for instance, would be three men manoeuvring an ungainly bundle? Yet against the odds, Reardon was inclined to believe what Sonny claimed he'd seen happening on what might have been Paul Millar's last evening on earth. In an odd kind of way, it hung together.

He stood up and reached for his jacket.

'Hadley Piece?' Gilmour asked with resignation.

TWENTY-ONE

They had left Matt's studio ten minutes ago, after finding it dark, shuttered and locked. Reardon wasn't sorry to leave the benighted spot behind. There had always been something about Hadley Piece and its aura of dereliction which challenged his belief that human emotions didn't cast evil shadows or inhabit inanimate things and places. Casa Nova was where he knew they needed to be now.

The white house stood out against a dark sky, its newness somehow more apparent than when Reardon had seen it in the light of day. Work on the as yet bare garden was evidently due to commence shortly. A small pile of gravel and bags of cement had been added to the waiting paving slabs. Shrubs and small trees in pots of varying size stood expectantly around.

The curtains hadn't been drawn, and a couple of lamps glowed behind the curved end windows, but no one answered when the bell was pressed. The door swung open when Gilmour tried the knob. A deep silence wrapped itself around them as they stepped inside, though not the unoccupied, inert silence of an empty house. A minute or so later the music started: slow, lonely and plaintive piano notes, sad and bittersweet, coming from the open doorway of the big sitting room. They moved towards it.

It was Thea who was playing, not expertly, but coping as efficiently with the Chopin etude as she did everything else, seated at a white upright piano. The small diamonds flashed sparks on her strong white hand as it moved. She looked up and in the darkened window in front of her saw their reflections and stopped playing. 'Come in, Inspector,' she said without looking round. 'We've been expecting you.'

Reardon had scarcely noticed the modern piano on his last visit. Perhaps it hadn't been here, for the big room was now transformed. All the old-fashioned, inappropriate furniture which had stood around like monoliths from another age had

vanished, leaving the room as it had been designed to be seen.
Not comfortable in the way he was used to, but clean, spare,
crisp and expensively modern.

The room's other occupant was Ted Millar, slumped back
in one of those low armchairs which had nearly cost Reardon
a slipped disc on his last visit. His hands hung loosely over
the arms, his legs were stretched out, his eyes closed. He'd
removed his collar and tie, and his jacket, and his waistcoat
was unbuttoned. He was in his own house, entitled to lounge
about in his birthday suit if he so wished, but the way he
looked now gave an overall louche impression which didn't
suit him, not lessened by the empty bottle and a tumbler with
an inch of whisky standing on the low table by his side.

His eyes flew open when Thea spoke. 'Inspector Reardon,'
he said, trying to ease himself into a more upright position
and only partly succeeding. His voice was slightly slurred. He
looked terrible, worse than he had when last seen at the Emscott
Hill site. The flesh on his plump face seemed to have caved
in, leaving it slack and ill-defined. His eyes were dull, and
even his hair seemed to have lost its inclination to curl. For
the first time since meeting him, Reardon thought he really
did look like a man who might have an ulcer. He wondered
how full the whisky bottle had been before he started drinking
and couldn't help thinking Mrs Chadwick's Ovaltine would
have been a wiser choice.

Thea, cool and immaculate as usual, in the same dark green
dress she'd worn previously, had swung round on the piano
stool and was watching them. 'Why were you expecting us,
Miss Millar?' Reardon asked.

'I assumed you would finally bring yourself to tell us sooner
or later about . . . that woman,' she replied, coldly sarcastic.

So, what he'd been afraid of had happened: Emily
Millar had made herself known, either to them or to Matt, or
maybe to all of them. Inevitable, perhaps. It would make little
difference now, but he wished she'd waited.

'She was wanting a . . . a pay-off, of course.' The contemp-
tuous, unaccustomed slang puckered Thea's lips as though she
tasted vinegar.

'Did Mrs Millar say that?'

'She didn't need to, it's obvious, isn't it? A woman like that, married to Paul? If she *was*! He came back here to Folbury only because she sent him, to see what he might get out of us. Have you considered she could have had a hand herself in what's happened to him?' she finished, failing to see the contradiction.

'No,' he said shortly. 'That's not why we're here.'

She merely inclined her head and indicated a sofa that didn't seem likely to repeat the sins of the easy chairs, one where they could sit reasonably upright. He and Gilmour seated themselves at either end, while Thea remained on the piano stool. Millar had flopped back into his own seat. No more than his sister could he hide the dismay – perhaps even fear – caused by the eruption into their lives of this Emily Millar, this hitherto unsuspected wife of Paul's.

Before Reardon could begin what he had to say, the front door was heard to open, quick steps sounded across the hall. Ted was galvanized again into a struggle to his feet, and this time succeeded, as his nephew strode in. 'Where the hell have you been, Matt? You said you'd be here hours ago. We have to talk. Has she . . . has that woman been pestering you again?'

Matt bent to remove the cycle clips from his trousers and stuff them in his pocket. 'Something else has happened,' he said abruptly. 'Nothing to do with her. It's changed everything. I came to tell you before I went to the police . . . but here they are. Inspector, Sergeant.' He gave them a jerky nod and moved stiffly towards the piano, where he directly faced his aunt. He seemed to find difficulty in speaking, until at last he said, in a low voice, 'I'm sorry, Aunt Thea, so sorry. I know how hard this is going to be for you, but it can't be helped. I wouldn't do it if I didn't have to . . . you know that . . .' He turned himself away so he wouldn't have to look at her face.

Her hand wasn't quite steady as it went out towards him and her sleeve slipped back. The scar on her arm stood out like a brand. 'Never mind me,' she said urgently, seeming to know just what he meant. 'You mustn't do this to yourself. Not another word.'

Millar was not being as quick as his sister to take in what was happening. 'You've been drinking, Matt, you fool!' he accused, notwithstanding the depleted whisky bottle by his own chair. More pacifically, he added, 'What's all this about? What's up?'

Matt looked nearly as bad as his uncle. His black hair was a rumpled mess. He was deathly pale, but he wasn't drunk. 'Only that I've buggered things up completely, haven't I? For both of us, me and Imogen.'

'Imogen? You *are* drunk!'

'I might feel better if I was. I've come to my senses, never been more sober.'

'What are you talking about?'

'Wesley's wife is dead, haven't you heard? Yes, of course you have.'

'We heard, yes. Poor old Wes. It's been a long haul. But what has Cora dying to do with anything?'

Perfunctory sympathy indeed, Reardon thought, but then her death had been expected. No doubt felt to be 'for the best'. Poor Cora, who couldn't have had the best of anything for God knows how long.

Matt gave an unamused laugh. 'It has everything to do with it. Seeing that at last they've decided to tell me . . . now of all times.'

'Tell you what?' Ted, still slightly fuddled, was struggling to understand.

'That Wesley – *Wesley* – is Imogen's dad, of course.'

If a feather had drifted to the floor you could have heard it. The silence extended until Millar found his voice. '*What?*'

He really hadn't known, Reardon thought, any more than Matt had. Despite what was to come, he pitied the young man. How long had he been harbouring the suspicion that he and the girl he'd fallen in love with might have the same father? And what had led him to think so in the first place? The same route, no doubt, Reardon himself had taken initially, if mistakenly. It wasn't as though Imogen was likely to have kept her romantic version of the youthful affair between her mother and Paul from Matt. And that legendary reunion of old pals in France, which had included both Paul and Connie, could have been no secret to anyone in Folbury. Enough, put together, to have aroused suspicions in Matt, particularly vulnerable on the subject of his father. Several emotions were now chasing one another across his face in rapid succession, leaving behind only the bitter realization that the truth had come too late, for him at least.

'They should have told her before,' Thea said suddenly. 'Imogen. They should have told the child.'

At that Matt spun round, caught sight of her face and for a moment was quite still. 'You knew?' he said. 'And you never said anything to me? You *knew*?'

'That Wesley was Imogen's father? Of course I knew. Do you think I am deaf and blind? It was always there to see . . . how he doted on that Connie girl when he was a boy, even though she preferred Paul. But Paul left her and found someone else to marry. And then, when she and Wesley found themselves together again, working in France . . . well! Never mind that Wesley was by then married to Cora Dennison . . . or she to that doctor. She came back from France with a baby, conveniently a widow.'

So that was how Thea chose to see that old quarrel. And how many more versions were there of those long-ago events? Reardon wondered. Structured, not only by those involved, but also by those who were outsiders, looking in, imagining what had gone on? He suspected none of them might ever approximate the exact truth, each version coloured by their own degree of involvement, their own prejudices.

Matt now couldn't take his eyes from Thea, as if she had suddenly become a being from another planet, this aunt who had taken the place of his own mother and whom he'd come to love as if she were. 'You knew how it was with me and Imogen . . . you must have guessed why I was holding off.' As if his legs had suddenly given way, he groped blindly for the nearest seat. The elegant folding chair, in maple and blond leather, rocked as he threw himself down, but then righted itself, sturdy enough to withstand the force. 'And you kept it from me. Seems the whole bloody world knew, except me.' He turned to Millar. 'You, too?'

'No! Good God, no, it never crossed my mind! Connie was a widow, she was married to that Dr Randall who died . . .' He stopped abruptly and passed a hand across his face, overwhelmed by his failure to realize what now seemed evident, and fell into a stunned silence. 'Are you sure?' he asked at last.

The three of them seemed to have become oblivious to the police presence. Gilmour, shifting uneasily and itching to get everything wound up, caught Reardon's eyes but saw he was holding back until more was said, or until he was ready to step in.

Thea was right, they should have told Imogen, Reardon was thinking, but they hadn't. Through a misplaced sense of loyalty to Wesley's wife? At what cost? He could only hope it was because neither of them had realized the real reason Matt might have been keeping himself at arms' length from Imogen.

'Of course I'm sure!' Thea was answering her brother impatiently. 'And what difference would it have made if I *had* told you, Matt? Connie Randall is never going to let her child marry a Millar. Not after Paul threw her over and then married someone else.'

Matt, who had been sitting hunched over with his hands clasped between his open knees, raised his eyes at last from the polished parquet. 'Imogen did know,' he said flatly. 'Her mother told her years ago. They didn't – couldn't – trust me with it before, not even Imogen. She was made to promise. I don't blame her, not really, she loves her mother, and Wesley too, for that matter. But if only she'd told me, before . . .'

'Have you let them know what happened, Matt?' Thea demanded with a sudden sharp urgency. 'I mean Imogen, and Wesley? Have you even *thought* what you're going to have to face? If—'

All the light left Matt's brilliant grey eyes, leaving them shadowed and heavy-lidded. Any fleeting hope vanished with her reminder. '*If?* There's no if about it. The game's up, well and truly now,' he said, staring into a bleak future.

It was the opening Reardon had been waiting for. Requesting silence from the other two, he spoke to Matt. 'When we asked you about the night your father visited you, you told us you spent half an hour with him and never saw him alive again.'

Matt blinked. 'What?'

Reardon repeated what he'd just said.

'Well, it's true. Everything I told you then is true.'

'Not entirely. What you didn't say is that he came back later.' Matt threw him a dark, troubled look, but didn't deny it. 'Isn't that why you were coming to see us, to confess what went on between you then?'

It took him a while to answer. 'If I was, I don't see that it matters now, it's better forgotten. I said things I shouldn't have done if I hadn't been so furious.'

'We'll be able to judge that better if you tell us what it was.'

He still had to struggle with himself before he could answer. 'All right, then. It really doesn't matter now.' He was desperately trying to pull himself together. 'I asked him why, if he'd been happy enough to keep away from me for all this time, he should expect me to receive him now with open arms. I reminded him I'd got on with living my life very well without him so far and I didn't see why him turning up like a bad penny should make me feel otherwise.'

It was an understandable reaction, although simply having his father out of his life again would at that point have made no difference to the problem of his relationship to Imogen. Why had he not confronted Paul with that? Afraid of facing the truth and having his fears confirmed? As long as it was only suspicion, he could learn to live with it?

'What did he say to that?'

He scratched hard at a stubborn yellow paint stain on his thumb until it drew blood, as if the discomfort would make what he had to say less painful. After a moment he looked up. 'He had the nerve actually to agree with me, said I'd every right to feel that way, but he could explain everything. I told him to go on then, explain, tell me why he'd abandoned me, but he wouldn't. Not then. He said he was going straight back here to see my aunt and uncle and I should go along with him because he wanted all three of us to hear what he had to say. As if I would.'

'You refused?'

'I told him flat out I wanted nothing more to do with him, so help me. He could get out of my life again and stay out. I pulled the drawer open where I keep all the letters I ever had from him when he was at the front . . . all half dozen, in four years! Told him that I'd kept them because I'd always looked on him as a hero and I was so proud of him. I started to tear them up one by one. He just stood there, watching. "Think about it," he said. Then he left.'

'Matt, you don't have to—' Thea tried again.

'Miss Millar, please.'

She gave him a freezing look but she subsided and Matt went on as though he hadn't heard the interruption. 'That was when Wesley came in. He saw I was upset and in the end I told him what had happened.'

Pugh had lied, or omitted to say anything, about that – and what else? Reardon asked himself.

'He'd just seen someone he'd thought was a ghost leaving the studio, so he was as shocked as I'd been when I walked into this room after Uncle Ted had sent for me, and saw the father I'd thought dead. But Wesley's response was better than mine. I know there had been no love lost between the two of them when they were young, but still . . . He spoke to me like a Dutch uncle, he said I should at least hear what he had to say. I told him there was no chance. I'd arranged to take Imogen to the pictures that night, one she particularly wanted to see, and there was no way my bloody father was going to stop that. In the end, he saw I wasn't going to change my mind and he left.'

It took a moment or two before he could carry on. 'But I kept seeing the way he'd looked when I tore the letters up and you know, I suddenly remembered . . . Once, when I was at school, no more than a little kid, five or six, I was accused of something I didn't do. The teacher wouldn't let me explain and he took his strap to leather me and told me to hold my hand out. I'd never been strapped before and I was terrified. He was just about to give me six of the best when he saw my face and said he'd give me a chance to explain what had happened. So . . . well, in the end I cycled over to see Imogen and told her we couldn't go out that night. She was annoyed at first, of course, especially since I couldn't tell her why, but she could see something was up, something important. She looked scared but she said all right, we'd go another time. I promised I'd talk to her the next day.'

Whatever he'd told her hadn't allayed her fears. She'd come to Reardon seeking reassurance. Despite her protestation of Matt's non-involvement, she'd suspected something. She hadn't known what it was, and it had frightened her. And with good reason, poor child, he thought.

'I left her,' Matt went on, 'and came straight here, but there were no lights, the house was empty. So I just went back home.'

Millar had risen to his feet and begun pacing restlessly round the room while Matt had been speaking, picking things up at random, putting them down again. At last, he came to a halt, a slender bronze figurine, a graceful dancing girl, still held in one hand.

Reardon turned to him. 'Your nephew came here, expecting to find you and his father here, but found the house empty. How do you account for that, Mr Millar?'

Millar didn't answer. He stood where he was, clutching the statuette, rubbing his thumb over the smooth bronze. At last he said, 'I can explain.'

'Don't be a fool, Teddy! Be quiet and leave this to me.' It was Thea, she who must be obeyed, echoing the words she'd once said to Reardon: *It will come better from me.*

'I'd rather hear it from you, Mr Millar,' he said. It was not a request.

'Well—' Millar began.

'For God's sake, Teddy! I can't – I won't let you do this.'

Millar turned to face Thea and astonishingly, without raising his voice, he said, 'You can, and you will.'

The way he said it, in the voice he used to his workmen, acted like a douche of cold water. Momentarily shocked into silence, she was the first to look away, turning abruptly and stretching out her arm to switch off the modern standard floor lamp which threw light on to the piano. It left her in silent shadow, but as she drew back Reardon saw why she turned the lamp off. He thought he saw tears in her eyes. He would not have believed it if he hadn't seen it himself.

He was still waiting for explanation from Millar. 'All right. Where were you when Matt came here that night and found the house empty?'

Millar didn't answer at once, but simply stood where he was, looking at nothing, his unprecedented moment of self-assertion over, it seemed. Then he unclenched his hands from around the dancing girl and put it carefully back on the window sill. It was a pretty thing, the arms and legs were slender and delicate, and it looked as though it might have cost a lot, so perhaps he was wise to do so. At last he said, 'One thing I want to make clear from the start is that Matt had nothing to do with . . . what happened.'

'That's not—' Matt started to say, but his uncle stopped him.

'Leave it, Matt for now. Hmm?' Matt made a strangled sound which might have been a protest. Millar's glance rested on him for a moment. Whatever it said, Matt gave up the attempt to speak.

'Please sit down, Mr Millar,' Reardon said.

Obediently, he dragged forward a companion chair to the one Matt had chosen and seated himself, facing Reardon. Gilmour judged it was time to open his notebook, but it took Millar some time to begin. Eventually, he said, 'He came back, that night, you know . . .'

'Paul, I suppose you mean?' Millar nodded. 'Where, and when?'

'Where? Oh, here, of course . . . that same night we're talking about, after he'd been to see Matt . . . the night after he arrived in Folbury.'

'And you quarrelled?'

Millar blinked. 'What gave you that idea?'

'You were overheard.'

Nothing came from the shadowy space where Thea sat, but Reardon knew she must be putting two and two together and guessing the witness had been Ivy Pearson. Millar merely shook his head, seemingly not interested in, or bothered about who might have heard.

'We had words,' he admitted at last. 'As Matt's just said, he'd refused to come here with his father, to hear what he had to say, but Paul insisted he would be joining us later, when he'd thought about it and seen sense. How could he possibly be sure of that, I said, when he didn't know the first thing

about his own son. That made him very angry and he began
to shout. I was fast losing patience with him, but I had the
sense not to start a row and I said no more. It was obvious to
anybody Matt was going to stay where he was, at home, and
I for one wasn't going to wait forever, so . . .' He hesitated,
perhaps regretting what he had begun.

'So you went to find Matt at Hadley Piece. All of you?'

'Well . . .' He reached out for the whisky glass on the table
and drained what was left in it. 'Well, yes. We went over to
Matt's studio.'

'How did you get there?' Gilmour asked.

'What? Oh . . . the truck. It was parked outside the house.
Billy Sturgess had delivered some garden-work supplies to us
on his way home. He lives not too far away from here and
I'd told him he could leave the truck overnight and pick it up
in the morning. It was there, handy.' He turned to Reardon.
'You've seen my car. No room for three.'

The 'truck' presumably meant that small flatbed which had
driven into the yard at Inkerman Terrace, when the barking
dog had triggered such a reaction in Thea. Certainly, neither
Ted's elderly Morris nor Thea's red Alvis Tourer could have
accommodated three people without an uncomfortable squeeze,
but the truck would have taken the three of them.

'So what happened when you arrived?'

'Matt wasn't there. But I have a key and we went in to
wait.' He threw a glance at Matt, who was still sitting silent
and grim-faced, his arms folded across his chest. 'We hung
around for about fifteen, twenty minutes. I was pretty fed up
by then, and I backed my sister up when she told Paul flatly
that it was time he stopped playing games with us.' The whisky
seemed to have loosened his tongue. 'I felt as exhausted as
she seemed to be. I think neither of us had slept the previous
night. Like me, she'd probably been tormented by wondering
how he'd been living during all those years, imagining what
had been happening to him, how he'd lived . . . To tell the
truth, I didn't much like the look of him that night, either.
Something I didn't understand. But I'd had enough of hanging
around. I told him he could please himself what he did, I was
taking my sister home. He wasn't having that. He said he

didn't think so, not until we'd heard what he had to say. At last! I had thought the whole point was that Matt should be there to hear it as well, but when I said so he laughed. "What I'm going to say has nothing to do with Matt. You can hear me out, then I'm going to kill you, Teddy Bear.'"

TWENTY-TWO

'It meant nothing – coming from Paul,' Millar said into the silence which followed. 'Simply the sort of thing he used to say, for effect, when I was little, not to be taken literally: "I'll kill you if you do this . . . or don't do that . . . if you tell what time I came in last night . . . If you sneak to Father about the bottles of beer in the cupboard under the stairs, I'll kill you." It didn't bother me, he'd say it with a laugh and I knew he didn't mean it. It was that "Teddy Bear" I minded.' And hated it, said the flicker in his eyes, and had never forgotten.

The words were almost tripping over each other now. Yes, he'd minded, but he was the baby of the family, a little boy, and who would have listened if he'd complained? Thea assured him it was only a pet name, and he'd pretended it didn't matter, because Paul was his hero, the big, grown-up brother he looked up to: handsome, daring, afraid of nothing – he even dared to stand up to Father and argue with him. He was kind to Teddy in a casual sort of way, encouraging him to do things, not to be afraid – but Teddy wasn't like Paul, he was physically timid and most of all frightened of getting into trouble with Father. At one time Paul had tried to teach him about cars and engines, too, but since Teddy couldn't get the hang of anything mechanical, he soon lost interest.

Reardon let him carry on without interruption while he was still feeling the need to get it off his chest. The urge for people to unburden themselves when questioned wasn't unusual: a need to unload the guilt; wanting to show themselves in a good light; self-justification. Even if what they came out with wasn't a confession, it was almost sure to have a bearing on what was to come.

It was Millar himself, appearing to realize how he was rambling, who pulled up short. 'I'm sorry . . . lost it there for a bit. Where was I?' He rubbed a hand across his face. 'Oh, yes. Well, he obviously thought he had some bone to pick with me, and since he wasn't saying what it was, it seemed up to me to set the ball rolling. So . . .'

Gilmour's shorthand was pretty good, but it was all he could do to keep up, now that Millar's words were tumbling out in his eagerness to tell of his exchanges with Paul.

'I may have been laying it on a bit thick, but I didn't care. It had never entered his head to let us know whether he was alive or dead, and he had to be told what it had been like for us, knowing nothing. No orange envelope telling us he'd bought it, no letter of condolence from his CO regretting the loss. The War Office, cagey as hell when we tried to find out more.'

The brass hats? Paul had laughed. What else would you expect from them? When they were dealing all day with men from all sorts of different units, packed into temporary barracks, kicking their heels and waiting for their demob papers, most of them in a mood for insubordination, if not rebellion? Everything was at sixes and sevens – which was why and how Paul's luck had changed. By some fluke, it so happened that amongst the four hundred men stationed with him at that time there was another man with the same name, although a stranger to him: the same initial 'P' although he was Peter and his surname was spelt in the usual way, Miller, with an 'e'. Their papers had somehow got mixed up – a not exactly unknown occurrence in that post-war chaos. It was risky. The absence of Paul Millar would be noted pretty soon and his namesake would be raising hell, but if he moved fast there was a chance. So he'd taken it while the authorities still believed they were discharging the right man. By the time they found their mistake, he would be long gone, and he reasoned that any charges against him would be conveniently forgotten, while they wiped the egg off their faces. He reckoned he'd served his country for four years and was entitled to his freedom – such as it was. For, lurking in the background, was always the fear that he might not quite have got away with it, that what he'd done might, just might, catch up with him. That was what had kept him away from Folbury . . . at least until circumstances forced him to return.

Compelled to pause and take breath, Millar looked for his

whisky but found both glass and bottle empty. He wiped a hand across his face and went on. 'The circumstances being money, of course. A share in Father's will, to be specific. He became furious when I told him pretty roundly what I thought of his nerve, asking – *demanding* – what he considered his entitlement.' His mouth had a bitter twist, but his eyes for a moment said something different as he added slowly, 'We didn't know then that . . . that his days were numbered. Maybe that was what was making him act as he did . . . I don't know. I do know that he was mad, that night anyway.' He swallowed, hard. 'We had no idea that he was . . . so ill,' he repeated.

Nor had they known then about Emily, thought Reardon, the wife to whom Paul had nothing to leave when he died – or not unless he could bring himself to appeal to his brother and sister who, in the event, had shown themselves disinclined to share anything with him after the last years of estrangement. Would it have made any difference if they had known either fact at the time? he wondered.

'Are you saying he was threatening to kill you simply because you refused him money?'

'Yes, I am,' he said, albeit not with the same certainty. 'Though I have to say I didn't think he could be serious. Until he said it again, that he was going to kill me. And that time it wasn't so funny. Not when he put his hand in his pocket and pulled out a gun – a *gun*! I thought at first he was just trying to frighten me, that it must be a toy, or at any rate not loaded. I told him to put it away, guns were dangerous things, there might be an accident. And he laughed. "Accidents happen around you, don't they, brother?"'

'What did you think he meant by that?'

For the first time since beginning, he hesitated. 'Could have meant anything, I suppose. That I was accident-prone when I was a child – which was true—or, well, anything.'

'But you knew he meant the accident where your father was killed. And your sister-in-law, too, I understand.'

Millar drew in his breath and looked at where his nephew was sitting hunched on the chair, elbows on his knees, staring at the floor again. 'You don't need to hear all this, Matt.' To

Reardon he said, 'Matt has nothing to do with this. He wasn't there, he only came home after it was . . .'

Up to that point, Matt had kept resolutely quiet. Reardon doubted he'd even been listening. He seemed to have removed himself from what was going on, but when he heard his mother's name and what Millar said, his head jerked up. He gave Millar an outraged stare. 'Don't you think I've had enough of being kept in the dark? All this mess wouldn't have happened if I'd known the half of it from the beginning.'

Millar shrank into himself as if he were being physically attacked. And something which might have been a stifled sob emanated from the dark corner where Thea sat. Ignoring both, Matt said, 'I want to hear it all – everything. Please carry on, Inspector.'

Reardon thought that whatever Matt was about to hear could be no worse than what he had been thinking and imagining. He took up where he had left off with Millar. 'You were in the car, too, when it happened, I believe – but you managed to survive. Something of a miracle, considering how bad the accident was. You must count yourself extremely lucky.'

'Luck had nothing to do with it. I survived because I used my wits, that's all.' He had summoned up a show of bravado but his voice betrayed him.

'Oh? Tell me, then, how did that happen?'

'That's asking a lot. It's something I've tried not to think about since. I'm not sure I remember the details.'

'Try.'

Beads of sweat appeared on his face. He wiped them off with his shirtsleeve but his voice had steadied and when at last he spoke it was to Matt. who was staring at him, his face stony. 'Your mother was driving, Matt. For some reason, the car went out of control as we were going downhill. It was that damned road. The old coach road, fit for man nor beast, certainly not motors. The surface was terrible. So perhaps it was a puncture that caused it, maybe the brakes failed, impossible to say. Liesl . . . she was paralysed with fright – she hadn't been driving long and she just didn't know what to do. The car wasn't going that fast at first, just lurching and bumping all over the place, but it was gathering speed. I yelled at them to open the door and jump out before it was too late, but they didn't, either of them. My father couldn't, I suppose. It was an open tourer, he was in the dickey seat at the back and besides, he was lame. But your mother, Matt . . . she just froze, and clung on to the steering wheel for dear life. I opened my door and rolled out. Bloody risky. But it saved me.'

'Quick thinking. If your sister-in-law had done the same . . . instead of hanging on to the steering wheel . . .' Reardon gave Millar a hard look 'Though I don't see how she could have done that when she wasn't driving.'

'But she was. I just told you she was.'

'So you said. But I think you were the one who was driving that day, were you not?'

'No. I didn't have a licence to drive.'

'I know you didn't. We found that out when we saw it on the report of the inquest.'

It was illegal to drive a car without a licence, although one could be bought by anyone over seventeen. There was much talk at present of a test being introduced for intending drivers to demonstrate their ability to drive before they could be issued with one, before they were allowed out on the roads in charge of potentially lethal machinery such as a motor car. That day hadn't yet arrived but with the increasing number of vehicles on the road, and the consequent rise in traffic accidents, it couldn't be long before it did.

'If you know so much about the inquest,' Millar said, suddenly sharp, 'you must know it was also established that it was impossible to say what had happened, never mind who had been sitting where. The car was a total wreck, the bodies . . .' He couldn't go on.

'It wasn't a verdict that satisfied Paul, though, was it? He suspected you'd been driving and he knew how hopeless you would have been in an emergency. He wasn't wanting to kill you for refusing him money, but for his wife's death.'

Millar suddenly put his head in his hands. Reardon waited and at last he looked up, his face ravaged with tears. 'You can't blame me. The truth was,' he said brokenly, no longer able, or perhaps not even wanting to hide anything, 'he had some bee in his bonnet, he'd had it there for years, ever since

that damned accident . . . maybe before. Totally wrong ideas
about me and Liesl. He'd got it into his head we were having
some sort of affair . . . so far from the truth it was ludicrous.
Oh, I liked her, who could help it? Fox Close became a different
place the moment Paul brought her home. There'd never been
much laughter there before, but even Father was charmed . . .
and she was kind to me, we used to share a joke . . . maybe
I *was* a little in love with her, but to be truthful . . .'
He stopped, his glance falling on Matt. 'Lovely as she was,
she was a natural flirt, and I think she led me on. She was very
attractive and liked men to admire her, though that didn't mean
. . . she would never have cheated on Paul, Matt. Never.' His
face worked with emotion. 'But he had to have someone to
blame for the accident and he fixed on me. It became an
obsession, he couldn't leave it alone. We met one night, in
France, you know, unbelievably, and even there he carried it
on. He got me on my own and tried to get me to admit the
accident had happened because it was me, not Liesl, who'd
been driving.'

That would have been the strange wartime evening which
had made such an impression on Connie Randall that she
recalled every detail vividly. She had remembered how Paul
had taken his brother outside the *estaminet* where they'd all
met, ostensibly to sober him up. When in actual fact it had
been to harangue him, a half-drunk youth already terrified out
of his wits at what the next day's fighting might bring. Paul's
dreams of flying shattered, he had taken out his frustration by
clinging on to an imaginary wrong done to him.

All pretence had left Millar. 'Liesl didn't want me to drive.
She must have heard Paul's opinion of my abilities in that
direction. I knew all I needed was a bit more practice and I
wanted to show her I was quite capable. I begged her, and in
the end she let me.'

'What about your father?'

'He didn't object. It was Liesl, after all.'

'Then why did you take that road?'

'God knows,' he said. 'I've asked myself a thousand times
since then.'

TWENTY-THREE

He had never been blamed for the accident. So complete was the wreckage which had marked the end of that fatal plunge into the river that nothing was left to indicate which of the people involved had been driving the car. A verdict of accidental death had been recorded on Ernest Millar and his daughter-in-law, Liesl. A lot of sympathy had been extended to Ted, the astonishingly lucky survivor, as he recovered from his multiple injuries and the trauma of being involved in such an appalling accident.

It was only now that the repercussions were coming back to face him, nearly two decades later, and he was still dodging them. The urge to talk about Paul confronting him with a gun was far stronger than his guilt for involvement in the death of either his father, or Paul's wife.

'He held that gun pointed straight at me! He said if either of us thought it was unloaded we should think again! That was what he said. I couldn't believe what I was hearing, I suppose I thought he was joking. I don't remember exactly what happened then, but I knew I had to get the gun off him. He was taken by surprise and I got hold of it quite easily, but then, somehow . . . oh God, somehow the damned thing went off. He wasn't the least bit afraid when I snatched it, just astonished . . . so sure *Teddy Bear* would never hurt him! I saw it right there in his face.'

'He was shot in the *back of the head*,' Reardon said.

'I can't account for how that happened. God knows, I never meant that.'

How many times had Reardon heard that same justification? *I never meant to pick up the carving knife . . . I never meant to dip my fingers in the till, it was just open . . . She asked for it, but I never intended . . . The fight he had started got out of hand, I didn't mean it . . .* And yet, there must, there surely must have been that one split second, with any of them, Ted Millar included, when the intention had been real.

The spill of emotion had left him spent, physically exhausted. All at once he sagged, boneless as a rag doll which had lost its stuffing, and just as speechless. He was gazing at Thea, who had sprung up from her seat in the shadows and come forward to defend him. 'It wouldn't have happened at all if Paul hadn't had that gun! It was entirely his own fault. He staggered. He seemed drunk, though I know he wasn't. He must have felt suddenly ill – he looked terrible, anyway – and that was how he had his back to Teddy when the gun went off. It must have been.'

She was almost spitting in her vehemence. All her tight-held composure had deserted her, and she looked what she was: middle-aged, plain, and frightened. But still able to draw on some reserves of strength, for after a while, she stopped talking, raised a hand and put it gently to Millar's cheek. He grasped it like a small boy, bewildered and looking to his mother for comfort, but this woman, previously so sure she was in charge of her emotions, was losing control of them, and looked almost as anguished as he did. Reardon hadn't expected such a collapse from either of them, not from her brother and certainly not from her, but he needed to know more. He motioned her to sit down again and was surprised when she obeyed and dragged herself heavily back to her seat at the piano.

Reardon turned his attention to Matt. 'You were there. You saw what happened.'

'No. I wasn't. I only came in afterwards, when he . . . I came in and saw my father was lying on the floor.'

'Why didn't you, any of you, call an ambulance, the police?'

'He was dead! Anybody could see that. How bad would it have looked – a hole in his head and my uncle with a gun in his hand? What were we expected to do? Call the police and have a rope put around his neck?'

Reardon understood the anger and frustration, and the stubbornness he had sensed in Matt before, evident now in the set of his jaw and the fury as he spoke. 'Didn't it occur to you that it would look worse than that if you got rid of his body? Who decided to do that?'

'Well, I did,' he admitted after a moment or two, his chin raised in defiance. 'I wrapped him in a blanket off my bed and then I got him down the steps into the truck.'

'You managed to do that, alone?'

'I managed, yes.'

'That won't do. There were three of you.' Two men, and as he now knew, a tall woman whom Murfitt had mistaken for a man in the dark. The sound he had heard had come from her – a muffled scream, a shout of fear, a consequence of the uncontrollable paranoia which had pursued Thea Millar for half her life. A glance at her face showed the old, deep-rooted phobia reflected there even now as she sensed what was coming next. 'We have a witness who claims he saw three people manoeuvring a body down the steps.'

'The dog!' she exclaimed. 'The man with the dog beyond the fence – I knew someone was there.'

'Yes. So, you got the body into the truck and the three of you took it—'

'No!' Matt said violently. 'My aunt had nothing to do with it. She stayed behind.'

'All right.' Thea had presumably stayed to clear up the mess. 'You took the body down to the river and threw it into the water. Where?'

Through his teeth, Matt said, 'The *body* was my father!'

'I'm sorry.' He was hearing insensitivity where none had been intended but there was no room for hurt feelings now. 'Where did you put your father's body into the water?' he repeated.

Matt glowered, refusing to speak, but in the end he saw he had no choice. 'There's a small sand and gravel works, just above Cooper's Lock, below the Laverocks . . .'

Of course. The sand and gravel pits, worked, Reardon recalled, by the husband of Maura Chadwick. Where there would be places for a vehicle to get to the river, if you knew where and how. Where Maura worked at night – and which might possibly have been a clandestine meeting place for her and her lover, Ted Millar. A pat on the back Constable Dawson! It answered a question hanging over the enquiry from the start, though knowing the place where Paul Millar's body had been consigned to the water would yield little evidence at this stage. Putting it there had been an act of panic, not even considering weighting it down. Reardon noted that Chadwick's works were situated at least half a mile below the Laverocks swimming place, round the river bend from it and out of sight, but he still felt it must be a form of masochism which enabled Matt to continue to swim in the river at all. He could only assume it might well be an endurance test, a way of confronting his demons.

Millar, still sitting slumped in the chair, suddenly muttered that he needed a drink, reached towards the low table, groped for his whisky glass and found it still empty. It took no more than a moment before he was on his feet, lurching towards the cocktail cabinet, where his reflection could be seen in the mirrored interior as he stood with his back to the rest, fumbling among the bottles, glasses, slots and pigeon holes. Several things then happened at once. With a cry, Thea leaped forward, the piano stool crashing down behind her, beating Matt to Millar's side by a split second, with Gilmour only a stride behind. But Millar had the gun which had been concealed in the cabinet to his temple and even as Thea grasped his arm, a deafening report filled the room.

Reardon could not have said, hand on heart, what had happened, whether Millar had pressed the trigger, or if it had gone off when Thea had jerked his arm. Or when Matt had tried to pull her off. He only saw there was blood all over Thea's white hand as it covered her mouth, the silent scream written across her face.

And Ted Millar, lying on the floor, indisputably dead.

EPILOGUE

It had rained on and off throughout the day, rain which had been such a relentless feature of this last winter. But today it had been softer, kinder, and the April sun had come out in the late afternoon. The trees were greening over and the air held a lingering warmth still, at this time of day which always felt nostalgic to Ellen – slightly melancholy, the day not quite over, the night not yet begun; the twilight hour before dusk, *l'heure entre chien et loup*, as the French so aptly had it, the hour between dog and wolf.

Reardon drew her arm through his as they walked down the garden, keeping her close to his side, their fingers interlaced. She wanted to show him the place she'd chosen for a rose bed, at present nothing more than a tangle of old brambles, nettles and other recalcitrant weeds. 'About half a dozen would do, I think,' she told him, eagerly pointing out the advantages of such a situation, wondering whether hybrid tea or shrub roses would be best. 'Either would be lovely there.'

He looked at the enticing prospect of the digging that lay ahead. 'Lovely,' he agreed.

Reaching the crumbling wall at the garden boundary, they found a perch not altogether comfortable, and it was still too cold to sit for long, but worth it for the familiar panoramic view stretched out in front of them. Watching the hundreds of lights gradually beginning to prick the sky's growing darkness over the great Black Country sprawl, they fell into a companionable silence.

'What are you thinking?' he asked presently. In the way they had of picking up the vibes between them, he'd guessed she was no longer thinking about roses but reflecting on what they'd been talking about before they'd left the house.

The conversation had concerned the Millars, of course, a subject which had never been far away since the climax of the investigation, when Ted Millar had shot himself. The way

it had happened still horrified Ellen. She hadn't known any
of the family herself, except for Matt, her former art teacher,
who was still awaiting judgement for his offence in aiding and
abetting, or being an accessory after the fact, or whatever the
official charge was. And she had met his father, of course, in
that casual encounter up there at Fox Close, a meeting as
unforgettable as it had been fleeting. Yet their lives had crossed,
however peripherally; Fox Close had been home to all of them,
the discovery of that biscuit tin in the chimney here at the
Lodge had stimulated her interest further and she had formed
an unexpected concern for the Millars.

Samuel Trust had finished his work on the sun room, its
new function providing it with a kinder name than glory hole.
Its capacity to get most of the day's sun and the view over
what was to be the garden, the new lightness and brightness,
the reinstated step down from the living room had opened it
up and had banished, forever one hoped, the horrid memory
of what had once happened there with the dog, and its unhappy
aftermath.

'I can't help wondering what's going to happen to her now,'
she answered his question.

'To Thea? Oh, she'll carry on running Millars.'

He sounded certain, but truth to tell, he was no longer as
sure of Thea as he had once thought himself. While still dealing
with practicalities in the aftermath of what had happened, he
had caught glimpses of another woman which disturbed him,
because it brought his own judgement into question. He had
thought of her only as a cold and frigid spinster, concerned
only with protecting the good name of the Millar family. Even
perhaps capable of killing her own brother for that reason.
But he saw desolation in her eyes now whenever he had reason
to speak to her. If he had looked beneath the surface, then he
might have seen her in another way, as a more perceptive
Charles Purbright did – although it might be said that if
Purbright himself had been more persistent in following his
instincts as a young man in love, there might have been
a different outcome to all their lives.

Of one thing he was certain however: Thea Millar was a
practiced survivor. She would eventually do well enough, as

long as she had Matt. He had come to see how much her
nephew had meant to her in her childless life. But she would
have to learn the meaning of the word compromise, and that
meant accepting the daughter of Connie Randall.

Had Millar killing himself been an act of cowardice, a fear
of facing up to the consequences? Or was it a kind of courage?
It had meant that those of his family left behind, Matt and Thea,
had been spared the anguish of the case being brought to
prosecution.

They had all been in it together, but Matt was the one
who would have to pay, and face charges for the part he'd
played. He was tough, however, or at least resilient. At the
moment, he was more concerned with what it was all going
to mean to Imogen. Reardon didn't think he need worry. She
would wait for him. As Ellen had said, the world would turn
again for them.

Reardon relinquished his uncomfortable perch on the wall
and eased his stiff limbs. He had never been guilty of allowing
worries and concerns about his work to dominate his private
life and the answer now was to get back to the ordinary things
which mattered; like finishing the Boswell, he thought wryly;
he and Ellen perhaps taking little Ellie on an outing somewhere,
buying Ellen a new dress, or a new hat, or whatever she wanted,
turning the gramophone on and listening to the new Louis
Armstrong record he hadn't had a chance to hear yet . . .

He held out a hand and said briskly, 'Come on, it's getting
cold. Supper, and a quiet night. I've an early start tomorrow.
There's a call I have to make on my way to work.'

'Where to?' she asked as she let him pull her up.

'I need to take a look at garden tools. I don't suppose that
old spade I have would be up to digging that rose bed you
want.'

'No,' she said, with a smile that lit up her face. 'I don't
suppose it would.'